INSIDE PARADISE

Nathan lay wide awake wondering what it would have been like to make love to her. He studied her as she slept. Not even the starless night could dim her vibrant beauty. Her brilliantly colored hair flowed across the dusky green pandanus leaves like liquid fire. He thought of how he loved watching the blue of her eyes deepen to smoky amethyst whenever he touched her. And her mouth. Sweeter than passion fruit.

But virgins were nothing but trouble.

With the stars as his witness, Nathan resolved not to let the situation get out of control. To do so would be lunacy. Absently he smoothed her hair. The fragrance of exotic blooms fogged his senses.

Sweet Lord, he groaned silently, who was seducing whom?

Other AVON ROMANCES

CAPTIVATED *by Colleen Corbet*
FRANNIE AND THE CHARMER *by Ann Carberry*
HIGHLAND FLAME *by Lois Greiman*
THE OUTLAW *by Nicole Jordan*
REMEMBER ME *by Danice Allen*
TAKEN BY YOU *by Connie Mason*
TOO TOUGH TO TAME *by Deborah Camp*

Coming Soon

FOREVER BELOVED *by Joan Van Nuys*
THE MACKENZIES: LUKE *by Ana Leigh*

And Don't Miss These
ROMANTIC TREASURES
from Avon Books

HEARTS RUN WILD *by Shelly Thacker*
JUST ONE KISS *by Samantha James*
SUNDANCER'S WOMAN *by Judith E. French*

Avon Books are available at special quantity discounts for bulk purchases for sales promotions, premiums, fund raising or educational use. Special books, or book excerpts, can also be created to fit specific needs.

For details write or telephone the office of the Director of Special Markets, Avon Books, Dept. FP, 1350 Avenue of the Americas, New York, New York 10019, 1-800-238-0658.

Inside Paradise

Elizabeth Turner

AVON BOOKS · NEW YORK

If you purchased this book without a cover, you should be aware that this book is stolen property. It was reported as "unsold and destroyed" to the publisher, and neither the author nor the publisher has received any payment for this "stripped book."

INSIDE PARADISE is an original publication of Avon Books. This work has never before appeared in book form. This work is a novel. Any similarity to actual persons or events is purely coincidental.

AVON BOOKS
A division of
The Hearst Corporation
1350 Avenue of the Americas
New York, New York 10019

Copyright © 1996 by Gail Oust
Inside cover author photo by Gorback Photography
Published by arrangement with the author
Library of Congress Catalog Card Number: 95-94915
ISBN: 0-380-77372-4

All rights reserved, which includes the right to reproduce this book or portions thereof in any form whatsoever except as provided by the U.S. Copyright Law. For information address Joyce Flaherty Literary Agency, 816 Lynda Court, St. Louis, Missouri 63122.

First Avon Books Printing: April 1996

AVON TRADEMARK REG. U.S. PAT. OFF. AND IN OTHER COUNTRIES, MARCA REGISTRADA, HECHO EN U.S.A.

Printed in the U.S.A.

RA 10 9 8 7 6 5 4 3 2 1

*For two special little girls,
Brianna and Caitlin,
who always bring me sunshine*

Prologue

New York, 1845

The late summer roses she had swiped from a neighboring yard were beginning to wilt. Jasmine Kincaid trusted God would forgive her small transgression. Her pang of conscience faded at the memory of the fleeting smile the dusky pink blooms had brought to her mother's pain-ravaged face. But not even the sweet odor of the flowers could hide the miasma of impending death.

Jasmine perched on the edge of the straight-backed chair that had been pulled alongside the bed and resumed her vigil. The roses were the only bright spot in the otherwise cheerless room. Faded muslin curtains billowed in the gentle easterly breeze. Elsewhere in the boardinghouse, she heard a door slam and people exchange greetings. The ordinary, everyday sounds of life continued to go on around her. A life that, until her mother's illness, she had always taken for granted. Jasmine clenched her hands together and fought back tears. Now was not the time for cowardice. For her mother's sake, she willed herself to be strong.

Although she was only twelve, she felt old beyond her years—immeasurably old—as she faced the ordeal ahead of her. She knew her mother didn't have much longer to live. When the doctor had visited earlier, he had told her that she probably wouldn't survive the night. Jasmine deliberately kept her mind blank. She didn't want to think about how she'd manage on her own. The two of them had always been so close that even without family they had seemed invincible.

Emily Kincaid stirred restlessly upon the bed. Her blue-veined lids flickered open. Upon finding her daughter seated at the bedside, she reached for her hand. "We need to talk, sweeting. I have a confession to make."

Jasmine applied gentle pressure, aware of the frail bones beneath skin as thin as parchment. "Save your strength, Mother."

"If I don't tell you the truth, others will. I'd rather that you hear it from me." Pain distorted her features, then eased.

Jasmine jumped to her feet and reached for the brown-stoppered bottle on the nightstand. "The doctor left this—"

"No, child." Emily forestalled her with a shake of her head. "I don't want my mind fuzzy before I tell you what I must."

"All right." Jasmine returned to her seat, dread churning in the pit of her stomach. "Just remember, nothing you can say will change the way I love you."

Emily clutched her daughter's hand with surprising strength. "The truth is, child, you were born out of wedlock. Throughout the years, everything I told you about your father is nothing but tales that I invented. I'm sorry for the lies, but I wanted to protect you. I planned to wait until you were older and better able to understand the vagaries of the human heart."

Jasmine blinked, then swallowed once, twice. "I had begun to wonder...."

"I was young, inexperienced in the ways of love, and desperately unhappy. Then your father came to town, and it became a summer of endless wonder." A bittersweet smile flitted across her parched lips. "He filled my foolish head with sweet promises, then when autumn came I discovered I was with child. He abandoned me."

"I'm sorry," Jasmine murmured, trying to imagine what it must have been like for her mother.

"Don't you fret. The shame isn't yours, but mine," Emily said fiercely. "Looking back on my life, I have few regrets. I'd willingly pay the price all over again to have you as my daughter. You've brought me nothing but joy. After I'm gone—"

"No!" The ragged denial burst from Jasmine.

"After I'm gone," Emily resumed calmly, "you'll find an envelope in the top drawer. In it, you'll find money and directions to your grandparents. They'll take you in, see that you have food and shelter. Promise me just one thing, sweeting...."

Unshed tears clogged her throat. "Anything, Mother."

Emily struggled to a half sitting position. "Don't let your grandfather ever make you feel ashamed. You've done nothing for which to apologize. The sin was mine—not yours."

"I p-promise," Jasmine agreed brokenly.

Relieved, Emily fell back weakly. Pain contorted her pale countenance. She grabbed the bedclothes, twisting and bunching them in her skeletal fingers as knifelike pains repeatedly stabbed her thin body.

Jasmine snatched the stoppered bottle of laudanum and poured a dose of the painkiller. Raising her mother's head, she spooned the thick syrup down her throat before she could muster a protest. As she waited for the medication to take hold, she bathed her mother's face in cool water. Gradually the lines of suffering smoothed. Jasmine marveled at the change. Traces of Emily Kincaid's former beauty were apparent. In repose, she looked almost youthful.

Believing her mother asleep, Jasmine sank down once more on the chair next to the bed. The chair creaked beneath her slight weight.

Emily opened her eyes and smiled dreamily. "Don't be afraid of life, sweeting. Think of it as a journey, a grand adventure, in which the road is a series of twists and turns and is filled with surprises. It's often rough and strewn with obstacles, but be strong and you'll reach your destination."

As Jasmine watched in growing horror, Emily's eyes became unfocused and she stared off into space. "Don't go, Mother. Please don't leave me."

"It's so cold," Emily mumbled so softly Jasmine had to bend close to hear. "Winter is coming. I must get you a new coat to keep you warm."

Jasmine drew the thin blanket higher around her mother's shoulders, but her efforts were for naught. Her mother would never be cold again.

Bright daylight streamed into the room, but the sun lacked warmth.

Jasmine buried her face in her hands. This time she didn't try to hold back the sobs.

Chapter 1

Lahaina, Maui
Hawaiian Islands, 1853

Mindful of her grandfather's uncertain temper, Jael Kincaid quickened her step. She was late, and her grandfather, Reverend Silas Kincaid, pastor of the First Hawaiian Church of the Holy Spirit, would be furious. Not out of concern for her safety, but because his dinner would not be on time.

As she stepped through the stand of hala trees and gazed at the vista below, her need for haste was forgotten. Sunset . . . that narrow bridge between day and night brought a soft smile of pleasure to her face, and she succumbed to the temptation to tarry. Beyond a stretch of bleached sand, the world burned with color. The sun, a flaming orange medallion, hovered above the horizon, setting the sky ablaze and torching the becalmed ocean in the same vibrant hues. Mountain peaks of the neighboring island of Molokai formed a purple smudge against the brilliant canvas of sea and sky.

She loved the islands passionately—and hated them in equal measure. They were her joy; they were her jailer. She never wanted to leave them, yet she couldn't wait to go. Her smile vanished. The struggle raged within her unceasingly, filling her with confusion, anger, frustration, and a sense of hopelessness. She watched the sun drop lower and lower until, only a sliver of fire, it slipped from sight. She sighed. It was time to face her grandfather's wrath.

It wasn't a noise that alerted her, but the stillness.

Jael felt the small hairs along the nape of her neck stiffen. A portent, the islanders called it, a foreboding of danger. Intuitively she sensed that she was no longer alone. Beyond the dense cover of trees and ferns she had emerged from minutes ago, someone was watching. Slowly she turned around.

"Who is it?" she called, trying to sound more confident than she felt. Narrowing her eyes, she searched the pathway that sloped from the mountainside and into the town of Lahaina. Now that the sun had set, darkness quickly shrouded the island in thick, heavy shadows. She tried to calm her mounting fear by reminding herself that the islands were safe. And her imagination overactive. "Who's out there?" she tried again.

A breeze rustled through the palms. Or was the sound she heard a man's heavy breathing?

Fear skated down her spine. *Scared of the bogeyman?* an inner voice taunted. *If you're a bad girl, Mu will get you.* "What do you want?" Even to her own ears, her voice sounded reedy and strained.

No response.

Jael's heart slammed against her ribs. She edged backward, slowly inching away from the unseen menace. She was certain someone was there, lurking, just out of sight. If the person she sensed watching so intently was truly harmless, why didn't he identify himself? The answer that flashed to mind wasn't reassuring. She picked up her muslin skirt in both hands and whirled to flee down the sloping track into town.

Ignoring her grandfather's admonition to avoid the Lahaina Roadstead with its rowdy sailors, Jael made straight for the busy waterfront and the protection a crowd offered. Her bonnet flew off as she ran past the Wainee Cemetery and would have been lost had it not been for the ribbons tied beneath her chin. Veering right, she cut through a churchyard. Wainee Church, the first stone church in the islands, stood silent witness to her flight. Her precious whalebone combs slipped from their moorings and fell to the ground unheeded, sending her waist-length red hair streaming behind her.

Twigs snapped underfoot. Her heart beat harder, faster, pumping blood so forcefully it pounded in her ears like a primitive drumbeat. The sound nearly obliterated the heavy thudding footsteps in the brush behind her... nearly, but not quite.

A sharp pain stitched through her flank as she raced past a pond with a tiny island in its center, once a favorite spot of Hawaiian royalty. She pressed her hand to her side but didn't slacken her pace until she spotted the masts of a hundred ships crisscrossing the night sky. As she had hoped, Front Street with its many grog shops teemed with seamen of every nationality. For the first time during her headlong flight, she risked a glance over her shoulder to see if she was still being followed—and collided with something solid. A pair of rough hands clamped her upper arms. "Well, what 'ave we 'ere?" a gravelly voice drawled.

Jael looked up and found herself staring into a face seamed by countless years of sea and sun. "I'm sorry, sir," she apologized breathlessly. "I wasn't watching where I was going."

The man smirked at his companions. "Sir, eh? Did you hear that, mateys? This tender young thing called me 'sir.'"

The remark was greeted with ribald humor. "She must have ol' George confused with some other gent," one of them offered.

"Either that or the poor girl's blind in one eye an' can't see out of the other," another guffawed.

Jael tried to pull free of the seaman's bruising grip. "Please, sir, kindly release me."

"What's yer rush, sweetheart?" A broad gold peg gleamed boldly where a tooth had once been. "Hellsafire, yer the best thing 'appened to me fer a month of Sundays."

"I really must get home. I'm already late," Jael insisted, worry over her grandfather's anger overriding the sailor's unwelcome flirtation.

"How about lettin' me buy you a drink?"

By now, Silas Kincaid would surely be pacing the parlor, one eye on the clock. "No, thank you." Jael frantically shook her head, sending her hair cascading around her shoulders. "I don't imbibe. The Bible forbids it."

The men circling her roared with laughter.

Jael looked into the men's expressions with stunned dismay. All of her grandfather's tirades against whaling men came rushing back. A godless lot, he had labeled them, men who came ashore only to drink, fight, and fornicate. Good Lord! What had she done? Had she escaped trouble of one sort only to land in the midst of another? The realization dawned on her with sickening clarity.

"Pretty little bird, ain't she, mateys?" George looked to his cronies for confirmation.

"Let go of me this instant," Jael demanded, doing her best to sound stern even though her voice quavered. When the seaman ignored her demand, she placed both palms against his barrel chest and pushed. The man didn't budge. He was built as solid as a giant koa tree.

George grabbed a handful of her hair and twisted it round and round his meaty fist.

"Been a long time since I had me a redheaded woman."

Jael blinked back tears at the stinging pain in her scalp. Tears of pain ... and fright. Tears she wouldn't give this rowdy group the satisfaction of seeing her shed. After all, she'd suffered worse at her grandfather's hand. As Jael watched horrified, George brought his mouth toward hers. She twisted her head in time to avoid the contact, and the slobbery kiss skidded across her cheek to land beside her right ear. Acting on pure instinct, she drew back her leg and kicked him with the toe of her serviceable black shoe.

George howled as her foot connected with his shinbone, then let loose a long stream of profanities.

Jael stared up at him, shocked as much by her actions as by the man's colorful obscenities. After what she had just dared, the man would surely beat her senseless. Grandfather wouldn't have hesitated. To her utter amazement, the seaman threw his head back and howled with laughter. "Never met me a redhead yet that ain't had a temper. Need a little tamin', is all."

"And ol' George is just the man fer the job," a shipmate gleefully egged him on.

The growing crowd of boisterous sailors clustered around them, calling out advice. A man with a nasty scar disfiguring one side of his swarthy face aimed a stream of tobacco juice at the ground. "When yer done with 'er,

George, I'll pay next month's wage to take a turn."

Jael's mouth went dry with fear. Eyes wide, she searched the faces of the men surrounding her, but she found nothing but lust carved on the weather-beaten features. Twisting and turning, she desperately fought to break free of her tormentor. "Please," she begged. "Please, just let me go."

"All right, George, you've had your sport. Now do as the girl says and let her go."

Jael ceased struggling and looked over her shoulder. The mob parted as a man pushed his way through the knot of seamen. He was followed by a sandy-haired companion of slighter build. She judged the taller of the pair to be about thirty. In spite of the man's relatively young age, he possessed an air of command that silenced the grumblings of much older men. He looked a little rough—and a lot dangerous.

"Who do you think you are, givin' me orders? King Neptune?" George jutted his chin and assumed a belligerent stance.

"Nathan Thorne, captain of the *Clotilde*." The man's engaging grin widened. "Now kindly release the girl."

"And if I don't?" George challenged.

"I'll personally see to it that no shipmaster in the harbor will hire you." The threat, issued with quiet confidence, hung in the sudden quiet.

George quickly recovered a degree of insolence. "That right? What makes you so bloody important?"

"I happen to have friends in high places. A well-placed word and you'll number among the scruffy lot without a ship who litter the islands like flotsam."

George cocked his head to one side as he pondered the matter. It was common knowledge that Lahaina was home to countless derelict sailors with no visible means of support. These displaced seamen lived in squalor unless a kindly islander took pity on them. On the other hand, George conceded, the girl was the prettiest thing he'd seen since signing on. And after months at sea, he was as horny as the devil. His face screwed into a frown as he weighed his choices.

Captain Nathan Thorne took advantage of George's quandary to inspect the hapless young woman who had the misfortune of falling prey to a bunch of whaling men. His first impression had been correct, and his concern justified. She wasn't a whore at all, but an innocent. The poor girl looked terrified—and rightly so. This was a sea-hardened lot who wholeheartedly subscribed to the whaler's credo of "No God west of the Horn." Lord only knew what might have happened to the girl if he hadn't passed by.

What still might happen...

Nathan shot a glance at his best friend and first mate, John McFee. John gave a slight nod of acknowledgment. The almost imperceptible bunching of John's shoulders signaled Nathan that his friend was ready and eager to back him if need be. A regular scrapper was John. Nothing his friend liked better, Nathan well knew, than a good brawl. Not even the prospect of a night or two in Lahaina's prison dampened his first mate's enthusiasm for a fight.

Nathan shifted his attention back to the burly seaman holding the girl. He tried for a conciliatory tone. "She isn't worth the aggravation, man. Allow me to share a bit of personal advice: Virgins are nothing but trouble."

The ring of whaling men chortled their approval. Nathan's lips twitched in amusement at the girl's startled gasp. But even without the involuntary outburst, the bright rush of color in her otherwise pale cheeks signaled that his guess had been correct.

"I diddled a virgin once meself," a man in the audience piped up. "Afore I knew whot happened, I had two snot-nosed brats in diapers and a third on the way. Hired out on the *Norma Rose* and ain't been back since."

"Find yourself a woman more seasoned," Nathan advised George. "They're much more satisfying than a green girl." Firmly taking hold of Jael's arm, he started to pull her away.

"Not so fast," George objected. He tightened his grip on Jael's arm lest his prize be wrested from his grasp.

"Look, mates," John cried suddenly, pointing beyond the ships to the open sea. "Thar she blows." Reacting automatically to the phrase that meant a whale had been sighted, the men turned as one.

Before they could recover from the ruse, Nathan hooked his arm around Jael's waist and darted to the right. "Stay behind me, sweetheart," he instructed in a low voice. "Duck when I duck, and don't look back."

Balling his fist, Nathan connected a punch to the jaw of the scar-faced man. On cue, John McFee sprang into action, landing a blow to George's midsection. This was the only cue necessary for everyone to join the fracas. Flailing fists and salty curses flew in syncopated rhythm.

"Latch onto me and hold fast," Nathan said to Jael seconds before he slugged a bandy-legged sailor who had just entered the fray.

Jael didn't need any coaxing. She clung to Nathan Thorne like lichen on a rock as he fought his way clear of the brawling seamen. She cringed when a man nearly twice his size blocked their path. The man hauled back his arm, but Nathan dodged and the blow glanced harmlessly off his shoulder. But Nathan, no stranger to brawls himself, gave as good or better than he got. Before the man could strike again, Nathan kneed him in the groin. The man doubled over in agony, clutching his privates with both hands.

Gaining the periphery of the fighting, Nathan pulled Jael out from behind him and grinned down at her. "Let's clear out of here, sweetheart, before anyone notices we left the party."

Clasping her hand firmly in his and pulling her along with him, he loped down the dirt road away from the harbor and turned down a sandy trail that led to the beach. With the town a safe distance behind, they paused to catch their breath.

Jael struggled to control her ragged breathing. Her composure felt unraveled, her nerve endings frayed and exposed. Pursued by an unseen assailant. Accosted by drunken seamen. And finally rescued by a stranger. The series of events had shaken her.

She braved a look at her gallant rescuer from beneath her lashes and found him gazing toward the ships anchored in the harbor. Tipping her head back, she studied him more boldly. His hair was a rich golden brown liberally streaked with blond and worn a shade longer than deemed fashionable. Broad shoulders teased the seams of the dark jacket he wore over a bronze brocade waistcoat and fawn trousers. A crisp white shirt contrasted sharply with sun-bronzed skin. Tall, lean, and muscular, he presented a fine figure of a man.

As the final vestiges of her fright dissipated, Jael gradually became aware of her surroundings. A full moon bathed the beach in a silvery glow. Waves tumbled onto the shore in an unbroken melody, then surged back in a froth of white. Trade winds rustled through the palm trees. And a warm and callused hand encased her smaller one. The man's grip was strong yet gentle. A strange combination, she thought wistfully. With odd reluctance, she disengaged her hand from his and stepped away.

Her action drew his attention from the ships bobbing at anchor and back to her. "I don't believe we've been formally introduced. Captain Nathan Thorne of the *Clotilde*." His teeth flashed white as he executed a short bow. "Pleased to be of service. And who might you be?"

Jael felt a warmth suffuse her cheeks and hoped the darkness would hide the telltale flush. "J-Jael," she stammered. "Jael Kincaid." Nathan Thorne possessed a pirate's wicked grin and the charm of a fairy-tale prince. A rogue dressed in gentleman's clothing. He was everything she had been warned against her entire life. The type of man who had lured her mother down the path of sin and eternal damnation.

"Jael..." he mused thoughtfully. He observed her with frank interest. She appeared small and slight—a waif clothed in dark, ill-fitting clothes. But there was nothing drab about the vibrant fall of red hair that framed her delicate features. The rich color hinted of zest and passion. "You have a most unusual name."

"It's from the Old Testament," she volunteered softly. "When I came to live with Grandfather, he thought a biblical name more suitable than the one my mother chose for me."

"Ah..." Nathan nodded as though he understood her explanation. "And what name was it that your grandfather saw fit to change?"

"Jasmine."

Jasmine... "The Hawaiians call it pikake," he said thoughtfully. The name conjured up images of a fragile white flower. Delicate, haunting, incredibly sweet. Yes, the name definitely suited her.

Jael belatedly remembered her manners. "Thank you for coming to my rescue, Captain Thorne. I don't know what would have happened to me if you hadn't chanced by when you did."

Nathan had a very clear idea of what her fate might have been, but saw no sense in frightening her anew. "Well, Jael Kincaid, what brought an innocent like you down to Rotten Row after dark?"

"Rotten Row?"

"It's how we seafaring men refer to that ramshackle row of grog shops along Front Street." He tilted his head to one side and found himself enjoying the sight of her bright hair lifting in the evening breeze. "You're avoiding my question, Jael."

"I...ah..." Jael's voice trailed off.

The girl looked as nervous as a greenhand his first time up the mast. He adopted a soothing tone. "What brought you so close to the docks this time of night? Surely someone must have warned you of its dangers."

She scuffed her shoe in the sand. "I was late returning from Wainee and I stopped to admire the sunset."

"And lost track of the time?" he prodded gently.

"No." Jael avoided his gaze and traced a strand of seaweed lying on the beach with the toe of her shoe. "I ran into town because I thought it safer there."

"Safer?" Nathan frowned. "Safer than what?"

"From whomever was chasing me."

Nathan reached out and caught her chin, gently canting it upward until she was forced to meet his gaze. "You're certain of this? Did you get a look at whomever it was?"

"No." Jael shivered at the memory. "I felt someone staring at me from the bushes. It scared me so that I turned and ran as fast as I could."

Nathan's frown deepened. With the exception of the area near the harbor, the island was one of the safest spots on earth. A virtual paradise where crime was almost nonexistent. "Did you actually see anyone?"

"No," she admitted grudgingly.

The tension melted from Nathan's stance. "Is it possible that your scare was the product of an active imagination?"

"But I heard footsteps behind me." Jael nibbled her lower lip, weighing the possibility.

"Are you absolutely certain?"

The entire evening was rapidly assuming a dreamlike quality. How much was real? she wondered. How much imagined? She was beginning to have difficulty separating the two. "At least I thought I heard footsteps."

Nathan heard doubt creep into her voice. "Being scared of the dark is nothing of which to be ashamed. I've known grown men who fall asleep with a candle beside them."

Suddenly angry with his patronizing manner, she jerked free of his grasp and stepped back. "You don't believe me, do you?"

"I believe you *think* you were being followed," he answered diplomatically. "Maui is safer than a church during Sunday services. Unless, of course, you venture down Rotten Row after sunset."

"But someone *was* watching me. I'm certain of it."

For a long moment, he studied her closely, his expression solemn. "In that case, you shouldn't go out alone, especially after dark. Promise me from now on that you'll be very careful."

Jael was touched by the concern that crossed his shadowed face. No one—and certainly not her grandparents—had truly cared about her well-being since her mother had died. "I promise," she said, summoning a small smile.

"Good," he said with obvious relief. "Now, I'd best see you home before your family fears for your safety."

"That won't be necessary," she protested in alarm as another problem loomed ahead of her. What would she tell Grandfather? How could she explain her tardiness? And how would she explain Captain Nathan Thorne?

"Nonsense. I insist." Nathan fell into step

alongside her. "Friends look out for each other."

Friends? She could sorely use a friend. The notion warmed her heart.

"Tell you what." Nathan's words broke through her reverie. "I have some influential acquaintances here in Lahaina. I'll ask them to be on alert and report any suspicious characters to the constable."

"That's very kind of you, Captain Thorne." Jael replaced her bonnet as she walked, stuffing her hair inside until it was once again concealed beneath plain black straw.

"My friends call me Nathan."

She darted a glance at him. The sight of his impertinent grin made her lips twitch in response. "Then thank you ... Nathan."

He playfully caught a wayward strand of hair that had escaped its demure confines. "You look prim and proper as a Puritan."

Jael snatched it back and tucked it under the brim.

Nathan halted suddenly as a thought struck him. "You're one of the missionaries, aren't you?"

"My grandfather is Reverend Silas Kincaid, pastor of First Hawaiian Church of the Holy Spirit." Jael quickened her pace. By now Grandfather would be absolutely livid that his dinner wasn't on the table.

Nathan quickly caught up with her. "Your grandfather has his work cut out for him. He must have to beat your suitors off with a stick."

No, she answered silently, *he beats me instead.* Aloud, she said, "I don't have any suitors."

"Then the young men on Maui must all be fools."

Jael was grateful the cottage she shared with her grandfather came into view and she was spared a retort. Pausing, she turned and held out her hand. "Thank you for escorting me home, captain...." She broke off at the almost imperceptible shake of his head, then began again. "Thank you for escorting me home ... Nathan ... but it isn't necessary for you to go the rest of the way."

Nathan folded his arms across his chest. "After your experience tonight, I don't want to risk anything else happening to you."

Jael gnawed her lip in frustration while her mind sought ways to discourage him. *The truth shall set you free.* One of her grandfather's favorite sermons sprang to mind. Drawing a deep breath, she decided to heed his advice. "Grandfather has a terrible temper." The admission came out in a rush. "He'll be angry that I'm late and won't understand why we're together."

"Then I'll simply explain the situation."

"You don't know Grandfather...."

His jaw firmed into a stubborn line. "A gentleman always sees a lady to the door."

"But ..."

"Jael!" Light spilled from the cottage door. "Damnation, girl, is that you?"

"Yes, Grandfather, it's me." Jael hurried forward with Nathan close behind.

Silas Kincaid scowled into the darkness, his pale blue eyes squinting behind wire-rimmed glasses. "Better have a good explanation, girl. My supper is long past due."

"I can explain, sir." Nathan stepped forward, intending to defuse the old man's anger.

"Who the blazes are you, young man? And who gave you leave to walk with my granddaughter?"

"If you'll permit me to introduce myself, Reverend Kincaid. I'm Captain Nathan Thorne of the bark *Clotilde*."

Silas curled his bony hands around the lapels of his shiny black broadcloth frock coat. "A whaling man," he sneered. "One of the godless heathens who come ashore to plunder the riches and corrupt the unspoiled. Well, sir, I have little use for men of your ilk. Kindly leave my doorstep immediately and never show your face again."

"Grandfather, Captain Thorne very generously offered to escort me home...."

"Don't talk back to me, you pagan hussy!" Silas's face purpled with rage. In his agitation, his trencher-style beard bobbed up and down like a stiff white ruff beneath his sagging jowls. "The minute my back is turned, you take up sinful ways with the first man you meet. Just like your wicked mother."

Nathan watched in helpless fury as Jael fled up the steps, swept past her grandfather, and disappeared inside without a backward glance. Reverend Kincaid gave him a final glowering stare, then turned and slammed the door in his face.

Impervious to the beauty of the tropical evening, Nathan headed back toward town. For the second time that evening, Jael Kincaid had managed to arouse his dormant sense of chivalry. He felt cowardly leaving her to fend for herself against a fanatical old man. If ever anyone was in need of protection, it was her.

The sweet, elusive image of jasmine drifted across his mind like a haunting fragrance that once experienced was never forgotten.

Chapter 2

Jael hurried to the small bedroom she occupied at the back of the house. She tugged at the ribbons fastened beneath her chin and quickly removed her bonnet, sending her hair tumbling around her shoulders in wild disarray. She hastily pulled it back and twisted it into a tight coil at the nape of her neck, knowing its unkempt state would only aggravate her grandfather's temper. The very thought of his reaction caused her hands to tremble.

She dropped a hairpin and stooped to pick it up. While Captain Thorne's intentions to escort her home were honorable, his chivalrous act could have disastrous repercussions. It had been a long time since she had seen Grandfather quite so furious. Hoping a hot meal would circumvent his anger, she jabbed the hairpin in place and left the bedroom.

"Why the rush, girl? Guilty conscience?"

Jael paused in her tracks. Silas, leaning heavily on his hickory cane, stood in the center of the Spartanly furnished parlor. His usually pasty complexion was suffused with color; his pale eyes gleamed with unholy fervor.

"I haven't done anything to feel guilty about, Grandfather."

"Can't trust you out of my sight for a second," Silas continued as though she hadn't spoken. "Minute my back is turned, you have men sniffing around your skirts. Just like your mother."

Just like your mother. How often had she heard that phrase? Jael wondered, feeling a sense of hopelessness pervade her spirit. Hundreds? Thousands? She braced for the tirade to come.

"She, too, had a fondness for anything in pants," he sneered. "Got herself pregnant by the first man to smile at her. Might've had enough sense to know the chap wouldn't marry her. Why buy the cow when the milk is free?"

Shame and humiliation twined around her like a parasitic vine squeezing the life from her soul. Jael felt her mother's disgrace as if it were her own. She didn't need a reminder that she was the result of that illicit union. Pagan issue, as her grandfather liked to call it.

Fighting the urge to hang her head, she resolutely met his look. "I had better prepare dinner," she said quietly.

As she was about to pass him, Silas caught her in a clawlike grip and spun her around. "Don't run away when I'm talking, girl. Disrespectfulness is a sin in the eyes of the Lord."

She swallowed back the bitter denial. Experience had taught her it was pointless to argue with him. "I'm sorry, Grandfather."

Silas wedged the head of his cane beneath her chin and forced her head back. "Who is this sea captain of yours? And how did you meet him?"

"On F-Front Street," she stammered. "Near the docks."

"The docks!" His hand on her arm turned bruising. "How dare you parade yourself on the docks like some common hussy."

"I know you forbid me to go near the docks, but . . ."

"Don't interrupt me! I won't stand for it." He gave her a vicious shake. "I swear, girl, you get more like your fornicating mother every day. Good Christian women don't loiter in that heathenish place."

"I wasn't loitering, Grandfather. I swear."

"First blatant disobedience, now back talk. You're an ungrateful little wretch."

They stood toe-to-toe, so close that Jael could see the fine drops of spittle that flecked her grandfather's thin lips. With increasing alarm, she realized how close he was to losing control.

"Have the pair of you been meeting behind my back?"

"No, Grandfather. We met tonight for the first time quite by accident."

"Accident, eh?" He let out a harsh bark of humorless laughter. "I'll be the judge of that.

You still haven't explained what you were doing on Front Street."

"Someone followed me from Wainee. I was frightened and started to run. I thought I'd be safer in town."

He wagged his head in disgust. "Following you, girl? Who in their right mind would follow a ninny like you?"

"I don't know," she admitted in a small voice. The more she repeated the incident, the less plausible it sounded—even to her own ears. How could she hope to convince others when she harbored doubts as well?

"Maybe a good caning would beat some sense into you."

Jael's mouth went dry with fear. Good Lord, no, not this. Would this horrible day ever end? she wondered with mounting panic.

Silas Kincaid dug his skeletal fingers into Jael's upper arm and started to drag her in the direction of his study. "Sinners must pay for their transgressions!"

After everything else that had happened since leaving Wainee, the thought of being forced to bend over the settee in her grandfather's study and expose her backside to the bite of his cane was too much to bear. More than the actual pain, the humiliation was intolerable. Jael dug in her heels. "No, Grandfather. No more . . . never again."

"What?" Silas stopped and stared at her in amazement. "How dare you defy my authority?"

"Remember what happened last time," she

pleaded, desperate to avoid a caning.

Faded blue eyes clashed with those of a more vibrant hue. They stood unmoving in the center of the room, two longtime foes engaged in wordless combat. Jael knew he recalled the incident as well as she. It had occurred nearly two years ago, shortly after her grandmother's death. Even though her vision had been distorted by tears, Jael would never forget the self-righteous gleam in her grandfather's pale eyes each time the thick hickory cane struck her flesh. While she had still been struggling to control sobs of pain and humiliation, Silas suffered a spell that had left him bedridden for over a week. Apoplexy, the doctor had later called it. When he was finally up and about again, he leaned more heavily on his cane. His vigor was never restored in full measure—a fact for which Jael was extremely grateful.

After what seemed a small eternity Jael felt the grip on her arm ease, saw the angry flame in her grandfather's eyes flicker and dim. Breathing a sigh of relief, she tugged free of his grasp and offered up a prayer of thanksgiving. "I'll start supper." She moved toward the door.

"Jael!" He stopped her midway across the room.

Reluctantly she turned to face him. "Yes, Grandfather?"

"You need to get down on your knees and pray Almighty God helps you overcome your wanton tendencies."

"Yes, Grandfather." She kept her eyes

downcast to hide their flash of resentment.

"You can begin your penance immediately after you prepare *my* evening meal. You can go without. Fasting cleanses the soul."

Once inside the small building used as a cookhouse, Jael leaned against the rough stone wall. Her knees felt rubbery. She trembled like a leaf in the wind. Where had she ever found the courage to challenge her grandfather? she marveled. Even Grandfather had been surprised that she had stood up to him. She shoved away from the wall and tied a starched white apron around her waist. A missed meal was a small price to pay for the caning she had narrowly escaped.

Her actions guided by rote, she cleaned and sliced vegetables grown in a small garden behind the cookhouse. She cautioned herself that she shouldn't celebrate her small victory prematurely. The Reverend Silas Kincaid had numerous ways to inflict pain without resorting to physical violence.

She set her jaw in determination. If she planned to escape from the islands before Grandfather succeeded in killing her spirit altogether, she would have to be more diligent. Her gaze strayed to the earthenware container on a shelf above the dry sink. It held the small cache of money she had been able to save thus far. Escape money. Her forehead wrinkled. Exactly how much was passage on a ship bound for New England? Perhaps she should choose a closer destination. Miners had discovered gold in California a few years back.

Hundreds, perhaps thousands, were flocking there. Maybe she, too, should seek her fortune there. It was definitely worth considering.

Jael sat beneath a gnarled hau tree near Lahaina's marketplace. She closed the worn Bible in her lap with a decisive snap. Much to the delight of the brown-skinned children who sat cross-legged in a semicircle around her, she reached into a large woven basket at her side and withdrew an equally worn book. The children nudged each other, giggling and grinning in anticipation.

"Now," Jael said with a smile as wide as one of their own, "this is your reward for listening so quietly."

Nathan, his arms casually folded across his chest, leaned against an open-air stall and enjoyed the sight of the lovely young woman reading to an enraptured ring of children. The sound of her laughter had first drawn his attention. Lilting and musical, it was as pleasing to listen to as a babbling brook in early spring. The animation in her voice was also evident in her expression. All traces of somberness had melted from her delicate features, leaving a piquant curve to her lush little mouth, a beguiling sparkle to her flower-blue eyes. She looked ... happy. The transformation from the frightened, uncertain girl he had rescued nearly a week ago to this fetching sight was truly remarkable. Barely more than a child herself, Jael Kincaid was clearly in her element.

"Once upon a time..." Jael began as the

children scooted closer. "There lived a beautiful princess and a handsome prince."

Nathan felt a strange tightening in his chest. The children obviously adored her—and she them. She looked as though she were born to be surrounded by a loving, merry brood of her own. All she needed to complete the picture was a doting husband.

Jael lowered her voice and put on a sad expression. "But the beautiful princess had a wicked stepmother."

More likely a wicked grandfather, Nathan thought grimly. Finding a husband would be no easy task given her grandfather's savage guardianship. What Jael needed was a gentle, loving mate. Not someone stern like her grandfather, not someone footloose like himself, but someone ready to settle down. A man who appreciated home and hearth. Another missionary, perhaps, with an unassuming, nurturing nature such as hers.

Jael's voice rose and fell as she narrated the tale.

The children listened, mesmerized.

He had tried married life once, and it had been a terrible mistake. His mouth tightened briefly at the unpleasant memory, then relaxed. The experience had taught him a valuable lesson: He wasn't cut out for married life. But he was content. He had the sea. And he had the *Clotilde*. The two constants in his life. Unencumbered by responsibility, he was free to come and go as he pleased. No wife to answer to. No one to complain if he was gone for years at a time. No one at all. That suited him just fine.

"... and the wicked stepmother was banished from the land."

Nathan sauntered closer as the story drew to an end. "Then the lovely princess married the handsome prince, and they lived happily ever after." He grinned, completing the fairy tale.

Jael glanced up, her eyes widening in surprise. Nathan watched bemusedly as startled pleasure gave way to embarrassment. When the children scampered off, she tucked the book of fairy tales deep into the basket, then rose to her feet and brushed off her skirt.

"You and the children made a pretty picture. You need a brood of your own to mother."

"I don't plan to marry."

"Never?"

"Never," she said firmly.

"That's a pity. You have much to offer children." *And a husband as well*, he added silently.

Jael cast a nervous glance over her shoulder. "How long have you been watching me?"

"Long enough," he replied noncommittally. What was the reason for her unease? he wondered. Did she expect to find her grandfather brandishing his cane like a sword of Damocles? Or was she worried about a shadowy figure spying on her? Either way, she needed a protector. Someone to watch over her. To keep her out of harm's way.

"I've tarried long enough." Jael picked up

her basket and turned toward the market. Nathan fell into step alongside her.

Not giving her the opportunity to object, he took the wicker hamper and slung it over his arm. "I'll walk you home."

"No!" Her refusal was swift. Emphatic.

Nathan paused and regarded her with a frown. "Why not?" he challenged. "Because of your grandfather?"

"Yes," she admitted in a small voice.

"I see." Nathan fought to stem the anger surging through him. Anger directed at Silas Kincaid and his irascibility. The ornery preacher had no right to terrorize the girl. Though he had only met the man once, he couldn't help but feel that as long as her grandfather lived, Jael Kincaid could never claim a life of her own.

And the old buzzard seemed too mean to die.

"Besides, I'm not going directly home," Jael explained in a rush of words. "I have to go to the market first."

"Then at least allow me to keep you company while you conduct your business."

His lazy grin disarmed her. Jael felt the corners of her mouth curve upward in reluctant response. Her suddenly befuddled senses registered that his eyes were a clear golden brown liberally flecked with green. Arresting eyes—as arresting as the man himself. "All right," she agreed shyly.

As they strolled toward the marketplace, she studied him with a series of sidelong glances. He was dressed more casually than last time. With snug-fitting trousers molding long, muscular legs and a white shirt open at the throat to reveal a mat of chestnut curls, he looked more like a pirate than ever. Very masculine... and very appealing.

Resolutely she pulled her attention away from Nathan Thorne's physical attributes and back to the matter at hand. She searched her mind for a way to discourage him short of seeming rude. "I don't want to detain you. Surely you must have more important matters to attend to."

"Nothing pressing. Tell me about yourself."

"There isn't much to tell."

"How long have you lived in the islands?"

"Since I was twelve."

"What about your parents?" Nathan persisted. "Were they missionaries, too?"

"No." Jael gazed out across the Auau Channel. White-capped waves danced restlessly in shimmering sapphire waters. Waves restless as her mother had been as a young girl. "My mother died shortly before I came to live with my grandparents."

"And your father?"

"I never knew him," she confessed. "My mother never wed."

She dragged her gaze back to Nathan. She expected shock, censure—or disappointment—to register on Nathan Thorne's handsome face. Instead, it reflected sympathy and understanding. A lump rose in her throat at this unanticipated reaction.

"Forgive me for prying." He caught her hand and squeezed it reassuringly. "Your mother's mistakes should be no reflection on you."

A bitter laugh escaped. "Not a day goes by in which Grandfather lets me forget her sin."

"The fault lies within your grandfather, not you. Though I'm not a regular churchgoer, I know the Bible teaches forgiveness—not vengeance." He increased the pressure on her hand, then released it.

At a loss as to how to respond, Jael was glad when they arrived at the marketplace, as it hindered further conversation.

The market consisted of a large straw house extending the entire length of the canal. Enterprising Hawaiians sold fish, vegetables, fruit, and dry goods of all sorts. Jael ignored the stalls that lined both sides of the wide center aisle and headed directly for a booth at the far end.

Mrs. Ka'ano, a Hawaiian woman nearly as round as she was high, greeted Jael with a broad smile and a merry twinkle in her black eyes. "You bring more for Mrs. Ka'ano to sell, pretty lady?"

Jael returned the smile. It was Mrs. Ka'ano's inherent friendliness that had first given her the courage to approach the woman six months earlier. Jael cast a quick glance at Nathan, fervently wishing he would find something to occupy his attention while she conducted her business. An unwelcome flush crept into her cheeks. As though sensing her unease, he turned away to study the goods at a neighboring stall. Breathing a sigh of relief, Jael reached into her basket and extracted a neatly wrapped bundle.

Mrs. Ka'ano showed no hesitation. She whipped off the wrapping and carefully inspected the stack of delicate feminine undergarments, some skillfully embroidered with soft pastel threads, others intricately smocked and trimmed with satin ribbons. Each was sewn with painstaking attention to detail. All were exquisitely feminine.

"Ah, very nice," Mrs. Ka'ano said at last, holding a camisole of fine cambric between thumb and forefinger. "Ladies buy plenty fast. Please themselves and," she winked broadly, "please their gentlemen."

Satisfied with the handiwork, the rotund Hawaiian pulled out a tin box concealed beneath a display table, counted out currency, and delivered it to Jael. "Come next week. Maybe more money for pretty lady."

"Thank you, Mrs. Ka'ano." Jael took the money and quickly stuck it in her pocket.

"Who is your handsome man, lady? Maybe he buy you trinket." Mrs. Ka'ano waved her chubby hand over the wide variety of wares spread across a cloth-draped table.

Jael gasped. Hectic color flooded her cheeks. "Mrs. Ka'ano, no."

But the woman was nonplussed. "Hush, you. Men like to buy presents. Like to make their ladies smile."

Hearing himself being discussed, Nathan

swung around. "A trinket is a small price for a smile. Somehow, I have a feeling that the young lady doesn't smile nearly enough."

"Really, Captain Thorne," Jael protested, growing more uncomfortable with each passing minute.

"Let me see...." Nathan scanned the table of baubles. He examined shell necklaces, lacy handkerchiefs, and even a silk parasol with a Japanese motif.

Jael tried again to dissuade him. "Truly, Captain, this is unnecessary. Certainly Mrs. Ka'ano was merely jesting."

Nathan lifted a brow askance. "Certainly, Miss Kincaid, even an innocent like you must realize Mrs. Ka'ano possesses a shrewd business sense. She can probably smell a sale a mile away."

"Ah, Captain," Mrs. Ka'ano beamed, "you are indeed as wise as you are handsome."

"And you, madam, are also skilled in flattery," Nathan countered.

The Hawaiian woman acknowledged the compliment with a regal tilt of her head. "I have special items reserved for special customers." Again she reached beneath the table and, this time, produced a case of polished teak.

Jael, curious in spite of herself, edged closer. Mrs. Ka'ano flashed a sly smile at the two young people and then with great ceremony slowly opened the lid.

Jael expelled a soft sigh of pleasure at the sight of beautifully carved scrimshaw jewelry displayed on lush black velvet. Nathan scrutinized the items with a critical eye before reaching inside and picking up a small brooch carved with what appeared to be a tiny rose.

"A particularly fine piece," Mrs. Ka'ano concurred. "That is pikake, or jasmine, as haole call it."

"Yes, I know," he replied absently as he inspected the bit of jewelry resting in the palm of his hand.

"It's lovely," Jael murmured. A lump rose in her throat. Jasmine—her namesake. Impulsively she reached out and traced the delicate carving with a fingertip.

"If you like it, it's yours." Nathan dug into his pocket for money with which to complete the transaction.

"No, please, Captain. I don't want it."

Nathan stared at her quizzically. "If you don't share my taste in jewelry, you're welcome to choose something else."

It struck her that he might not be offended, but hurt at her refusal of his gift. The realization rendered her momentarily speechless. "It's lovely, but I can't accept it," she managed when she found her voice again. Her eyes entreated him to understand.

He frowned thoughtfully. "But if you like it as much as you say you do..."

"Please," she forged ahead. "If Grandfather ever discovered..."

His expression cleared as understanding dawned. He replaced the brooch on its velvet bed and closed the lid of the teak case with a decisive click. "I wouldn't want to do anything that might cause any repercussions."

Jael's spirits lightened. After promising a disappointed Mrs. Ka'ano to return soon, she bade her good-bye, then left the market with Nathan determinedly at her side.

"Sew more quicker. You make bigger dollar," Mrs. Ka'ano called after them.

For a time, Jael and Nathan walked in silence. Out of habit, Jael nervously scanned the shrubbery that bordered the narrow path leading away from town. Never far from her mind was the notion that someone observed her every move, all the while careful never to reveal his presence. Her palms grew damp at the thought; her pulse jerked, then settled back in its usual rhythm.

"I'll only walk you halfway."

Jael started at the sound of Nathan's low voice, then silently berated herself for being skittish. Switching the basket to her other hand, she surreptitiously wiped her sweaty palm on her dun-colored cotton skirt.

Nathan pretended not to notice her nervous gesture. Pausing, he plucked a blossom from a nearby bush and presented it to her with a flourish. "Pikake."

Smiling, Jael accepted the flower. "Thank you, Captain."

"My friends call me Nathan," he reminded her.

"Nathan." She stared into his compelling hazel eyes and felt suddenly giddy. "Nathan," she repeated slowly, liking the way it rolled off her tongue, liking the way it made her feel.

She dragged her gaze from his and, closing her eyes briefly, inhaled the honeyed fragrance of jasmine.

Watching her delight at his simple offering, Nathan felt inordinately pleased with himself. This woman-child had a strange effect on him. One minute she made him want to shower her with gifts. The next, like a knight of old, mount his charger and ride to her rescue, ready to slay dragons if need be.

Then and there he made a vow. After he walked Jael partway home, he'd return to the marketplace and quiz Mrs. Ka'ano. He had glimpsed the exchange of clothing for money and was curious to learn exactly what business dealings his prim little missionary had with the Hawaiian woman.

And why?

Chapter 3

Sew more quicker. You make bigger dollar.

Jael yawned and tried to concentrate on the row of tiny, precise stitches. The hour was late. Grandfather slept soundly. Just as his loud snoring reverberated through the walls, Mrs. Ka'ano's advice echoed through her mind. How much money did it cost to book passage to Fairhaven, New Bedford, Nantucket, or any of the whaling towns along the eastern seaboard? she wondered. Whatever the price, the amount was probably more than she had managed to save thus far. Captain Thorne—Nathan, she corrected—would know. She had been remiss not to ask him when she had the chance.

She rested her head against the back of the chair. Her thoughts drifted to a smile as bright as sunlight. To a man as tempting as sin itself. For the first time in her sheltered existence, she had an inkling of the attraction that could exist between a man and a woman. But such weakness had led to her mother's downfall. From an early age she had decided that she wouldn't fall victim to the same fate. Once she escaped her grandfather's tyranny, Jael vowed, she would never—ever—allow another to subjugate her.

Not even one who stole her breath with a smile.

Her resolve bolstered, Jael neatly folded the camisole she was embroidering, then stood. She stretched, her body stiff after sitting for hours. Her glance swept the small, sterile room she had occupied since childhood. A pine chest held all her worldly possessions in its three drawers. Above the chest hung a picture of vengeful angels wielding pitchforks and spears as they cast the wicked into the bowels of hell. As a child, she had laid awake nights fearing she would be their next victim. Once she removed the picture from the wall and hid it behind the chest. Her grandmother had found it the next morning. Jael considered herself fortunate to get off with a lecture on not touching what did not belong to her. But if she persisted, her grandmother had warned, she would be forced to tell Silas. Could the Lord's wrath be any worse than Grandfather's? Jael wondered. In her mind, they were one and the same.

The narrow iron bed with its hand-stitched counterpane and gauzy mosquito netting beckoned. But she still had several things to do before retiring for the night. She must creep out to the cookhouse, return the sewing basket to its hiding place, and add the money Mrs.

Ka'ano had paid her to the small cache she had already saved. She had long suspected her grandfather periodically searched through her belongings, but knew he never invaded the cookhouse.

Careful to avoid squeaking floorboards, she tiptoed through the house. Upon reaching the doorway, she paused and looked about. Sooty clouds scudded restlessly across a murky sky, often obscuring the pale silver crescent of the moon. The wind beat against the palm trees, sending them swaying and dipping like drunken sailors. Shifting shadows transformed familiar shapes into sinister forms. A storm was brewing; rain would fall before first light.

Driven by a sense of urgency, Jael left the shelter of the cottage and hurried toward the cookhouse. The crushed shell walkway bit into the soles of her bare feet, but she barely noticed the discomfort. Midway along the path, she stopped suddenly, her body tense. The hair along the nape of her neck prickled—the same sensation she had experienced returning from Wainee.

The bogeyman will get you.

The childhood taunt ran in sing-song through her mind. Jael's fist tightened reflexively, and the coins she clutched dug into the palm of her hand. The pain sliced through the immobilizing torpor. *Stop behaving like a frightened child*, she chastised herself. After all, she was a grown woman. If she wasn't brave enough to venture out of her own home at night, where would she ever find the courage to leave the islands?

Jael drew a steadying breath and quickly traversed the remaining distance to enter the cookhouse. Two narrow windows on either side of the open doorway allowed light to seep in. Even so, darkness hugged the corners. Jael fervently wished she had brought a candle with her. Nerves on edge, she stashed the basket of sewing beneath the dry sink, then dragged a three-legged stool over to a tall cabinet, climbed on top, and took an earthenware jar from the top shelf. She took off the lid and dropped the money inside.

She was about to replace the lid when the feeble light dimmed and was then snuffed out by an invisible hand. Thick gloom blanketed the cookhouse.

Jael froze. Her heart seemed to stop beating. For a long, terrible moment, she ceased to breathe as every fiber in her body reacted to a numbing fear. Gradually her heart resumed a reluctant, heavy thudding against her rib cage and her oxygen-starved lungs labored to suck in air. She tried to convince herself there was nothing to be frightened of. Clouds drifting across the moon, nothing more. Yet she trembled. She pivoted slowly, not really wanting to see what was behind her, but compelled to look. Just as she did so, a silhouette moved across the window. A man's silhouette, one far too large to belong to her grandfather. Footsteps crunched on the shell walkway, then grew muffled and disappeared. Once again the cookhouse was bathed in eerie light.

Jael scrambled from the stool, sending it toppling to the stone floor, and ran for the relative safety of the cottage. The night was as before. Full of shifting shadows. Shapes without substance. Forms without faces. The wind twisted the white muslin nightdress around her legs as she made her way toward the house. Suddenly she stopped short. At her feet, in the center of the walk, was a beautiful lei held in place by a chunk of lava.

She stared at it for a long moment, then slowly stooped to pick it up. Its soft petals felt like lush velvet in her cupped hands. Drawn by its sweet perfume, she dipped her head and inhaled the heady aroma. She recognized the feathery red blossoms as being ohia lehua. At one time, they were considered sacred. It was said that Hawaiian chiefs made leis of them for Pele, the volcano goddess. Grandfather despised them, calling them the heathens' flower. Yet someone had deliberately plucked these exotic blooms, made them into a lovely wreath, and then placed it directly in her path. Fear and confusion spread through her.

The lei dropped from her nerveless fingers.

She ran into the house, closed the door, and drew the shutters, shaken by the unwanted gift. Who would do such a thing? Who lurked in the bushes careful to keep his presence a secret?

And why?

* * *

Alice Hadley stopped in front of each guest with a tray laden with generous slices of her renowned pineapple cake. "I must confess my conscience is bothering me."

"Do unburden yourself, dear," urged Phoebe Skinner, a handsome woman in her forties.

"At Thomas's urging, I invited Reverend Kincaid and his granddaughter Jael to join us for dinner, but when he said he was conducting a prayer meeting this evening, I was secretly relieved." Alice waited patiently while Phoebe perused the entire selection before choosing the largest piece. "I realize that was a very uncharitable reaction, and I should be ashamed. But I'm not the least bit sorry he couldn't join us."

Edmund Skinner, captain of the schooner *Sunflower*, declined dessert with a shake of his head. "What's wrong with the man?"

"Silas can be rather..." Reverend Thomas Hadley accepted a cup of tea, stalling while he searched for the appropriate word to describe his colleague.

"Argumentative," Alice supplied. "Silas Kincaid is without a doubt the most contentious person I've ever met. I feared he would ruin a pleasant evening with one of his endless diatribes on the lack of moral fiber among seamen."

Thomas aimed a meaningful look at his wife over his wire-rimmed glasses. "Silas is a man of strong convictions. In light of the recent spate of rowdiness in town, I fear he's become quite outspoken on his views of whaling men."

"Poor Jael." Alice wagged her head in sympathy as she offered tea and cake to her daughter Corinne, then moved on to Nathan. "I don't understand how she puts up with his abuse."

"Alice, you mustn't say things like that." Thomas gently but firmly rebuked his outspoken wife. "You have no way of knowing for certain whether or not Reverend Kincaid mistreats the girl."

"Women have a sixth sense, Thomas." Alice Hadley settled on the sofa next to her husband.

Nathan leaned forward, a frown drawing his brows together. "Are you intimating that the old man beats his granddaughter?"

"Goodness gracious." Phoebe clucked her tongue, her eyes darting between Alice Hadley and Nathan. "Do tell all."

"My wife suffers from an insatiable curiosity." Edmund Skinner gave his companion of twenty-five years an indulgent smile. "It's her only flaw."

"Well, of course, I can't say for certain, but I have my suspicions." Alice Hadley daintily stirred her tea while Nathan barely restrained his impatience to learn more about Jael Kincaid.

"You're her friend, Corinne." Reverend Hadley turned to his daughter for verification of the many rumors. "Has Jael ever mentioned her grandfather harming her in any way?"

"Jael isn't the sort to speak ill of anyone, especially her family."

"How well do the two of you know each other?" Nathan persisted. He set his cake aside untouched while he studied Corinne with frank interest. There was such a wide disparity between the two young women that he found it difficult to imagine them as friends. Corinne struck him as sensible and self-confident, able to hold her own in any given situation. According to her father, she was about to return to the States, unaccompanied, where she would marry her fiancée, a medical student at Yale. Jael, on the other hand, possessed a vulnerability that, to his chagrin, both irritated and attracted him.

Alice Hadley didn't share her daughter's reticence on the subject. "While Silas Kincaid seldom allows Jael out of sight, there have been occasions over the years when the girls have spent time together."

Corinne's expression clouded. "There was one incident..."

"Go on, dear," Phoebe prodded, leaning forward in her eagerness to hear more details.

"I'm afraid you'll have to forgive my wife." Edmund Skinner helped himself to another cup of tea. "Phoebe has spent entirely too much time of late restricted to shipboard. She has sorely missed the chance to gossip."

Corinne addressed her comments to the gathering at large. "Several years ago, Jael and I were asked to deliver medical supplies to Wailuku. It was very hot that day, so on the way home we decided to cool off by wading in the ocean. We had to raise our skirts above our knees to keep them from getting wet, and..."

"... And?" Nathan prompted.

"I still remember the backs of her legs." Corinne's troubled brown eyes swept her rapt audience before resting on Nathan. "They were covered with welts."

"Did you question her about them?" Nathan asked, uncaring that his persistence was drawing quizzical looks from the others.

"Yes, as a matter of fact, I did." Corinne frowned into her teacup. "Jael said her grandfather had used his cane on her, but that I wasn't to blame him. She insisted the fault was hers."

Reverend Hadley looked appalled at his daughter's revelation. "Did she say what she had done to provoke such harsh punishment?"

"No." Corinne shook her head. "Jael simply refused to talk about it and changed the subject."

"I suspected as much." Alice Hadley nodded smugly. "Remember, Thomas, when Bishop Willery came from Honolulu to administer confirmation to our converts? Jael must have been about fourteen at the time." She adjusted a small pillow behind her back and absently stirred her tea. "The ceremony and reception lasted an entire day, and not once did the poor girl sit down. Not that I didn't ask, mind you, but she refused, saying she'd rather stand. I remember remarking about it to her grandmother, but Esther Kincaid seemed unconcerned at the child's odd behavior. Said the girl was sulking after being disciplined the day before. Then Esther complained how the girl was a trial to them in their advancing age, but that she and Silas felt it was their Christian duty to raise her since her mother was dead."

In the wake of Alice Hadley's story, a heavy silence fell over the group. Frowning darkly, Nathan clenched his jaw. He had seen the fanatical gleam in the clergyman's eyes, so allegations of mistreatment shouldn't have come as a surprise. Yet it greatly disturbed him to think of the lovely girl as the victim of a vicious old man.

Phoebe Skinner cleared her throat. "I don't know the young lady, but she sounds like a fragile creature."

"Sometimes it's strength, my friends, not weakness, that enables us to endure life's hardships," Reverend Hadley quietly reminded the gathering.

Nathan's mouth curled into a cynical twist. Spoken like a man of the cloth, but he wasn't buying into the preacher's bag of platitudes. Minister or not, Silas Kincaid was evil hidden under the guise of piety. And Jael an innocent lamb thrust into a lion's den. If anyone ever needed a champion, it was she. As he had thought earlier, the girl needed a husband to look after her. What was wrong with the young men on Maui? Where was their backbone? Rather than pursue her hand in matrimony, they had allowed Silas Kincaid to scare them off.

A loud banging sounded on the front door, interrupting further discussion. Thomas Hadley rose to his feet, crossed the room, and opened the door. Not waiting for an invitation, Silas Kincaid stepped into the parlor with his granddaughter in tow.

Angry red smeared the sharp planes of Silas's high cheekbones. "I tried to warn you," he intoned theatrically. "This town is crawling with godless heathens who reek of rum."

"What's the problem, Silas?" Thomas adopted a mild tone.

Silas drew his reed-thin body to its full height. "A drunk, unruly crowd disrupted my prayer meeting. Drove off every potential convert."

Alice Hadley went to her husband's side. She glanced worriedly from one man to the other. "I baked a pineapple cake just this morning. Please, Silas, why don't you and your granddaughter sit down and join us for dessert."

"This is not a social call, madam, but one of utmost importance," Silas declared pompously.

Aware his guests avidly watched the unfolding scene, Thomas strove for a modicum of cordiality. "Before we adjourn to my study where we can discuss the matter, allow me to introduce my guests."

Silas glowered at the group. Jael stood behind him, her eyes demurely downcast.

Thomas Hadley quickly made the introductions. "Captain Skinner and his wife, Phoebe, are old friends of ours," he explained, "and Captain Thorne is the son-in-law of my brother, who also happens to be the owner of his ship, the *Clotilde*."

Son-in-law? Jael's heart plummeted to her heels. Nathan... married? It stood to reason that a man as attractive as he would have a wife and probably children waiting for him back home. She had even dreamed about him, she thought with self-loathing. Grandfather was right. She was a ninny. A naive little fool! She twisted her fingers together and kept her gaze averted.

Silas viewed Nathan with open disdain. "You again, eh?"

"The two of you have met?" Thomas asked.

"In a manner of speaking, you might say that. Captain Thorne brazenly escorted the girl home from town after she defied my specific order to avoid the Lahaina Roadstead."

Jael wasn't listening to her grandfather's tirade. What an easy target she had been for Nathan's breezy charm—how ridiculously easy. He must have found her amusing. She had been hopelessly infatuated with the first man to smile at her. Her mother's daughter through and through.

Silas's chin whiskers bristled in self-righteous indignation. "There's serious work to be done if we're to save the heathen from Satan's fires. Yet you, Hadley, sit here engaged in idle chatter consorting with the enemy."

"The enemy," Edmund Skinner choked in indignation, his tea sloshing over the rim of his cup. "Now just a minute, sir."

"The enemy is not just at your doorstep. He is here inside your home." Silas pointed a spindly finger dramatically at the two ship's captains.

Thomas Hadley bit back a sharp retort and prayed for forbearance. Silas Kincaid was a trial sent by the Almighty to test his patience. "If you continue to insult my guests, Silas, I'm going to have to ask you to leave."

Silas was undeterred by the threat. "Time has come to take a stand against the defilers of God's laws."

Jael felt Nathan watching her, but resolutely kept her gaze trained on her grandfather's back.

"Which specific laws are you referring to, Silas?" Thomas asked with admirable restraint.

"Men—seafaring men—come ashore whoring after the heathens. Then they consume great quantities of rum in the grog shops that line the streets of town. It's sinful, I tell you. Sinful! God will bring His wrath down on the entire population of Hawaii just as He did to the citizens of Sodom and Gomorrah." Silas's voice quivered with fervency.

Jael moved to stand next to her grandfather and placed a restraining hand on his arm. "Grandfather, please," she cautioned. "It isn't good for you to get so upset."

Silas shook off her touch.

Jael instinctively stepped back. "I-I'm sorry, Grandfather," she stammered. "I was merely concerned about your welfare."

"Be concerned about your eternal soul, girl. That is in more danger than my well-being. Don't think I didn't notice those men ogling you tonight." Silas thumped his hickory walking stick against the floor. "Remember, Granddaughter, the Lord will reward His humble servant and punish the wicked."

Unable to ignore Nathan's penetrating gaze any longer, she turned her head to meet his look. With uncanny ability, she read pity in his arresting hazel eyes. Her pride smarted. It was a look often cast her way, one that made what little was left of her self-respect shrivel still more. *Be proud*, Mother had always told her. *Hold your head high, sweeting, for you've done nothing to feel ashamed of.* Remembering, she squared her shoulders.

Nathan had heard enough of the old man's self-righteous fervor. He stood abruptly, arms folded across his chest, head to one side. "I trust the Lord has the wisdom to discern who is wicked and who is pure of heart."

Silas glared at Nathan with undisguised loathing. "When, Captain Thorne, did you last attend church?"

"I've been taught that only the Lord can see into men's hearts," Nathan replied quietly.

"Hrmph!" Silas tugged on the lapels of his jacket. "God has granted some of His servants more wisdom than others."

"At last we agree," Nathan concurred wholeheartedly.

Jael felt the urge to smile. Nathan had adroitly managed to end her grandfather's tirade—at least temporarily.

Uneasy silence fell over the small assembly. Alice Hadley looked to her husband for direction. Captain Skinner and his wife exchanged glances while Corinne fidgeted with the handle of her teacup. Jael studied the needlepoint sampler on the wall. Of the group, Nathan appeared the least disconcerted. He calmly met Silas Kincaid's pale glare with a smile that a casual observer might even describe as pleasant.

Thomas Hadley belatedly took command of the drama being enacted in his parlor. "Let's adjourn to my office, Silas. There we can discuss the matter and decide on a time for a future meeting."

Silas Kincaid allowed himself to be steered from the room. "Every grog shop in Lahaina—indeed every den of iniquity on the island needs to be banned. The longer this is allowed to continue..." The office door closed decisively on the rest of his sentence.

Nathan instantly stepped into the lull by catching Jael's hand and drawing it through the crook of his arm. "If you'll excuse us," he said, bestowing a winning smile on his hostess, "Miss Kincaid and I have a small matter to resolve."

Before Jael could collect her wits or one of the guests could voice an objection, Nathan propelled her from the parlor and out onto the veranda.

Chapter 4

"What will people think?" Jael cast a worried glance over her shoulder.

Nathan muttered something under his breath. "What could I possibly do to jeopardize your reputation with a roomful of people not ten feet away?" he shot back, irritated at finding himself whispering.

Jael, equally irate, whispered back, "Grandfather will be furious if he discovers us alone together."

"What I have to say won't take long."

"Very well," she returned with a crisp nod. "Get on with it." She stationed herself near the edge of the veranda.

Nathan cursed himself for a fool. What did this slip of a woman-child matter to him anyway? Why take her problems upon himself? If the tight-knit community of missionaries was unconcerned about her welfare, why should it bother him? He tunneled his fingers through his hair. *Damn!* He was an easy mark when it came to a pretty face and trusting blue eyes.

"I heard some rumors this evening that disturbed me."

Jael glanced into the lamplit room behind her. The people who remained in the parlor had resumed their conversation in hushed, animated tones while Mrs. Hadley efficiently refilled teacups. There was still no sign of her grandfather or Reverend Hadley, though they could emerge at any moment. "What did you hear tonight that bothered you?"

Nathan blew out an impatient breath, then took the plunge. "Does the old man beat you?"

Jael tensed. So that was Nathan's burning question. That explained his pitying glance. Apparently she had been the object of gossip before their untimely intrusion. Even Corinne, her closest friend, had been telling tales behind her back, she thought with a growing sense of betrayal. "Whatever transpires between my grandfather and me is none of your business—or that of anyone else."

Nathan scowled down at her. Beneath the straw brim of her bonnet, her expression was wooden. Jael had neatly evaded his question and, in so doing, had provided the answer. "The bastard," he breathed, clenching and unclenching his fists. "He ought to be horsewhipped."

Jael stared back defiantly. This man had no right to ask her personal questions. No right whatsoever. He should save his precious concern for the wife who patiently awaited his return in some distant seaport. "How Grandfather treats me is no concern of yours, Captain Thorne."

He scowled into her upturned face. Her reply irritated the hell out of him. So did the fact that she was absolutely correct. Soon as whaling season began, he would sail from Lahaina. The last thing he needed—or wanted—was a woman clinging to his coattails. "You're right. Your safety is no affair of mine."

"Rest assured, Captain, I can fend for myself."

"Pardon me, *Miss* Kincaid," Nathan replied in a voice dripping sarcasm, "but you hardly look strong enough to defend yourself against a swarm of mosquitoes." Nevertheless, he admitted reluctantly, she was right about one thing. She was none of his business. Absolutely, positively none.

Her chin raised a notch. "Muscle and brawn aren't the only measures of strength."

Nathan recalled Thomas Hadley's earlier words along the same vein. Missionaries, he knew, also preached that when struck by an opponent one should turn the other cheek. Another philosophy he didn't adhere to. He ascribed to the belief that when attacked the only solution was to fight back with both fists. Folding his arms across his chest, he rocked back on his heels. "Forgive my foolish concern."

Jael felt a stab of remorse. In spite of his biting sarcasm, she hoped she hadn't unwittingly offended him. Dropping her voice, she sought to make amends. "I didn't mean to sound ungrateful, Captain, but there is no cause for worry on my behalf. I have plans to leave the islands."

"Plans?" A frown drew his brows together.

"Shh." She glanced nervously over her shoulder as though half expecting her grandfather to descend upon her, his cane raised in retribution.

"What kind of plans?"

She already regretted her impulsive admission. "I'm not obligated to relate the details to you or to anyone else. I'm legally of age to do as I please."

"Bah!" he scoffed. "You're scarcely more than a child."

"Child or woman, Captain Thorne, I'll do whatever it takes. I will leave Maui—and soon."

Jael Kincaid's words, though softly spoken, were laced with steel. She was certainly turning out to be an obstinate little creature, he thought, half amused, half chagrined at the discovery. He felt respect burgeon for the mere slip of a girl. Perhaps he had underestimated her. Perhaps she was capable of dealing with her grandfather's cruelty. Perhaps she was less fragile than he feared, and he didn't have to worry about her. *Worry?* He grimaced. Why should he care what happened to a girl he barely knew. One who had informed him in no uncertain terms that she didn't need— or want—his concern?

"I am prepared to do whatever must be done, Captain Thorne, and I will find a way."

Jael repeated the avowal as much for her benefit as for Nathan's. She savored the sound of the words, liking their ring of resolve, the promise of freedom. This marked the first time she had said them aloud. Doing so lent them credibility—even to her own ears. Strange that Nathan Thorne, not Corinne Hadley, should be the first she had confided in, she mused.

A smile softened the stern line of Nathan's mouth. "Such passion, little one. I'm beginning to wonder if the name pagan doesn't suit you after all."

Her eyes widened with amazement as they searched his face. When he spoke the word, pagan sounded like a compliment and not an epithet.

Impulsively he reached out and gently traced a forefinger across her cheekbone. "There are shadows beneath those bewitching blue eyes, little pagan flower."

An alarm sounded in Jael's head, but she ignored it. Nathan Thorne made it seem as though it really mattered whether or not she was rested. How long had it been since anyone had cared? She couldn't remember the last time. A lump lodged in her throat, painful and tight.

"Have you been sleeping poorly?"

The truth was she hadn't been sleeping well, and when she did sleep her dreams were haunted by nightmares. Dreams in which she was pursued by a mysterious phantom. She felt a strong temptation to confess her fears to a sympathetic listener.

Then suspicion surged to the surface, and she edged back beyond his reach. Could this man be trusted? If anything, experience had taught her to be wary of men. Perhaps she had already revealed far too much to a virtual stranger.

And a married one at that, she recalled belatedly.

The revelation had come as a shock. Her first instinct had been to loudly refute the claim. But Reverend Hadley was an honorable man of the cloth. He would never say anything that wasn't truthful. If he said Nathan Thorne was his brother's son-in-law, then Nathan must surely be exactly that. She wrestled with the perverse need to hear Nathan admit or deny his marital status—and lost. "Is it true, Captain, that you're married to Reverend Hadley's niece?" Her words came out in a rush.

Nathan regarded her, somewhat bemused. "Married or not, what difference does it make?"

"N-none," she stammered a shade too quickly to be convincing. "I was merely curious."

"Then allow me to set the record straight." A hint of a smile tugged at his mouth before his expression turned serious. "I am a widower. My wife—Catherine—died less than a year after we wed."

"Oh-h." Jael linked her fingers together and

nervously worried her lower lip with her teeth. What had she been thinking to ask such a personal question? A question that undoubtedly opened old wounds. "I'm so very sorry."

"Don't be." Nathan's manner was abrupt. "It all happened a very long time ago."

Unsure how to respond, Jael turned and walked to the far end of the porch. Poor Nathan. She saw him then as a tragic figure, heartbroken and grieving for a lost love. The pain must have been unbearable. "How tragic to lose your beloved so soon."

"I hate to disabuse your girlish fantasies, Jael, but Catherine and I quickly learned we were unsuited for each other. While marriage is fine for some, it's definitely not for everyone."

"I see," she murmured, not really understanding at all.

After some deliberation, Nathan looked as though he was about to explain more when, their meeting concluded, Silas Kincaid and Reverend Hadley emerged from the study. Their raised voices carried to the two young people regarding each other thoughtfully from opposite ends of the veranda.

"Mark my words, Hadley, the Lord will visit His wrath upon the islands if people continue to ignore the dens of iniquity that crowd the waterfront. Churches—not grog shops—should line the streets of a town."

"While I agree there is a problem, Silas, our primary goal should be to convert the natives to Christianity, not to condemn Christians because of their fondness for rum."

"You, Hadley, are a disgrace before the eyes of the Lord. The time has come to take a stand. Instead, you mumble mealy excuses."

Jael sucked in her breath, mortified by her grandfather's accusation. Never had she heard him openly criticize one of his colleagues. It was an unspeakable affront to do so before others. Reverend Hadley didn't deserve to be vilified. He was a fine man, understanding and patient, and held in high esteem by the *alii*, the Hawaiian royalty. Through the window, she saw him struggling to maintain his composure.

Silas's faded gaze swept the room and discovered Jael was missing. "Where's that girl run off to now?" he growled. Leaning heavily on his cane, he stomped from the parlor. He paused in the doorway, and picking Jael's figure from among the shadows on the long porch, glared at her accusingly. His piercing stare shifted from her to Nathan.

"I might have known I'd find you and the girl together," he sneered. "You're like a dog sniffing after a bitch in heat."

"Grandfather," Jael protested, shocked at his outburst.

"Really, Silas," Thomas Hadley remonstrated, "it's only natural for two young people to seek a measure of privacy for a conversation."

Silas threw the other clergyman a scornful look. "I doubt conversation is the only thing on the captain's mind." He walked over to Nathan and poked a thin, bony finger into his chest. "Keep your whoring ways away from my doorstep. I won't tolerate lecherous behavior. Stay away from the girl, Captain Thorne."

He hobbled down the steps and turned in the direction of home, not looking back to see whether or not his granddaughter followed. Her cheeks flaming, Jael hurried after him.

Nathan stared after the pair with mounting frustration. Whether he admitted it or not, there was certain merit to Silas Kincaid's advice. Instead of castigating the old man, he should give him a vote of thanks. He had already gotten more involved with the flame-haired slip of a girl than logic dictated. He'd appointed himself her protector. How noble. How commendable.

How totally unlike him.

Disgusted with himself, Nathan swung away and reentered the Hadleys' parlor.

Unnoticed, a hulking figure slipped from behind a clump of bougainvillea and, careful to keep in the shadows, followed Jael and Silas Kincaid.

Mu crept along silently. The wind whipped his iron-gray mane about his stern-featured face. Weeks of watching and waiting were nearly over. Soon the red-haired enchantress would be his. He had prepared a special place for her. A sanctuary deep in the bowels of Mauna Kea. A place where no one would disturb them.

Since the first time he laid eyes on her, he knew he must possess her. For years, ever since the old ways had been abolished, he had entreated the gods Kane, Lono, and Ku to restore the ancient *kapu* system. A system in which he had held great power. When he had spied this woman transfixed by a sunset, her hair catching fire in the dying rays, he knew his prayers had been heard. It was as though the goddess Pele stood before him, incarnate as a beautiful young woman. A sign from the spirits. An answer to his prayers. He would steal her away and convince her of his worthiness as a mate. Together they would form an alliance. Together they would rule the islands. It would be like days of old.

. . . Before the hated new religion of the missionaries.

His obsidian eyes gleaming in anticipation, Mu stationed himself behind a clump of bushes outside his victim's bedroom and prepared to wait. Just as Pele devoured the land of his ancestors with her flames, this woman consumed his mind until she burned in every thought, every desire. Soon she would be his.

It took Jael a long time to fall asleep and when she finally did, she slept restlessly. In slow, measured degrees, fear poisoned her fragmented dreams. She felt overwhelmed by the sensation that she was no longer alone. That someone loomed over her. Watchful. She tried to surface from the heavy lassitude that immobilized her. Her limbs felt leaden. Panic cast its net and captured her in an unnamed fear. She murmured aloud. Desperation spurred her struggle to awaken. Ever so slowly, she clawed through thick layers of torpor toward consciousness.

She sat bolt upright, heart racing. Perspiration plastered her dress to her skin. Terror brought an acrid taste to her mouth. She shoved her hair away from her face with trembling hands and cautiously searched the shadows.

Trade winds drifted through the partially opened shutters, the night breeze raising goose bumps along her damp flesh. Nervously she chafed her arms and was surprised at finding herself fully clothed. She must have dozed off at last still wearing her dress. She tried to calm the frantic beating of her pulse. Dregs of a vaguely remembered nightmare still held her in its thrall. Impending danger lingered in the room like a disagreeable odor. Something had frightened her badly.

Or someone.

The mosquito netting around the bed danced in the breeze. She stared at the swaying curtain, her mind still fuzzy, trying to figure out what was amiss. Then it dawned on her. Upon retiring, she had drawn the curtains around the bed.

Now they hung partially open.

Her pulse jerked, then speeded. Renewed fear coursed through her veins. It made her dizzy, nauseated. *Stay calm, Jael. Think.* She started to take a calming breath when her worst nightmare materialized from the gloom. But the man who invaded her room was no dream.

Before she could react, a large hand clamped over her mouth, stifling her scream.

At precisely noon the following day, Nathan stormed into Reverend Thomas Hadley's study. His first mate, John McFee, followed close on his heels. "I came as soon as I got your message."

"Sit down, Nathan. You, too, Mr. McFee." The minister gestured toward two low-backed Windsor chairs in front of his desk and waited until the men were seated.

"Your missive said you needed to see me immediately. What is so urgent that it couldn't wait?"

Thomas laced his fingers together on the top of his teakwood desk. "Jael's missing."

"Missing?" Nathan sprang to his feet. "How? When?"

Hadley regarded him thoughtfully, mentally weighing the sea captain's involvement with the girl.

"Out with it, man." Nathan braced both palms against the minister's desk and leaned forward. "Where do you think she went? How does her grandfather explain her disappearance?"

Uneasiness crossed the clergyman's features. Thomas dropped his gaze and shuffled then reshuffled a pile of papers on his desk. "Actually," he said, clearing his throat, "Silas Kincaid is the reason I sent for you."

Nathan was in no mood for riddles. "I'm afraid I don't follow you, Thomas."

Thomas steadfastly met Nathan's question-filled look. "Silas charged that his granddaughter might have run off to be with you."

"Ridiculous!" Nathan banged his fist on the desktop so hard the inkwell rattled in protest.

"Is it?" Hadley asked mildly.

"Of course it is." Nathan straightened and made a broad sweeping motion with one hand. "I hardly know the girl."

"Forgive me if I've insulted you, Nathan, but I felt it my duty to investigate the charges." Thomas Hadley adopted a conciliatory tone. "Seeing how you and Jael seem to be friends, I thought it not completely unreasonable that the girl might have sought your ... protection. After all, she is a comely miss, and you do have a reputation with the ladies."

John snickered at the clergyman's comment, unperturbed by the scowl Nathan shot in his direction.

Hadley sighed wearily. "It's common knowledge the man mistreats the poor girl. No one could blame her if she did run away."

"I can vouch for the captain here." The first mate stretched his legs out and crossed one ankle over the other. "Captain Thorne was aboard ship last night and all morning seeing to the new rigging. The crew can attest to the same."

Child or woman, Captain Thorne, I'll do whatever it takes. I will leave Maui—and soon.

Jael's words swept across Nathan's memory

like a cold ocean breeze. Damn! Why hadn't he been more insistent that she reveal her plans to leave the island? When he had questioned her, she had refused to give any details. "How long has she been missing?" he asked tersely.

"According to Silas, since last night. When his breakfast wasn't on the table, he went looking for her. He checked her room and found it empty. He searched all over, but found no trace of the girl."

Nathan paced the confines of the small office. He felt cramped, hemmed in. He needed space to walk, to think. "With that kind of head start, she could be on a ship halfway to Honolulu."

"Or one bound for Boston or Singapore," John offered.

Thomas drummed his fingertips on the desktop. "We've already checked the passenger lists on all ships that sailed since dawn."

Rest assured, Captain, I can fend for myself, Jael had boldly proclaimed. But somehow Nathan doubted it. Jael Kincaid was truly an innocent cast adrift in a cruel, capricious world.

Thomas reclined back in his chair and observed Nathan thoughtfully over the tips of steepled fingers. "Did Jael ever mention plans to leave Maui?"

Nathan gave a noncommittal shrug, reluctant to reveal Jael's secret. "Who could blame the girl for wanting to escape the old buzzard?" he hedged.

John took a pragmatic approach. "Well, the

miss couldn't have gone far by herself. Someone must have seen her."

"You'd think so, wouldn't you?" Thomas said with a trace of exasperation. "We've questioned half the population on the island, yet no one claims to know anything about her disappearance."

"People just don't disappear." Nathan's unease grew as he continued to pace the study. Where could Jael have gone in the middle of the night? Where? He ceased his restless prowling and glanced up as Corinne Hadley entered the room.

Corinne paused, startled at finding Nathan in her father's study. "Is Jael with you, Nathan? Please tell us she's all right."

Nathan's brows drew together. What had come over everyone? Just because he and Jael had a brief conversation out of earshot of a roomful of people, they assumed he was romantically interested in the girl. What sheer and utter nonsense! It seemed everyone in Lahaina had him pegged as a seducer of innocents. A fine reputation indeed. If he wasn't so distracted by Jael's disappearance, he'd feel downright insulted. "No," he snapped. "I haven't seen her since the night of your parents' dinner party."

"Oh, dear," Corinne sighed. "I was afraid of that."

Nathan looked at her sharply, alerted by something in her tone. Suddenly, his mouth felt dry as a desert. "Is there something you haven't told us, Corinne?"

Corinne swallowed hard, then nodded. "When I spoke with Jael, she admitted to being frightened. She thought she was being followed."

"Followed? Why, that's ridiculous!" her father scoffed. "No place on earth is safer than the islands. I've never heard of such a charge in all my years here."

Belatedly Nathan recalled that on their very first meeting Jael had claimed she was being followed. Instead of taking her fears seriously, he had brushed them aside, blaming them on an overactive imagination.

"I beg to disagree, Father," Corinne continued. "Jael believes she has a secret admirer. I teased her about it, but I could tell that she was clearly frightened by the whole affair."

"A secret admirer, eh?" John chuckled, trying to lighten the mood. "Probably some poor chap afraid to show his hand lest her grandfather bite it off."

Corinne wasn't diverted by John's feeble attempt at humor. "I've known Jael since childhood, and I've never seen her quite so nervous."

"What made Jael believe she had a secret admirer?" Hadley asked, still skeptical.

"Jael told me she'd been receiving gifts—a lei, a shell, a carved figure. These presents were always left where she was certain to find them."

"There must be some reasonable explanation," the clergyman insisted doggedly. "Surely no one meant the girl harm."

"Then where is she?" Corinne cried, her usual calm deserting her in the face of her friend's disappearance. "Where would she have gone in the middle of the night without telling a soul?"

Thomas Hadley rose and went to his daughter's side to put his arm around her shoulders. "There, there, my dear. We'll find her."

A pall fell over the four people, each of them lost in thought.

Footsteps clattered across the veranda. Moments later, Alice Hadley, wearing an apron over her dress and a smudge of flour on her cheek, ushered in a strapping young Hawaiian in his early twenties. "We have a visitor. He said his name is Inaika and that he has brought important news."

"Nice to meet you, Inaika." Hadley extended his hand in a warm greeting.

Encouraged by the friendly welcome, Inaika grasped the missionary's hand in return. "I bring news of pretty wahine."

"Out with it!" Nathan wanted to grab the Hawaiian and shake the information from him.

"I fish late at night. Heard noise, then saw Mu carry Pele to boat. She struggle, kick, but Mu is big and strong. He not let Pele go."

Nathan shot Hadley a quizzical look. "What is he talking about, Thomas?"

"Pele is the fire goddess highly revered by the Hawaiian people. When she is angry, they often describe her as a beautiful young woman with flowing red hair."

INSIDE PARADISE 75

"Jael..." Corinne murmured, the name a mere whisper of sound in the hushed room.

John sat straighter in his chair. "Who is this Mu character?"

Thomas Hadley's forehead creased with worry. "Under the old religion there were two orders of priests, the priests of Lono, who were concerned with peace and agriculture, and the priests of Ku, who were concerned with war and killing." Hadley walked over to the side window and, hands clasped behind his back, stared out at his garden. "Mu was a powerful priest, a kahuna, of the Ku. People refer to him as the public executioner. His job was to procure victims for human sacrifice and to execute *kapu* breakers, those who violated the sacred law."

Nathan's gut twisted into a knot at the disclosure. "But the old religion was abolished years ago."

"Yes." Alice Hadley absently tucked a strand of gray hair behind one ear and added another smudge of flour to her cheek in the process. "Liholiho, the son and successor of Kamehameha the Great, abolished the old religion in 1819, the year before the arrival of the first missionaries."

Her husband picked up the story again. "Many Hawaiians opposed the abolition of the old religion. They rallied under the leadership of Kekuaokalani, a priest under Kamehameha. Kekuaokalani gathered an army to fight the destroyers of the ancient gods and temples. A battle was fought on the plains of

South Kona. Kekuaokalani was killed and his followers dispersed."

"Mu not dead," Inaika insisted stubbornly, his expression earnest. "I see Pele. I see Mu carry her to boat."

"We've got to find her." Nathan's words, full of energy and determination, exploded the quiet. Jael, frightened and perhaps injured, was in the hands of a madman. The thought sent dread coursing through his veins like deadly venom.

"Don't worry." John quickly rose to his feet and stood beside Nathan. "We'll organize a search party."

Thomas Hadley picked up on the suggestion. "A friend owes me a favor. If you man it, Nathan, I'll ask for the loan of his two-man skiff. Meanwhile, I'll conduct a land search."

John squeezed Nathan's shoulder. "If anyone can scour the coast, you're the man for the job. I'll see to the *Clotilde* while you're gone." The look he gave Nathan spoke of the affection he held for his ship's captain. With a friend's insight, John sensed Nathan harbored more than a passing interest in the flame-haired girl, in spite of denials to the contrary.

Chapter 5

Terror bubbled through Jael's veins like a brook in early spring, ready to burst through the flimsy dam of calm and sweep her over the brink of hysteria. She strained against the ropes tying her wrists around the stout trunk of a tree. The rough hemp abraded her wrists until the skin was scraped raw and bloody. Her head throbbed unmercifully from the blow she had received earlier when she had tried to escape. All the while, her eyes were fixed on her captor.

Even by Hawaiian standards, the man was a giant. The average Hawaiian was large, she knew, often reaching a height of six and a half feet and weighing two hundred and fifty pounds. This man was every bit that big and then some. An iron-gray mane trailed wildly over his shoulders and framed a wide face with broad features. His gladiator's body, the color of oiled teak and clad in a tapa loincloth, was powerfully muscled as though honed by years of rigorous physical activity. He wasn't a young man, neither was he old, but rather one who wore a mantle of timelessness with careless authority.

Unmoved by her distress, the man boldly returned the stare.

Jael fought hard against the panic that threatened to engulf her. "Please," she begged, unable to keep her voice from quavering. "Untie me. Let me go."

Her abductor stepped closer until he loomed over her. Jael shrank back until the bark of the tree gouged her spine. He reached toward her, and she flinched.

His derisive snort mocked her fear. With fingers thick as sausages, he plucked the pins from her hair and tossed them away with disgust, growling low in his throat when her hair tumbled over her shoulders. He picked up a thick strand and rubbed it between his fingers, examining its texture. Intrigued, he held it up to the sunlight, twisting it and turning it first one way then the other until the rays caught hold and shimmered like fire.

"Pele," he grunted.

"No." Jale shook her head in vigorous denial. "Not Pele, Jael."

"Pele." He wound a hank of hair around and around his fist so roughly it brought the sting of tears to her eyes. "You—Pele."

Jael bit her lip to keep from crying out and bravely met her captor's look. Instantly she regretted the impulse. She felt as though she were plummeting into a bottomless abyss. The obsidian eyes boldly meeting hers were as stark as barren lava. Cunning. Evil. Tottering on the brink of madness. Her grandfather had limits to his cruelty, but this man, she sensed, had none. A shiver rippled through her.

Satisfied he had established his mastery over her, her abductor relinquished his tight hold on her hair, but not his fascination with it. He stroked the red tresses almost reverently, then before Jael could guess his intent, he pinched several hairs at the base of her scalp and jerked hard.

Jael sucked in her breath at the sting of pain. Warily she watched him hold the hairs up to the breeze. A possessive gleam shone in his dark eyes. A sly smile curved his mouth. Then, with utmost care, he added the hairs to a pouch he wore tied around his neck.

He stood back, arms folded across his massive chest, and inspected her from crown to toe with an intensity that made her want to cringe. Only sheer willpower kept her from cowering. Summoning all her courage, she stiffened her spine and returned his stare. His gaze lingered approvingly on her face and hair, then darkened as it traveled downward. Scowling, he hooked a forefinger into the neckline of her serviceable gray cotton.

"No," Jael gasped, divining his intention.

"Haole dress," he sneered. With a vicious swipe, he tore the dress from neckline to waist. "No like haole."

Jael clenched her jaw and endured the indignity. With calculated moves, her tormentor yanked on the skirt until the fabric parted with a loud rent. She prayed for forbearance as she waited for the ordeal to end.

Grunting in satisfaction, Mu tugged and tore at her dress until it was nothing but shredded strips of cloth. He ground the tattered remnants in the ground beneath his feet. "Haole gone. Pele stay."

Clad only in drawers, chemise, and muslin petticoat worn thin by repeated launderings, Jael felt naked under his perusal. Naked and defenseless. She shivered, chilled in spite of the brilliant afternoon sunshine.

Her abductor jabbed his breastbone. "Mu," he proclaimed.

Jael's eyes widened.

Mu. The public executioner?

The name Jael had feared since childhood was suddenly no longer phantom, but flesh and blood. Whispered tales of human sacrifice and torture scuttled through her mind like maggots. Under the old religion there were many *kapus*, or taboos. Stoning, strangulation, clubbing, and burning were common sentences meted out to *kapu* breakers. Even touching the king's shadow meant swift, certain death. Women in particular were forced to remember an endless list of *kapus* if they wanted to survive. A simple act, such as eating a coconut or a banana, could lead to instant strangulation. But the old ways had ceased to exist years ago. Or had they?

"You'll never get away with this," she said with false bravado. "People will be searching for me."

Mu snorted in contempt. "Grandfather no like Pele. He no look."

Cold truth rang in his words. At this very moment, her grandfather probably secretly rejoiced that she was missing. While he would publicly voice a concern he didn't feel, she knew his true feelings all too well. He hated her. Had hated her from the moment he had set eyes on her when she was a frightened child who had recently lost her mother. Even Grandmother, during her lifetime, had blamed Jael for the disgrace that had caused them to flee thousands of miles to escape the stigma of an illegitimate grandchild. Battling down a sense of futility, she cleared her throat and tried another approach. "Where are you taking me?"

"I take far. Place where no one find."

"This is a small island. You can't hide forever and never be seen."

"No one find." He made a broad gesture toward the sea. "Tomorrow we go big island."

The big island? Hawaii? A sinking sensation settled over her. Should her grandfather feel obligated to instigate a token search, it would never stretch beyond the confines of Maui. Though she had never been there, she knew Hawaii to be a vast lava wasteland dominated by two mountains, Mauna Kea and Mauna Loa. The fire goddess, Pele, was said to reside there in Kilauea, an active volcano. To Mu's warped thinking, this would represent an appropriate destination. She bunched her hands into fists. "I'm not Pele," she cried, her voice strident.

"Mu go. Find food." He turned and disappeared down the rocky slope behind her.

Jael tugged again at the bonds that secured her to the tree, but to no avail. The knots held fast. She had to find a way to escape. But how? It was difficult to think when hammers pounded incessantly inside her skull. Mu said he was taking her to the big island. Once there, they would vanish without a trace.

She rested her head against the tree, closed her eyes, and tried to formulate a plan. The wind teased her petticoats and whipped her hair across her face. Despair settled over her, smothering the last faint glimmer of hope. If Mu did kill her—as she suspected he would— no one would mourn her passing. It was a brutal realization. *No one to care. No one to mourn.* The sorrowful lament seemed borne on the breeze.

Nathan narrowed his eyes and searched the rugged coastline. The sun was already beginning to drop low in the sky. There weren't many hours of daylight left. He had sailed halfway around the island, stopping at villages along the way to inquire about a red-haired girl and a large Hawaiian man, but no one reported seeing the pair. Rounding Kalahu Point, he stopped to investigate Piilanihale, a centuries-old temple. It was a slim chance, and he knew it, but there was no telling where a man who considered himself a kahuna might carry his ill-garnered prize. The huge terraced platform, once the site of ancient rituals and human sacrifices, dozed undisturbed in the sunlight. Ghosts, not mortals, walked the stone ramparts. Nathan left, equally relieved and disappointed.

At sea once again, he peered at the shoreline through his telescope. If he didn't locate Jael soon, chances of finding her were slim. Where could the devil have taken her? Did Mu dwell on Maui? Or make his home on Lanai, or Molokai? Or perhaps on inhospitable little Kahoolawe? The day suddenly seemed less bright. He glanced skyward and was mildly surprised to find no clouds in sight.

By his calculations, he was nearing Hana, a tiny village situated at the eastern end of the island. From there, the northernmost tip of Hawaii was directly across the Alenuihaha Channel. He gazed across the open expanse of water that separated Maui from the big island of Hawaii, and wondered if at this very moment Jael and her abductor were headed there.

Heaving a sigh, Nathan concentrated on navigating the borrowed craft along a coastline that was becoming increasingly rocky. Pailao Bay, a pretty little cove fringed with black sand and considered haunted, was directly ahead of him. He adjust the telescope and scanned the shore. Suddenly he drew in a sharp breath, then swung the tiller about for a better look. His eyes hadn't betrayed him. There, he glimpsed an outrigger canoe partially concealed by boulders along a deserted crescent of beach.

And not a soul in sight.

Strange, he thought as he steered the skiff closer. Fishermen seldom ventured far from their crafts. For the first time all day, he felt a ray of optimism. The minute the skiff scraped bottom, he leaped into the water and pulled it ashore. Squinting against the glare of the sun, he looked about. Beyond the strip of black sand, the earth climbed steeply and quickly became wooded. No telltale movement rustled the thick vegetation. With his pistol tucked into the waistband of his pants, he started up the imposing bluff.

At the top, he paused and looked about again. There was still no sign of the canoe's owner. Or of Jael. He cupped his hands around his mouth, ready to shout her name until it echoed off Haleakala's towering crater, then a thought occurred to him. What if his cries served no purpose other than to alert her abductor? He dropped his hands to his sides in frustration.

Cautiously he continued along the bluff. To his left, the Pacific touched the horizon, blue meeting blue. On the right, verdant foliage marched up the ramparts of Haleakala, or "house of the sun," as natives referred to the dormant volcano. Another time he would have appreciated the beauty of his surroundings, but not now. Not when his mind was preoccupied with Jael's safety. Discouraged by his fruitless search, he was about to return to the skiff when his eyes fell upon a barely discernible path of downtrodden grass. Responding to a tightening in his gut, he drew his gun and proceeded to follow the trail. He broke through a thick copse of trees and stumbled to a halt.

Jael stood lashed to a tree in a small clearing. Alive. He had found her *alive*. Dressed in flowing white, her hair fluttering like a brilliant banner in the breeze, she resembled an ancient pagan offering to the gods. Driven by a need to reassure himself that she was unharmed, he returned the gun to his waistband and ran to her side.

He pushed aside the thick curtain of hair and gently cupped her face in both hands. Moisture shimmered at the tips of her lashes, making them dark spikes around eyes that were enormous in her pale, delicate face. He stared into twin pools of blue violet and felt as though he were drowning. Relief slammed into him, so profound, so forceful, it made his knees weak.

Jael blinked in disbelief. "Nathan," she whispered, uncertain whether or not to trust her good fortune.

A lump rose in his throat and he swallowed it back. He was staggered by how much this woman-child had come to mean to him in such a short time. He wiped traces of tears from her cheeks with the pads of his thumbs. "Are you all right?" he asked huskily.

"Yes," she managed with a tremulous smile. "I am now."

He whipped out a pocketknife and slashed the ropes binding her to the tree trunk. Hurtling into his arms, she buried her face in the curve of his shoulder and clung shamelessly.

"Thank God you're safe." He wrapped his arms around her, his voice hoarse with emotion.

Jael snuggled against him as though seeking his warmth. "I was so scared." Her words sounded muffled against his chest. "I thought I was going to die."

The urge to comfort warred with the instinct to retreat. Prudence fought against impulse. The wisest thing to do would be to keep her at arm's length, not pull her closer. Nathan groaned inwardly. But when had he ever been wise? Or prudent? Ignoring the warning his brain telegraphed, he tightened his arms around her. "Don't think that way. You've nothing more to fear now that I'm here." He pressed a kiss into her tumbled curls.

Safe, Jael marveled as she continued to cling. Numbed with fear, she held fast, trying to absorb his heat, his vitality, his strength. Suddenly life seemed unbearably sweet, indescribably precious. She drew a shuddering breath. Nathan smelled of sea and sun and healthy male. His musky scent mingled with the heady exuberance of her rescue to form an intoxicating brew that made her want to laugh and weep at the same time. "How did you ever find me?" she asked, drawing back slightly to look up at him.

At the shift in her position, the hard barrel

of the pistol jabbed into Nathan's midriff, a grim reminder of the gravity of the situation. "Luck," he admitted ruefully. He stepped back and examined her for injuries. He frowned at the darkening bruise along her jaw, then explored the lump with a gentle touch. "The bastard! I could kill him for this."

Jael's temporary sense of well-being vanished in the blink of an eye. Even now Mu could be lurking in the foliage, watching. Always watching. The thought was sobering. "Let's go, Nathan," she pleaded, frantically clutching his shirtsleeve. "We have to get away—far away—before he comes back."

"Are you worried that I can't protect you?" Nathan's pride balked at the implication. His jaw hardened with resolution. He'd protect her with his life if need be. The knowledge stunned him.

His mind quickly scrambled for a reasonable explanation before placing the blame on Thomas Hadley's stooped shoulders. Hadley was responsible for this uncharacteristic surge of protectiveness. He had promised his friend that he'd find the girl and return her safely— and as his crew well knew, Nathan Thorne was a man of his word. Jael Kincaid, after all, was no different than anyone else given into his charge. Absolutely no different.

"Mu's a giant." Jael caught Nathan's hand and tugged impatiently, unable to understand his obdurateness. "And he's evil, truly evil."

Nathan rested his hand on the butt of the pistol. "Even a giant doesn't stand much chance against a man who's armed."

"Please, Nathan, don't argue. There isn't time." Eyes bright with worry, she darted a look over her shoulder.

Jael was right, Nathan conceded reluctantly, they needed to get away before Mu returned. By all accounts, the man would be a formidable opponent should a fight ensue. He clasped her hand, but before he could take a single step, he heard Jael's gasp of dismay.

Mu, his features as impassive as a carved tiki figure, stood outlined against the cloudless blue sky at the edge of the bluff, cutting off their retreat.

Nathan instantly released Jael's hand and, whipping out the pistol from the waistband of his pants, leveled it at Jael's abductor. "I don't want to hurt you. Just let the girl go."

Mu flicked his gaze at the gun pointed at him, his expression one of disdain. "Mu not scared of white man's fire."

"Then Mu is a fool."

Mu took a step forward. "Mu is great warrior. Haole can not hurt a priest of Ku."

"I'm warning you. Stay away!"

Mu boldly narrowed the distance. "You steal from Mu, haole. Now you die."

Was the man extraordinarily brave? Or incredibly stupid? Nathan's grip tightened on the pistol. His index finger curled over the trigger, ready to fire. He had never shot a man in cold blood, never fired at point-blank range. And he was reluctant to do so now.

As though sensing his foe's dilemma, Mu's

mouth twisted with mirthless humor. "Mu is favorite of the gods. Haole not."

Only five feet of rocky ground separated the two men. His jaw hardened with resolve, Nathan squeezed the trigger.

The pistol misfired. A metallic click sounded above the pounding of the waves against the base of the bluff.

For a split second, Nathan stared at the gun in disbelief, then hurled it aside with an oath. Dropping into a crouch, he retreated several steps. Careful to keep his back to the ocean, he lured Mu farther away from Jael and closer to the edge of the cliff.

Jael clamped her hand over her mouth to stifle any involuntary sound. Any cry, she knew, however slight, could prove a fatal distraction. And she sensed this would be a fight to the death. She watched in morbid fascination as the men circled each other like two ancient gladiators in an arena. The pairing looked mismatched. Nathan was lean and agile as a poplar, while Mu was sturdy as an oak and nearly as large.

Nathan's face wore a mask of fierce concentration. Mu grinned broadly, a smile that could turn blood to ice. Nathan patiently waited for Mu to strike the first blow. All the while, the men edged closer and closer to where the earth dropped to the sea below. Jael followed at a careful distance, not wanting to witness the forthcoming match, yet unable to look away.

In a macabre choreographed dance, the

combatants circled each other. Nathan dodged and feinted, his movements as light as a jungle cat's. His muscles flexed, bunched; his tawny eyes gleamed. Jael was reminded of a sleek tiger, ready to pounce.

Mu's iron-gray mane fluttered around his shoulders. His pleased smirk signaled his supreme confidence. Suddenly tired of the game, he hurled himself at Nathan. "Die, haole!" he shrieked, his face distorted with hatred.

The men rolled about, arms flailing as they fought to land telling blows. Mu's superior weight acted to his advantage. The tussle was brief. Mu easily pinned Nathan to the ground while one giant hand circled his throat, cutting off his airway. Jael bit her lip as Mu's fist slammed into Nathan's face with sickening force. Nathan lay unmoving.

Mu rose to his feet and stood over him, gloating at his easy victory. He lashed out with his foot and sent Nathan's inert form tumbling toward the cliff's brink. Nathan grunted with pain and groggily tried to rise to his feet when Mu kicked him the second time.

Jael knew she had to act quickly. Not giving herself time to weigh the consequences, she dove for the pistol, which had landed beneath a low-growing shrub. "Stop!" she yelled, grasping the gun with both hands to keep the barrel from wobbling. "Stop or I'll shoot."

The total unexpectedness of her command caused Mu to momentarily cease battering Nathan. Nathan took advantage of the temporary lapse. Grabbing Mu's foot, he unbalanced the giant by heaving upward with all his might and sending Mu toppling backward into space.

A shrill scream followed his descent onto the rocks below.

Jael rushed to Nathan and helped him to his feet. "Oh, Nathan, I was so frightened. I thought he was going to kill you." She shivered uncontrollably.

"It's all right, pagan flower. Thanks to your quick thinking, we're out of danger." He put his arms around her, and they drew comfort from each other. Cautiously Nathan peered over the edge of the cliff. Far below, Mu's body was bent like a broken matchstick over a projection of lava. The impact of the fall had driven the sharp point though his massive body like a giant spike.

"Mu will never bother you, or anyone else, ever again." Blocking the grisly scene from her view with his body, Nathan led her away.

Chapter 6

"Watch your footing," Nathan directed, already halfway down the path. "A friend of Thomas Hadley's loaned the use of a skiff. I beached it near the canoe."

The notion of returning to Lahaina in a small sailing vessel added yet another worry to Jael's already lengthy list. She had been terrified during the canoe trip from Lahaina. During the voyage, Mu had forced her to sit directly in front of him on a narrow seat. She had quickly discovered waves that looked perfectly harmless at a distance could reach formidable heights in open waters. She had been afraid to move lest they overturn and drown in the churning sea. The wooden sides of the craft must still carry the imprint of her fingers.

Jael blocked out thoughts of a return voyage. Instead she concentrated on her footing as she descended the steep slope. The narrow path required all her attention. Vines as thick as her wrist tried to snag her feet and trip her. A third of the way down, the heavy undergrowth gave way to rocks and loose stones.

Agile as a mountain goat, Nathan reached the ribbon of sand before she did and crossed to the small sailing craft. "Is anything the matter?" she inquired anxiously, seeing his scowl.

But even as she voiced the question, she followed the course of his gaze and the answer to her question quickly became evident. A large, jagged hole in the hull of the boat gaped back. A hefty rock lay nearby. Even a landlubber such as herself knew the damage was extensive. Appalled by the destruction, she stared in dismay.

"The bastard. That dirty, rotten bastard," Nathan muttered under his breath. Not only had that madman destroyed the stuff, but the outrigger had disappeared as well.

Jael shot him a look. What she saw frightened her. A muscle twitched ominously in his jaw. His hazel eyes spit angry green sparks; his hands gathered into fists. No longer the charming rogue, he suddenly appeared a stranger. A man to be treated with caution. A man to fear. Carefully she inched away, loath to do or say anything that might inadvertently direct that rage at herself.

"What'll we do now?" Jael finally asked in a small voice when the silence became unbearable.

"There's little choice in the matter," Nathan replied grimly. "We walk."

"Walk?" Jael echoed, the prospect daunting.

A wry smile tugged at a corner of his mouth. "Unless we sport wings or sprout fins, I can't think of a better way."

The full import of their situation struck her. Though still on Maui, miles and miles of rugged terrain separated them from Lahaina—and civilization. "But it'll take days, maybe weeks."

"Can you come up with another plan?"

She stared dismally at the shattered hull of the skiff, then shook her head. "No," she murmured.

"Then let's see what that scoundrel left behind." Nathan stooped down and began sorting through the small cache of supplies that Mu hadn't bothered to steal or destroy. His wool jacket, a small supply of foodstuffs, and a water pouch were all intact. He placed these items in a pile. Then a frown tugged his brows together and his search intensified.

As Jael watched mystified, he rummaged through the debris, carelessly flinging splintered bits of wood onto the beach. She took a tentative step closer. "What are you missing?"

His frown deepened as his gaze alighted on an object partially hidden by a pile of rocks. He strode over and picked up the shattered remains. "That devil destroyed the most valuable item of all—my telescope." Angrily he flung it aside. "An instrument of that caliber will be hard to replace."

Nathan turned his back to the sea. Hands on hips, head to one side, he regarded her thoughtfully. She looked on the verge of collapse, pale and strained. Her skin was the color of parchment. Violet smudges of fatigue shadowed her huge sky-blue eyes. He felt a twinge of pity—and something more. A fierce surge of protectiveness swept through him.

"Damn!" he swore fiercely under his breath. *Damn*, he repeated inwardly, seeing her flinch at the expletive. He didn't need a woman complicating his life—and that's all they were. Complications. Hindrances. Ruthlessly he tamped down this unwanted surge of feeling. But in spite of his resolve to the contrary, a part of him was secretly pleased that he had been there when she needed him most. If anyone had ever been in need of a rescuer, it had been Jael. And she had been magnificent. He'd never forget the look of sheer determination on her face when she aimed that pistol at Mu. She had shown a rare courage he couldn't help but admire.

"There's a cave close by. It'll afford us shelter for the night. Here," Nathan said as he draped his jacket over her slender shoulders.

Jael grasped the lapels and pulled the coat tighter. "Thank you," she replied solemnly.

"The sun's already sinking behind Haleakala," he said, adopting a brisk tone. "We'll spend the night there and start fresh in the morning." He spun on his heel, leaving Jael to follow.

Jael gamely scrambled after him along the narrow beach. The coarse sand crunched loudly beneath the thin soles of her shoes, the spongy texture sucked at her feet, slowing her steps. She stumbled as the full import of the situation hit her with the force of a hurricane. They were miles from nowhere. Stranded. And Nathan didn't sound pleased with the situation. The prospect of days on end in a man's company was unsettling.

Men weren't to be trusted.

The warning slithered through her mind. Men had unpredictable tempers that often exploded without warning. Men were physically stronger than women and often brutal in their strength. Men used. Abused. They were to be feared, avoided.

But Nathan wasn't like that, a small inner voice insisted. He'd never take advantage of her. *Or would he?*

"This is where we'll spend the night." He gestured to a volcanic tunnel that had been formed more than a century ago by a violent eruption on Haleakala. The cylindrical tube was large enough for a man to stand upright in and appeared quite deep. "Rest a bit while I get a fire started."

Jael wearily sank to the floor of the lava tube, leaned her head against the rough cinder wall, and hugged her knees against her chest. There was nothing she'd like better than to curl into a tight little ball and fall fast asleep. For a time after Nathan disappeared from view, she stared down at the black sand beach below, her mind blank. Waves curled onto the beach like frilly strips of lace decorating a matte black canvas. Beyond, the ocean stretched out, an unending bolt of sapphire blue. Pretty, she thought, in an eerie sort of way. Her eyelids felt weighted with fatigue. Lulled by the steady rhythm of waves breaking on shore, she nodded drowsily, yawned once, then dozed off.

When she woke an hour later, the sun had slipped behind Haleakala's craggy rim, leaving the landscape smothered in darkness. Several feet away, a fire crackled and snapped around a mound of dry sticks. Orange flames leaped into the air. Shadows danced like faceless puppets against the back wall of the cave.

A delicious aroma of roasting food assailed her nostrils, and Jael realized she hadn't eaten since the previous night. Nathan squatted in front of the fire with a fish speared on a stick over the flames. Slices of sweet yellow guava and a small bunch of bananas rested on a low flat-topped rock. He glanced up as she drew nearer.

Jael felt apprehension coil in the pit of her stomach. Instead of preparing the evening meal, she had been sound asleep. Nathan had had to do all the work himself. Grandfather would have been livid. She clenched her hands to still their nervousness. "You should have awakened me."

"Why?" Nathan cocked an inquisitive brow.

"Because..." She shrugged her shoulders in confusion. If anything he sounded more amused than angry. "Because," she said, "cooking is women's work."

"I'll let you do the dishes." She was regarding him as though he were some sort of ogre. He hoped his bantering would erase some of the tension from her face.

If Nathan could conjure a meal out of nowhere, the possibilities were boundless. Jael glanced around, half expecting to see fine china and stemmed glassware glitter in the firelight. Then she blushed lightly as she realized he was merely teasing.

Grinning, he made a sweeping motion with his hand. "Please be seated. Our banquet table awaits."

Self-consciously she lowered herself to the ground and tucked her knees demurely beneath her.

"Madam, dinner is served." With a flourish, he placed the fish on a ti leaf and held it out for her inspection.

To her mortification, her stomach gave a loud, unladylike rumble of hunger. He laughed and sat on the ground opposite her. After breaking the fish apart with his fingers, he nudged a portion toward her to sample.

Daintily using her thumb and forefinger, she popped a small morsel of grilled fish into her mouth. "Mmm," she sighed, closing her eyes in appreciation. Tender, juicy, utterly delicious. Never had fish tasted this good. She wasn't sure if the unique flavor resulted from being cooked over an outdoor flame, the fact that someone other than herself had prepared the meal, or perhaps she was simply famished. She only knew this was the best meal she had ever experienced.

"I gather my culinary efforts meet with your approval." Nathan grinned as he helped himself to a portion.

"Absolutely amazing. A man who cooks."

She daintily licked the juice from her fingers. "Grandfather would starve before he'd prepare a meal."

Nathan found the innocent gesture oddly disturbing. She had the sweetest mouth—it brought to mind a succulent, sun-ripened strawberry.

"I've never tasted anything quite so good." She helped herself to another piece of fish.

"Surely you must have eaten grilled fish before?"

"Never." She shook her head for emphasis. "Grandfather viewed cooking outdoors as barbaric. He forbade any partaking of heathenish ways and insisted all our food be either boiled or fried."

Ah, yes, that sounded like Silas Kincaid. Nathan barely knew the man, yet knew him all too well. The clergyman's dour disposition tainted the air of everyone around him. To his twisted mind, sin and evil lurked around every corner.

Jael reached for a slice of fruit. "Besides cooking, do you have other talents as well?"

"Many," he replied. "Having spent most of my life at sea, I've had to become adept at many tasks, including doctoring, cooking—and sewing."

"Sewing... You?"

"Don't look so shocked," he chided. "Out of necessity, a whalingman must be skilled at mending sails if he's to be at sea for months on end."

She chewed thoughtfully. "I never thought of that."

"Once back in civilization, we could have a contest," he proposed. "I'll wager my row of neat stitches against yours." Then his expression turned serious. "Care to tell me what happened last night?"

His question triggered the return of Jael's anxiety. She hugged Nathan's jacket tighter to ward off a sudden chill. "It must have been after midnight when I woke."

"Go on," he encouraged.

"At first I thought it had all been a nightmare, but..."

Nathan waited patiently for her to continue.

Jael swallowed hard, the scene still vivid in her mind, lingering there like an uninvited guest. "Then I noticed the curtains around my bed were open. I distinctly remembered closing them before I went to sleep."

He digested the information in silence. This Mu character had been a hunter, silently, stealthily stalking his unsuspecting prey.

"Before I could even scream, Mu appeared out of nowhere. He must have struck me, because the next thing I remember he was carrying me toward an outrigger canoe he had left down the beach." Reflexively she touched her bruised jaw.

He leaned forward earnestly. "I'm ashamed of myself for not putting more credence in your story when you said you were being followed. Maybe if I had, all this never would have happened. Can I make it up to you?"

She summoned a small smile. "You already have." Gazing into the distance, she watched waves ripple ashore. The full moon cut a silvery swath on the darkened ocean. Silver and black, sullen and brooding, the night reflected her mood.

"Its late," Nathan said at last, breaking into her thoughts. "If we plan to get an early start in the morning, we need to get some rest."

"Where will I sleep?"

Nathan climbed to his feet and added more sticks to the fire. "Why, in the lava tube, of course."

"But where will you sleep?"

"Right next to you."

Appalled by this total loss of privacy, Jael started and her eyes widened in shock. Her mouth went dry. "But that's impossible."

"Not impossible, just practical," he replied, unruffled. "Unless you have another suggestion . . . ?"

She watched him gather an armful of pandanus leaves and pile them into a soft mound on the rocky floor. "It's a sin for unmarried couples to share the same bed," she pointed out, knowing she sounded self-righteous, but her strict upbringing demanded she voice her protest.

"Then don't think of this as a bed, merely a pile of leaves," he replied equably.

Her chin raised a fraction. "But it's a bed all the same."

"What do you think I'm going to do? Ravish you?" Nathan asked, exasperated that she'd balk at the sleeping arrangements. The day had been difficult at best, and tomorrow they would have to start the grueling trek to Lahaina. After all they had been through, where was her trust? Had she forgotten how he'd rushed to her rescue like Sir Galahad, ready to slay dragons if need be? Instead of gratitude, all she wanted to do was quibble about who was going to sleep where.

Jael cast a dubious glance at the makeshift sleeping bower, but remained obstinately silent.

Nathan tunneled his fingers through his hair and tried a different tack. "We should consider ourselves fortunate that tonight we have the protection of a cave. Tomorrow we'll be sleeping under the stars."

Unresolved fears materialized to plague her anew. Jael swallowed hard, then wiped her suddenly clammy palms along her petticoat-clad thighs. The smooth, worn texture reminded her anew of her current state of undress. Warmth crept up her neck. *She was practically naked.* Grandmother's tales of men preying on defenseless women flashed through her mind. *Men are after only one thing, girl*, Grandmother had warned time and again, *one thing only*. Another fear was added to her already heaping plate of worries. Not only did she have to worry about her physical safety, but her virtue as well.

"I'll give you my word that I won't lay a finger on you." He held both hands up in a gesture of surrender and dropped his voice to a conciliatory tone that one might use to calm a small child. "It turns cold at night. Since we don't have a blanket, we'll need to share the warmth of the jacket you're wearing."

Jael studied him warily for a long moment, then wordlessly lowered herself to the thick mat of fronds. Grateful that darkness hid the telltale flush of embarrassment, she hastily slipped out of Nathan's jacket and tossed it to him. "Pardon me. I didn't mean to monopolize your coat," she apologized stiffly.

He caught it with one hand, chuckling at her display of pique. Maybe there was still some spirit under that demure, docile exterior that the old bastard hadn't beaten out of her. "I hardly thought you'd be guilty of such an uncharitable act." Nathan lay down next to her and spread the fine woolen coat over both of them.

Inches apart and miles away. They lay stiffly, back to back, neither speaking nor touching. Nathan suspected Jael, too, was wide awake and unable to sleep. His mind churned with unruly thoughts. He should have been more attuned to her needs, more understanding. Considering the circumstances, she had borne up remarkably well. She had been abducted from her home by a madman and nearly killed. Many women would have been hysterical, yet her only complaint was their sleeping arrangements. And why shouldn't she object? She was a young girl and had led a sheltered life. He reminded himself that just because he had rushed to her rescue didn't necessarily mean he had earned her trust. Now all he wanted to do was relieve the tension between them.

With a sigh, he half turned toward her. "Look, Jael, I know this isn't easy for you, but if you want to return to Lahaina safely, we need to work together. We need to be practical, not prudish. Once we get back to civilization, you can go back to being the granddaughter of a preacher and I'll return to the *Clotilde*. But until then we're just two people doing what they must to survive in the wilderness. Agreed?"

Jael considered his words. As uncomfortable as she was at the situation, her innate practicality and sense of fair play prevailed. She had to admit his reasoning was sound. They were totally dependent on each other. "Agreed," she said softly.

"Good girl," he approved. What she needed to do was put the day's events behind her. To relax. He searched his mind and finally came up with what he hoped would prove a distraction. "If you waken to the sound of crying in the middle of the night, don't be alarmed."

"Crying . . . ?"

"Did you know that this place—Waianapanapa—is a legendary meeting place for lovers?"

"No," she replied, instantly intrigued. "Tell me about it."

"Legend has it that a Hawaiian princess fleeing from her jealous husband hid in a cave that could only be reached by diving into a pool and swimming underwater. The husband eventually found her hiding place and, filled with rage and jealousy, killed her."

"How horrible," Jael gasped.

"Every April, the month the killing took place, the water turns blood red. Natives insist it's to commemorate her murder."

Jael inched closer to him, and Nathan smiled in the dark. His strategy had an unforeseen benefit.

"How tragic for both of them," she murmured. "He must have loved her to the point of madness."

"Man is a fool to allow a woman to have so much influence over him that he can't think straight. I'd never fall into that trap."

Shadows bobbed against the wall of the lava tube. Wind soughed through the trees. Or was it the mournful wailing of a murdered Hawaiian princess? The night—this place—seemed haunted with sinister shapes and spooky sounds. "Nathan . . . ?" she began tentatively, needing conversation to reassure herself of his presence beside her.

"Mmm . . ."

"Nothing." She wanted to ask if he had ever loved a woman so much that he'd do anything to keep her, but lost her courage.

It would be all too easy to fall under this man's spell. He had an easy charm, a way of making her feel special. But men weren't to be trusted. Her mother had trusted a man once and had been left abandoned and disgraced. Her grandfather was another example of why men couldn't be trusted. They presented one face to the public and another behind closed doors. No, Nathan Thorne was no different. He was to be treated with utmost caution. Lying on a rocky floor with sleep eluding her, Jael vowed to keep her guard high. She wouldn't fall prey to his roguish grin or to the devilish twinkle in his hazel eyes.

Chapter 7

Jael awakened to the patter of falling rain. She had slept soundly, dreamlessly, in spite of the gruesome tale of a slain Hawaiian princess. Just as she had as a small child in a cot under the eaves, she found the sound of rain comforting. Unlike her grandparents, her mother had never scolded her for dawdling on a rainy morning. Though they never had much money, her mother always laughingly insisted that they were rich as long as they had each other. Why had she nearly forgotten the happy times they had shared together? she wondered sadly.

Stretching lazily, she gradually became aware of her surroundings. Memory of the day before—and the night—flooded back. Cautiously, her senses alert for a sound, a scent, a clue to Nathan's whereabouts, she rolled onto her back. The craggy ceiling of the lava tube greeted her. She raised herself up on one elbow and scanned the shelter. There was no sign of him anywhere. She was alone with only the sound of the rain as her companion. Ordering herself not to panic, she quickly got up to investigate.

A silvery curtain of rain streamed over the lip of the lava tube. Clouds the shade of tarnished pewter crowded the sky. Water rolled from broad leaves of foliage and plopped to the ground. Sea and land perfumed the air with the tangy scent of brine mingled with the fecund smells of damp earth and thick foliage. The outline of the battered skiff was barely discernible on the beach below. She clutched Nathan's jacket tighter around her shoulders to ward off the dampness. It was warm and comforting—like the feel of his arms around her after he had rescued her. The wool smelled of sandalwood—and Nathan's own unique male essence. If she closed her eyes, she could almost imagine him holding her.

She shook her head to clear away the fanciful notions. Where was he? Surely he wouldn't have abandoned her. Not after all the trouble he had gone through to find her. But where could he have gone to? Jael dragged a hand through her tangled mane and tried to think clearly. She glanced over her shoulder and noted that the supplies were still just where he had left them the previous night.

"Afraid I deserted you?"

Jael whirled around, startled. His entrance muffled by the steady rain, Nathan now stood directly behind her, water dripping from his rain-darkened hair and down his lean cheeks.

"The possibility crossed my mind," she confessed.

Her words brought a scowl to his face as he stepped farther into the lava tube. "Your lack of faith wounds me."

"I'm sorry. I was only being honest." She watched him warily, uncertain of his mood.

"There are times I'd prefer less honesty," he muttered, shaking droplets from his hair. "While you were sleeping, I went into Hana. I thought perhaps one of the villagers would have a sailing vessel he'd loan us."

Her eyes lit up hopefully. "And did they?"

"No—or at least none they're willing to entrust to a haole. But my efforts weren't totally a waste of time." He held up a mesh sack filled with fruits and vegetables. "I was able to barter for enough food to see us through the next few days."

His words barely registered. She absorbed the sight of him as thirstily as the earth absorbed rain. His cotton shirt was plastered wetly to his broad chest, and his pants molded his narrow hips, leaving little to the imagination. He looked very male. Dangerous in a way that had nothing to do with physical assault. She averted her gaze with effort. "You're soaking wet." She grasped the first words to pop into her mind, then wanted to bite her tongue at their inanity.

He swept a quick glance downward. A rueful smile tugged at one corner of his mouth. "Well, so I am," he drawled.

Jael couldn't be sure if he was teasing or being sarcastic. "You should get out of your wet things before you catch your death."

"If I get out of my wet things, darling," he retorted, his eyes holding a devilish twinkle, "you're the one who's likely to die—of embarrassment."

Her flush deepened and she strove to assume a more businesslike tone. "At least take your shirt off and slip into your jacket while I get a fire started."

Using the remainder of the dried sticks from the previous night, Jael managed to start a small fire. Nathan peeled off his wet shirt and spread it in front of the blaze to dry. She slipped his jacket off and handed it to him, all the while trying not to stare at his bare chest. But curiosity prompted her to look.

A smattering of chestnut curls covered a hard-muscled expanse that was tanned the rich hue of oiled teak before tapering into a trim waist. He looked fit enough to perform heavy labor without breaking a sweat. Strong enough to sweep a woman off her feet. Her fingers tingled with the urge to stroke the bronzed flesh, to comb through the nest of curls. Her heart skipped a beat.

Nathan refused the return of his jacket with a shake of his head. Instead he reached into the sack and brought out a papaya. "Breakfast." Taking out a pocketknife, he slit the fruit in half, then offered her a piece. "Eat up, it's nearly noontime."

"Noon!" She accepted the slice of papaya. "I thought you said we'd get an early start."

He shrugged carelessly. "I didn't hear any rooster crowing a wake-up call, did you?"

It wasn't like her to oversleep. She was used to being up early to bake bread before the day got too warm. Her grandfather expected a hearty breakfast waiting for him every morning.

Nathan hunkered down on the pandanus leaves and peeled a banana as though the late hour was no problem. Hesitantly Jael sat opposite him, drew up her knees, and hugged them to her chest. His presence—and state of undress—was disconcerting. She stared out of the cave and pretended a great interest in the mist-shrouded world beyond their shelter.

"Looks like the sky's getting lighter," Nathan observed, his gaze following the direction of hers. "The rain's just about over. We won't get as far as I planned today, but we can get a few miles behind us."

While he gathered up supplies, Jael pulled a narrow blue ribbon from the neck band of her chemise. Using her fingers, she plaited her hair into one long braid and tied the end with the ribbon. She silently brushed off Nathan's jacket and handed it to him. She felt naked without it. Naked and vulnerable.

Nathan stared at her strangely for a long moment, and she resisted the urge to shield her breasts with her hands. She felt as though he could see straight through her chemise and slip. His expression grew taut, strained. A muscle jumped in his jaw.

"You keep it." Slinging his damp shirt negligently over one shoulder, he turned and left the lava tube.

Grateful yet vaguely disconcerted, Jael shrugged into the jacket, rolling up the too-long sleeves as she hurried after him.

The sun came out in full force and burned off the mist. The day quickly became warm and humid. Nathan set a steady but grueling pace as they picked their way along a path so faint it was barely discernible.

Damn! he muttered under his breath.

Jael Kincaid had looked utterly fetching standing there clad only in her undergarments. It had taken every bit of self-discipline he could muster to offer her the use of his jacket. Seemed a shame, he thought, to cover up such feminine pulchritude under a bulky wool coat. It was one thing to think of her as the granddaughter of a missionary when she was clothed in a frumpy high-necked black dress demurely buttoned to her chin. Or with that god-awful ugly straw bonnet hiding that glorious fall of red hair. Prim, proper, and definitely off limits. When she dressed like that, he could easily think of her as the daughter of a friend—or even a little sister.

Impatiently he batted a low-hanging branch out of the way. Who would have guessed that swathed beneath yards and yards of dreary muslin was the body of a bewitching temptress? He must have been blind back in the lava tube not to notice the enticing curves and enchanting valleys. And her breasts. Desire snaked through him. He couldn't help but notice the dusky pink nipples nudging the soft, thin fabric of her chemise. They reminded him of tightly furled rosebuds waiting for the first kiss of the sun.

Damn, he swore again as he kicked a rock out of his path. The girl had him waxing poetic. How his crew would roar with laughter if they knew the limits their captain could be driven to by a comely wench. He had to get control of himself before things got out of hand. After all, he had appointed himself as her protector, not as a despoiler of innocence. What he was experiencing now was nothing more than lust. Plain and simple. Unbridled physical attraction. If he wasn't careful, his baser instincts would threaten to play havoc with his good intentions. Hadn't his ill-fated marriage to Catherine taught him a lesson?

Sophisticated. Sensuous. Seductive. Catherine Hadley was as different from Jael Kincaid as night to day. Summer to winter. No, he wouldn't repeat his previous mistake. It was his strong attraction to a woman that had landed him in trouble before. He had refused to listen to common sense. Not even John's counsel could sway him from the course he had set for himself. He had been so blinded by lust that he had failed to see the flaws in Catherine's character, failed to see her for the selfish, faithless woman she really was.

Nathan paused to wipe the sweat from his brow. He cast a glance at Jael over his shoulder, ostensibly to see how she was faring along the steep trail, and she flashed him a friendly smile in return. He turned his attention back to navigating through the thick foliage. Yes, he agreed silently, lending her the use of his jacket had been a wise choice.

As the afternoon wore on, Jael lagged farther and farther behind. Sweat trickled between her shoulder blades. Only a strongly ingrained sense of propriety prevented her from taking off the woolen coat. Wearily she brushed back curling tendrils of hair that had escaped her braid. She looked at Nathan far ahead of her and felt a twinge of envy. His shirt still dangled over one shoulder and trailed down his tanned back. He looked at ease, completely in his element. And impervious to the heat.

"How much longer?" Unable to go another step, Jael eased herself down on a rock. Though they probably hadn't walked more than five miles, it felt like twenty.

Nathan studied her with a worried frown. Her cheeks were flushed from a combination of sun and exertion. Her slender shoulders slumped wearily beneath the bulky jacket. He knew he couldn't push her any harder without her collapsing. Until she grew accustomed to the pace, it would be better to let her get a good night's rest and start fresh in the morning. Tomorrow they'd have another long, arduous hike ahead of them. "I know a place not far from here where we can spend the night."

Jael pushed to her feet with a sigh. Too tired to complain, she concentrated on putting one foot ahead of the other and followed Nathan. Her mind had ceased working. Not even the lush scenery merited her attention.

Nathan led the way around a bend and up an incline. Jael picked up her petticoats and stumbled after him. "Well, what do you think?" Nathan asked, drawing to a halt and making a sweeping gesture toward the crest of a ridge.

Jael stared in awe. Primitive and majestic, a stone structure hundreds of feet in length rested atop a bluff. Terraces that towered fifty feet high flanked both sides. A thick wall encircled the other two sides.

"Piilanihale," Nathan announced. "The largest *heiau* ever discovered in Hawaii."

"*Heiau*?" Jael repeated, searching her memory. "Isn't that a temple?"

Nathan nodded. "It's believed this one was built by a Maui chief in the sixteenth century."

Fascinated, her fatigue momentarily forgotten, Jael trudged the remaining distance to investigate. She looked around in wonder, half expecting ghosts of previous victims to appear. Once the site of ancient rituals—and human sacrifices—the place was silent as a church. Or a tomb. "I can't help but wonder how many hapless victims lost their lives on its bloodied altar."

The question was the same one Nathan had asked himself only the day before. This was the same place he had stopped yesterday, hoping—praying—that her deranged abductor hadn't planned to make her yet another sacrificial offering at this centuries-old site.

"We'll spend the night here."

"Here?" Jael repeated, dismayed by the prospect. It would be like spending the night in a church. Or worse yet—a cemetery.

"It'll at least afford some degree of protection." Nathan appeared unperturbed at the notion. "You don't believe in ghosts, do you?"

"N-no," she demurred, "but ..."

He shaded his eyes with one tanned hand and looked up at the *heiau*, then down to the ocean, before resting his gaze on Jael's troubled face. "Look," he sighed. "I respect Hawaiian tradition as much as the next person, but we need to take advantage of every opportunity. We have nearly fifty miles of rugged terrain ahead of us. We don't need to make them more difficult than they already are."

"Well..." She was unable to find a flaw in Nathan's practicality.

"Listen, Jael, I give you my word we'll leave this place exactly as we found it. We'll sleep inside its shelter, but that's all."

"All right," she agreed reluctantly.

"Find a spot and rest a while. I think I'll try my hand at fishing."

He retraced his way to the beach, whistling as he went along. Jael resisted the urge to nap, and gathered firewood instead. When Nathan returned an hour later with a fat fish wriggling on a line, she had a small fire going and yams roasting on the coals.

After a tasty meal of fish and vegetables,

Nathan lounged on his side, propped on one elbow. A smile of satisfaction curved his lips. "All we need now is my favorite dessert. No one makes a better pineapple cake than Alice Hadley."

Pineapple cake. The Hadley parlor. Nathan's words vividly recalled the night her grandfather had interrupted the Hadleys' dinner party. He had looked completely at ease in their parlor, sipping tea and sharing gossip. Gossip in which she had been the prime subject.

Bitterness and shame flooded through her at the memory. She dropped her gaze to her lap and fidgeted with the folds of her petticoat. She hated being the target of pity. It diminished her. Made her feel more of an object and less of a person. Soon, she vowed, her mouth firming with determination, soon she would leave Maui for good and start a new life. Unfettered by the past, she would be free to start anew. Far removed from her grandfather's domination.

Far from pitying glances.

"I spoke with one of the natives at Hana who knew a smattering of English," Nathan said. "Tomorrow we'll climb to a trail on higher ground that will eventually lead to Wailuku."

Jael glanced at him reclining negligently against a stone fortification, looking totally self-assured and relaxed. It was simple to picture him on the deck of a ship, giving orders to a crew who scrambled to do his bidding.

She wondered a bit enviously if he ever suffered pangs of indecision and inadequacy. He was beyond a doubt the most attractive man she had ever met. Though her experience was limited, she sensed he was a man who effortlessly appealed to women.

But she could resist a man's blatant charm. She wouldn't fall into the same trap that her mother had. She wasn't like her mother. Not one whit. No man would ever take advantage of *her*. As soon as she had enough money saved, she would leave Maui and never look back. For the first time ever she would be free—unencumbered by anyone or anything.

"The trail is primitive at best, but not impassable."

"Fine," she murmured. She spoke little during the remainder of the evening.

Nathan cast questioning glances her way, then with a shrug gave up his attempt to engage her in conversation.

That night they slept back to back in the shadow of Piilanihale. Jael's spine was ramrod stiff. She was more determined than ever not to let her defenses down, to maintain a distance—even in her sleep.

Jael sat on the bank of a pool fed by a mountain stream and waited while Nathan went off to investigate Nahiku, the small village situated far below on the water's edge. The respite was a welcome one. For two days they had hiked nonstop from early morning to sundown, pausing only long enough for a quick meal at noon. Savoring the rare moment of privacy, Jael tugged off her shoes and wriggled her toes in the cool, crystal-clear water. She smiled to herself. The pool looked tempting. It had been a long time since she had been swimming. Not since she was fifteen. Not since that horrible afternoon when one of her grandfather's parishioners innocently divulged he had watched her swim near Black Rock at Kaanapali beach.

Grandfather, his face pinched with fury, had been waiting.

"Satan's spawn," he had hissed the moment she had returned home. "How dare you make an exhibition of yourself. I'll teach you a lesson you'll not soon forget."

"Please, Grandfather, I didn't do anything wrong," she had pleaded.

But he was beyond reason. He had wrapped his bony hands around her forearm and dragged her into his study and pointed to a small settee. "Bend over," he ordered.

Trembling, she had done as she was told. Her dress had hiked up and her thin cotton drawers had stretched taut over her buttocks, leaving her feeling exposed and humiliated.

"I will not be made a laughingstock!" His voice quivered with fervency. "As the Lord is my witness, you'll learn never to bring shame down upon my household."

The hickory cane had made a whirring sound as it slashed through the air.

Spasmodically clutching the opposite arm of the settee, Jael had bitten back outcries as his cane repeatedly lashed her backside and thighs. Writhing in agony, she had struggled to contain the sobs, the pleadings for him to stop. Then guilt or innocence ceased to matter. In the end, arcing white pain had seared through her flimsy defense, incinerating bravado to ash. By the time the caning had ended, she had been sobbing convulsively and pleading incoherently for her grandfather's forgiveness.

"Pagan issue! Devil's child!" Breathing heavily, Silas Kincaid had leaned on his cane and pointed a spindly finger at her. "Get out of my sight."

Blinded by tears, Jael had crawled from his study.

For three days and nights, she had kept to her room, too racked by pain to do more than use the chamber pot or take a sip of tepid water from a pitcher at her bedside. She had dozed fitfully, the slightest movement reawakening the burning, throbbing agony that latticed her hips and legs. Careful lest anyone overhear, she sobbed miserably into a pillow. Neither of her grandparents cared enough to bring her food or ease her discomfort. Even more devastating, however, was their total indifference to her suffering. Unloved. Unwanted. Those two words sang through her brain like the refrain of a hymn. Scalding tears rivered down her cheeks and dampened her pillow.

On the fourth day, she had slowly gotten up from bed, dressed, and neatly braided her hair, then painstakingly made her way to the parlor. Each step sent a fresh burst of pain jarring through her.

Silas had been working on a sermon while her grandmother applied herself diligently to a cross-stitched sampler. Both had ignored her entrance.

"Grandfather," she had begun haltingly.

He had glanced up from his writing.

She had tried again, her voice faltering. "G-grandfather, I'm sorry if my actions displeased you. I didn't mean to embarrass you."

His pale, unblinking eyes had stared right through her, making her feel small and insignificant. Nonexistent. From the corner of her eye, she had caught the glint of a needle as her grandmother viciously jabbed it in and out of the linen square.

"It wasn't I, girl, but the Almighty that you offended." He came out from around his desk and stood over her. "It was not my hand but the Lord's that smote you for your wickedness."

Jael had laced her fingers together and hung her head, retreating behind silence out of fear her words might inflame his temper.

"You are made in His likeness, and it angers Him to see you take up heathenish ways." He caught her chin and jerked it up so that she was forced to look at him. "Look at me when I speak! Are you listening, girl?"

Jael had been afraid he might strike her again and didn't think she could tolerate another beating. "Y-yes, Grandfather, I'm listening."

"Good." He had nodded, pleased with her meek reply. "You are never—ever—to do anything that might bring shame upon my name, nothing that might set idle tongues to wagging. Nothing that might even remotely recall the shame and disgrace your mother brought crashing down upon our heads. Understand?"

"Yes, Grandfather," she had agreed eagerly

while inwardly despising herself for being a spineless coward.

"Then get down on your knees, girl, and pray for your mortal soul."

For the next hour, Jael had been made to kneel in front of him on the hard wood floor, head bowed, while he prayed over her. Weakened by the caning and lack of food, she swayed unsteadily, hoping she wouldn't faint. She had clung tenaciously to the fine thread of consciousness. Silas had never suspected the rebellious thoughts that raced through her mind. When she had finally been permitted to rise, it wasn't contrition but a sense of determination that filled her heart. Someday, somehow, she vowed to be free, totally independent, of a man's domination. Someday she'd have no one to answer to but herself.

Gradually the welts had stopped seeping blood and changed to ugly purple bruises. It was weeks before she finally stopped eating her meals standing up and even longer before she could sit with any degree of comfort. But during this whole time, her resolution to gain her freedom never wavered.

With a shudder, Jael shrugged off the unpleasant recollection and climbed to her feet. With her grandfather on the other side of the island and Nathan visiting a native village, there was no one to stop her. A strange exhilaration swept over her. The pool looked inviting, and it had been a long time. Much too long. Without further hesitation, she stripped off her clothes and dived into the water.

Chapter 8

Playful as a dolphin, Jael cavorted in the crystalline pool. With carefree abandon, she repeatedly dived deep, then glided through the water, experiencing an exhilaration she had been denied for years. She bobbed to the surface and shook the water from her eyes. She realized that unless she wanted Nathan to catch her swimming nude, it was time to bring the pleasant interlude to an end.

Wading ashore, she walked to the spot where her freshly laundered garments were drying on a bush. She stepped into her drawers, slipped the chemise over her head, and wriggled into her petticoat. She reached for Nathan's jacket, but changed her mind. The afternoon was warm, and she was alone.

A rustling in a nearby bush startled her. Her mouth dry, her heart hammering, she forced herself to slowly turn toward the sound.

"Nathan?" Her voice quavered. "Is that you?"

No one stepped forward. Dear Lord, why hadn't she insisted on accompanying him to the village? Her eyes darted about for signs of an intruder. The rustling sounded a second time, this time in the foliage to her right. With a startled gasp, she swung toward the noise.

A honeycreeper flew from a branch of lobelia. Its crimson plumage matched the brilliant shade of the flowers. Jael let out a shaky laugh as she tracked the bird's flight across the wooded glade. What a spineless coward she had become. It was time to put a rein on her runaway imagination. She had started imagining villains behind every plant and tree. She had been scared silly by a bird. Next she'd jump at her own shadow. What was keeping Nathan anyway? she wondered. Still feeling a trifle skittish, she decided to go look for him.

The switchback trail snaked down the deep descent. Now and then she stopped and, shading her eyes with one hand, admired the view. Far below, breakers pummeled rocky outcroppings, sending a salty mist spreading across a vista that spanned three bays. Beyond, the earth dropped away, leaving an endless expanse of water and sky.

She continued on her way, but had only gone a short distance when she rounded a bend and came to an abrupt stop. There, seated on a flat rock by the side of a stream approximately twenty feet away, was a young Hawaiian. Jael's first instinct was to flee, but curiosity made her hesitate. The man, scarcely out of his teens, seemed intent on a wooden object he held in his hands. As she stood rooted in indecision, the young man glanced up. He smiled at her, then went back to his task.

He certainly didn't appear to be a threat. Emboldened by his friendliness, Jael edged closer. He was carving a figure of some sort from ohia wood that vaguely resembled a bird. For a while she was content to watch quietly as his dexterous fingers gave shape to the wood. When he was satisfied with his handiwork, he held it up for her inspection.

"It's very nice," she complimented.

"Owl good *aumakua*." He turned it first one way, then the other, for her to admire. "Bring luck."

She reached out and traced the smooth wood with her fingertip. A wistful smile curved her mouth. *Good* luck? The only variety she seemed to have was bad.

"You like, missus? You keep."

For a moment, Jael stared at the unexpected gift in disbelief. "No, but thank you. I really can't accept your gift."

"You don't like?"

The young Hawaiian looked so crestfallen at her refusal that Jael relented with a smile. "Thank you..." She looked at him quizzically, waiting for him to supply his name.

"Manuku." He pointed first at himself, then at her. "You Pele?"

"No, I'm not Pele." She shook her head in denial. "Not Pele."

Manuku put his head to one side and appeared to ponder her words. Disappointment crossed his face, then he broke into a broad grin. *"Nani wahine."*

Pretty woman. Jael recognized the compliment. "Thank you again," she said, returning his smile.

The sound of footsteps crunching the rocky soil preceded Nathan's appearance. He halted abruptly at finding Jael engaged in conversation with a stranger. All defenses down, her face was alight with animation. The sparkle in her blue eyes matched that of the sun glinting on the Pacific. Why had he never noticed before how lovely she looked when she smiled? A scowl crept over his face as he experienced a totally unexpected stab of jealousy. "Well, well, what have we here?"

"Nathan..." Jael turned and held up a crudely carved wood trinket. "Look what Manuku just gave me. He said it was an *aumakua* to bring me good luck."

He barely glanced at the object in her outstretched hand. Instead he glowered at the pair. She acted as though she had just been given the crown jewels. It galled him to think that while she readily accepted a gift from a virtual stranger, she had refused his earlier offer of a scrimshaw brooch. It didn't matter one iota that one was more costly, more personal, than the other. "Don't you know better than to wander off? I would think after everything that's happened you'd have more sense than to put your trust in strangers."

Jael looked stricken by the sharp note of censure in his voice. "But Nathan..."

"Manuku not harm *wahine*." Jael's new friend was quick to come to her rescue. "She like *aumakua*. Like Manuku."

Nathan quickly closed the distance between them and belligerently shoved his face in Manuku's. "If you're smart," he snarled as he poked the young man's chest for emphasis, "you'll clear out of here before I lose my temper. The lady is my responsibility—and none of your business!"

Jael pushed between them. "Nathan, what's come over you? You're being totally unreasonable."

"*I'm* being unreasonable?" he sputtered. "I leave you alone for a few hours, then come back and find you flirting with some stranger."

"Flirting?" Jael's voice rose in indignation.

"Yes, *flirting*," he said, placing both hands on his hips and perfectly imitating her tone. "The way you were looking up at him and smiling, it's no wonder you attract unwanted attention."

The unfairness of the accusation ignited her temper. She flung her hair over her shoulder and crossed her arms. "I was doing no such thing. I was merely being friendly."

"I gave Thomas my word I'd see you safely to Lahaina. How do you expect me to protect you if you make cow eyes at every man we meet along the way?"

"Cow eyes!" She stamped her foot in utter

frustration. "Nathan Thorne, you're the most exasperating man I've ever met."

The young native took advantage of the diversion to disappear into the thick undergrowth, shaking his head as he went. A wise man didn't anger Madam Pele. She could make the lava flow, fill the air with sulfur, and turn the sky black with smoke.

A muscle bunched ominously in Nathan's jaw. Turning away, he strode toward the pool.

Unreasonable? Exasperating? *Damn!* he swore under his breath. He was guilty of both. He liked to think of himself as a rational man, but something inside him had snapped upon seeing Jael with another man. *Damn*, he swore again. What was it about the comely little redhead that made him behave like a jealous lover?

Stretching out his long legs, Nathan studied Jael from across the campfire. On one of his first trips to the islands, he had witnessed Mauna Loa's violent but spectacular eruption. Now he found himself comparing the color of Jael's hair to that of molten lava. Both shimmered, glowed. Mesmerized. He ached to bury his hands in the lustrous strands, to let them sift through his fingers like spun silk.

She sat with her head bent, her expression hidden behind a curtain of fiery curls. Since their angry exchange, she hadn't spoken more than a half dozen words. He couldn't help but notice that she had only picked at her food.

He hurled a stick into the fire. The flames

crackled and orange sparks leaped skyward. Jael cast an uncertain glance in his direction. Nathan noted her reaction and instantly regretted startling her. Jael, he reflected, was like some untamed forest creature, wary and slow to trust.

Fact of the matter was, he admitted ruefully, he felt ashamed of himself for losing his temper when he found her talking and smiling with the Hawaiian. Remorse stirred to life. She must think him a brute, probably in the same category as her grandfather. Next he'd be kicking helpless kittens.

Knowing he was wrong didn't make his task easier. He loudly cleared his throat. "I apologize."

Jael stopped pleating the folds of her petticoat to stare at him. "Apologize for what?"

"I'm sorry that I barked at you earlier." He got to his feet and walked to the edge of the pool. The clouds cleared, leaving the heavens spangled with a million pinpricks of light. A quarter moon hung high in the sky. The night air was fragrant with the unique elixir of the tropics. She wasn't helping him any by her silence. He picked up a pebble and sent it skipping across the still water. "Dammit, Jael," he growled. "I apologized. What do you expect from me?"

"Nothing," she replied softly. "Absolutely nothing."

Her admission stunned him. The simple truth of her statement couldn't be disputed. She asked for nothing and expected nothing in return. Her total honesty disarmed, then irritated him. "Stop playing the martyr. You have a right—everyone has a right—to expect more from life than a slap in the face."

"I'm not seeking sympathy." She rose from the ground and joined him at the water's edge. "I've merely come to the realization that a person must ultimately rely on one's own wits—not someone else's."

"Thus far, you've done a fine job of taking care of yourself," he observed dryly.

Jael flushed as the barb hit home. She didn't need the reminder that he had rescued her on several occasions. It would be a simple thing to lean on Nathan Thorne in times of crisis rather than develop resources of her own. But the time had arrived to renew her resolution to become totally independent. She carefully overlapped the front of his jacket over her chemise. "How much do you charge for passage on your ship?"

He eyed her speculatively. "So," he drawled, "the money you earn from sewing for Mrs. Ka'ano doesn't go into the church coffer?"

Her eyes widened in surprise. "How did you find out?"

"I paid another visit to the enterprising lady. She was quite happy to supply the details."

She stubbornly held his gaze, refusing to back down. "How much do you charge, Captain?"

"More than you can afford."

She ignored his slightly mocking tone. "Right now perhaps, but I intend to save enough to book passage on a ship and sail to New England."

"Where is it, specifically, that you wish to go?"

She shrugged. "It doesn't matter. Any town will do."

"My advice is to devise an alternative plan."

"Why?" she asked, her voice unusually sharp. Something in his tone alerted her to trouble. What had she overlooked in her plan to escape? She had tried to make allowances for all possibilities.

"Whaling ships don't return to their home ports on a regular basis," he informed her. "Most are gone for three or four years at a stretch."

Jael expelled a sigh of relief as a solution became obvious. "Then I'll book passage on a merchant ship instead."

"Besides the expense, the journey is long and arduous." As a seaman accustomed to the rigors aboard ship, he studied her for signs of weakness or uncertainty. "Rounding the Horn is the most treacherous journey faced by a seaman. The westerlies from the Pacific whip the waves into mountains. Ships by the dozen have been battered to kindling against the rocks. It's no voyage for a sheltered young woman such as yourself."

"You've overlooked one important fact," she told him with a trace of smugness.

"And that is?"

"I've already made the journey once before. Surely if I could weather the passage as a child, I can do it again as an adult." The voyage to Hawaii was an experience she had never forgotten. And never would. Even without her grandfather's urging, she had gotten down on her knees and prayed that God spare her life. But even remembering this, it was a journey she would gladly undertake again if it meant escaping Grandfather's tyranny. "I've endured more than you know. Need I remind you, muscle and brawn aren't the only measures of strength."

Nathan folded his arms across his chest and regarded her thoughtfully. "What are your plans once you arrive? Do you have family in the East?"

"No," she replied reluctantly. She gazed past him to where a path of moonlight slanted across the mirrored surface of the pool. "At least no relatives that I'm aware of."

"Then how do you intend to survive?"

"As soon as I arrive in New England, I'll find a position."

"Doing what precisely?"

She snapped off the top of a fern, then shredded the fronds. "There are a good many things I'm capable of doing."

"Such as?"

Without looking at him, she could predict the skeptical lift of one eyebrow. Unconsciously she squared her shoulders. "I intend to apply for a position as a seamstress. Or perhaps a governess or teacher."

"Suitable positions aren't easy to find. You'll quickly learn many wives are hesitant to hire attractive young ladies such as yourself for fear they might capture the attention of their husbands."

Jael stared down at the denuded fern in her hand. "I've heard house servants are in high demand."

"Ah, yes. Quite true." Nathan nodded in agreement. "That is due to the fact that capable girls refuse to stay on because of the enormous workload. Many prefer factory work to being on tap from six in the morning until eleven at night."

"Those hours aren't much different from the ones I keep now," Jael retorted, airily dismissing his warning.

Nathan sighed with exasperation. For someone who appeared exceptionally vulnerable, she was proving extremely mulish. "And just where will you live while you're looking for work?"

Jael nudged the wet grass at the edge of the pool with her toe. Nathan had struck upon yet another problem area. Until she actually arrived at a port, she couldn't begin looking for a job, much less a place to stay. She couldn't risk alerting her grandfather for fear he would foil her plans. If Grandfather caught wind of her scheme, there would be hell to pay. Other than Nathan Thorne, no one knew of her plans to leave Maui. And the only reason she had confided in him was because he might be helpful. "I'll use whatever money is left from the voyage to pay for lodging while I find work," she said, trying to sound more confident than she felt.

"My poor little innocent." Nathan wagged his head sympathetically. "After living all these years in the islands, you'll find living conditions in the cities appalling. With the influx of immigrants, housing is pitifully scarce. At best, tenements are overcrowded, roach-infested firetraps. Instead of air fragrant with blossoms and sea as you've become accustomed to, some streets smell like bad eggs dissolved in ammonia."

She swallowed hard at the graphic description. "Say what you will, Captain, but my mind is made up."

Nathan was relentless. Better she know the hard facts beforehand, he reasoned, than to discover them at journey's end. "Big cities like New York or Boston aren't kind to young girls with no means of support. Many a country girl has had to forfeit her morals in order to survive."

Barely able to suppress a shiver of revulsion at the thought, Jael spat out, "That's enough! I don't want to hear any more."

"I know how unhappy you are." Nathan caught her hand as she turned to flee. "It wasn't my intention to discourage you, only to inform you of the realities you'll face so that you can be prepared."

"Don't underestimate my determination to leave Hawaii. I *will* leave the islands. Regardless of the cost."

"Regardless of the cost, eh?" Her words floated on the night breeze like clouds over the West Maui Mountains. She surprised him. Instead of retreating from his attack, she had countered it brazenly. The keen edge of determination in her voice sliced through the angry tension that seemed to bind them. Tension of another sort began to build inside Nathan. His grip gentled, his tone softened. "Beware, my little pagan flower, the price may be more than you're willing to spend."

"I'll do whatever it takes."

"Then allow me to help you."

She blinked in rapid succession, unable to comprehend his offer. "Help?"

The impulsive offer had slipped out of its own volition. Just as quickly, Nathan realized his desire to be of assistance was genuine. "I have friends in Boston. Perhaps a letter of recommendation. Or..."—he hesitated—"... money to tide you over until you find a position."

Jael searched for a way to thank him. Slowly she became aware that he still held her hand. She rather liked the feel of his callused palm pressed against hers. She wondered what it would feel like, if only for a moment, for him to hold her. To feel his hard, lean frame against her smaller, softer one. Wondered what his kiss would feel like.

Frightened not by him but by her reaction to him, she tugged her hand free. "That's very kind of you."

"Listen, Jael, we have a long way to go before reaching Lahaina." Placing both hands on her shoulders, he stroked her arms from shoulder to elbow, then back again. "I don't want to spend our time together quarreling."

Pleasure rippled through her at his touch. A yearning that had begun as a slow, smoldering warmth deep within her grew hotter. Exerting every ounce of willpower she possessed, she battled the urge to tip her face upward and invite his kiss. "I don't want to quarrel either," she finally admitted, her voice husky.

She left him standing by the pool, his tall figure silhouetted in moonlight. Nathan Thorne, she reflected, was a man not without his share of faults. He could be arrogant, temperamental. Strong, yet surprisingly gentle. And above all, he made her feel—for the very first time in her sheltered existence—every bit a woman.

Chapter 9

One day blurred into the next. They traveled along an ancient trail barely wide enough for one person that clung to the edge of a pandanus-covered cliff. On the lava shore far below, jagged rocks glistened from their constant bathing by the pounding surf. Tropical blooms and exotic birds added bright splashes of color to the verdant green foliage. Waterfalls formed by mountain streams were too numerous to count. Jael marveled at the sheer beauty surrounding her.

This must be what paradise is like, she thought in awe. Days of beauty and wonder. Days of buttery-yellow sunshine interspersed with brief episodes of rain; showers so gentle and benevolent that they felt like a benediction. Jael loved the periods after the brief rains best of all. That was a time of rainbows. Rainbows strung like gay bands of ribbons, so exquisitely beautiful they took her breath away.

"Nathan, look," she cried, unable to suppress her excitement as she pointed to a crescent of black sand far below.

He paused on the trail ahead of her and peered over his shoulder in the direction in which she was pointing. He smiled indulgently at her unbridled enthusiasm. "It was near here that the legendary god Kane thrust his spear into the lava rock and released the fresh water that provides an abundance of taro, yams, and breadfruit."

"How is it you know so much about Hawaiian legends?"

"Hawaiians have served in the crew aboard the *Clotilde*. They're eager to talk about their homeland and the ancient beliefs of their people." Nathan resumed their hike, navigating a particularly tricky portion of the trail. "How is it you've lived in the islands most of your life and know so little?"

The treacherous heights made her lightheaded. Jael carefully picked her way over the narrow, uneven path. "Grandfather forbade any discussion of their ancient culture even among his converts. He called it wicked and heathenish."

Nathan said nothing.

"But I find their old ways fascinating. Tell me more."

"One local legend tells of a spirit that took the form of a giant shark that grew to full size from a fish in a farmer's pond. Greatly respected by the neighbors, the shark served as a powerful *aumakua*."

"*Aumakua*?" Jael dipped her hand into her

pocket. Her fingers curled around the smooth wood figure of an owl.

"A spiritual ancestor, a protective spirit."

"Or a guardian angel of sorts."

"*Aumakuas* can be very powerful," he explained, warming to the subject. "They can assume many forms, such as a bird, an eel, or a rock. Take the shark, for example. Ancient Hawaiians believed that a shark could change from fish to man at will. As a man, he lived unnoticed by his neighbors, recognizable only by the tapa cloth across his shoulders. When his predictions of impending death weren't heeded, he would change from a protective spirit to a vengeful one, killing those who had not heeded his warnings."

"Thus fulfilling his own prophecy," Jael ended.

Nathan grinned at her over his shoulder. "Precisely."

"Perhaps the *aumakua* Manuku gave me will protect me against bad luck." *Or against Grandfather*, she added silently. Fear formed an icy lump in her stomach each time she thought of her homecoming. Minor infractions had routinely met harsh consequences. And knowing her grandfather, she knew he would consider her abduction a major transgression. That she was the innocent victim would be of little or no consequence. He would blame her for everything that happened. To her grandfather's warped mind, her sinful ways had drawn unwanted attention to herself—and to him.

At this very moment he was probably on his knees praying her presence would never again darken his doorway. Publicly, of course, he would bemoan her disappearance, but privately he would congratulate his good fortune. Silas Kincaid would undoubtedly be disappointed at her safe return.

"Watch your footing," Nathan warned from up ahead as he disappeared around a bend.

A strand of hair escaped the thick braid that hung down her back, and she tucked it behind her ear. Deliberately she set thoughts of her grandfather aside. She searched for a more pleasant topic, and her mind rested on Nathan.

Nathan Thorne just didn't fit her preconceived notion of a widower. He was much too young, too carefree. And much too handsome. While part of her sympathized with his loss of a loved one, another part of her, a very selfish part, rejoiced that he was unmarried. She ought to feel ashamed of herself, but she didn't. Remembering his moonlight caress, she felt a warm glow start deep inside and begin to spread. For the first time in her life, someone made her feel attractive. Desirable.

Made her feel . . . special.

Intuitively she knew such heady sensations could be dangerous. She wondered for the first time if that's what had led to her mother's downfall. Had she, too, grown weary of Silas Kincaid's tyranny? Had she escaped with the first man to show an interest in her—maybe the first one who had made her feel special?

Ever since she was a young girl, Jael had listened to her grandparents condemn her mother's wanton behavior. Maybe her mother hadn't been wanton at all, but had loved unwisely. Under her grandparents' tutelage, Jael, too, had condemned her mother's rash actions. Now, at last, she was beginning to view things differently. Now—because of Nathan—she was beginning to understand.

And with understanding came forgiveness.

A light mist started to fall. Jael turned up the collar of Nathan's jacket. While she had been lost in thought, he had gotten a good distance ahead of her. She caught an occasional glimpse of him through the trees. The trail had become practically indiscernible as it twisted, then switched back on itself as it snaked its way up a steep cliff. Jael glanced downward and instantly regretted it. The sheer drop made her dizzy. She concentrated on placing one foot ahead of the other.

She stopped abruptly as a hoarse shout echoed from above. The cry was followed by the clatter of sliding rocks. She tensed, waiting, listening, all senses alert. Her heart pounded painfully against her ribs. After a silence that seemed longer than eternity, she heard the rocks crash to the shore below. The sound released Jael from immobility.

"Nathan..." she shouted. Caution aside, she scrambled up the embankment. Her petticoat caught on a rock and the muslin tore. She tugged it loose, not looking down to assess the damage, and hurried on. Her eyes anxiously scanned the path ahead. "Nathan!" she called again, fear lending a sharp edge to her voice.

After rounding a turn, she stumbled to a halt. A section of the trail was missing. In its place was a ragged, gaping hole. Eroded by days of rain, the ground must have crumbled beneath Nathan's weight. A sick sensation filled her stomach as she forced herself to peer over the edge, expecting to see his battered, broken body. There was no sign of him, and a tiny kernel of hope took root.

She inched closer. Her foot sent pebbles and chunks of dirt hurtling soundlessly through space before crashing on the larger rocks below. Biting her lip to keep it from trembling, she bent forward and craned her neck for a better look. Hundreds, maybe a thousand feet below, waves beat against jagged rocks, spewing spray skyward. The sight made her head swim. "Nathan!"

Rain and tears streaked her cheeks. Where was he? What if . . . ? She couldn't bear to complete the thought.

Coward. She sniffed back tears. If Nathan was alive—and he had to be, he just had to be—he needed her. For his sake she had to remain calm, to keep her wits about her. Carefully she eased onto her stomach and inched forward.

Panic clawed its way toward the surface, and she held it at bay with sheer willpower. *Dear Lord,* she prayed desperately, *please let him be alive.* Blinking back tears, she twisted her head to the right and noticed a scrap of white snagged on the side of the cliff. She wriggled forward another inch and recognized it as a piece of Nathan's shirt. Her gaze tracked downward, then came to rest on a narrow shelf of rock.

Nathan lay in a heap on a ledge far below. Only a trio of stunted trees had prevented him from plunging to his death. Jael couldn't tell from this distance whether he was breathing or not.

"Nathan," she cried shrilly, "please be all right." Her plea was answered by a soft moan. In her mind, the sound was sweeter than birdsong. She held her breath and waited. At last, he opened his eyes and stared up at her. Though his expression was dazed, he was alive, and for the moment that was enough.

"Lie still. Don't try to move."

His eyes drifted shut, giving no indication if he had understood, or even heard, her admonition. Terrified that any movement, however slight, would send him plunging onto the rocks, she huddled as close to the edge as safety permitted. A feeling of utter frustration swept through her. Nathan had come to her aid countless times. Now for the very first time, he needed *her*—and she didn't know how to help him.

Talk to him, an inner voice prompted. *Say anything, everything, but talk to him.*

"Nathan, you're frightening me. Please, wake up." Jael brushed damp tendrils of hair off her forehead, then swallowed hard. "I never told you this before, but you're the bravest man I've ever known. You've been coming to my rescue since the night we met. I'm afraid to think what might have happened if you hadn't saved me from that rowdy group of sailors. Then when I was certain Mu was about to kill me, you appeared suddenly, as if by magic."

A light rain continued to fall, its patter soft and soothing. She laced her fingers together and doggedly continued. "I have a confession to make. When you told me your wife had died, I was glad. This is all my fault. It's God's way of punishing me for my sinful thoughts."

Growing more desperate when there was no response, she lowered her voice and forged ahead. "Nathan, dammit," she said, unconsciously borrowing his favorite expletive, "don't you dare desert me now. I need you." Her voice broke. "You're the only friend I have, and I don't want to lose you."

A groan, clear and unmistakable, came from below. Quickly she peered over the edge and found Nathan staring blankly at the gaping wound in the trail above. When he saw her peering down at him, he started to drag himself into a semireclining position. Jael's initial joy quickly turned to concern. She bit her lip in uncertainty as a new problem debuted. Nathan looked unable to walk, much less scale the side of a cliff.

"Be careful, Nathan," she called in warning. "You're on a narrow ledge. Any sudden movement could send you falling the rest of the way."

Nathan looked around cautiously. His close brush with death immediately became apparent.

Jael was on her hands and knees, leaning over the edge as far as safety permitted. "How badly are you hurt? Is anything broken?"

Nathan experimentally flexed his muscles, and when all four limbs responded appropriately to his commands, gave Jael a lopsided grin of victory. "Sore as the devil, but it seems I'm all in one piece."

"Are you able to climb?"

He eyed the steep wall of the cliff skeptically. "I think sprouting wings would be easier."

Jael slipped out of his jacket. "If you can catch onto a sleeve . . ."

He shook his head. "Even if I could reach it, you don't have the strength to haul me up."

"Surely there must be some way."

"What we need is a rope, a long one."

She frowned thoughtfully, then her expression cleared. "I have an idea!"

"Jael, what are you up to? Don't take any chances." His warning fell on deaf ears. She disappeared, leaving him gazing at the space she had occupied only moments before. In her absence, he cursed his carelessness. If he had been paying attention to where he was walking instead of being preoccupied with thoughts of her, this situation could have been averted. He was still bemoaning his stupidity when Jael returned, her face alight with enthusiasm, her arms laden with roots and vines.

He raised a skeptical brow. "What do you intend to do with those? Weave them into a sleeping mat?"

"I've been tripped one time too many. Now is my chance to finally put these to good use." Ignoring his cynicism, she sat down and selected vines of comparable lengths. "I once watched one of Grandfather's parishioners fashion these into a rope of sorts. I remember it being surprisingly strong."

Nathan watched dubiously. "If they're not long enough, they'll be of little use."

She shook her head at his lack of imagination. "But they will be once the ends are knotted together."

He regarded her with new respect. "It just might work. Do you know how to tie knots?"

"No." She gave him an impertinent smile. "But any sailor worth his salt ought to."

Nathan watched her nimble fingers deftly plait the strands. It took nearly an hour, but at last all the vines and roots were twined together. "You'll need a secure knot if you expect it to maintain my weight," he warned. "A sheet bend ought to do it. Listen carefully. First thing to do is . . ."

He proceeded to instruct her in the sailor's art of knot tying, advising, encouraging, and praising her efforts. When finished, she held her handiwork up for his inspection. "Good girl." He nodded approvingly. "Now see what you can find nearby to anchor it to."

Jael quickly secured one end around the base of a tree and tossed him the other. "Are you certain you feel well enough to make the climb?"

"I've experienced worse falls from the riggings during a gale." Nathan failed to mention the broken bones he had sustained. At the time, he had been grateful it had been his collarbone and two ribs and not his neck. He caught the makeshift rope with one hand and jerked hard, testing its strength. Satisfied, he twisted it once around his wrist, then gamely, hand over hand, began the ascent.

Every muscle tense, Jael watched his slow progress. Nathan used his feet to search for toeholds in the rocky cliff, finding precious few to ease the nearly vertical climb. Midway he found an outcropping of lava that appeared solid enough to sustain his weight while he took a moment to catch his breath.

The lava crumbled and dropped to the sea.

Horrified, Jael clamped her hand against her mouth to stifle a scream. For heart-stopping seconds, she watched Nathan dangle precariously. He was close enough for her to see his white, shiny knuckles, the corded muscles in his arms, and the beads of perspiration on his brow. Finally, after what seemed aeons, he recovered. His features a mask of intense determination, he painstakingly inched up the rope.

The instant he was within reach, Jael leaned over and grabbed onto him. Pulling and tugging with a strength she didn't know she possessed, she hauled him over the edge and into her arms. They lay in an untidy sprawl of arms and legs, drawing solace from each other and filled with gratitude for the simple fact that they were alive.

Jael kept her arms around Nathan as though afraid to let go. Slowly recovering from her fright, she trailed her fingertips over his face, at first to reassure herself that he was indeed safe, and then because of the pure pleasure it brought. She lightly traced the well-defined ridges of his cheekbones, the roguish arch of his brow, the firm thrust of his jaw. Already bruises were beginning to discolor one cheek. Blood leaked from a gash on his forehead. He might have been in a waterfront skirmish or fallen from a cliff. It didn't matter. Neither would have altered her opinion. In her eyes, he appeared even more dashing—and infinitely dear.

He gave her a tender smile. "When I opened my eyes and saw you looking down at me, I thought I had died and gone to heaven."

"You must have struck your head when you fell." Jael threaded her fingers through his hair, ostensibly feeling for lumps, but secretly wanting to sift through the rich brown strands liberally streaked with gold. "You're not making sense."

He captured her wrist and held her hand against his cheek. "I don't know how I managed to cheat the devil," he murmured. "But I do know an angel when I see one. A lovely one with flaming hair and eyes the color of a summer sky."

The compliment made her go warm inside—and soft. He was doing it again, effortlessly, artlessly, making her feel special. Emotion clogged her throat, making her voice husky. "Ah, Captain, you turn a simple maid's head with your pretty words."

He brushed his lips across her fingertips and chuckled. "You're doing yourself an injustice, Jael Kincaid, by thinking yourself simple when in fact you're a very complex young woman."

When at last he stirred and bit back a groan, Jael reluctantly withdrew and pushed herself into a sitting position. Nathan did likewise. They sat side by side, close but not touching. Gradually she became aware that the rain shower had stopped and the sun had come out. Glancing back toward the path they had traveled earlier, she drew in a sharp breath. A rainbow of iridescent pastels spanned the sky from mountainside to ocean. Clear, vibrant shades that rivaled an artist's palette.

"Look!" she exclaimed, clutching Nathan's arm. "Have you ever seen anything more beautiful?"

"Yes," he replied quietly.

Jael was too enthralled with the spectacle to notice that his gaze wasn't directed at the rainbow, but at her.

Chapter 10

That evening they camped a safe distance from the cliff-side trail. Nathan lounged against a log and looked on as Jael collected water from a mountain stream. He loved watching her. She moved with the fluid grace of a ballerina. He could easily imagine her in a ballroom, dressed in fine silks, gliding effortlessly to the haunting strains of a waltz. In his mind, he pictured himself as her partner, holding her lithe body and smiling into guileless blue eyes. He shook his head. What had come over him? It had never been his nature to pine after a woman. Where women were concerned he could take them or leave them with equal ease. He let out a snort of disgust. Next he'd be composing sonnets.

He shifted, trying to get more comfortable, and bit back a groan. Damn, but he ached all over from that blasted fall. He had more cuts and bruises than a shark had teeth.

Jael looked at him, worry deepening the hue of her eyes. "Are you in much pain?"

"Only when I move," he returned with a wry smile. "Or breathe too deeply."

"Those cuts need tending." She poured water into a hollowed gourd, then came over to where he half reclined and set it next to him. "I wish I had some disinfectant, but at least there will be less chance of infection if they're clean."

He eyed her warily, not sure whether or not he liked the notion of someone fussing over him. It certainly was a novel situation. As shipmaster, doctoring chores usually fell to him. Carpenters' or sailmakers' tools sufficed for sewing, cutting, and occasional surgery. "I don't need pampering," he replied more gruffly than he intended.

"It isn't my attention to pamper you, merely tend your wounds."

He told himself it would be churlish to refuse when she only wanted to help. "All right," he agreed reluctantly. "Since you insist."

"Good. Now, let me help you out of your shirt, or," she frowned at the tattered strips of cloth, "rather what's left of it."

"I'm not an invalid," Nathan grumbled irritably. "I don't need a mere slip of a girl helping me undress." He straightened and started to shrug off his shirt. A grimace of pain distorted his features and stilled his efforts.

"Are you always this obstinate?"

Nathan pondered her question, then grinned unabashedly. "Always."

Jael blinked, taken aback by his forthright answer.

Nathan's grin broadened. "Don't forget, my pretty little pagan flower, I'm a ship's captain and used to being in command."

Jael cocked her head to one side and studied him. "What kind of ship's captain are you? Are you harsh or lenient when your crew disobeys your orders?"

"My men don't disobey my orders—at least not more than once."

"Ohh..." Her voice betrayed disappointment.

Seeing fear flicker in her gaze, he sobered. He should have tempered his words, but he had felt compelled to be truthful. "On the seas, one man, and one man alone, is in command of the ship. My crew doesn't have to like me, but I demand their loyalty—and their respect. In exchange, they find me a fair and knowledgeable captain. There's no task I ask of them that I haven't mastered myself. Now," he cajoled, "stop looking at me as though I'm some sort of ogre and help me off with this blasted shirt."

Jael moved closer and eased off his torn shirt.

Her actions provided him with tantalizing glimpses of creamy round breasts with dusky rose centers straining against thin fabric. Silently he cursed the gallant gesture that had prompted him to loan her the use of his jacket. The blasted coat was obstructing his view of femininity at its sweetest. How long had it been since he had had a woman? Too long, he decided. A situation he intended to remedy as soon as he returned to Lahaina.

As Jael knelt in front of him, the tantalizing aroma of tropical flowers drifted up to him. In spite of their hardships, she still managed to smell good. Good enough to make him long to bury himself in her unique fragrance. Good enough to set common sense aside and satisfy the demands pulsing through his body with increasing urgency.

With maddening thoroughness, she traced his ribs with gentle hands. Thoughts of her touching other parts of his body with the same agonizing slowness flitted through his mind. Beads of perspiration dotted his brow. He flinched when she located a particularly tender spot along his flank.

"A rib or two may be cracked," she murmured. "It's a wonder nothing was broken."

"It's a miracle I wasn't killed."

She bent her head and resumed her examination. "Do you believe in miracles, Nathan?"

"Miracles?" Here he was as horny as hell, and she wanted to discuss philosophy. Perhaps, he admitted reluctantly, that was a far more prudent path for his wayward thoughts. He concentrated on her question before answering. "I believe a man must create his own miracles. That he's responsible for his own destiny."

"Are you an atheist?"

His lips twitched in amusement. She was

transparent as glass. "Are you thinking to convert me?"

"I-I..." Her face reddened.

"You can harness that missionary zeal. I'm no heathen."

Embarrassed, she started to rise. "I never meant to imply..."

He caught her hand before she could flee. "Though I don't ascribe to any given religion, I do believe in the Almighty. It's hard not to when you gaze up at the heavens on a clear night and recognize the order in the universe. Or observe the perfect harmony of the tides as they ebb and flow in a ceaseless rhythm."

She gazed at him thoughtfully. "I never thought of God in quite those terms."

He ran his thumb lightly over the base of her wrist and felt her pulse leap in response. "And after today, I even believe in angels."

She moistened her lips with the tip of her tongue and, unsure how to respond, waited for him to continue.

"I owe you a debt of gratitude. It isn't easy to swallow my pride and admit that I owe my life to a slip of a girl. If it wasn't for you, I wouldn't be sitting here now having a philosophical discussion with a pretty young woman." His mouth drew into a grim line as he thought of what might have happened if not for her ingenuity. None of the possibilities were pleasant. "Thank you," he told her solemnly. "You saved my life."

"You're welcome," she replied, equally solemn. She tore off a small piece of cloth, dipped it into the water, and began cleansing a laceration on his chest. "Anyone would have done the same."

"I beg to differ with you." He wagged his head in disagreement. "Not everyone would have exhibited the presence of mind you did. You performed like an old salt."

"Is that a compliment?" Jael wrinkled her nose in distaste. "You make me sound like something used to preserve a barrel of cod."

He chuckled. "An old salt is a seasoned sailor—one you can depend on in times of crisis."

"You've come to my rescue often enough. It was time I repaid the favor. After all," she concluded with a smile, "if we don't look out for each other, no one else will."

"I guess that makes us a team."

"Team..." she repeated thoughtfully, then nodded. "I rather like that idea. It's nice knowing that someone is looking out for you and cares what happens. That you're not alone."

He rested his back against the log. Her words struck a deep chord. He, too, could relate to loneliness. Like a shadow, loneliness had stalked him all of his life. He had entered marriage thinking a wife and family would fill the deep, aching void. Unfortunately, by the end of his brief marriage he had been more alone than before its beginning. Alone with empty promises. Shattered dreams.

"By morning, I expect you'll be a mass of bruises." Jael rinsed the rag in the pink-tinged water and applied it to a nasty-looking abrasion on his shoulder.

Nathan sucked in a sharp breath, not so much from pain as from reaction to her delicate, sensual touch.

"Am I hurting you?"

"No," he grunted, lying through his teeth. Her touch was pure torture.

He was too distracted by her nearness to feel more than a sting. Her slightly turned head exposed the tempting nape of her neck. The glow of the campfire lent her skin the color of a ripe peach. Succulent, tempting, begging to be tasted. Backlighted by the fire, her hair was a fiery nimbus around her head. The color as brilliant as a Maui sunset. He tugged at the scrap of fabric that fastened the braid.

Her eyes flew to his, mirroring an emotion he couldn't define.

"You have beautiful hair." He leisurely unplaited her waist-length braid. "Let me see how it shines in the firelight."

"Grandfather says it's wild and unruly."

His lips curved wickedly. "Certain things, pagan flower, are meant to be wild and unruly."

"But..."

"Ssh..." He silenced her protest by placing his index finger against her lips. "Humor a sick man."

When her hair was unbound, he burrowed both hands through the thick tresses and slowly raked his fingers from scalp to tip, savoring the feel, memorizing the texture. "It has the same richness as raw silk," he said in a thick voice.

Jael's eyelids drifted shut. With unconscious sensuality, she arched her neck and moved her head side to side, making her hair sway and dance in the glow of the fire.

Unable to stop himself, he cradled the base of her skull and lowered his mouth to hers. His lips brushed hers in a kiss so light it might have been a breeze. Her mouth was perfect. Sweet as sugar, intoxicating as rum.

"Nathan..." She sighed his name against his mouth as he deepened the kiss.

When he reluctantly pulled away, the rosy bloom in Jael's cheeks told him that she had been affected by the kiss. He spread her hair about her shoulders like a luxurious cape. "There," he said. "I've wanted to do that for a week."

Her expression dazed, she rose gracefully, then picked up what was left of his shirt and tore it into strips. Flustered and embarrassed, she wanted to ease the current of tension between them. "I don't think any ribs are broken, but just in case I'm wrong, it might be wise to bandage them."

"I feel like I've been flogged with a cat-o'-nine-tails." Nathan painfully dragged himself to his feet and stood in front of her.

Jael kept her glance averted. "If you place your hands on my shoulders, I'll wrap these around your rib cage."

The top of her head came barely to his chin. Scant inches separated their bodies; they stood close enough to feel each other's body heat. Nathan wanted to prolong the moment.

Touching, smoothing, then touching again. Her fingers moved purposefully at first, then with increasing lethargy as if she, too, relished the contact.

Drawn by her heat, Nathan pulled her closer. "You were right," he whispered in her ear. "That does feel better." He slipped one hand inside the jacket she always insisted on wearing, splayed his fingers against the small of her back, and held her close. Her soft breasts flattened against him. Through the thin chemise that separated their bodies, he could feel the tight buds of her nipples nudge his chest. His self-control hung by a hair-thin strand. A strand ready to snap.

She shuddered as his body brushed hers. "We shouldn't..."

Nathan stole the objection from her lips with a kiss. His mouth moved over hers. Sampling. Tasting. Savoring. Her arms twined around his neck and she melted in his arms like candle wax. His hunger grew.

He spread playful, nibbling kisses along her jaw, pausing to nuzzle the sensitive junction near the base of her ear. A shiver rippled through her. He gloated at her responsiveness to his touch. Pure masculine satisfaction pulsed through his veins. He lifted a heavy lock of her hair and explored the tempting site at the nape of her neck that had enticed him earlier.

"Nathan..." she breathed. It wasn't a name

but an entreaty, infused with wonder and awe.

Drawing upon reserves of willpower dangerously near depletion, Nathan returned his hands to her shoulders and set her aside. "I think it best if neither of us do anything that we might later regret."

Jael gazed at him, perplexed by his sudden rejection.

"It's been a long, very harrowing day." Even as he uttered the words, he cursed himself for a fool.

"Yes, of course," she murmured in a choked voice. She turned away and began gathering up the bowl of water and remnants of his shirt and walked to the other side of the campfire.

Nathan dragged his hand through his hair. His manhood throbbed painfully at being denied. Damn! She had been his for the taking. A flower ready to be plucked. Why had he suddenly turned noble?

Later, in too much discomfort to sleep, Nathan lay wide awake wondering what it would have been like to make love to her. He studied her as she slept. Not even the starless night could dim her vibrant beauty. Her brilliantly colored hair flowed across the dusky green pandanus leaves like liquid fire. He loved watching the blue of her eyes deepen to a smoky amethyst whenever he touched her. And her mouth. Sweeter than passion fruit.

She shifted position and presented her profile for his inspection. John McFee would find her delicate silhouette a perfect subject for one of his scrimshaw carvings. Pretty as a picture, all purity and innocence. Purity, innocence, and slumbering sensuality. A sensuality that nagged at him to be awakened. He suspected a passionate nature existed below the puritanical exterior.

But virgins were nothing but trouble.

Jael sighed in her sleep, a sound almost like a purr. Rolling onto her side, she rested her head comfortably on his shoulder, then flung one leg partially over his. Her action stunned him. Slow to trust, Jael carefully maintained a distance even while asleep.

With the stars as witness, Nathan resolved not to let the situation get out of control. To do so would be lunacy. Absently he smoothed her hair. It felt like rumpled silk beneath his callused fingertips. The fragrance of exotic blooms fogged his senses.

Sweet Lord, he groaned silently, who was seducing whom?

The day was balmy. Barely a breeze sifted through the trees. Jael flipped a strand of hair out of her eyes, then stumbled to keep up with Nathan. She felt as if she were on a forced march. A field general, she grumbled under her breath, would have shown more compassion to his troops. Ever since his near fatal accident, Nathan had set a grueling pace and expected her to match it. If his injuries caused any discomfort, he was careful to hide it. While she could understand it, she didn't share his urgency to return to Lahaina. With each mile traveled, her heart grew heavier, her feet more reluctant. She dreaded confronting her grandfather. Fury would quickly overcome disappointment, and she shuddered to think of the possible consequences. She determinedly shoved the unpleasant thought aside.

In spite of the hardships, the journey had been a glorious adventure. Knowing Mu no longer posed a threat to her well-being, she actually began to enjoy the trek from Hana. Day after day, she and Nathan traveled across an island of incredible beauty. Each minute all her senses were bathed in a plethora of sights, sounds, and scents. She delighted in the foliage. Exotic blossoms peeked from beneath leaves larger than dinner platters. Trees, some familiar, many strange, grew in thick profusion. Rain forests, jungles of bamboo, tangled hau, paperbarks, wild ginger, and African tulip trees, all were a source of endless fascination. Birds with bright plumage chirped as they flitted through their boughs.

She slowed to wipe the perspiration from her face with a sleeve. Nathan's wool jacket was stifling, but modesty's sake prevented her from taking it off.

"Don't fall behind," Nathan called from up ahead. "We still have miles to go."

Jael glared at his bronzed back, then trudged after him. Grumble as she might about their fast pace, she had to admit that following Nathan was no hardship. He moved with surefooted masculine grace, conditioned by years of scaling masts in raging seas. She loved watching his muscles ripple and seeing the wide expanse of his bronzed shoulders. She often caught herself staring unabashedly, but couldn't seem to stop. She was as drawn to him as a kitten to cream.

She shook her head in despair. Her thoughts were scandalous; her behavior shocking. Just this morning, she had awakened to find his bare chest against her back, his arm around her waist, the pair of them cozy as two spoons in a drawer. Careful not to disturb him, she had hastily withdrawn from his uninvited embrace. She, the granddaughter of a minister, was acting with flagrant disregard of propriety. She was no better than a common trollop.

Nathan stopped on the trail and waited for her to catch up. His look encompassed her flushed face and the unkempt strands of hair straggling down her face. "Perhaps I've pushed too hard," he said, taking pity on her. "There's a place up ahead where a mountain stream divides into twin waterfalls. We'll spend the night there."

Jael napped in the shade while Nathan went off in search of food. When she awoke a short time later feeling refreshed, she decided to go exploring. The site Nathan had chosen was absolutely idyllic, she decided. A small slice of paradise. A thick grotto of ferns surrounded an emerald green pool formed by cascading waterfalls. Flowers in brilliant splashes of pink, yellow, red, and white adorned trees and shrubs.

Wanting to investigate further, she climbed the embankment leading to the top of the falls and gasped in delight when she spied what she thought was jasmine growing on the opposite side of the bubbling mountain stream. She picked her way across a series of smooth rocks that formed a natural bridge over the water. Midway across, her feet slid on a slippery moss-covered rock. With a shriek of surprise, she plummeted into the pool below.

When she surfaced, she shook the water from her eyes and was about to strike out for shore when Nathan charged through the bushes.

"Don't panic," he shouted to be heard above the waterfall. Not bothering to remove his clothes, he dived into the pool.

Flabbergasted, Jael tread water and waited for him to emerge.

"I've got you," he said as he bobbed up next to her. "You're safe now." Grabbing her by the braid, he began paddling toward shore with her in tow.

"St-stop," she sputtered.

"Dammit, Jael," he panted. "I'm not a strong swimmer. Fight me and we'll both drown."

There was truth in his warning, she quickly realized. For a man who eked his livelihood from the sea, he was clearly out of his element. His arms clumsily splashed the water, his feet churned awkwardly. He could barely keep himself afloat, much less two people. She willed her body to go limp.

Grimly Nathan released her hair and wrapped an arm around her neck just below her chin. Jael could barely breathe in his stranglehold, much less protest his treatment of her. She was gasping for air when he finally dragged her to shallow water.

"I heard you scream and came running." Even though they were now standing in hip-deep water, he held on to her as if she might vanish below the surface any second.

A lump rose in her throat. Not knowing that she was the better swimmer, he'd risked his life to save hers. She lacked the heart to disillusion him. "If you hadn't come when you did, I might have drowned."

His hands strayed from her waist and roamed up and down her back. "Are you sure you're all right?"

"I'm fine." Her voice was oddly breathless. She tried to smile, but failed.

"You're certain?"

Touched by his concern, she reached up to smooth the furrow from his brow.

The action directed Nathan's attention elsewhere. His expression became intense, almost fierce. She glanced downward and her mouth dropped in dismay. Soaking wet, her garments had become virtually transparent. Cotton worn thin by repeated laundering molded her breasts, hips, and buttocks like a second skin. To her mortification, the dusky rose nipples poked at the flimsy barrier, taut, erect, almost inviting. Reflexively she crossed her arms over her chest to shield her breasts.

"Never be ashamed of your body, love. Think of it as a temple, a place of worship." His voice deepened, roughened by emotion.

Cool water swirled around her legs, but inside she felt fire consuming her. The pounding of the waterfall was deafening. Or was it the beat of her heart? Her thoughts muddled, she could only stare at Nathan, fascinated by the gold sparks of desire dancing in his hazel eyes.

His gaze dropped to her mouth, and he hungrily followed the pink tip of her tongue as it nervously traced the full lower lip. "Sweet Jasmine, share your nectar."

Jael accepted his kiss. Accepted, then returned in full measure. Her mouth opened eagerly, joyfully as a blossom to the sun. She felt his tongue glide over hers, engaging hers in ancient love play. Tremors raced along nerve endings. The world slanted beneath her feet, and she clutched at his shirt to steady herself. If this was sin, she could understand why her mother had fallen under its spell. Wrapping her arms around his neck, she clung tightly.

He dragged his mouth from hers, then scooped her up in his arms, carried her from the pool, and laid her on a bed of ferns. With his eyes locked on hers, he lowered the shoulder strap of her chemise, first one side, then the other.

Jael knew she should muster a protest, but when light butterfly kisses drifted along the same course his hands had charted, her mind emptied. "Don't...," she sighed, "... stop."

"Which is it? Don't?" He flicked his tongue

lightly over the hard bud of her nipple. "Or don't stop?"

She arched against him in an unguarded response. Wanting. Needing. Seeking.

"Ah, my pagan flower, your body gives the answer your lips refuse."

His warm breath fanned fires that were already raging. "Please..." she moaned, the sound almost like a purr. "Please, don't stop."

"I don't think I could if I wanted to." Nathan stripped the remaining garments from her slender form and let them fall in a soggy heap. "God, but you're beautiful."

Though she knew she wasn't, he made her *feel* beautiful. Made her feel wanted, desirable. Right and wrong, good and evil, ceased to exist. There was no past, no future, only the glorious present. She wanted him as much as he wanted her.

He cupped her breasts, his touch gentle, reverent, then using his thumbs circled their peaks. They puckered instantly. "So lovely, so responsive." He drew one of her nipples into his mouth and sucked.

Pleasure, so exquisite it was almost painful, speared the core of her femininity. An unfamiliar dampness leaked from the apex of her legs. She was caught up in a vortex, spinning faster and faster, out of control. Her hands roamed up and down his back. Desire, hot and potent, pumped through her veins.

Nathan reached between their straining bodies and fumbled with the buttons of his pants.

A familiar male voice, raised loud enough to be heard above the falling water, sounded behind them. "And here, gentlemen, are the falls I was telling you about. We'll camp here for the night."

Startled, Jael and Nathan raised their heads as a small contingent of men entered the clearing. Shock and outrage registered on the men's faces as they noticed the entwined lovers for the first time. In that startled instant of recognition, Jael realized that for as long as she lived she'd never forget the censure on Thomas Hadley's face.

Nathan scrambled to his feet, and pulling Jael behind him, he used his body to screen her from their lewd and accusatory stares.

Chapter 11

Reverend Thomas Hadley led the way into his study and motioned for both his guests to be seated. Before Jael could comply, Silas jerked the chair away and shoved it across the room. "Let the bitch stand," he snarled. "She needs to do penance for her sins."

Jael stood in a corner of Reverend Hadley's study and stared dejectedly at the braided rug. Chairs scraped the wooden floor as both men took seats on opposite sides of the teak desk. The remainder of the trip to Lahaina had been sheer torture. Jael had felt like an escaped felon being returned to prison. Under the stringent chaperonage of the small search party, she and Nathan never had a minute alone. They had been given no opportunity to discuss their predicament. She had often felt his gaze rest on her and wondered what his thoughts were.

"Always said she's the devil's child." Silas

Kincaid thumped the floor with his cane for emphasis.

"Now, Silas, you're being too harsh," Thomas remonstrated. "True, the girl made a mistake..."

"You, a man of the cloth, call fornicating with a whoremongering whaling captain a mistake?" Silas's face turned an alarming purple.

Thomas took off his wire-rimmed glasses and pinched the bridge of his nose. "It was an error in judgment. Two young people got caught up in the heat of the moment. A sin, yes, but a very human one."

"I tried to mold her in the ways of the Lord, but she's evil. Just like her mother." Hatred emanated from Silas Kincaid as he glared at his granddaughter.

Jael shifted uncomfortably. She had never seen her grandfather as angry as he had been after hearing Reverend Hadley's description of finding her and Nathan. Not even the time he learned she had been swimming at Black Rock.

"She's wicked. She needs to be punished." Silas gripped the head of his cane. His fingers flexed the handle spasmodically as though already relishing the thought of slashing it across her backside.

"Have you arrived at a solution to our problem, Silas?"

Silas's pale eyes blazed as he leaned forward. "That blasted sea captain is a friend of yours, a relative of sorts, isn't he? Do what you must, but make him marry the girl."

Jael sucked in her breath. *Marry?*

Thomas ignored her shocked gasp. "Silas, I can hardly coerce Captain Thorne to wed your granddaughter if the man's unwilling."

"Unwilling?" Too agitated to remain seated, Silas rose to his feet. "Your fine, upstanding young captain wasn't unwilling to lie with her, was he?"

Jael cringed. Shame and embarrassment swirled through her, devastating any remaining shreds of pride. She wished she could just vanish in a puff of smoke. That the floor would open and swallow her. How could she ever again hold up her head in public?

Thomas drummed his fingers against the desktop, his brow knit in a thoughtful frown. "I'll do what I can," he said at long last. "That's the reason I asked that Nathan join us."

A rap on the study door signaled Nathan's arrival.

"Come in, lad," Thomas called out.

Nathan entered the room, his expression glum. If he was surprised to find Jael and her grandfather already there, it didn't show. "You sent for me, Thomas."

"You randy, no-account..." Silas's chin whiskers bobbed in agitation. "You ought to be horsewhipped. I hope you plan to do right by the girl."

"Silas," Thomas interjected smoothly, "if you don't object, I'd like to speak to the two young people—in private."

"All right," Silas agreed reluctantly. He limped from the room without a backward glance.

"Please sit down, both of you," Thomas bade them kindly.

Nervously Jael perched on the edge of the chair her grandfather had just vacated and laced her fingers together to still their trembling. Except for a bright dot of color in each cheek, her face was devoid of color. Ignoring her, Nathan lowered himself in the chair alongside hers.

"This is a serious situation, my children." Reverend Hadley steepled his fingers contemplatively. "I've known you, Jael, since you first came to the island as a child, and it pleased me to see the fine young woman you've become. It pains me to have this discussion."

Eyes downcast, she felt too ashamed to meet his look. His words only made her feel worse—if that was possible, which she seriously doubted.

The clergyman cleared his throat, then continued. "And, Nathan, I've known you for years and have felt nothing but affection and respect for you. Until now..."

"Don't be angry with him," Jael interrupted. "It was as much my fault as it was his."

Thomas replaced his eyeglasses. "That's very generous of you, my dear, but Nathan is older—and far more experienced than you. I expected him to show restraint, rather than exploit a young woman's innocence."

"Perhaps Grandfather is right after all." Jael

swallowed painfully and stared down at her laced fingers. "Perhaps I am no better than my mother."

"Now, now, don't go loading all the blame on your shoulders," Thomas counseled.

Nathan crossed, then uncrossed his legs. "Speak your piece, Thomas. I have duties that require my attention aboard ship."

Thomas leveled a stare at him. "I suspect you fully realize the gravity of this situation. I shouldn't need to point out that Jael's reputation is ruined beyond repair. When word gets out what happened between the two of you, she'll be a social outcast. A pariah. No decent man will have her. Is that what you want?"

Nathan leaped to his feet. "No, of course not!"

"Well, then, what are you willing to do to rectify the problem you created?"

Hands clasped behind his back, Nathan paced the length of the study. There was only one solution. He had realized it from the outset, though he hated to admit it. Marry the girl. Give her his name, thus safeguarding her reputation. Still, being forced into marriage galled him. He valued his freedom, prized his independence. True, he liked the girl, was attracted to her even, but that didn't mean he wanted her riding his coattails into eternity. Yet, what was he to do? His honor was at stake. As was hers.

He heaved a sigh of resignation. "I'll marry her."

"Good." Hadley picked up his pen, dipped it into the inkwell, and began scrawling across a document of some sort. "I'll waive the banns. The wedding will take place before the day is over."

"No." Jael was instantly on her feet. Her furious gaze darted from one man to the other. "Has the fact escaped you that no one has bothered to ask my opinion? I don't want to get married to you or anyone else."

Both men were speechless at her outburst. An angry flush crept into Nathan's face. Who did the chit think she was to refuse his generous offer? Thomas Hadley peered at her over the rims of his glasses as though she had taken leave of her senses.

"But, my dear, you must look at this matter rationally. Even should you leave the islands, gossip of this sort will follow wherever you go." Thomas made a sweeping motion with one arm. "It'll spoil any chance you'll ever have to lead a normal life. And," he pounced on what he hoped would be his winning argument, "should you stay here and choose not to wed, your grandfather would live in the shadow of your shame. Your actions are a poor reflection on his teachings."

Jael's shoulders slumped in defeat. Grandfather would make her life a living hell.

Thomas Hadley shoved back his chair. "I'll leave the two of you alone to discuss your decision." With that, he got up and left the room.

Awkwardness spun a long, taut silence.

Jael fixed her gaze on the floor while nervously twirling the ribbon holding her bonnet in place. Nathan paced restlessly before coming to stand in the far corner of the small room.

He regarded her carefully from a safe distance for the first time since entering Hadley's study. Had it only been that very morning that they had made their ignominious return from Hana? It seemed like a century ago.

Jael didn't even look like the same person who had accompanied him on that trek. Once again her vibrant beauty was hidden beneath drab black homespun and a hideous straw bonnet more suitable to a matron twice her age. Even her demeanor had undergone a change. She appeared subdued and unhappy. Already he missed her bright smile and bursts of exuberance.

The transformation saddened him.

And aroused all of his protective instincts.

He cleared his throat to draw her attention. "Jael, please believe it was never my intention to compromise your morals. I'm truly sorry for what happened. Thomas was right, I should have known better."

"I could have stopped you." Jael's voice sounded strained. "But I didn't."

They regarded each other warily, each battling guilt and inner conflict.

Nathan took a step forward, then stopped. "Allow me to make amends in the only way possible. Say that you'll marry me."

"But..."

He cut her off before she could object. "I

promise I'll provide for you and that I'll never raise a hand to you in anger."

Jael caught her lower lip between her teeth and blinked back an unexpected sting of tears. Her breath came out in a soft rush of air as she bowed to the inevitable. "Then I accept your offer, Nathan Thorne."

Trapped!

Nathan felt trapped. Knowing there was no one to blame but himself was scant consolation. His neck was stretched across the chopping block, and the ax was about to fall. And all because he couldn't keep his pants buttoned.

Nathan clambered aboard the dinghy and began rowing out to where the *Clotilde* lay bobbing at anchor. Leaning forward, he pulled on the oars with all his might. The little boat fairly danced through the choppy water. He felt the prospect of marriage hang about his neck like a millstone, seemingly heavy enough to drag him beneath the waves and put an end to his misery.

Dammit! He had been married once and had vowed never to do so again. Yet in a space of hours, he was about to repeat vows that would bind him to a woman for the rest of his days. Marriage might be fine for some men, but it definitely wasn't for him. Who the hell was it anyway who referred to women as the weaker sex? Where the institution of marriage was concerned, *he* was the simpleton. He had showed no sound judgment whatsoever, blundering into a situation that had been the brunt of numerous jokes. Getting caught with his pants down like some callow youth trysting in a hayloft with the farmer's daughter. Wait until John learned the outcome of his so-called meeting with Thomas Hadley. He would laugh himself silly.

It wasn't that he disliked Jael Kincaid. He didn't. Quite the contrary, he was fond of the girl. She was sweet, charming, and pretty as a picture. A man could do far worse than to choose her for a bride. The problem was, he didn't want a bride.

Not Jael. Not anyone.

Nathan tugged mightily on the oars. The muscles in his arms burned from the demand made on them. Gentle and unassuming, Jael was the direct opposite of Catherine. Like storm clouds gathering on the horizon, unhappy memories drifted across his mind. Memories of wedded hell. Memories of Catherine. While Jael had lured him with unintentional guile, Catherine had been a conniving huntress, baiting the trap with cunning and skill, then crowing in glee when the catch snapped shut.

Because she was different from the young women in her social circle, Nathan was fascinated by her from the beginning. Her father had tried to discourage the match, but the more he opposed it, the stronger became her determination to wed. Nathan, too, had harbored reservations about their engagement. He had proposed they wait, test their feelings, until he returned from a scheduled voyage. But by feigning pregnancy, Catherine had bested both men. Neither could muster any objections to a precipitous wedding.

The following week she had jubilantly announced that her fears were unfounded.

Not only had she never been pregnant but, Catherine had announced with a meaningful look at Nathan, she had no intention of finding herself in that condition in the near future.

Marriage had provided Catherine the vehicle by which to leave her father's house. Unfettered by paternal rules and regulations, she would be free to come and go as she pleased. To her way of thinking, a doting husband could be more easily managed than a strict parent.

Spoiled and willful, Catherine viewed Nathan as a child did a coveted toy in a shop window. Something she just had to own, but once possessing it, quickly tired of and set aside. Much to Catherine's chagrin, husbands weren't as easily discarded as toys.

He frowned, recalling the scene in Thomas Hadley's study. Jael hadn't looked any happier at the prospect of matrimony than he did. There had to be a solution to this dilemma. There just had to be. If so, he was determined to find it and set them both free.

Thomas Hadley had dreaded confronting Nathan. He knelt in the coral stone church he had helped construct and prayed for divine guidance. It was always his intention to offer guidance, not interference. What he had told Jael was true. He liked and respected Nathan Thorne—and still did. While he didn't condone their behavior, he could understand it. Jael Kincaid was a comely young miss, and Nathan a charming rogue with an eye for the ladies. He was aware that since becoming a widower, Nathan scrupulously avoided emotional entanglements.

He squeezed his eyes shut. The pressure building behind his eyes would soon be a full-blown headache. Under normal circumstances, he would rejoice in a match between such fine young people. But the situation was far from ideal. The girl's reputation was sullied beyond repair. After what had transpired between the two of them on their journey from Hana, no decent man would have her. She'd be condemned to spinsterhood. Denied a husband. Children.

And if that prospect wasn't grim enough, she'd spend it under Silas Kincaid's roof. It terrified him to think what might happen to the girl when Silas got her alone. If Alice and Corinne's assumptions were correct, the old goat had beaten her severely for far less serious infractions. He didn't want her innocent blood on his hands. Jael Kincaid needed a defender.

And that someone might just as well be Nathan Thorne.

Nathan, he knew, was not likely overjoyed at the prospect of becoming a bridegroom. He preferred his life unencumbered. The pounding in Thomas's temples increased. He despised having to use his influence to coerce Nathan into marriage. Sighing heavily, he realized he had little choice in the matter. He rose stiffly and left the church.

This was all a bad dream, Jael thought. A nightmare. Any minute she'd wake up and find herself in the small bedroom at her grandfather's house.

"There." Alice Hadley snipped a piece of thread, then stepped back to admire her handiwork. "I brought this dress with me when I came to the islands as a young bride."

"That shade of violet is just perfect with your coloring." Corinne pinned a spray of tiny white flowers in Jael's red curls.

Jael looked at her own reflection in the mirror, and a stranger stared back. Gone was the drab, serviceable dress she usually wore and in its place a lovely gown of violet taffeta trimmed with blond lace. After brushing her hair to a high gloss, Corinne had pulled it away from her face and arranged it into a cascade of loose curls. Jael barely recognized herself.

"Who would have thought you'd be married before me?" Corinne clamped her hand over her mouth, horrified to have let such an unfeeling remark slip.

"The world is full of surprises, dear," Alice tried to smooth her daughter's gaffe. "Nathan is a lucky young man. Doesn't Jael make a beautiful bride?"

Bride? Though she might look like one, Jael definitely didn't feel like one. A bride was supposed to be happy, excited. In love. All she felt was a coldness that seeped straight to the marrow of her bones.

All her dreams burned to ashes. She wished fervently she had never set eyes on Captain Nathan Thorne. What had her attraction to the man gained her? A lifetime of bondage, she answered, her mouth turning down bitterly. For the remainder of her days, she was to be subject to Nathan Thorne's whims and foibles.

"It's time," Alice Hadley announced with a cheery smile. "Goodness, child, you're pale as a ghost."

"Don't look so gloomy." Corinne pinched Jael's cheeks to bring some color into them. "Nathan is quite a catch, you know."

The three women walked the short distance to the church without speaking. Jael was vaguely aware it was twilight, usually her favorite hour. Somehow the time of day seemed symbolic, just as the sun set on another day, an old way of life was ending.

Corinne handed her a Bible, then took a seat on one of the benches. Besides the Hadley family, Nathan's good friend, John McFee, and her grandfather were the only witnesses to the nuptials. Jael cast an anxious glance at Nathan, but he didn't appear any happier than she was with this arrangement.

Candlelight added a benevolent glow to the small church. Someone, probably Corinne, had thought to pick a bouquet of flowers, which perfumed the air. Jael moved woodenly up the aisle.

Silas Kincaid glowered at her as she passed. Two vertical lines of disapproval bracketed his thin lips. Even his chin whiskers bristled with disdain. "Satan's spawn," he hissed just loud enough for her to overhear.

The cruel barb brought tears to her eyes. She had foolishly thought she had grown impervious to his insults, but he still wielded power to hurt her.

Reverend Hadley favored those assembled with a benign smile. "My dear friends," he began as he opened the Book of Common Prayer. "We are gathered here this evening..."

Dazed, Jael barely heard him.

"...not to be entered into unadvisedly or lightly, but reverently, discreetly, advisedly, soberly, and in the fear of God."

Jael felt like a fraud. She didn't love Nathan, and he didn't love her. She didn't even know if love existed. Perhaps true love was only a substance of fairy tales.

"Wilt thou, Nathan Benjamin Thorne, forsaking all others..."

As though from a distance, she heard Nathan's clipped, emotionless response. Jael felt as though she were encased in a block of ice. Gradually she became aware that an expectant hush had fallen over the church. Everyone seemed to be waiting, watching. Belatedly she recited her lines, "I, Jael Elspeth Kincaid..."

From behind, she heard the rhythmic thump of her grandfather's cane on the hard-packed earth floor. The sound unnerved her. Her voice faltered. It required little imagination to feel the hickory stick striking her repeatedly. She cleared her throat and tried again, this time making it through the vows without stammering.

Still in a fog, she extended her hand while Nathan slipped a wide gold band on the ring finger of her left hand. If he was suffering an attack of nerves, it didn't show. His hands were rock steady. In contrast to the icy coldness of hers, his skin was warm, almost fevered.

The clergyman brought the brief ceremony to a close. "Those whom God hath joined together, let no man put asunder."

Once again Jael was cognizant of the expectant hush from the small group of witnesses. They were waiting for Nathan to kiss his bride, and the realization sent rosy color spreading across her cheeks.

Silas didn't wait for the traditional token of affection. With a loud snort of disgust, he limped from the church while muttering under his breath.

Jael watched him disappear, then slanted a cautious look at Nathan. Not a hint of a smile softened his mouth. Taking her firmly by the arm, he steered her down the aisle, leaving Jael filled with an aching disappointment. In spite of the uncertainty, in spite of the resentment, she had been secretly hoping he would kiss her. She desperately longed for the touch of his lips on hers.

Chapter 12

"Have another piece of cake, Jael dear. It's Nathan's favorite."

"No, thank you, Mrs. Hadley. In all the excitement, I'm afraid I'm not very hungry."

"Ah, yes, weddings play havoc with a girl's appetite. That's why I was once as tiny as you and could fit into that dress." Her round face beamed a maternal smile at Jael. "Then I quickly became pregnant, and my waistline hasn't been the same since."

Jael's mouth went dry. Babies? She hadn't given a thought to married life beyond the actual wedding. Strange, she reflected, instead of alarming her, she found the idea of children a pleasant one. And children meant shared intimacies. A trace of color crept across her cheekbones as she remembered the intoxicating sensation that spread through her at Nathan's slightest touch.

"I hope I haven't embarrassed you. Thomas is forever scolding me for my blunt speech." Alice Hadley patted her hand. "By the way, dear, you made such a lovely bride."

"Thank you," Jael murmured. Her eyes sought out Nathan, who was across the room talking with Reverend Hadley and Corinne. Judging from the size of the slice on his plate, the day's turn of events hadn't affected his appetite in the least.

Alice Hadley moved off to refill the punch glasses. Jael felt like an outsider at her own wedding. Though she had never envisioned herself as a bride, this wouldn't have been the way she imagined it. The weddings she had witnessed had been joyous occasions filled with talk and laughter. This was such a solemn affair. Here, bride and bridegroom remained as far apart as possible within the same room, she alone and unsmiling at one side, Nathan at the opposite end.

She absently shredded the cake with her fork. What had prompted her to go through with the ceremony? She should have just refused. No one had held a gun to her head or a knife to her throat. Yet she had been maneuvered as easily as a puppet on a string. In her heart she knew the real reason. She couldn't lie to herself when the answer was crystal clear. She was a coward. The choice had been either Nathan Thorne—or her grandfather. Not really a choice at all. Even a hellish marriage held more appeal than remaining another night under her grandfather's roof.

Enough! she rebuked herself. She had wallowed in self-pity long enough. It was time to start looking for a way out of this untenable situation. Surely if she remained calm, rational, and patient, she could find a solution. At the least, marriage to Nathan provided time to explore other options. Although she didn't fully understand it, she had heard the term divorce whispered on rare occasions. If that failed, she would continue to stitch garments for Mrs. Ka'ano until she had enough money saved, then vanish. One way or another, she didn't intend to meekly relinquish her plan for independence.

John McFee strolled over to where Jael stood off to one side. With a quick glance, he took in the pile of yellow crumbs on Jael's plate and shook his head in mock dismay. "Considerin' how you just destroyed the pride of Mrs. Hadley's kitchen, am I safe guessin' you won't be askin' for the recipe?"

Jael looked down at what had once been dessert, then smiled sheepishly. "I guess I'm just not very hungry."

John took her dish and set it on a nearby table. "I don't believe we've been properly introduced. McFee's the name. John McFee, first mate aboard the *Clotilde*."

"It's a pleasure to meet you, Mr. McFee." In spite of a nose that looked as though it had been broken a time or two in a waterfront brawl, he had an appealing, boyish face. Jael felt herself responding instinctively to his infectious grin and the merry twinkle in his brown eyes.

"Call me John. In case you've forgotten, I

was with Nathan the night he rescued you from a scoundrel named George."

"Ah, yes." Jael smiled slowly. "If I recall the incident correctly, you were the gentleman who spotted the whale."

John gleefully rubbed his hands together and grinned. "Nothing I relish more than a good fight. Gets the blood circulatin'."

Jael's mood lightened a bit. "Your observation that night was most timely, Mr. McFee... John," she quickly amended, "and most appreciated."

John's grin faded somewhat. "Don't mind the cap'n none, miss. Nathan's as good as they come, but he's just not the marryin' kind. This wedding goes against his grain. Don't take it to heart."

The steel band around her chest tightened. "Whether you believe me or not, it goes against my grain, too."

He gave her a long, considering look. "One could hardly blame a body for wantin' to get away from the miserable old coot you call a grandfather."

"I never intended..." Jael licked her suddenly dry lips. "I didn't..."

John continued, all traces of merriment wiped from his face. "I remember gettin' knocked around plenty by my old man and bein' too small and too puny to fight back. I would have done anythin' to get away from the bastard's fists... anythin'. That kind of life is tough on a boy. Must be even tougher on a female."

Jael blanched. John knew. Indeed everyone must know. They must all think her a spineless weakling. That she was so intimidated by her grandfather she would do anything, agree to anything, rather than face his wrath. The truth stung. Besides being angry with her for forcing him into an unwanted marriage, Nathan must hold her in contempt.

Out of the corner of her eye, she saw Nathan excuse himself from the Hadleys and make his way toward them. He flashed his friend a quick grin. "Leave it to John to single out the prettiest lady in the room."

"Trouble is"—John winked at Jael—"the cap'n's already staked his claim."

"I should warn you." Nathan placed his hand possessively at the small of her back. "Don't believe anything John tells you. He's a born yarn spinner."

John gave Nathan's arm a playful punch. "No better than the cap'n."

It was obvious to Jael that the two men shared an easy camaraderie, which she envied. She wished she, too, could feel at ease, but the slight pressure of Nathan's hand sent nerve endings jangling up and down her spine.

"Here," Nathan said, turning his attention to Jael. He handed her a glass of fruit punch. "I thought you might like a cool drink."

"Thank you." She accepted the punch, hoping he wouldn't notice the tremor of her hands.

"My pleasure."

She had feared his anger. Instead he was . . .

kind. She gazed up at him, her eyes searching his, seeking hidden truths in the green-flecked hazel depths.

"Think I'll get a drink myself," John said, a faint note of humor in his voice as he ambled off.

Before Jael could create order out of her confused thoughts, Corinne Hadley came up to her with outstretched arms and caught her in a hug. "I've been so busy helping Mother, I haven't had a chance to congratulate you two."

"Don't I get a hug, too?" Nathan asked.

"Of course, you do." Corinne wrapped her arms around him and gave him a peck on the cheek. "Have you ever seen a bride more beautiful?"

A hot rush of color stained Jael's cheeks as she was forced to endure Nathan's leisurely perusal. She took a sip of fruit punch to hide her discomfiture.

"No, never," he agreed at length, his eyes fixed on Jael's flushed face.

Corinne nodded her approval of the pair, then hurried off in search of extra plates and glasses, leaving Jael and Nathan alone once again.

Jael stared at the particles of pulp swimming in her punch glass, then she drew a deep breath and asked Nathan the question foremost in her mind. "I thought surely you would hate me for trapping you into marriage. Why are you being so nice?"

"Always slow to trust, aren't you?" he murmured. He reached out, crooked his index finger beneath her chin, and tilted her face to his. He discarded the glib reply on the tip of his tongue in favor of an honest answer. "When I saw you across the room looking so lost, so forlorn, I just wanted to make you smile. Every bride is entitled to be happy on her wedding day."

Seeing her tentative smile blossom, he ruthlessly squashed pangs of conscience. Soon enough he would inform her of his plans.

He caught her elbow and steered her toward the Hadleys. "It's time we thanked our hosts and went on our way."

"On our way to where?" Jael asked in alarm.

He shot her a bemused look. "Did you expect we were going to be permanent houseguests of the Hadleys?"

"No, of course not," she answered hastily.

Further inquiries were postponed as they had to bid their farewells out on the veranda, where Corinne hugged Jael a final time as Alice and Thomas Hadley looked on.

Then, Thomas turned to Nathan and pumped his hand. "Jael is a fine young woman. Once the two of you get past this initial awkwardness, you'll thank me."

Nathan muttered something indistinguishable. With Jael's hand clasped firmly in his, he led her down the steps to the shell walkway. Jael glanced over her shoulder and waved to those who stood watching their departure.

Nathan headed up the beach. Jael lengthened her stride to match his brisk pace. "You still haven't told me where we're going. Will we be staying aboard your ship?"

"No," he retorted brusquely. "The *Clotilde* is being reoutfitted and happens to be off-limits at the moment."

Jael let go of his hand to pick up the skirts of her borrowed dress, and half ran to keep up with him. "Then where?"

"There's a cottage down the beach that houses visiting clergy. It happens to be vacant at the moment. It'll serve the purpose for the time being."

She trudged along, her feet sinking deep into the soft sand. A cottage? Just the two of them? She found the thought oddly appealing. Perhaps marriage wouldn't be as bad as she had dreaded. Marriage to Nathan, that is. After all, he was her friend. Her protector. Her knight in shining armor. Ever since their first meeting, he'd always come to her rescue. Always been there when she needed him. Maybe, just maybe, she could lead a life like other women. Until now, a loving husband, children, and a home of her own had been a fantasy she rarely permitted. She glanced downward. The gold band on her left hand glittered in the moonlight.

The faint glimmer as fragile as her dream.

Jael stopped to dump sand from borrowed slippers a size too large. By now Nathan was far ahead of her. He seemed oblivious of the increasing distance separating them. A frisson of unease shimmied down her spine, so barefoot she hurried to narrow the gap.

Fifty feet farther, he turned up a path. Slippers in hand and out of breath, she tagged after him to a small cottage set back from the beach. Nathan was waiting for her on the front porch. Flinging open the door, he made a sweeping gesture with one arm. "Our honeymoon cottage," he declared.

Jael hesitantly stepped inside, then waited while he struck a match and lit an oil lamp. She let out a gasp of delight. The small dwelling was similar in size and layout to the one she had occupied with her grandparents. But there the similarity ended. This one was cheerful, not gloomy. Gaily colored rag rugs covered the floor; throw pillows in bright blues and greens were piled on the settee. The shutters were ajar to allow a light breeze to circulate. Someone, perhaps Corinne, had filled a pottery bowl with vibrant coral hibiscus.

"It's perfect," she pronounced with a smile.

Nathan watched her move about the room with the effortless grace of a dancer, pausing to trail her fingertips over the surface of a table, to plump a pillow, to sniff a flower. Corinne Hadley's observation had been right on target. Jael did make a beautiful bride.

It didn't make his task any easier.

"Jael, sit down. We have to talk." He tugged off his striped neckcloth and tossed it toward a chair. It missed the target and slid to the floor.

Jael gave him an inquisitive look, then perched on the edge of the settee, her hands folded primly in her lap. "I didn't know what to expect, but I never imagined a place half this nice," she said to fill the awkward void.

He loosened his collar as though it were suddenly strangling him. "I've done a great deal of thinking since we spoke with Thomas this afternoon. And I've come to a conclusion."

Her eyes mirrored uncertainty—and fear. "What is it you're trying to tell me?"

He lowered himself to the settee, but, too restless to sit still, he bounded to his feet a moment later to pace the confines of the small room. "The sea has been the only life I've known since I was just a lad. I'm not the sort to marry and settle down. I like to see new ports, and I'm often gone for years at a stretch. So I came up with a plan—"

"A plan?"

"I'll set you up with a small house here on the island—this one, if you like—and see that you're well provided for. Your grandfather will never lay another hand on you. You'll have your independence and," he added on a triumphant note, "I'll have mine. What could be more perfect?"

Jael bit her lip as she fought for control. She kept her gaze lowered and clutched her folded hands so tightly that the knuckles shone white. Nathan had married her out of a sense of obligation. Now he planned to abandon her. *And she had been naive enough to hope there might be a future with this man.* She didn't know whom to be more angry with—him or herself.

Well, she was going to gain her independence all right. But it wasn't going to be according to his script. Time had come to take control of her own destiny.

She was quiet so long that Nathan grew worried. He sank down next to her and placed his hands over her icy ones. "Try to understand, Jael. This is the best possible solution for both of us."

A choked sound escaped, but she still refused to meet his gaze.

Nathan felt lower than a skunk. He hated like the devil to hurt her, but he had to be honest. He owed her that much. "I'm very fond of you, Jael, but I don't want to be married. Not to you—not to anyone. What do you say? Can we come to an agreement?"

"No!" Her head came up with a snap.

Nathan stared at her in amazement. This was not the response he had anticipated. Tears, hysterics maybe, but not blatant defiance.

"You arrogant, insufferable man! Has it ever occurred to you that *I* might not want to be married to *you*?" Though her face was chalk white, her eyes blazed with a hot blue light. "My entire life I've been the object of pity, but no more! I'll not allow you to abandon me while you go on your merry way. I refuse to have people whispering behind my back how my husband only married me because he was forced to. That he deserted me first chance he got."

"What do you want from me?"

"Take me with you." Jael's mind worked feverishly to devise a plan designed to assuage her pride and soothe her hurt. "California, or New England, it hardly matters where. Once there, I'll find a position and will no longer be your responsibility."

Nathan stood, feeling a bit dazed. "All right. After the *Clotilde*'s next voyage, we return to New Bedford. Be ready to sail when she does."

"Fine." She could barely get the word out. A steel band seemed wrapped around her chest, making it difficult to breath. She felt the sharp sting of unshed tears behind her eyelids. Any second her control would snap. Having Nathan witness how deeply he had wounded her with his rejection would be the final humiliation. She turned and fled into the bedroom.

The village of Lahaina receded with each stroke of the oars. Behind him, the mast of the *Clotilde* pointed a scolding finger heavenward. Nathan raised his face to the sea breeze and inhaled a deep draught of briny air. He should be elated that Jael didn't want to hold him to marriage vows grudgingly made, but all he felt was a queer little pain in the region of his heart.

The dinghy nudged the side of the *Clotilde*, the slight movement dragging him away from his brooding thoughts. Nathan grabbed onto a rope ladder and climbed aboard. He found John McFee smoking his pipe on the aft deck.

The first mate looked up in surprise. "I hardly expected you here on your weddin' night."

Nathan rested his arms on the rail and gazed toward Maui. "Don't be funny. You know my feelings on the subject of matrimony."

"Ain't the bride willin'?"

"Virgins are nothing but trouble. It's time I heed my own advice."

John squinted at him through a stream of pipe smoke. "You mean to tell me the whole time you never laid a hand on her? She's still pure as the day she was born?"

"I've never made love to the girl," Nathan snapped. *But he would have if it hadn't been for those damn clergymen interrupting when they did.* He shifted his weight uncomfortably. The knowledge didn't sit well with his conscience.

"Not that I'd blame you if you had. She's pretty as a picture with those big blue eyes."

Nathan didn't want to think of those gentian-colored eyes. The memory of them swimming with tears made his gut wrench. He felt slimier than bottom-feeding scum. He wasn't proud of his actions that night.

"She don't seem a bad sort." John puffed his pipe thoughtfully. "Can hardly blame the girl for wantin' to get out from under her grandfather's thumb. Mean ol' cuss, from what I hear."

Nathan whipped his head to glare at his friend. "Whose side are you on? If anyone, you should know how I feel about marriage."

"Might not be as bad as all that, Cap'n. Maybe you oughta give it a chance."

"Never!" Nathan pounded the rail with his fist.

John gazed across the stretch of water to the West Maui Mountains, darkly silhouetted against the night sky. "If you feel that strongly, maybe it's not too late to wiggle out of it."

Nathan glanced at him sharply. "What are you talking about? Spell it out, man, I'm in no mood for games."

"There is a simple way out."

"A way out? What kind of way out?"

"An annulment." John waited for his words to sink in. A grin tugged at one corner of his mouth. "If what you say is true—that you never touched the girl—a lawyer can draw up papers to that effect, have both parties swear to it, and have a judge annul the marriage."

Nathan slapped John heartily on the back. "That's it. That's the answer."

"Whoa!" John held up a hand in caution. "First you have to get Jael to agree."

"She'll agree quickly enough. She wants her freedom as much as I want mine." Nathan's mouth firmed into a hard line. "I'll take her back to New Bedford and, after we see a judge, I'll give her enough money to tide her over until she finds a decent job."

"For a man who just got his neck out of a noose, you don't look none too happy."

Muttering expletives under his breath, Nathan barked orders to the man on watch, then strode off in the direction of his cabin.

John stayed at the rail, puffing thoughtfully on his pipe. A broad grin split his weathered face as a realization struck him. Whether the cap'n wanted to admit it or not, he had been harpooned by the little red-haired wench.

A fine way, indeed, to spend a wedding night, Nathan thought, as he lay on the wide bed in his quarters. He mulled over John's advice. An annulment. The perfect solution to a prickly problem. But an annulment was only valid if the marriage was never consummated. It was becoming increasingly difficult to spend time in Jael's company and keep his hands to himself, he acknowledged with a rueful twist of his mouth. He liked stroking her silky skin, liked sampling her sweet kisses.

He laced his hands behind his head and stared at the overhead beams. All he needed to do was find exactly the right moment to broach the subject with her. She had been a regular little spitfire earlier when he had offered to set her up here on the island. He grinned at the memory. His docile little wife had a redhead's temperament all right. He'd give her temper time to cool. In the meantime, he needed armor to gird himself against the growing attraction. Until then, he needed to maintain a safe distance between them.

Chapter 13

Jael sat in the center of the bed and rested her forehead against her raised knees. Her eyes felt gritty; her head pounded. She caught a tangle of hair and shoved it behind her ear.

Her resolution hardened. She didn't want to be married—ever. Marriage was definitely not for her. She didn't want to be under any man's thumb. She wanted to be free. Independent.

She parted the mosquito netting that surrounded her bed and peeked out. Instinct told her she had slept later than usual. She tossed back the covers and swung her legs over the edge. Buttery yellow sunlight slanted through the half-open shutters, hinting of another beautiful day. Birds warbled cheerily. She looked around with interest. Like the rest of the cottage, the bedroom was light and airy with whitewashed walls and wood shutters and doors painted bright blue. In addition to the large bed draped in netting, there was a small dressing table, a chair, and a chest of drawers.

She spied a battered valise stuffed with her meager belongings on the floor near the door. As she reached for it, she heard movement in the outer room. Nathan? she wondered. Dread churned her stomach. What could she say to him after last night?

Before she could make up her mind, there was a hesitant knock on the bedroom door. Not waiting for a response, a smiling native girl pushed the door open. She carried a bamboo tray spread with a plate of sliced guava and a china teapot. While Jael watched speechless, the girl placed the tray on the bed.

"Morning, missus. I bring breakfast."

"Who are you? What are you doing here?" Jael asked when she found her tongue.

"My name Mahie. Captain send."

Jael settled back against the pillows and studied the lovely girl. Mahie was probably several years younger than herself, with lustrous black hair that fell to her hips and eyes like liquid ebony. She was dressed in a long flowing dress splashed with crimson flowers.

"Captain say missus tired. Told Mahie not to wake." Mahie started unpacking Jael's things, wrinkling her nose in distaste at the plain drab-colored garments. "You no like pretty dresses, missus?"

"Yes, but these are the only dresses I have."

"Captain tell Mahie to take care of pretty lady."

Jael was unexpectedly touched by his concern. "That was very kind of the captain, but I can take care of myself."

The girl shook her head obstinately, making her long hair sway. "Captain say Mahie cook and clean for pretty missus."

Jael poured a cup of tea. "That isn't necessary, Mahie. I won't be needing your services."

Mahie's dark eyes filled with disappointment. "You no like Mahie?"

Jael felt guilty. She had never intended to hurt the girl's feelings, but she was perfectly capable of doing her own cooking and cleaning. "I like you fine," she amended. "It's just that I'm used to taking care of myself."

The native girl broke into a wide smile. "Then you let Mahie stay?"

"Well, I . . ."

"Captain promise Mahie this many dollar to take care of missus." She held up both hands. "Mahie soon marry Inaika. Dollar be present to Inaika."

Jael bit into a sweet slice of guava. If Nathan chose to spend his money hiring a servant, then so be it. Besides, it would be mean spirited to snatch a wedding gift from the young couple and it would be pleasant to have another woman's companionship. "It will be good having you here, Mahie."

"Eat now, missus too skinny. Mahie go heat water for bath."

Jael ate slowly. In spite of the strain between them, she felt warmed knowing that Nathan cared enough to provide her with a companion during his absence. No one had showed that much consideration in a long time. Not since her mother had died. For the first time in years, fond memories of her mother surfaced. Memories not tainted with anger or bitterness—or sadness.

Don't worry your pretty little head, sweeting, Mother won't let anything bad happen to you. I'll always take care of you.

It shamed her to know that where her mother had been concerned, she had become like her grandfather. Quick to criticize. To condemn. Then an even more stunning realization struck her. Jael's hand trembled so violently that she had to set the cup down. All these years she had blamed her mother not for her actions but for abandoning her by dying. A tear trickled down her cheek.

It was time to forgive.

The day passed pleasantly with Mahie for company. The Hawaiian girl repeatedly bemoaned Jael's inadequate wardrobe. "Why all your dresses like dark clouds on rainy day?"

Jael was hard-pressed to give a suitable reply. "I like bright colors, Mahie, but have no money for pretty clothes."

Mahie held up Jael's black bonnet, eyeing it critically from every angle. "This ugly. You ask Captain. He give you dollar, you see."

Mahie left just before sunset after promising to return the next day. When there was still no sign of Nathan, Jael ate dinner alone. Now that the sun had set, she felt a vague sense of unease. Miles from town, the cottage was isolated. The episode with Mu had shaken her complacency. Evil lurked everywhere. Not even the islands were immune. Every sound seemed magnified. Her imagination churned with unpleasant thoughts. What if Nathan didn't plan to return? For all she knew, he might have already pulled up anchor and set sail. She tried to convince herself that would be just fine as far as she was concerned. That she didn't want a husband any more than he wanted a wife. Once he left Lahaina, they'd both be free.

Distracted, she brought out her sewing. The thread kept knotting, and twice she stuck her finger with the needle. "Ouch," she muttered, then sucked her fingertip to keep it from staining the delicate garment she stitched.

Suddenly she stiffened. In the distance, she heard men's voices, which grew louder as she listened. The chorus of a bawdy ballad rang through the night. She set her sewing aside and stepped onto the porch as the group stumbled up the beach. She immediately recognized Nathan, who towered half a head above the rest. He had one arm draped loosely over John McFee's shoulders. A bottle dangled from his fingertips. As she watched, he raised the bottle and took a long swig.

Nathan glanced up and spied her standing in the open doorway with her arms folded. Undaunted, he lurched toward the cottage. The other three members of the group exchanged uncertain looks when they saw Jael waiting. Nathan reeled unsteadily up the steps and across the porch, a lopsided grin on his face. "Well, if it isn't my pretty little bride come to greet her new husband." Before she could object, he looped an arm around her waist, pulled her hard against him, and planted a sloppy kiss on her mouth.

Jael pushed away in disgust. With a slack-mouthed grin, Nathan reached out and pinched her buttocks. "Stop," she gasped. "How dare you?"

"I can dare anything I like." He leered at her lecherously from beneath a sun-streaked shock of hair. "You're forgetting, sweet, I have a legal document granting husbandly rights 'til death do us part."

Jael wiped his kiss from her mouth with the back of her hand. Nathan tasted hot, wet—and reeked of rum.

He wound an arm around her stiff shoulders. "Zeke, Charlie, allow me to introduce my dutiful bride, Mrs. Nathan Thorne. She's already met John here."

"Gentlemen," Jael murmured politely. The smaller of the two doffed his cap. The other bobbed his head and muttered a greeting. John McFee managed a sheepish smile.

Nathan swung Jael around and gave her a playful swat on the behind. "What's for dinner, woman? We're starving. I promised my friends a good meal before we got down to a serious game of poker."

The men cleaned her out of food in record time, then settled down to cards. She could hear their off-color jokes and raucous bursts of laughter from the cookhouse as she washed dishes. When she returned to the cottage, the air was blue with cigar smoke. Bottles of rum and mugs of ale littered the table. Nathan didn't look up from his cards. "Don't mind us. Just go to bed and forget we're here."

Jael bade the men good night, then disappeared into the bedroom and closed the door behind her. She slipped into her nightdress and climbed into bed. Though she was tired, she wasn't able to sleep for all the noise in the adjoining room. She rolled onto her side and punched her pillow. She hadn't thought it possible for four people to make such a racket.

And, she sighed, they showed no sign of leaving.

In the morning, Jael cracked the bedroom door and peeked out. Bodies were strewn from one end of the cottage to the other. One man, Zeke, if she remembered correctly, was slung across the settee, his booted feet dangling over the edge. Charlie was curled in a ball on the braided rug, the tablecloth draped across his shoulders. John snored peacefully from a makeshift bed consisting of several chairs shoved together.

The cottage looked a shambles. It smelled of stale smoke and spilled ale. Empty liquor bottles and saucers overflowing with ashes were everywhere. She took a cautious step out of the bedroom, and her foot encountered a sticky puddle.

Just then, Nathan, his hair tousled, his eyes

bloodshot, came out of the spare bedroom. A day's growth of bearded stubble covered his jaw. He rested an arm against the doorjamb and yawned broadly. "Sure is nice having a woman around the house. Makes a man want to invite his friends home more often."

"Surely you don't plan..."

"Don't worry. You needn't fuss on our account." Scratching his chest, he turned and disappeared back into the bedroom.

Jael stared after him in dismay. Was he going to make this a habit? If so, she might as well be a barmaid in a grog shop.

Her grandmother had been fond of saying that a man expected three things from marriage: a spotless house, tasty meals, and a modest wife. If that was true, Nathan was due for a reckoning. Every single night this past week, she had witnessed his drunken revelry, prepared hot meals for his hard-drinking, poker-playing cronies, and cleaned up after them. Her jaw firmed with resolution. Tonight, she vowed, she would bring this pattern to a halt.

With a rebellious gleam in her eyes, she added a generous sprinkle of hot spices to the simmering pot. She sampled a spoonful of stew, and her face screwed into a grimace. The food was indeed as terrible as she hoped. Pity to waste good food, but drastic measures were called for. Next she checked dessert. Pineapple cake. Pineapple pancake, she giggled, would be a more apt description. Toasted near black on the outside, it had come out of the oven flat and lopsided. Previously Nathan's favorite, he might lose his taste for it after tonight.

Now for a final check on the cottage. Jael had met Mahie at the door that morning and insisted that she spend the day with her young man, assuring her she could manage alone for a single day. Although puzzled, Mahie had gone off, eager to enjoy the company of Inaika. Jael had left the cottage in the exact condition she had found it upon rising. She hadn't picked up a single dirty dish or emptied an ashtray. Empty bottles from the night before littered a floor that was none too clean.

She glanced into a mirror. Instead of its usual prim coil, her hair, unbound and uncombed, fell in loose tangles around her face and shoulders. The heat of the cookhouse had twisted curls into corkscrews that framed her face and temples. She had purposely neglected to wear an apron while cooking. Now her dress was spattered with stains and smudged with flour. The top four buttons were left unfastened, and the bodice gaped at the neckline. So much for the most important duties of a wife, she gloated.

At the sound of footsteps on the porch, she turned her back on the havoc she had created and went to greet Nathan. He stood on the threshold, his broad shoulders filling the doorway. Seeing his look of stupefaction, she was hard-pressed to hide her smile of triumph. He scanned the messy room, then his gaze landed on her, and she felt a twinge of guilt that she quickly stifled. "You're looking at me strangely, Nathan, is anything wrong?"

"Your clothes look as though they've been slept in. Have you been ill?"

She smiled sweetly. "No, I feel fine. In fact I've never felt better."

He looked beyond her to the messy cottage as though not quite believing what he saw. "What have you done to the place?"

"Done?" She assumed a guileless expression. "Why, nothing, nothing at all. You and your friends seem to prefer it in this condition, and I want them to feel at home when they visit."

He seemed to pale beneath his tan. "I brought company with me."

"You know that your friends are always welcome. I prepared a special meal tonight."

"That's good, because I invited them for dinner."

Nathan stepped aside, and for the first time Jael noticed their guests. Her eyes widened in dismay.

"Hello, dear." Smiling, Alice Hadley came up the walkway trailed by her husband. "I hope we're not intruding."

Jael gulped. "No, of course not."

Thomas Hadley removed his hat as he mounted the steps. "Nathan insisted we join you for dinner."

"Please, come in." Her voice was faint.

"Yes, please do," Nathan echoed, shooting his bride daggers with his look.

Jael felt as though she were going to be ill.

The shocked expressions on the Hadleys' faces would be engraved in her memory forever. Alice Hadley's mouth dropped, her eyes bugged. Reverend Hadley frowned blackly. Jael cut a glance at Nathan. He was tight-lipped and scowling. He would probably strangle her the minute he got her alone. And she deserved it. Whatever made her think that she could get away with such a stunt?

Jael swallowed nervously, then spurred into a frenzy of motion, she raced about like a mad woman, fluffing pillows and clearing piles of debris from the settee. "I was just about to tidy up. Sit down, rest. I'll check on dinner. Nathan," she squeaked, giving him a look of desperate pleading, "would you serve our guests refreshments while I see to dinner?"

"Yes, of course." Eager to forestall Thomas Hadley's questions, Nathan gratefully grasped Jael's suggestion. "You must be thirsty. It's quite a walk from town. Be right back." Grabbing Jael's elbow none too gently, he hustled her from the room.

He waited until they were in the cookhouse, well out of the Hadleys' hearing range, before he exploded. "What the hell is going on?"

Jael was too frantic to worry about Nathan's irritation. "Nothing," she snapped, adding water to the simmering pot in an effort to dilute the spicy stew.

He shoved an impatient hand through his hair. "What the devil's come over you? The house is usually neat as a pin, and you're dressed as prim as a nun. Tonight of all nights, you decide to look like a..." he gestured wildly, searching for the right word, "... a harridan."

"Not now, Nathan." She sampled the stew, shuddered, then added more water and stirred frantically. "The Hadleys will wonder what's keeping their drinks."

He groaned in frustration, then rummaged through the cupboards. "Glasses? Where do you keep the glasses?"

"There aren't any clean ones. You'll have to fetch the ones off the table and wash them." She shoved a strand of hair back from her face, wishing she could slip inside and change clothes.

Nathan speared her a look, but he didn't argue. He dashed off, returning with an armful of dirty glasses, and dumped them into a basin of soapy water. Wordlessly he and Jael worked side by side, washing, rinsing, and drying with an economy of movement.

"There's a pitcher of juice on the counter behind you," she said, indicating an earthenware container. Just as he was about to race off with pitcher and tumblers, her voice stopped him. "Nathan, ah..." She hated to be the bearer of bad news, but it couldn't be helped. "Bring back any plates you find. There aren't enough clean ones."

He rolled his eyes. "Wait 'til I get you alone. You better have a good explanation ready."

But Jael had more immediate problems to contend with than Nathan's temper. When he rushed back with a tray filled with plates of caked-on food, she immediately set to work scrubbing them clean. "Go entertain the Hadleys. I'll join you shortly."

He squinted at her suspiciously. "All right, but don't be long."

In a whirlwind of activity, Jael washed dishes, tied back her hair with a piece of cord, and buttoned her dress up to her chin, all the while praying the stew had been watered sufficiently to dilute the potent spices.

When she entered the cottage carrying a tray loaded with plates, flatware, and a steaming tureen of stew and vegetables, she found Nathan chatting amiably with their guests. She pinned on a smile. "Dinner's ready."

"Let me help you, darling." Nathan jumped up and relieved her of the tray. Bending his head, he whispered, "Let's just concentrate on getting through this evening without further mishap."

Alice sniffed, trying to identify the aroma. "It smells . . . interesting."

"Nothing I enjoy more than a good savory stew." Thomas Hadley infused heartiness into his tone. "Reminds me of long New England winters."

Alice Hadley rose from the settee and started across the room, then stopped dead in her tracks. She tried again to advance, but to no avail. A mystified expression crossed her plump face. "Goodness gracious! I seem to be stuck."

"Allow me to assist you, my dear," Thomas offered.

Nathan and Jael watched, frozen in embarrassment, as the clergyman gamely reached down, grasped his wife's ankle, and gave it a mighty tug. Her foot popped free, leaving her shoe still fastened to the floorboards.

"I'll be right back with a rag." Nathan hurriedly left the room.

An uncomfortable silence fell over the group. Even the usually loquacious Alice Hadley seemed to be at a loss for words. Jael's face burned with shame—and resentment. She refused to take sole responsibility for this fiasco. If it wasn't for Nathan and his nightly poker parties, she never would have been driven to such extremes. She fidgeted with a button on her dress. What was keeping him? It seemed to be taking him forever.

His expression harried, Nathan returned with a dripping rag. He scrubbed frantically at the floorboards and pried the shoe from the gummy residue. "There, problem solved," he announced with forced cheerfulness. "My wife must have missed a spill."

After Alice wiggled her foot into her shoe, they all took their places around the table. Reverend Hadley offered up grace while they sat with bowed heads. From across the table, Jael felt the sting of Nathan's glare. She darted a defiant look back at him.

The prayer finished, Jael ladled the concoction onto plates, knowing the biggest hurdle was still ahead.

Alice attempted polite conversation as the plates were filled. "I thought Nathan had found a young Hawaiian woman to help with the housekeeping."

"Yes, Mahie," Jael answered absently, her attention on the stew. Chunks of meat and pieces of vegetable swam in a thin, pale gruel. She caught her lower lip between her teeth. It looked runny, but . . .

Nathan improvised to fill the gap in the conversation. "Mahie's getting married soon, so Jael gave her the day off."

Thomas spread a napkin across his lap. "That was very generous of you, Jael, but clearly you could have used her help."

"That's my wife, generous to a fault. Eat hearty, everyone." Nathan rubbed his hands together. "My bride made enough to feed a small army."

Jael wiped sweaty palms on her skirt as Thomas Hadley picked up his fork, speared a piece of meat, and began to chew. His face turned beet red; his eyes widened, then watered. In his haste to reach his water glass, he knocked over the salt cellar.

Alice Hadley encountered similar problems with her food. She cut a dainty morsel and popped it into her mouth. She chewed and swallowed, she gasped and wheezed. Tears streamed down her face, as she, too, groped for water to quench the fire.

Nathan watched the proceedings with morbid fascination. He raised his eyebrow questioningly and leveled a stare at his wife that had caused seasoned sailors to quake. Jael determinedly kept her eyes downcast.

"My wife's cooking skills are no match for yours, Alice, but I'm sure with more experience she'll do just fine." Nathan gave his guests a conciliatory smile, then bravely sampled the cuisine.

Jael held her breath and waited as Nathan chewed thoughtfully. Even the Hadleys watched with amazement as he took a second bite, then a third. Their awe turned into respect with each morsel he consumed.

"A little too much salt, dear, but otherwise delicious."

His comment was so completely unexpected that Jael didn't know whether to hoot with laughter or to hug him. Instead, she flashed him a grateful smile. "Thank you, Nathan. I'll keep your advice in mind next time."

Alice and Thomas Hadley moved meat and vegetables around their plates with the dedication of small children sailing their handmade boats around a pond. Jael nibbled on a potato that had mercifully escaped the brunt of the seasoning and watched Nathan polish off his entire serving.

"Would you care for more, dear?" she asked sweetly, admiration warring with irritation.

Nathan shoved back his plate. "As delicious as your stew was, dearest, I'm going to decline. I'm saving room for dessert. I did see a cake, didn't I?"

Nathan seemed to delight in embarrassing her even further. She would have gleefully kicked him under the table if she hadn't been afraid of missing her target and striking one of the Hadleys instead. "My baking can't compare with yours, Mrs. Hadley," she said, hoping they would decline dessert.

Alice reached over and patted her hand. "No need to fret, Jael dear. Baking takes many years to master."

Nathan leaned back in his chair, his arms crossed over his chest. "My bride learns very quickly, Alice. She's constantly amazing me."

Jael excused herself and, after gathering the dinner plates, hurried to the cookhouse. Would this evening ever end? she wondered as she prepared tea. And did she want it to? Once Nathan got her alone, he'd probably wring her neck as he threatened to do earlier. After the horrendous meal she had just served, no court in the land would convict him of unjustified homicide.

When Jael returned with dessert, she found Nathan regaling the Hadleys with tales of his adventures in exotic ports. All eyes turned to her expectantly as she entered the room. "Pineapple cake." She smiled weakly. "Nathan's favorite."

Thomas Hadley nodded approvingly. "I knew Jael would make some lucky man a good wife."

"I just wonder how much more luck I can stomach," Nathan grumbled under his breath, just loud enough for Jael's ears.

Jael set the cake on the table and grimly sawed through its crusty exterior.

Nathan watched, a wicked smile curving his

mouth. "Remind me, dear, to sharpen the knives. I had no idea they were so dull."

She sawed harder. "You've been so busy, *dear*, I didn't want to bother you with such small details."

An uneasy quiet ensued as she served each of them a slice of cake.

Nathan studied his fork as though selecting a weapon, then sampled his piece. "Mmm," he chewed slowly, "interesting. The inside reminds me of custard."

Her slice untouched, Alice Hadley pushed her plate aside and stood. "It's getting late, Thomas. Perhaps we should start back."

"Quite right," her husband agreed promptly. "We've imposed on the newlyweds far too long as it is."

Alice leaned over and whispered in Jael's ear. "My pineapple cake recipe is a carefully guarded family secret, but I'll gladly share it with you. Your efforts are commendable, dear, but you need all the help you can get."

Nathan and Jael walked their guests to the porch and waved them off. Nathan kept his arm securely around his wife's shoulder to prevent her from fleeing. Anyone watching would think the gesture one of husbandly affection. They stood side by side until Alice and Thomas Hadley disappeared around a curve of the beach.

A wave of gratitude that their guests had finally left engulfed her, leaving Jael's knees weak. She sank down on the top step and put her head in her hands. The evening had been an ordeal; the meal a disaster. A nightmare straight from hell.

And there was still Nathan to deal with.

Chapter 14

What type of punishment did whaling captains mete out to a mutinous crew member? Did they make them walk the plank? Toss them in irons? Flail them with a cat-o'-nine-tails? Or if sufficiently provoked, all three?

Jael nervously laced her fingers together. The small amount of food she had consumed threatened to come back up. Summoning her courage, she hazarded a glance at Nathan.

"I have to hand it to you," Nathan said. "I have never tasted a worse meal in my entire life. Did you see the look on Thomas's face when he took his first bite?"

Jael studied him appraisingly. He didn't look angry. Didn't sound angry. His lips twitched as though trying to contain a smile. Wicked green and gold sparks danced in his hazel eyes. "Or how red Mrs. Hadley's nose turned?" she ventured, encouraged by the amusement that underscored his words.

"I didn't know two people could drink that

much water at a single sitting." His shoulders shook with mirth.

A giggle escaped before she could stifle it. "I was afraid Mrs. Hadley was going to be permanently cemented to the floor."

"Goodness gracious, I seem to be stuck." Nathan perfectly mimicked Alice Hadley.

To Jael's surprise, he threw back his head and roared with laughter. For a split second, Jael could only stare at him dumbfounded. Then, as all fear of reprisal fled, the humor of the situation struck her as well. She made no attempt to stop the merriment bubbling inside as her laughter joined Nathan's. Tears streamed down her cheeks. Nathan held his sides, doubled over.

They sobered slowly, their laughter fading into a fitful series of giggles and grins. Jael dabbed at her watery eyes with the hem of her skirt. She felt better, freer, than she had in days, weeks. Years. A lifetime. Laughter, she discovered, provided a glorious release from tension.

Nathan slumped on the bottom step, rested his elbow on the one above, and grinned at her. "Well, you definitely managed to even the score. I'll think twice before ever inviting friends home for dinner unannounced."

"Can I assume that you'll no longer bring friends here to drink and play cards 'til dawn?"

"Sweetheart," he drawled, "if I caroused like that every night, I wouldn't be fit to pilot a ferryboat across Long Island Sound." All traces of humor fled, and his expression grew somber. "Seems to me we both want the same thing—our freedom. What if we join forces, work together instead of on opposing sides?"

Hope flared in her eyes, making them as bright and incandescent as blue flames. "Just tell me what I have to do."

"Agree to an annulment." Nathan watched her intently, attuned to every subtle nuance of her expression.

"An annulment?"

"Return with me to New England. Once there, we'll have a lawyer draw up annulment papers. All you have to do is swear in front of a judge that our union has never been consummated. In return, I'll give you enough money to help you settle or find a suitable position if you like."

She studied him, equally as intent, silently repeating his offer and weighing the benefits. "All right," she agreed slowly. "On one condition."

He nodded tersely, his voice clipped. "Name it."

"Any money from you is to be considered a loan. I promise to repay as soon as I'm able."

"And that's all?" His tone conveyed skepticism, suspicion.

"That's all."

"Agreed."

Scarcely believing her good fortune, Jael flung her arms around his neck. "Oh, Nathan, how can I ever thank you?"

Her supple, eager body fit his like the second half of a mold. Doubt swarmed through him. If this felt so good, so right, why had he rejected their union? And having rejected it, why wasn't he rejoicing in the decision? He should be thrilled, ebullient, that she had accepted his proposition without a fuss. What was wrong with him? He had just regained his prized independence. He should be running along the beach, leaping into the air, and clicking his heels. This is what he plotted, schemed, and even prayed for. But instead of satisfaction, he felt a growing sense of loneliness build in the region of his heart.

He put his arms around her and held fast, fearing that he had already lost that which he held so tightly.

Clouds wreathed the peaks of the West Maui Mountains like a misty bridal veil. Waves surged to the sugar-sand beach. Restless and full of energy, they mirrored Jael's own nagging discontent as she made her way homeward.

Jael knew she ought to be ecstatic over her arrangement with Nathan. Instead, unsettled, dissatisfied, and vaguely disappointed, she felt far from happy. She kicked a clump of seaweed with the toe of her shoe. Everything she had always wanted was practically in the palm of her hand. Soon, Nathan promised, they would set out on a whaling voyage that would culminate in their return to New England. Far from her grandfather, she would have more freedom than she had ever dared dream.

She owed it all to Nathan—her husband. *Husband.* That word tasted foreign on her tongue. He wasn't a husband at all. Merely a companion, a protector, a generous godfather. Thinking of him brought a smile to her lips. Nathan Thorne was kind and generous to a fault. Only yesterday he had gifted her with bolts and bolts of beautiful fabric. Jade green, teal blue, shimmering periwinkle, and her favorite, a lemony yellow muslin sprigged with tiny white flowers and green leaves.

The sack of sewing notions she carried—pins and thread, ribbon and lace—had provided the excuse she needed for a visit to town. It also provided an opportunity to visit the Hadleys and apologize for the horrid meal she had served on their recent visit. They had listened politely to her halting explanation, then both quickly declined her invitation to dine in the near future.

As she neared the cottage, she noticed a dull brown mound lying on the beach just beyond the water's edge. Thinking it a large coconut that had washed up on shore, she nudged it with her foot. She drew back in surprise when she realized her mistake. It wasn't a coconut at all, but a shaggy pup rolled into a ball. The little dog lazily opened its eyes and raised its head. One brown ear cocked toward the mountains; the other tipped oceanward.

Stooping down, she scratched between the puppy's ears and was rewarded when it licked her fingers with a rough pink tongue. "What are you doing way out here?"

She stood reluctantly and started toward home. The little dog bounded after her. "Shoo," she scolded. "Go home. I can't bring you with me." The pup stopped and gazed at her with soulful eyes. Jael paused and gnawed her lower lip in indecision.

The dog's coat was dull and matted. She didn't have the heart to refuse the canine. "All right," she relented. "Poor thing. You look like you could use a decent meal, but once your belly is full, it's back to town with you. Your owner is probably wondering where you ran off."

She slowly walked in the direction of the cottage, the pup trotting at her heels. It was unlikely that the little dog had an owner, she realized. Judging from its half-starved appearance, it had most likely been abandoned. For as long as she could remember, she had begged for a pet, but Grandfather had been adamant in his refusal. How did Nathan feel about animals? she wondered. Did he like dogs? And more importantly, how would he react when he learned she had adopted a puppy? Or rather, she glanced down at the shaggy mop of fur scampering at her feet, that a puppy had adopted her?

Mahie came out onto the porch to greet them, a wide smile on her face. "Missus, who is your friend?"

"I found him on the beach," Jael explained.

"Poor little creature looked half starved. I couldn't turn my back on him."

"Captain like dogs, missus?" Mahie knelt down to pet the puppy. As she looked from the dog, then back at Jael, a strange expression crossed her face. "Pele, people say, often seen with small dog. People also say you look like her."

The girl's comment was momentarily disconcerting. Then Jael dismissed it as more island superstition. "Mahie, could you find some scraps for the puppy before you leave?"

"Yes, missus. I do now."

The next hour was spent in a discussion of suitable names for the puppy. In the end, the two women decided to call him Niu, which was Hawaiian for coconut. After Mahie left for the evening, Jael bathed the dog and brushed its coat until it was glossy. Then she sat down on the porch and watched the sun bleed over the horizon, staining the ocean bright crimson. Absently she ruffled the pup's shaggy fur. The little dog rested its head trustingly on her lap and gazed at her with liquid eyes.

Hopelessly smitten with the puppy, she vowed she'd coax Nathan into letting her keep him. She'd argue that the pup could act as a watchdog in the interim after Mahie left and before he returned. The animal would be her trusty companion during the twilight hours.

Darkness fell, and Jael yawned broadly. Nathan was later than usual. The issue of a pet would have to wait until tomorrow. She smiled at the dog, who slept as soundly as a baby. "Well, my furry friend, a fine watchdog you are. I think it's time we turn in for the night."

The dog opened one eye and regarded her lazily, making her laugh at his comical expression. She picked him up, debating where he should spend the night, then decided in favor of her bedroom.

Making himself right at home, the pup crawled under the bed and was instantly asleep. Humming to herself, Jael reached for the plain cotton nightdress she usually wore, but changed her mind. Instead she slipped on a delicate batiste nightdress she had originally intended to sell in Mrs. Ka'ano's stall. It featured a rounded neckline, full cap sleeves, and a bodice of tiny tucks painstakingly embroidered with pale pink roses. The fabric was so sheer it was nearly transparent. Feminine and delicate, the garment would have outraged her grandfather.

She drew the mosquito netting around the bed, snuggled beneath the covers, and fell soundly asleep, secure in the knowledge Nathan would soon be home.

Nathan returned later than planned. He was driving both the crew and himself hard on final preparations. The *Clotilde* should be ready to sail by the end of the week. He flung his jacket carelessly across the settee and helped himself to the cold meal Jael had left waiting for him. God knew, he didn't like leaving her alone for extended periods of time. As usual she roused his protective instincts. Had, in fact, since their first meeting.

But being away from her was easier than being close. The less time spent with her, the better. Whenever she was near, he had to fend off his never-ending, ever-growing attraction. "Look but don't touch" was proving a difficult credo. Already he dreaded the months of close proximity aboard ship. Before the voyage ended, he'd be sharing John McFee's cramped quarters.

He started toward his own bedroom, but changed direction. He'd rest easier knowing she was safe. Just one quick peek, he promised. He eased open the door of her bedroom and stepped inside. Moonlight seeped through the shutters, casting silvery bands across the wood floor. Drawing closer, he parted the netting and stared at her sleeping form. His breath caught in his throat. Hair the shade of molten lava framed a cameo-perfect face. Lips slightly parted, hinting of innocent sensuality, begged to be kissed. She was a vision of purity and beauty. An angel. A temptress.

His gaze roamed downward, and he stifled a groan. Rounded breasts strained against filmy cotton and threatened to overflow. Ivory skin gleamed petal soft. He yearned to touch, caress, but knew it would fail to satisfy him. He'd be unable to stop with a single touch, a single caress. He wanted more. Wanted it all. A fine sheen of perspiration beaded his brow. Unable to resist, he picked up a fiery lock of her hair. The sweet fragrance of jasmine filled his senses. He raised it to his lips, closed his eyes, and...

...a loud snore ripped through the quiet.

Startled, Nathan's eyes flew wide and he dropped the strand. The awful sound effectively doused his ardor. He stared at Jael in disbelief, wondering how such an ungodly noise could rise from such an angelic source. She snored worse than a sailor after a weeklong bender. Maybe he should be grateful. Another minute and he would have put noble resolutions aside. As he was about to turn away, his eyes fell on a wisp of brown lying on the braided rug alongside the bed. Curious, he bent to investigate.

It looked like a piece of rope, or a lock of hair. He poked at it, and it twitched in response. "What the hell?" he muttered.

He tugged on the rug, and it slid from beneath the bed. In its center, curled into a tight ball, was a small, shaggy dog. As he continued to watch, the dog let loose another guttural expulsion of air. "Well, I'll be," he chuckled, sinking onto the edge of the bed.

The sagging of the mattress woke Jael. Half asleep, she stared at him in alarm, confusion and fear clouding her eyes. When she recognized the intruder as her husband, her fear quickly subsided.

Nathan held a finger to his lips and indicated she be silent. They didn't have long to wait before the puppy's snore rocked the bedroom.

Shock and dismay flickered across her face.

Her secret had been discovered, and she hadn't had the opportunity to lay the groundwork.

Nathan watched her expression with interest. "Did you know that there was a stray dog sleeping under your bed?"

"No..." She regretted the denial the instant it slipped out. "I mean, its not really a dog," she prevaricated.

His mouth quirked with amusement. "If it's not a dog, madam, what do you propose it might be?"

Jael's hand fluttered nervously on the counterpane. "Dogs are bigger," she explained lamely.

"Ah, I see." Nathan sighed with exaggerated patience. "Do you suppose this animal—whatever it might be—might eventually become a dog?"

She ran the tip of her tongue over her lower lip. "I suppose one could make that assumption."

He smiled slightly. "While my mind is relieved on that point, there's another matter that puzzles me."

Jael kept her eyes fastened on his face and waited expectantly.

He found her nearness distracting. She was all woman, warm and sleep-tousled. The nightdress she wore ought to be outlawed for what it was doing to him. He felt a burgeoning desire to explore the shadowed cleft between her breasts. He shifted his weight.

Best get back to the matter at hand, he

thought, clearing his throat. The dog. He had nearly forgotten the damn thing. "Perhaps you'd care to enlighten me as to how this *potential* dog happens to be sound asleep under your bed?"

Eager now to present her case, Jael pushed herself into a sitting position, her nightdress bunched around her bare thighs. "He followed me this afternoon. I don't think he belongs to anyone. He looked half starved, as though he hadn't eaten a decent meal in weeks. He'll make a good watchdog."

Nathan cocked a brow and regarded the slumbering animal skeptically. "A well-rested watchdog."

"I've always wanted a pet, but Grandfather refused to consider one. I swear I'll take good care of him." Words tumbled over themselves in their haste to be said. "You'll never even know he's around. Please, Nathan, can I keep him?"

She had never asked anything of him. This was such a simple request, but it obviously meant a great deal. "All right." He nodded. "But only until we sail, then you'll have to leave him in Mahie's keeping."

Her radiant smile robbed air from his lungs. Nathan doubted if she had any idea just how lovely she was. That was part of her charm, her considerable charm.

Jael impetuously flung herself into his arms and hugged him tight. "Thank you, Nathan."

"Just keep him from underfoot," he warned gruffly, already suffering the consequences of granting her wish. Feeling her slender body pressed against his was creating havoc with his self-control.

The bed ropes squeaked as she sat back on her heels, her face shining with happiness. Seeing how much pleasure she derived from such a simple gift made his heart ache. She was so fine, so lovely. She deserved far more than a stray dog. She ought to be showered with expensive jewels and costly silks by an adoring husband. A lump rose in his throat. She deserved far better than him for a husband.

At long last, the puppy stirred and opened his eyes. A low growl rumbled in his throat. Jael watched as Nathan held out his hand for the little dog to sniff. Accepting Nathan as an ally, the pup thumped his tail against the floor. "That's a good fellow." Nathan chuckled. "I see you're a fine judge of character in spite of your tender age." He bent down and ran a hand over the dog's fur.

The pup let out a loud yelp.

"What's the matter?" Jael peered at the dog anxiously.

Nathan scooped up the animal and explored along his rib cage with gentle fingers. "No wonder the mutt was looking for a new home. He has a knot the size of a goose egg where someone probably kicked him."

"The poor thing." Jael took the puppy from Nathan and cuddled it.

Nathan felt a jolt of envy at seeing the puppy snuggled against her breasts. He wished he could nuzzle against those creamy mounds. He almost groaned out loud when the pup licked his raspy tongue along the elegant line of her neck and jaw. Jael laughed happily. The nightdress slid down, baring one shoulder. Nathan reached out and slowly, deliberately, replaced the strap. Her skin was incredibly soft and warm. Instead of eliminating a distraction, the action only served to heighten his need to touch. To taste.

With the sleepy pup cradled in her arms, she stared at him with lambent eyes.

Damnation! he swore silently. Feeling like a greenhand in rough seas, he got to his feet and strode across the room. "We sail in less than a week," he called over his shoulder as he reached the door. "Keep the mutt out of trouble until then."

He left her abruptly and went to his small room with its narrow bed and lumpy mattress and slammed the door behind him. In his mind, he could still picture Jael lovingly petting the puppy—and wished she was stroking him instead. Another second in her presence and his control would have snapped.

Chapter 15

Torches flickered. Drums beat.

Dozens of people milled about, talking and laughing. Soon the dancing would begin. Jael sighed. If only Nathan were here, her enjoyment would be complete. But he wasn't. There was still much work to do, he had informed her, if the *Clotilde* was to sail the day after tomorrow. So Mahie had persuaded Jael to attend the wedding feast alone.

Jael's glance drifted to the bridal couple. Inaika's arm was draped across Mahie's shoulders; her arm circled his waist. Whenever their dark eyes met, they glowed with happiness. They couldn't seem to get enough of each other, sharing lingering looks and secretive smiles. So very happy, so much in love. Her heart twisted in envy.

How unlike her marriage to Nathan. Fueled by resentment and uncertainty, their wedding had been a solemn affair. There had been no smiling faces, no huge celebratory party for friends and family. There had been no laughing bride, no happy groom. She recalled her apprehension and Nathan's gloom. She wished things had been different then, could be different now. Now that she no longer had to contend with her grandfather's temper, independence didn't seem quite as important as it once had.

The bridal couple came over to where Jael sat on a woven mat, and Mahie placed a lei of *pua melia* around her neck. "This for you, missus."

"Thank you, Mahie. It's lovely."

"When women dance, you dance, too."

Jael shook her head. "Oh no, I couldn't."

"You no like dance?"

"It isn't that," Jael tried to explain to the puzzled girl. "I don't know how to dance."

"Mahie show you, missus." Inaika proudly beamed at his bride. "Mahie fine dancer."

Keohi, Mahie's plump aunt who was seated next to Jael, swept a disapproving look over the lilac muslin dress Jael wore. "No can dance hula in haole clothes."

"Auntie right, missus." Mahie grabbed Jael's hand and pulled. Keohi hoisted her bulk off the mat, latched onto Jael's other hand, and added her considerable weight to haul Jael upright.

Protesting halfheartedly, Jael allowed the two women to push and prod her into a thatched enclosure. Keohi waddled off, then reappeared minutes later with a loose-fitting flowered dress that had become popular among the island women. "You wear, missus.

Too much clothes bad for dance. Body needs to move. Can't move in haole clothes. Need to free body, free spirit."

When Jael emerged from the enclosure with Mahie on one side and Keohi on the other, her bare feet peeked from the flowered garment. Her hair lung loose to her hips, and a white hibiscus was tucked behind one ear. She not only looked changed, but felt changed.

Inaika was waiting for them. His gaze arrested when it fell on Jael. "You look like Pele, missus."

Having grown accustomed to the comparison, Jael accepted the comment with a gracious nod.

Inaika, his expression earnest, continued, "Inaika happy he see Mu steal missus. Happy missus safe."

Jael managed a feeble smile. "Thank you for going to Reverend Hadley and telling him what you saw. If you hadn't..." She shuddered.

"Come, missus, I show you hula." Keohi motioned impatiently for Jael to follow.

Inaika grinned. "Women now can dance. Before only men allowed."

"Watch. Keohi show hula."

In spite of her girth, the woman moved with astonishing agility as she demonstrated the dance. Fascinated, Jael closely observed the motion of her feet, hips, and arms.

Mahie placed her hands on Jael's hips to guide their movement. "Dance tell story, missus. Think story, not dance."

Jael repeated the steps, tentatively at first, then with growing confidence.

"Good, missus," Mahie encouraged. "Think story. Move hips to beat of drum."

Jael forgot that others watched. Her initial self-consciousness disappeared as inhibitions fled. Keeping time to the primitive beat, her body swayed gracefully in the torchlight. Her slender arms reached out, entreated; her hands beckoned, enticed.

Blood pounding through his veins with each beat of the drum, Nathan observed Jael from beyond the circle of torches. She was a vision. A pagan goddess performing an ancient ritual. Her hair rippled down her back, catching the light, shimmering like a flaming torch. She moved with the suppleness of flame, grace and sensuality in every gesture. Viewing her was like watching fire. Intriguing. Mesmerizing. Desire heated, simmered, sizzled.

When the dance ended, Jael stood poised, arms raised above her head, fingertips touching. Silently Nathan slipped from the shadows into the circle of light. He came up behind her and wound his arms around her slender waist. Unable to resist, he pressed a warm kiss to the tempting spot at the juncture of her neck and shoulder, bared by the loose-fitting gown. Smug satisfaction curled his mouth as she shivered in response. "You were wonderful."

Jael's eyelids drifted shut. She leaned against him, savoring his closeness. Her head lolled against his shoulder, a dreamy smile played on her lips. "Nathan," she breathed, his name a contented sigh.

"Expecting someone else?" His voice was rough, playful.

"No," she murmured, eyes still closed. "No one else could ever make me feel the way you do."

Her admission inflamed him further. He pulled her against him even more snugly. His arousal, painfully evident, nudged against her. He nuzzled her throat with his lips and felt her pulse leap. "You've bewitched me, pagan flower. After watching you dance tonight, never again will I think of you as my prim little missionary."

"Captain!" Inaika and Mahie came over to greet their newly arrived guest, unknowingly breaking the bubble of intimacy that enclosed Jael and Nathan. Inaika slapped Nathan's back. "So glad you come to wedding feast."

Jael's eyes clouded with longing. Nathan seemed in no hurry to release her. Both were reluctant to shed the intimacy of the embrace. Accustomed to uninhibited displays of affection, the Hawaiians didn't seem to find such behavior out of the ordinary.

Mahie gave Jael a knowing look. "Now Captain here, missus smile."

"Captain just in time." Inaika nodded toward a smoking pit that emitted a mouthwatering smell of roasting meat. "Feast about to begin."

"You eat plenty, good food."

Nathan lifted a skeptical brow and stared

down at Jael. "Only if you assure me my wife had nothing to do with the preparation. I'm not sure my stomach's up for another of her special meals."

At the reminder, Jael turned her laughing face up to him.

Nathan stole a kiss from her unsuspecting lips, then grinning broadly, placed a hand at her waist and guided her to a straw mat. With his legs folded beneath him, he sat cross-legged beside her while huge wooden platters of food were circulated. All the wedding guests sat on the ground in a wide circle. Along with roast pig, all the favorite Hawaiian dishes were there, including yams, breadfruit, and poi.

"I've heard of poi, but never tasted it." Jael regarded the pasty purple concoction in front of her with trepidation. "I asked Mahie to describe it, but she told me that poi tastes like poi."

"That about sums it up." Nathan chuckled. He helped himself to a piece of pork and placed it on a ti leaf, then selected a piece for Jael. "As you probably already know, poi is made from taro root. Even the men help in the preparation. It isn't unusual for some Hawaiians to consume as much as one or two pounds of poi a day."

"No wonder they're so large." Jael eyed the bowl suspiciously.

"Allow me to demonstrate the proper etiquette." Nathan scooped poi onto his second and third fingers, then ate from them.

Jael shook her head. "I don't think..."

"Refusing to partake of your host's food is considered rude." Nathan nudged the poi bowl closer. "You don't want to insult Mahie, do you?"

"No, of course not." Gamely Jael aped Nathan's actions. She sampled a dainty portion, finding it bland but not unpleasant.

His eyes smoldering and intense, Nathan watched as she licked her finger pads clean with the tip of her tongue. He suddenly imagined her small pink tongue flicking over him as she appeased a hunger that had nothing to do with food. His loins throbbed; his appetite fled.

Jael smiled winsomely, oblivious to the havoc she was creating. "I'm glad you were able to come tonight."

Nathan shifted, trying to find a more comfortable position. He wondered about the wisdom of his decision to attend the wedding feast. For a brief moment, he desperately wished Jael was garbed in her serviceable drab clothing, her brilliant hair concealed beneath an ugly straw bonnet. If so, maybe then he would stand a fighting chance in his battle against her overwhelming allure.

Jael looked about with obvious delight. Flowers were in abundance. Women wore them in their hair and around their necks. Many of the men were adorned with elaborate necklaces, some carved from kukui nuts, others made from dogs' teeth or boars' tusks, and wore colorful strips of tapa cloth about their hips. Everyone seemed to be enjoying themselves immensely. Including herself.

She cast a sidelong glance at Nathan and smiled, a purely feminine smile. She loved the tiny crinkles around his eyes when he laughed. She loved his pirate's grin. She sobered as a sudden truth struck her.

She loved him.

Completely and without reservation. She accepted this realization without question, knowing with a deep, abiding certainty that she loved him now and would all the days of her life.

Night deepened. More torches were lit, their smoke carried away by tropical breezes. Once appetites were sated, drums started anew, their beat louder, more insistent than before. Fashioned from hollowed-out gourds, coconut shells, and breadfruit logs covered with sharkskin, the drums made a primitive sound that echoed across the island. Other gourds and coconuts, decorated with feathers and tapa cloth and filled with shells and pebbles that produced a rattling sound, accompanied the drums. Male voices joined in an ancient chant. Excitement stirred as a young man with an untamed black mane leaped into the center of the ring.

"You're in for a rare treat," Nathan whispered in Jael's ear. "The *kahiko* hula has been outlawed since the missionaries arrived, but is still performed on special occasions among Hawaiians."

Jael watched, admiring the sheer masculine

beauty of the *kahiko*. The dancer's bare feet pounded the hard-packed earth in a staccato rhythm as he executed the intricate dance.

"In ancient times, the hula was performed only by men. It was man's way of communicating with the gods," Nathan explained when the dance ended. "Later it became a way of telling stories and legends."

Next, Inaika was shoved into the circle by laughing friends. He assumed a look of fierce concentration, let out a bloodcurdling yell that almost sent Jael running, then caught a flaming torch and began whirling it about. Mahie joined him as he gyrated, their bodies moving in perfect accord.

"What story are they telling now?" Jael asked, not taking her eyes from the pair.

Nathan laughed softly. "I've been told this is a fertility dance. Inaika is asking the gods for many fine sons."

"Oh," Jael replied in a small voice, her cheeks pink.

When the dance ended, Mahie and Inaika wandered off with their arms twined around each other's waist. Jael followed them with her eyes until they disappeared through the trees. She was no longer so naive that she didn't know they would soon be making love. A wistfulness swelled inside her. She yearned to discover the joys married couples shared. Would the sweet kisses, gentle caresses, and tender endearments of marriage forever be denied her?

"Let's slip away, too." Nathan's warm

breath fanned her cheek. "No one will miss us."

Jael nodded her agreement. Unnoticed by the other wedding guests, they disappeared through the thick screen of foliage. Nathan slung his jacket over one shoulder. Their fingers touched, twined, locked. Hand in hand they strolled along the beach in companionable silence. The tropical night wove its magical spell. Palm trees fluttered, rustled, their fronds whispering secrets in the night. Waves lapped against the shore, their sound as soothing—and seductive—as a lullaby. Moonbeams frolicked across black satin water.

"Look." Nathan stopped suddenly and pointed out to sea. "Dolphins."

Jael turned her eyes in the direction he indicated. As she watched, a dolphin made a playful leap, its wet body glistening like hammered silver in the moonlight. "How beautiful," she marveled.

"I couldn't agree more," Nathan answered, his voice thick with emotion.

Jael slowly turned toward him. It wasn't the sea he gazed at, but her. Her heart bubbled with happiness until it felt like it could burst.

They continued walking. As Jael scooted out of the foamy path of a wave, her body brushed Nathan's. The contact was electrifying, bringing an awareness so sharp it was painful. The air seemed charged with tension.

Dropping his jacket to the sand, Nathan framed her face with his hands and let his gaze leisurely roam her features. "You're so beautiful that you make my knees grow weak."

"And you make me feel . . . special."

He meant the kiss to be a slow, tender assault on her senses. Instead it was raw hunger, bordering on desperate. His mouth plundered and his tongue ravaged the honeyed cavern of hers. *Steady,* he cautioned. *Go slow, take your time. Don't frighten her.* But need skyrocketed out of control. Still he tried valiantly to corral his rampaging desire.

And might have succeeded if her passion hadn't matched his own.

She leaned into the kiss as though driven by the same raging hunger. Taking her cue from him, her tongue tangled with his in an age-old lovers' duel. With a groan that was part impatience, part frustration, he dragged his mouth from hers. His lips traveled over her face, tracing her cheekbones, nibbling a path from jaw to collarbone. She melted in his arms. Nathan drew back with the vague intention of regaining a measure of control.

"No, don't stop," she pleaded brokenly. Tunneling her fingers through his hair, she pulled his mouth down to hers. Her lips found his . . . and clung.

Not even his wildest fantasies had conjured anyone quite like her. A gift from the gods. So responsive, so exquisitely responsive. Tinder ready to burst into flame at his slightest touch. She quivered like the strings of a violin.

He dragged the loose-fitting garment from her body. Her undergarments quickly followed. Sweeping her into his arms, he laid her on the discarded pile of clothes scattered in the sugary sand. His eyes never leaving hers, he shed his shirt and pants and dropped down beside her. His hand, rough and callused, drew lazy circles around one nipple. Jael caught her lower lip between her teeth, but not before a ragged sigh of ecstasy escaped.

"You're a sorceress, pagan flower, and you've slowly been driving me crazy. I want you so badly that I'm not sure if I can hold off much longer."

"I'm not asking you to." She caught his wrist and flattened his palm against her breast so he could feel the rapid hammering of her heart. "Love me."

He muttered a strangled oath. Dipping his head, he laved her rosy nipple with the tip of his tongue, then drew the taut peak into his mouth.

She arched against him eagerly. Pleasure darted through her, sharp and swift. Her body grew increasingly impatient. Since their journey from Hana, she had been consumed with restless anticipation. Waiting. Yearning. But for what? Because of lack of experience, she wasn't entirely certain. Tonight—soon—she would discover the long-awaited answers to a thousand questions.

His mouth drove her wild with wanting. He swept a hand along the curve of her hip to the burgundy curls at the apex of her thighs. After a moment's hesitation, he slid his hand lower through the nest of curls to the soft petals that shielded her femininity. She was slick, hot, ready. He braced himself above her. "I feel as though I'm the virgin," he confessed, his voice low, husky. "That making love to you will be making love for the first time."

His words made her want to sing with joy. She tilted her pelvis in wordless invitation and rocked her hips.

He eased into her gradually, pausing when he felt the resistance of her maidenhead. Sweat beaded his brow. God as his witness, he hated to cause her pain. She was so sweet, so trusting. He wanted this to be as good for her as it was for him.

"Take me, Nathan. Make me yours." She put her arms around his waist, holding him tight.

He moved deeper. At her sharp intake of breath, he almost withdrew, but he felt her nails biting into his flesh. Urgency kindled, blazed. He stroked faster, finding a rhythm that excited, exhilarated.

She strained upward, his urgency communicated to her. Her hips meeting each thrust in wild abandon. Ripples of sensation grew into waves of pleasure. Pleasure so intense she felt as though she were drowning in its seductive depths. She clung to him with mindless desperation. He became her rock in a tumultuous sea as pleasure continued to surge. Riding the peak of a giant breaker, she hovered, suspended for a microcosm of time in breath-stopping anticipation, then the mighty wave crested.

"Nathan," she cried as she tumbled into ecstasy.

In the dark hours presaging dawn, Nathan lay awake, staring at the ceiling. Jael curled next to him on the wide bed, her head on his shoulder, her hand lightly across his chest. He never should have made love to her. His body simply refused to listen to logic when she smiled up at him with her big blue-violet eyes, sparkling like a sky full of stars. He had been too long without a woman, he reasoned—and she had been there. Incredibly sweet. Seductively innocent. Burning like liquid fire in his arms.

Though his thoughts teemed with regret, part of him, a very primitive, masculine part, gloried in the knowledge that he had been her first. She had surrendered her virginity with a sweetness and generosity that had moved him deeply. And just as he had suspected, behind that sweetness, that generosity, was a slumbering sensuality awaiting to be awakened. Never had he experienced anything quite so satisfying. Absently he stroked her hair.

Jael rubbed against him, lazily, contentedly.

Nathan knew he should leave while he still could. He knew it, yet he lingered.

"Don't go," she murmured drowsily as if sensing his wish to retreat.

He chuckled deep in his throat. "I think you've cast some ancient Hawaiian spell over me. I can't seem to budge from this spot."

"Good," she sighed. "My only regret is that I didn't discover one sooner."

Her words sent a warm tickle of air whispering across his bare chest. "And why is that cause for regret?"

"Because..."

"...because?" he prompted.

"If I had access to some secret spell, I wouldn't have had to remain a virgin long after we were wed."

For a stunned moment, Nathan didn't know whether to hoot with laughter or keen with despair. *An unwilling virgin?* For Chrissakes, what had he done? A self-appointed despoiler of innocence, he had solved her quandary while creating one of monumental proportions for himself. Too late for recriminations, he thought in disgust. The damage—he grimaced at his choice of words—had already been done.

"Nathan...?"

"Mmm..."

"Did I do everything right?" she asked, her voice tinged with uncertainty. "Did I please you?"

Oh dear Lord, how she pleased him. He brushed a lock of hair from her face, then leisurely ran his thumb along the curve of her cheek. "If you had given me any more pleasure, I'm not sure I would have survived to talk about it."

"Then I'm happy." She snuggled closer, her fingers idly sifting through the mat of hair covering his chest.

Happy? Nathan realized with a shock that he was, too. Happier, more lighthearted, than he had felt in years. Later, there would be ample time to castigate himself for his behavior, but at this moment all he wanted from life was to luxuriate in the warm bath of contentment.

"I like touching you," she confessed shyly as she traced his collarbone with a fingertip.

He caught her hand and brought it to his mouth, where he nipped the pad of her finger with his teeth, then soothed the small sting with his tongue. "And I like being touched."

A shiver raced through her. Feeling it brought Nathan a measure of pride and humility that his bride could be so perfectly attuned to every overture.

"You make it hard for me to think."

"This isn't the time to think, love. It's the time to let your feelings make you soar like an eagle."

He lifted the heavy fall of hair from her neck and planted a warm, moist kiss along her nape.

"Ah, yes," she breathed.

In one smooth move, he rolled over, pulling her beneath him. He framed her face between his hands and stared into it, committing it to memory, storing it in the private recesses of his mind where he could take it out at some future date to examine. "Your beauty outshines the stars."

His mouth claimed hers, gently, tenderly at first. Sampling, savoring. The fervor grew. His lips made maddening forays across her closed eyelids, then along the delicate ridges of her cheekbones, and down the slender column of her neck. Next he playfully dipped his tongue into the hollow at the base of her throat.

She shuddered at the wet rasp of his tongue against the sensitive flesh. "Nathan," she moaned as heady delight swept through her.

"Are you ready to fly yet, sweet Jasmine?"

A bubble of laughter, giddy and refreshing, rippled through her. "It takes more than a few kisses to make an eagle soar."

He drew up on one elbow, raised an inquisitive brow, and peered down at her. "Tsk, tsk." He clucked his tongue. "What have we here?" he mused. "Have you gone from a prim little virgin to a wicked, insatiable woman all in the space of one night?"

"I'm worse than wicked." She grinned, unabashed.

He pretended to look shocked. "Worse?"

She tunneled her fingers through his thick, tawny hair, then pulled his head down until his lips were inches from hers. "Where you're concerned, I'm shameless."

"Shameless," he murmured agreeably.

This time his kiss was ravenous, demanding. She surrendered to it completely. Arching her body to fit his, she was dimly aware of his hand skimming down her spine, then resting possessively at the small of her back.

His hands, his mouth, inflamed her senses. A thousand light touches. A million sparks of desire. Jael felt her breasts ache and grow taut from wanting. Heat coiled through her body and seeped between her legs. When Nathan's long, callused fingers touched the ultra-sensitive nub at the juncture of her thighs, she nearly sobbed with need. Seeking surcease from this exquisite torture, she tilted her hips and rubbed her pelvis against his.

"Spread your wings, eagle," he whispered hoarsely. "Let yourself soar."

She flung back her head and clung to his shoulders as he entered her. "I'm flying," she managed to gasp as she felt herself hurtled into space.

Shadows silently slid through the bedroom; silvery moonbeams speared through partially open wooden slats. In the distance, waves drummed against the beach in a rhythm more ancient than time. But inside the shuttered room, thunder crashed and lightning arced.

And magic fused two souls into one.

Chapter 16

Nathan lay with his hands propped behind his head and frowned up at the ceiling. One fact shone in his mind with startling clarity. He had been temporarily insane. Making love to Jael the first time had been folly. Making love to her a second time had been sheer madness.

Unfortunately for him, once initiated into the art of lovemaking Jael proved an apt pupil. He found her shy but sensual advances more potent than fine wine, her kisses more intoxicating than costly brandy. Like the fabled sirens of the sea who lured hapless sailors onto hazardous shoals, Jael's beauty beckoned him along a course of self-destruction.

But Jael wasn't to blame. He was.

He accepted full responsibility for his rash actions. Regardless of who was at fault, the results were still the same. Because of his unbridled lust, he must deal with the consequences. A muscle worked in his jaw. An annulment was now out of the question. Unless he came up with an alternative plan, and came up with it quickly, he would be permanently saddled with an unwanted bride.

He inched away from Jael, who lay curled next to him. He needed to be clear-headed, needed time to think, to plan, and proximity to the red-haired wench tended to muddle his thoughts. Careful not to awaken her, he eased one leg over the edge of the bed.

He stole another glance at her. It nearly proved his undoing. Pale golden sunlight streaming into the small bedroom illuminated her slender form. Lips still swollen from his kisses the previous night were slightly parted. Her skin glowed with healthy vibrancy. One arm was outstretched, the fingers curved, beckoning. His resolve wavered, and he nearly gave in to the urge to gather her close, to make love to her while sunrise heralded a new day.

He must have made a slight sound for she began to stir. She raised both arms above her head and stretched slowly, sinuously. Nathan looked on, bemused. Her actions made him think of a lazy house cat basking on a sunny sill. He wouldn't have been surprised to hear her purr. Her eyelids fluttered open, and she smiled when she found him watching her.

"Good morning, Nathan." Her voice caressed his name, and a wistful longing welled inside of him.

"Morning," he mumbled. Lord, she was a tempting sight. Warm and sleep-tousled. Desirable. He felt his body respond independently of his better judgment.

She raised up on one elbow and observed for the first time that he had been in the process of getting out of bed. Her mouth curved downward in disappointment. "Must you leave already? It's still early." Then she blushed at her forwardness.

Nathan almost succumbed to the impulse to crawl back into bed. Almost. "I—ah—need to check on my crew."

She caught his hand to forestall his leaving. "At least let me fix you some breakfast. I promise not to add hot spices to your eggs."

His lips twitched at the reminder of the disastrous dinner. "I thought I convinced you that I liked my food spicy."

She blushed again and gave him a winsome smile.

Sugar and spice and everything nice. The phrase from an almost forgotten nursery rhyme danced in sing-song through his head. That described Jael perfectly. Sweet, but with a captivating mischievous streak. Then he brought his thoughts up short. Impatiently he shoveled both hands through his hair. He was doing it again. Getting soft, turning to mush. Next he'd be quoting sonnets like some lovesick schoolboy.

"No thanks!" He jerked his hand free and swung out of bed.

Catching a glimpse of her crestfallen expression, he immediately felt remorse. "Don't bother about breakfast," he said, trying to soften his curt refusal. "Cook will have coffee ready by the time I board the *Clotilde*."

Jael sank back against the pillows and watched him step into his pants. She loved watching him perform even the simplest of tasks. He had a unique lissome grace she never grew weary of. This morning, with a light stubble shadowing his cheeks and his hair mussed from raking his fingers through it countless times, he looked very masculine. And very handsome.

He tugged on his boots. "Jael... about last night."

"It was absolutely wonderful." She yawned and stretched.

"Yes, but..." Nathan half turned, determined to set the record straight, and the remainder of the sentence stuck in his throat. The bedclothes had fallen nearly to her waist, leaving the creamy mounds of her breasts with their impudent rosy nipples exposed to his gaze.

"Never in my wildest dreams did I expect making love to be so... so... gloriously fulfilling." She pulled up the sheet, seemingly oblivious of the effect her nudity had on him.

Nathan swallowed hard, then wiped the beads of sweat from his upper lip. He had to get out of here—and fast—while he was still able to move. He grabbed his shirt and stuffed his arms into the sleeves.

"I've got to go. We'll talk tonight." Leaving Jael staring after him with a puzzled expression on her face, Nathan bolted from the bedroom.

Leaving the cottage behind, he headed toward town with long angry strides. He never should have allowed the situation with Jael to get out of hand. By doing so, he had made a mess of things. Now it was up to him to find a remedy.

His mind worked feverishly, forming plans and considering options.

As the *Clotilde* came into view, a grim smile twisted his mouth. While an annulment was out of the question, a divorce was not.

Jael's spirits felt as light and fluffy as the clouds that wreathed the West Maui Mountains. Not even the prospect of visiting her grandfather could dim the inner glow that warmed her. Last night had been the most wonderful night of her life. Each passing day had brought the realization that her feelings for Nathan continued to grow. Friendship that had begun as a tiny seed had taken root and developed into a certain fondness. And now... The fondness had blossomed into love. She loved him, and though he hadn't yet voiced his feelings, she hoped he loved her as well. Tomorrow they would leave Hawaii to begin a brand new life together. What could be more perfect?

She turned up the path leading to her grandfather's cottage, climbed the porch steps, and knocked on the door.

"Who is it?" her grandfather called querulously.

"It's me, Grandfather." She heard the thump of his cane as he crossed the parlor.

He opened the door a crack and stuck his grizzled head out. "What do you want?"

"May I come in?"

He grudgingly opened the door wide enough to allow her entry, but didn't invite her to sit down. "Make it quick. I'm busy."

Jael stood in the center of the parlor and surveyed the small house that had provided shelter but had never really been a home. Smaller and shabbier than she remembered, the cottage wore a neglected air. A thick layer of dust coated the furniture. Flies buzzed around the remains of a half-eaten meal sitting on the table. Piles of papers and books were scattered about.

Silas rested both hands on his cane and frowned with impatience. "Well, girl, don't waste my time. Spit out what you came to say."

"I came to tell you good-bye. Tomorrow when Nathan's ship sails, I'll be leaving with him."

"So? What do you expect me to do about it?"

"Nothing, Grandfather, nothing at all." Jael said softly. He appeared to have aged considerably in the short time since her marriage. She noticed a grease spot on the lapel of his shiny broadcloth jacket. His trencher-style beard was shaggy and in need of trimming. "You look as though you've lost weight. Have you been eating regularly since I left?"

"Fine time to worry!" he blazed. "Instead of doing your Christian duty and tending to family, you run off. Only person you care about is yourself. Ungrateful baggage! Selfish as ever." Turning his back on her, he limped to the table and gathered up a handful of papers.

"Grandfather, if you need..."

"Don't need you. Don't need anybody but the Lord."

To her amazement, for the first time ever she gazed upon him without fear. He no longer exercised any power over her. If anything, she felt sorry for him. He was nothing more than a feeble old man. "I'll write when I reach New Bedford."

"Don't bother." He stuffed his notes in a pocket, grabbed his hat from a chair, and jammed it on his head. "I've got a prayer meeting to conduct. Close the door behind you when you leave."

"Grandfather...!"

The sharpness in her voice made him hesitate.

"What have I ever done to make you hate me so?" There it was said. The burning question she had never dared ask was out in the open. Deep in her heart she knew the answer, but that didn't matter. She needed to hear the words spoken aloud.

He glared at her through pale blue eyes, his mouth working in agitation. He made no attempt to disguise—or deny—his loathing. "Because you're the spitting image of *her*!"

"Her? Do you mean my mother?"

"I see you, and it's like looking at her all over again. I tried to do right by her, tried to teach her the Lord's ways. But I failed. And everyone knew it, my bishop, my congregation, everyone! Then you arrived on my doorstep, a reminder of my shame, my failure. Got so I couldn't look them in the eye, couldn't hold my head up. Finally had to pack up and move to this godforsaken island to escape the disgrace. Promised myself I wouldn't fail a second time if I had to beat the evil out of you."

Jael flinched at the malevolence directed at her, but held her ground. "We all make mistakes, Grandfather, and Mother paid dearly for hers."

"She was a sinner!" he hissed. "A sinner!"

"Mother didn't preach Christianity, she practiced it," Jael fired back, incensed at her grandfather's unbending attitude. "She was good and kind and loving. She worked day and night to put food on the table and a roof over our heads. Never once did I hear her speak a derogatory word about you. Not even when she knew she was dying and was trying to prepare me for what life with you was going to be like."

"She was a sinner." Silas's reed-thin body quivered with righteous indignation. "A fornicating sinner."

"Aren't you forgetting one thing?" Jael asked as her grandfather's bony hand reached for the door latch.

"What's that?" he barked.

"We're all sinners . . . even you."

Her quiet reminder gave him pause, then he collected himself and stomped off.

Jael watched him hobble down the coral path. He didn't spare her a backward glance. "Good-bye, Grandfather," she whispered.

It was strange, she mused, though she couldn't summon a scrap of affection toward him, she did feel a certain . . . responsibility. She felt better knowing that Reverend Hadley would keep an eye on him in her absence. Grandfather's irascible temper had alienated all who had tried to befriend him. Except for her, he didn't have a soul in the world who cared if he lived or died.

No one to mourn. No one to care.

She recalled the desolation that had swept over her when she feared Mu would kill her. But Nathan had changed all that. Although he hadn't said that he loved her, she knew beyond a doubt that he did care. Turning her back on the unhappy home of her girlhood, she lifted her face to the sun. And her future.

As she neared the cottage she shared with Nathan, the puppy, Niu, ran out to greet her, yipping excitedly and dancing around her feet. His antics brought a smile of amusement.

Then Mahie came out to greet her, shaking her head. "Bad dog, missus." She held out a mangled clump of black straw.

Jael hardly recognized what was left of her bonnet. "Bad dog," she scolded, wagging a finger. The puppy cowered pitifully at her feet, and she hadn't the heart to discipline him further.

"Mahie sorry. Niu stole bonnet when back was turned."

"A bonnet can always be replaced." Jael scooped Niu up in her arms and absently scratched the pup behind his ears.

"Then missus not blame Mahie?"

Mahie looked so distraught, Jael wrapped her arm around the girl's shoulders and gave her a hug. "Thank you for being my friend. I'll miss you when we leave."

Later that evening after Mahie left, Jael sat on the top step and awaited Nathan's return. Niu, his transgression forgiven, snored peacefully beside her. Jael purposely set the disturbing encounter with her grandfather aside and dwelt on more pleasant subjects.

She smiled, thinking of the night before when Nathan made love to her a second time. If possible, the magic between them had been even more potent. She had summoned the courage to touch him as he had touched her. To her delight, he had grown taut like a bowstring in response to her tentative explorations. His manhood had felt like steel sheathed in satin, the combination both startling and intriguing. She was eager to know his body even more intimately than she knew her own. Blood rushed to her cheeks. *Pagan hussy.* Her grandfather's accusation rang in her ears.

The puppy raised his head, ears pricked and alert. Jael looked toward the beach and saw Nathan approaching. Her heartbeat quickened, leaving her suddenly breathless. Scrambling to her feet, she ran to greet him, her love shining in her eyes. Niu bounded after her, yipping with excitement.

Nathan tried to summon a smile, but didn't succeed. He gazed at her soberly for a long moment. He noticed that she had taken special pains with her appearance. With her hair a cascade of curls and wearing a gown of violet taffeta, she looked much as she had on their wedding day. Only happier. "Did I ever tell you what a lovely bride you made?"

She smiled shyly, pleased at the compliment. "I feel more like a bride now than I did then."

Unable to look into her glowing face without being racked by guilt, Nathan averted his gaze. He felt lower than pond scum for what he was about to do. But postponing the inevitable would only make it more painful. He slowly continued walking toward the cottage. "We need to talk."

His seriousness communicated itself to her. "Is there something wrong with the *Clotilde*? Will we still be able to sail tomorrow?"

"The ship's fine." He reached the porch, but made no effort to enter the house. Resting one foot on the bottom step, he buried his fists deep in his pockets.

"Then what is it?"

"You're aware that I was married once before," he began hesitantly.

"Yes, of course." Puzzled by his manner, Jael leaned against the porch rail. She had the uneasy feeling she'd need its support before their strange conversation ended.

"Believe me when I say my marriage was unpleasant. After Catherine died, I decided I'd never remarry. I'm much better suited to the single life than being tied to one woman for the rest of my days."

Jael dropped her gaze to her feet, where Niu contentedly gnawed the mangled bonnet. "What is it you're trying to tell me?" she asked in a small voice when the silence lengthened painfully.

Nathan wished he were in China. Or Bora Bora. Anywhere but here. He allowed the puppy to distract him from the subject at hand. "What's the dog chewing?"

"It used to be my bonnet." Jael's voice was thin, strained.

Nathan's mouth twisted into a parody of a smile. "Never did like that blasted thing."

Jael raised troubled eyes to his. "You still haven't told me what's wrong."

He sighed. "This isn't going to be easy for either of us, but I think we need to be honest with each other."

Jael went very still inside.

"I assumed you understood the way I feel about marriage. I *don't* want to be married. Above everything, I value my independence, my freedom."

"But Nathan, I thought last night changed things. I love you." She valiantly fought back tears. "I thought you loved me."

"You're confusing the issue. All we had last

night was sex." She winced at his bluntness, but he forged ahead. "That's what can happen between a man and a woman who share a strong physical attraction. It has nothing to do with love. Call it chemistry if you will, but never call it love."

Never call it love? She bit her lip to keep it from trembling. "You must think me terribly naive. I always believed the two went together." At least they did for her. *Why*, she cried silently, *couldn't it be the same for him?*

"I lost control last night, but I give you my word, it won't happen again."

His promise only made her feel worse. Her heart felt like it was being split in two with a dull blade. "Perhaps that would be best," she said, hoping he wouldn't see how deeply his words had wounded her.

"Listen, Jael, you're infatuated with me, nothing more," he explained earnestly, trying to convince them both with his logic. "It's not uncommon for a young woman who's led a sheltered life to fancy herself in love with the first man to come along."

Maybe that was true for some, but not for herself. She knew she loved him. Loved him enough to want to alleviate his pangs of conscience. "I suppose you're right." She forced a brittle smile. "In time, I'll get over this silly notion and recognize it as being only infatuation."

Nathan sighed in relief. "Good girl. I knew you'd see reason. Someday you'll thank me for being honest with you."

Jael gazed across the beach toward the horizon. The sun was sinking low in the sky, staining the horizon with glorious crimson stripes. "I-I think..." She faltered, then cleared her throat and tried again. "I think that I'll miss the sunsets most of all."

Nathan turned to admire the sight. The wistfulness in her voice tugged at his heart. "Yes," he agreed softly, "sunsets here are like no others."

Together they silently watched the blood-red sun slip behind the horizon, then Nathan turned away and slowly mounted the steps.

"I'm sorry I had to hurt you, but it was important that I make you understand. Don't take it personally, I just don't want to be married."

It took all Jael's willpower to refrain from putting her hands over her ears to block out the hateful words. "Yes, you've made that quite clear."

"Good." He nodded in grim approval. "Although an annulment is no longer possible, a divorce is. I'll speak to an attorney about the details when we dock in New Bedford. Now I'd better go inside and pack if we're to leave at dawn." He disappeared inside, leaving Jael staring bleakly at the fading sky.

She loved him; and he only lusted after her.

She wanted to weep, but pride dammed the tears. Finally pain seeped through layers of shock and penetrated her numbed brain. *Just like your mother*. The phrase repeated through her mind. Hateful words. Hateful ... but prophetic. Just like her mother, she, too, loved unwisely. But she didn't regret loving Nathan.

Only that he didn't—couldn't—return the emotion.

Which was worse, she wondered dismally, never loving at all or not having love reciprocated? Certainly the former would be less painful. But for her, the brief interlude of unparalleled joy had wrought a profound change. Loving Nathan had enriched her life beyond measure. Life without experiencing love would be like never witnessing a sunset.

And where there was life, there was always hope.

Though Nathan might not feel the same way about her as she did about him, she knew he cared. And that he was attracted to her. Months of sharing close quarters lay ahead of them aboard the *Clotilde*. Months in which to make him change his mind about marriage.

Chapter 17

Nathan's heart wrenched with sympathy. Jael looked small and forlorn as she stood alone at the rail. And very brave. Her shoulders were squared, her chin high and resolute. He had been watching her surreptitiously since they boarded the *Clotilde*. She had been withdrawn ever since their conversation the previous night. He half expected her to change her mind about leaving Hawaii and would have understood if she had. Much to his surprise—and relief—she hadn't suffered a change of heart. Her quiet courage drew his admiration.

After issuing final instructions to John McFee, he crossed the deck to stand next to her. Relishing the feel of the sea breeze in his face and the roll of the ship beneath his feet, he watched Lahaina grow smaller and smaller. A handful of frame buildings that appeared no larger than child's toys hugged the shoreline. Mist curled around the jagged peaks of the West Maui Mountains like plumes of smoke.

Deep ravines carpeted in lush green gouged their ramparts, the terrain so rugged it discouraged explorers.

"No matter how many times we drop anchor, Maui's beauty never fails to stir me." He spoke quietly, reflectively.

Jael kept her eyes trained straight ahead. "The first time I saw the island, I thought we had arrived in paradise."

The wistfulness in her voice provoked a fresh wave of sympathy. He'd seen homesickness take a heavy toll on hale and hearty seamen. "As beautiful as the island is, there's still much of the world for you to see," he said, attempting to divert her thoughts from leaving the place she called home.

"I barely recall living in New York. I have only vague memories of cold winters and crowded streets." She tucked a wisp of blowing hair behind her ear.

"Here in the tropics, there is only summer. You'll have to get accustomed to the change of seasons all over again." The strand immediately came loose from its mooring, and he struggled against the urge to smooth it from her cheek. "The brilliance of a New England autumn rivals a Maui sunset. Jack Frost turns the countryside into a winter fairyland. It's great fun to bundle up in blankets for a sleigh ride, then stop for mulled cider at a country inn."

"It sounds . . . very different."

"Spring is a sight to behold. Flowers poke up in every park and garden. Trees that have been bare for months sprout leaves and turn green almost overnight."

"Your words paint a pretty picture."

"There are hundreds of things to do and see. There are theaters and museums. People will be fascinated when they learn you've lived in the Sandwich Islands. Your social calendar will be full."

"And just who will be inviting me to theaters and museums? Aren't you forgetting I don't know a soul there?"

Nathan found himself wishing he could be the one to introduce her to the delights he had just described. "You'll soon meet people. Young men by the droves will be clamoring to squire you around town and show you the sights. You'll have to fend them off."

Jael dragged her attention away from the vanishing speck on the horizon and turned to face him. "Will these same young men still be eager when they learn I've been divorced?"

Rather than meet her look, he watched a foremast hand climb the mast to the lookout. Her blunt question made him uncomfortable. "True, society takes a dim view of divorce, but there's no need to advertise your state."

"I surmised as much," she said bitterly.

So, she hadn't been certain, but had tricked him into answering. "I'm not asking you to lie, Jael. I'm merely suggesting that you use discretion as to whom you tell."

"My imagination is quite good, thank you. It isn't necessary to spell out the details." She turned to him angrily, chin raised, eyes flash-

INSIDE PARADISE 267

ing. "Once divorced, I'll be a social outcast, a pariah, ostracized from polite society. Forgive me if I'm not enthused at the prospect."

True, Nathan admitted silently, divorce was looked upon as scandalous. Jael had just cause to be upset. He shifted his weight uncomfortably and avoided her eyes.

"Well, whatever, after the divorce my well-being will be no concern of yours. I can fend for myself. Now, if you'll excuse me," she said, her tone arctic, "I think I'll go to the cabin and unpack."

"Allow me to show you the way."

Her expression stony, she stared at his crooked arm, then pointedly ignored it. Accepting her snub with resignation, Nathan escorted her across the stern, led her down a companionway, then opened the door to the captain's quarters.

Jael gazed about in awe. The accommodations were far more luxurious than she had imagined. Beyond a tiny washroom was a stateroom dominated by a large bed. Her sea chest had been placed on the floor nearby. A tufted sofa of burgundy leather stretched across the after-end of the cabin. An oak desk, its surface hidden beneath a pile of nautical charts, resided against the forward bulkhead. A brass compass was positioned above the desk in such a fashion that it was equally visible from both the main and forward cabins.

Nathan gestured toward the bed. "Even merchant ships envy a whaling captain his comfortable berth. The bed is hung from gimbals, stone-weighted devices that allow it to swing freely. No matter how the ship rolls and tosses, the bed remains on an even keel. I'm sure you'll find it most comfortable."

"What about you? Where will you sleep?" The instant the words were out of her mouth she wished she could call them back. Her face flushed with embarrassment.

"I'll sleep on the sofa."

"Oh." She had half expected him to say he'd sleep elsewhere. Or offer to bunk with John McFee. But she was glad he'd be close. Though ashamed to admit it, truth was she didn't want him sleeping on the sofa. She wanted him in bed . . . next to her.

"I took the liberty of purchasing a few items I thought might be useful." He nodded at a stack of parcels wrapped in brown paper. "Meals are served in the main cabin. I'll introduce you to the rest of the crew at dinner. Now, I'd better oversee duties on deck. Make yourself comfortable."

Jael stared at the closed door for a long minute. Another facet of Nathan's personality was coming to light. As a ship's captain, he seemed to have undergone a subtle change. An air of command settled about his shoulders as comfortably as a well-tailored coat. She admired the way he dealt with his crew. He issued orders, never harshly and always without arrogance, yet men scurried to obey.

Curiosity overtook her, and she unwrapped the packages. She found several woolen shawls, yards of soft challis in both prints and solid colors, and two flannel nightdresses inside. She bent to pick a piece of string off the floor and noticed a hatbox for the first time. She lifted off the lid, then sighed with delight. A frilly bonnet nestled in a bed of tissue along with a note.

Feed that ugly piece of black straw you call a bonnet to the sharks.

Smiling, she lifted the bonnet out of the hatbox. Straw-colored with saucy pink roses decorating the brim, it tipped up in back and down in the front. Pink satin ribbons tied beneath the chin. Pretty yet practical, it would shade her fair skin from the sun's burning rays.

She ran the satin ribbons through her fingers, enjoying the smooth, silky texture. It was the prettiest bonnet she'd ever seen, much less owned. Niu apparently hadn't appreciated her old one any more than Nathan. The puppy had snatched a meal from the sharks. She'd sorely miss his company on the long voyage, but Nathan had been firm on the subject. A whaling vessel, he had insisted, was no place for a frisky pup constantly underfoot. Reluctantly she had left the little dog in Mahie's care.

Her expression clouded with uncertainty, she sank down on the bed still holding the bonnet and wondered what surprises the voyage held in store.

* * *

Jael was the first to arrive. The table was built about the mizzenmast in the main cabin. Racks, or fiddles as they were called, were fitted into the tabletop to prevent dishes from landing in unsuspecting laps. Long narrow benches with hinged backs were along both sides of the table. Nervous at the prospect of meeting the crew, she smoothed her hair. Each unruly curl had been tamed into submission. She had decided to wear a new gown of striped silk in a flattering shade of green. She wanted to look her best tonight. To make Nathan proud. She wondered how many of the men knew that he had been forced to marry her. Surely they must have heard tales and considered what type of woman she was.

When Nathan entered the main cabin, he spotted her standing indecisively at the far end. He hurried to her side, took her hands in his, and raised them to his lips. "You look beautiful."

"Thank you," she murmured, feeling a delicious tingle spread through her. Basking under the warm approval in his hazel eyes, the dregs of her earlier anger faded away.

The officers filed in according to rank. John McFee, as first mate, immediately came over to welcome Jael. "You're sure pretty as a picture. Always did accuse the captain of bein' the luckiest man alive."

"Remember, I saw her first," Nathan kidded good-naturedly. "Don't let him fool you, Jael. Under that rough exterior beats the heart of a smooth-talking ladies' man."

John grinned and slapped Nathan's back.

Nathan introduced her in turn to each of his officers. "This is Gunnar Iverson, otherwise known as Swede. Swede acts as my second mate."

"It's a pleasure to meet you, Mr. Iverson."

The blue-eyed giant who looked no older than twenty brushed a shock of white-blond hair back from his face and gave her a bashful smile. "Call me Swede, ma'am."

"Swede is absolutely fearless when confronting a killer whale, but quakes like an aspen around a lovely lady." At Nathan's ribbing, a flush crept up Swede's neck and he ducked his head in embarrassment. Nathan's indulgent smile faded as he introduced his third mate. "And this is Simon Pulver. This marks the first voyage Simon and I have made together."

"How do you do, Mr. Pulver."

Simon Pulver grunted an unintelligible response, then turned his sullen, pockmarked face to Nathan. "You didn't tell me when I hired on there'd be a woman along."

"I didn't think that was pertinent to our agreement, Pulver. With your record, don't make me sorry I hired you."

"Women ought to wait at home where they belong. They're nothing but trouble aboard ship."

Jael observed the man uneasily. His thinning dark hair looked greasy and his belly hung over his belt. Animosity brightened his close-set brown eyes.

"This is my ship, Pulver, and I'll thank you to keep your opinions to yourself." Nathan's tone was even but undermined with steel.

While the others watched in uncomfortable silence, the two glared at each other.

"You're the captain." Pulver shrugged and turned away.

Tension drained from the room as the steward carried in platters of steaming food. "The *Clotilde* boasts the finest sea cook in the Pacific," Nathan informed Jael as everyone took their seats at the table. "Believe me, good cooks are tough to come by."

John speared a chunk of meat. "Nothin' men like better than complainin' about the fare."

"Women start whinin' soon as they tire of salt beef and hardtack," Pulver mumbled around a mouth stuffed with food.

"Don't mind Pulver." John tore off a chunk of bread. "Many wives aren't content to sit home and write letters. They prefer to accompany their husbands instead."

"It's not unusual for a whaling voyage to last four years," Swede volunteered. "That's a long time for couples to be separated."

Pulver scowled across the table. "Just wish I'd knowed ahead of time. No way I'da signed on a hen frigate."

Jael's appetite vanished. She wasn't sure if she could attribute it to the roll of the ship or the third mate's surly attitude. "I'll try not to be a bother."

"The dinner table is no place to air grievances, Mr. Pulver." A muscle ticked ominously in Nathan's jaw. "In the future, should any complaints about how I run my ship arise, please direct them to me in private."

John stepped into the awkward breech. "Wait 'til you get your first taste of plum duff," he said, winking at Jael.

"Plum duff?"

"It's kind of a puddin' made from flour and lard and raisins." Swede popped half a boiled potato into his mouth. "Cook serves it as a treat once a week."

Much to Jael's relief, the remainder of the meal passed without incident. The men, as though eager to make amends for Pulver's boorish behavior, regaled her with stories of their adventures in exotic ports. With the exception of Simon Pulver, all were in good moods when dinner ended. After bidding her good night, the men took their leave in the opposite order they had entered.

The scratch of quill against paper could be heard above the creaking of timbers and the wash of waves against the ship's hull. A mellow glow spilled from an oil lamp mounted on a beam above Nathan's desk, where he sat writing in his journal.

Never having shared intimate quarters with a man before, Jael wasn't quite sure of the proper etiquette. She turned her back, then quickly undressed and slipped into a nightdress. Sitting on the edge of the bed, she proceeded to take the pins from her sleek chignon. Her hair swirled around her shoulders. She pulled a brush from roots to tips in slow, rhythmic motions until her hair crackled with electricity.

Feeling Nathan watching her, she paused in mid-stroke and looked up. In the lamplight, his eyes were a mysterious marsh green. His face wore an odd expression. "You're looking at me strangely. Is anything wrong?"

"No, nothing." He jabbed the pen into the inkwell, then swore under his breath when the ink formed a large, dark smudge over the neat column of figures. "Damn," he muttered again as he reached for the blotter.

Jael ignored him and continued to brush her hair. From time to time she darted a covert glance at him, trying to gauge his mood. He certainly seemed irritable for no apparent reason.

Nathan cast an eye at the compass suspended above his desk on the skylight, then entered calculations in the journal.

Bored and curious, Jael edged closer until she stood directly behind him, taking pains to be quiet so as not to disturb him. Raising on tiptoe, she leaned forward and peered up into the compass.

"Just what the hell do you think you're doing?" Nathan growled, tossing down his pen in disgust.

Jael froze.

Nathan turned to glare at her over his shoulder and found himself eye level with firm round breasts impudently thrusting against fabric so sheer he could see the rosy outline of her nipples. He felt an uncomfortable rush of heat. Dammit! She had him blushing like a callow youth.

Jael cleared her throat nervously. "I . . . ah . . . just wondered what you were looking at."

"Curiosity killed the cat," he muttered hoarsely.

The ship heaved suddenly. Jael lost her balance, grabbed for the compass to steady herself, missed, and twisting, landed with a plop in Nathan's lap. Nose to nose, they stared at each other. Anyone happening upon the scene would have been hard-pressed to tell who appeared more astonished.

Neither spoke. Indeed, both seemed incapable of speech.

Jael moistened her lower lip with the tip of her tongue, drawing Nathan's attention to the lush curve. The muscles in his throat worked soundlessly.

Tension charged the air.

Nathan moved his hand a fraction and encountered smooth, bare thigh. He bit back a groan as he felt his manhood harden in response. He watched in silent fascination as surprise gradually faded from Jael's gentian-blue eyes and the lids grew heavy.

Desire arced through the cabin like lightning before a summer storm let loose.

Grabbing the last shreds of his self-restraint, Nathan surged to his feet, nearly dumping Jael on the floor in his haste. "Think I'll go up on deck for some night air before retiring."

Jael leaned against the desk for support, her legs as unsteady as a newly foaled colt, and listened to the sound of his retreating footsteps. Among the conflicting emotions she had read in his face, she had also seen desire. This realization brought a measure of hope. In spite of his harsh words the previous night, she sensed that he still harbored feelings for her. Feelings that if carefully nurtured could deepen and bloom.

When she was confident her legs would support her weight, she crossed to the cabin and curled up in the center of the big, luxurious bed. She tried to wait up for him, but her eyelids grew weighted and closed. She was sleeping soundly when he returned.

Nathan stood for a long time staring down at her. Her hair rippled across the white bed linen like Oriental silk. Eyelashes, long and feathery, rested against her petal-soft skin like delicate burgundy fans. She looked like an angel in repose. Unable to curb the impulse, he traced his index finger along the delicate curve of her cheek. She sighed in her sleep.

Desire punched him in the gut like a heavy fist. Dammit! He didn't want to be married! Not even to a flame-haired enchantress with the face of angel and a body that could tempt a saint. And, God help him, he was far from saintly. Physical attraction was all he felt for her. Physical attraction. Plain and simple.

But it wasn't simple at all. The situation was damn complicated. How could anyone expect a red-blooded man to share a small cabin for months on end with a violet-eyed beauty and not be affected? Dragging a hand through his hair, he cursed under his breath. A man would have to be a monk.

Or better yet, a eunuch.

Days of glorious weather under a full spread of canvas lengthened into a week. Jael had been as excited as a child when she witnessed flying fish gather around the bow, then scatter like leaves before a wind. Dolphins frolicked in the ship's wake, their graceful bodies gleaming opalescent. Clouds banked the horizon like great mounds of whipped cream.

Once the whaling grounds were reached, sails were shortened and the *Clotilde* slackened to cruising speed. Gradually a pattern emerged. The officers kept the watches occupied. Spars were scraped and slushed, rigging overhauled, whaleboats patched, and sails mended. The two dogwatches from four to six and from six to eight in the evening were times of rest and relaxation. All hands came out on deck. It was during dogwatches that one of the crew produced a battered concertina. Men talked, smoked their pipes, and told yarns of their whaling adventures. Others made intricate carvings in the teeth and jawbones of whales, an art known as scrimshaw. John, Nathan had explained, was particularly skilled. Each time Jael approached him to see what he was working on, he'd quickly tuck it into his pocket.

Jael made another tour about the deck while Nathan remained in the cabin making entries in his log. Though he hadn't voiced an objection, she got the distinct impression her presence was intrusive. Simon Pulver, in charge of the watch, ignored her as she strolled past. That suited her just fine. She didn't like him any more than he liked her. She paused at the rail and, shading her eyes against the sun's glare, looked out to sea.

"Lookin' for a whale?"

Startled, she half turned to discover John beside her. "Well," she said, smiling, "it would be exciting to be the first to spot one."

"That's when all hell breaks lose. Pardon the expression, ma'am." He grinned unabashed. "Nothin' like a Nantucket sleigh ride to get the blood pumpin'."

Jael nodded knowingly. "Nathan mentioned how he likes to stop for mulled cider after a sleigh ride in the country."

John looked at her peculiarly for a long moment, then roared with laughter. "You truly are an innocent," he said between gales of mirth.

"I fail to see what's so funny." She drew herself up indignantly.

John brought his amusement under control. "A Nantucket sleigh ride is what happens sometimes after a whale is struck by a harpoon. The whale panics and makes a run for it, towin' the whaleboat at a high rate of speed. Heard tell once of a whaleboat that harpooned a sperm whale. Whale took off like a shot out of a cannon, and neither whale nor whaleboat was ever seen again."

Jael's eyes widened in horror. "It sounds dangerous."

"That's what I like about it. Man against beast. Or, if you will, like your Bible story David versus Goliath. Whaling's a challenge every time you step foot inside a whaleboat. Never know what's goin' to happen. Whales can become the aggressors when attacked. Several ships have been rammed head on and sunk in a matter of minutes."

Jael shuddered at the image conjured up by her imagination. "I had no idea they could be so vicious."

John saw her shiver and was instantly contrite. "But those things don't happen often, ma'am. No need to worry your pretty little head."

Jael was anxious to change the subject. "Have you sailed with Nathan very long?"

"Goin' on six years now. Never sailed with a better man."

"Then you knew his first wife?" Jael tried to keep her tone casual.

"Can't rightly say I knew her, but then I don't suppose Nathan did either."

Puzzled by his cryptic remark, Jael swung around to study him. "What was she like? Was she beautiful?"

"Guess you could say that." John rested both arms on the rail and stared at the unending expanse of ocean. "Always reminded me of one of those fancy dolls you see in shop windows come Christmastime. The kind with painted faces and fancy clothes. The kind made to look at, but not to touch."

"You don't sound as though you liked her very much," Jael observed cautiously.

"I didn't," he retorted with uncharacteristic sharpness. "I warned Nathan not to get tangled up with the likes of her, but the dang fool didn't pay any mind. All she brought him was heartache."

"He must have cared for her a great deal." Jael could hardly squeeze the words past the lump in her throat. She fervently wished she had never initiated the subject.

"Too much for his own good." John kept his gaze fixed on the rolling sea. "By the time of her accident though, he realized their marriage had been a mistake from the beginning. She was nothing but a spoiled, selfish woman."

Jael was startled by John's vitriolic attack on Nathan's first wife.

"Marriage to Catherine Hadley left a bad taste in the captain's mouth." He turned to Jael with a smile that managed to be both bitter and sweet. "Be patient with him, Jael darlin'. The captain can be as single-minded as a bull sperm whale, but if anyone can soften him up, I'd wager it's you."

Her mind adrift in confusion, she watched him amble off. She replayed their conversation in her mind. John had painted an entirely different picture of Catherine Hadley than the one she had imagined. Initially she had pic-

INSIDE PARADISE 281

tured Catherine a paragon of virtue, beautiful and charming—everything she was not. Apparently it took more than beauty and charm to sustain a husband's love.

Chapter 18

Rinsing her hair with rainwater had been a rare treat. Nearly dry, her hair swirled around her shoulders like a ruby cape. Dragging the hairbrush through it slowly, she paced back and forth. She slanted a look at Nathan as she passed his desk. The oil lamp overhead captured the golden highlights in his hair. An unruly lock fell across his brow, and she fought the urge to smooth it back.

She doubted he'd welcome her advances. She seriously doubted if he was even aware of her presence. If so, he certainly gave no indication of it. Instead he seemed intent on his work. He paused occasionally to squint through the compass, then busily scratch notations in his journal. She might as well be on another continent for all the attention he gave her.

Restless and edgy, she continued to pace. It was difficult sharing close quarters with someone determined to ignore you. The close confines of the cabin were getting on her nerves. She felt irritable, ready to snap at the least provocation. She and Nathan were constantly in each other's way, bumping into each other, then apologizing profusely. Cold intimacy.

She had foolishly hoped this voyage would bring them closer. That somehow she could find a way to break through his defenses. To force him to reconsider his decision to seek a divorce. But if anything, they were drifting further and further apart. Each day the tension between them seemed to increase to the point where a simple conversation was becoming impossible.

Nathan had erected an invisible wall, a barricade so high it was impossible to scale. As terrified as she was of being branded a divorced woman, she was even more terrified, however, of the hole Nathan's absence would leave in her life. Without him it would be an empty shell.

A muttered curse from Nathan drew her attention.

"Can't you sit still?"

"No," she fired back, uncharacteristically short-tempered.

He brushed the unruly lock from his brow with an impatient hand. "It's difficult to concentrate when you're parading back and forth."

"I'm not parading. I'm restless."

"Well, then," he said, turning back to his work, "find something to keep you occupied. Stitch a sampler, read a book."

Her lower lip jutted out rebelliously. "I've sewed so much my fingers are numb, and if I read another page my eyes will cross."

He glared at her, mumbled something unintelligible under his breath, then dipped his quill in the inkwell and returned to making notations in his journal.

Jael made another pass of the cabin. "I don't know why you forbid me to go up on deck alone," she grumbled peevishly.

"It's for your own good."

"You didn't object before."

"I overheard some of the crew complaining." He kept his eyes fixed on the page in front of him. "Seems that not all the men are accustomed to having a woman on board. I'm trying to avoid trouble."

Jael stopped to regard him questioningly. "Do you think my presence is going to cause a problem?"

"Not if I can help it."

His cryptic response was hardly reassuring. "Does that mean you're going to keep me confined to quarters unless you have the time—and the inclination—to accompany me on deck?"

"If that's what it takes..." Nathan replied through gritted teeth.

"I'm used to being active, not cooped up like some animal."

"Well, you better get used to it," he said, his voice tight. "We haven't even sighted our first whale yet. It's likely to be a long voyage."

She continued to walk back and forth, absently sweeping the brush through her hair. She didn't know what was wrong with her, only that she felt ready to explode. Nerves frayed, tempers on edge, it felt like a storm was brewing inside the cabin. The air seemed charged with electricity. Even an argument would be preferable to the awkward silences that punctuated fits of conversation.

At the far end of the cabin, she paused, trying to sort through her chaotic emotions. Without being aware of her actions, she tapped the brush repeatedly against her palm.

"Must you?" Nathan's voice lashed out, startling her.

She swung around and found him staring at her, his expression intense, formidable. Even hostile. It unnerved her. "Must I what?"

Must you be a constant distraction? he wanted to ask. His concentration shattered, he had just added the same column of figures for the third time. Each time he had arrived at a different sum. She was slowly but surely driving him crazy.

He expelled a long sigh as he tunneled his fingers through his already tousled hair. Did she have any idea of the effect she had on him? How desirable she was? Having her within arm's reach yet not being able to touch was wearing his control threadbare. Thoughts of her even disturbed his sleep. Just yesterday, he had wakened in the middle of the night to find himself cuddling a pillow and murmuring her name. Pathetic. Downright pathetic!

Jael nervously moistened her lower lip with

the tip of her tongue. "Nathan, you're making me uncomfortable. Stop staring at me that way."

"What way?"

"Like a hawk ready to swoop down and devour a rabbit," she retorted.

"Strange analogy."

Funny she should choose that analogy, but she had just described his feelings perfectly. At this moment, he wanted nothing more than to scoop her up in his arms, lay her on the gimbaled bed, and spend the rest of the night making love to her. Maybe then he'd exorcise her control over him. Maybe then he'd find some peace.

His jaw hardened with resolution. The time for a confrontation was at hand. He would tackle the problem like a man, not some spineless weakling. With deliberate movements, he replaced his pen in the inkwell, then rose from his chair and walked over to where she stood. "I've got a proposition."

Wary but defiant, Jael tipped her head and met his look head-on. "I'm listening."

By the stubborn tilt of her chin, Nathan knew he had his work cut out for him. "I've done some serious thinking."

"That sounds ominous," she replied with an undercurrent of sarcasm.

Nathan scowled at the cheeky rejoinder. Cocking his head, he studied her thoughtfully. She had become a feisty little thing. Her blue-violet eyes flashed with the same glint he had witnessed in John's eyes countless times before diving headlong into a fray. He was struck by the transformation that had taken place in her. Jael had changed dramatically from the timid little creature he had rescued from a crowd of unruly seamen. No longer meek and docile, she had become a woman with a mind of her own.

He fleetingly reconsidered the request he was about to make, then squared his shoulders with renewed determination. Nathan Thorne, captain of the bark *Clotilde*, never backed down from a challenge. Never veered from course.

Hands clasped behind his back, he rocked on his heels in an attempt to appear more confident than he felt. "We've already slept together, and the damage..." He bemoaned his inept choice of words, but forged ahead relentlessly. "The damage, so to speak, has already been done. What's the harm in our continuing to sleep together?"

"What's the harm?" she repeated in a deceptively mild tone.

He cleared his throat. "It's turning out to be a long voyage and..."

"...and?"

He looked down at her hopefully, willing her to accept his logic. "Since neither of us found the experience disagreeable, I thought..."

"You're suggesting we sleep together, and you fail to find a problem with that?"

A dull red flush crept across Nathan's cheekbones. This discussion definitely wasn't following the course he had routed. "What I'm suggesting is hardly immoral," he protested. "After all, we are married."

Jael tapped the hairbrush rhythmically against her palm. As the only sound in the small cabin, the noise was as annoying to Nathan as the ticking of a metronome or the buzzing of a mosquito. In morbid fascination, he watched her fury build.

"We'd be no different than two animals mating. I can't believe you even suggested such a thing." Her voice, her entire body, quivered with indignation. "You expect me to spread my legs like a...a...common trollop." When the term didn't seem quite strong enough, she borrowed one she had undoubtedly heard her grandfather use. "Like a cheap whore."

Nathan, realizing he had made a serious blunder, placed his hands on her shoulders. "Jael, please listen to me. I've never regarded you with anything but the utmost respect, and I never shall."

She angrily shrugged off his touch. "Did it ever occur to you that I might become pregnant?"

Her question caught him off guard. He had been too busy contemplating a way of alleviating more immediate problems than to give the possibility much thought. Embarrassed by the oversight, he adopted a conciliatory tone. "I'd willingly provide for both you and any child that might ensue from such an arrangement."

Jael sent the hairbrush flying. Nathan ducked as it narrowly missed his head, glanced off an overhead beam, then after striking the bulkhead, clattered to the floor.

"Not only would you leave me to contend with the stigma of divorce, but a child to raise as well. No, thank you," she informed him bitterly. "I learned firsthand the hardships involved in raising a child alone."

Nathan was at a loss for words. He had been an insensitive oaf, thinking of only his own needs.

Jael spun away from him, grabbed her shawl from the sofa, and marched toward the door.

"Where do you think you're going?" he called after her.

"I'm going up on deck for some fresh air—with or without your blessing. There's a decided stench in here." She banged the door in her wake.

Seemingly rooted to the floor, Nathan stared at the closed door. Jael had certainly succeeded in setting him back on his heels. And made him feel ashamed of himself in the bargain. What had he been thinking of to suggest such a thing? Had he gone crazy?

A bemused expression flitted across his face. Under her demure surface lurked an awesome temper. He had never imagined seeing her so riled that she practically spit fire. In her fury she had become Pele incarnate, ready to spew fiery lava and incinerate everything in her path. Him included.

Then all traces of amusement fled. He sank down on the bed and scrubbed his hand across his face, his expression sober. He owed her an apology. But right now he didn't think she was ready to listen to one. He'd give her some time alone, time to cool down, then he'd seek her out and ask her forgiveness.

He should have known, should have realized, Jael wasn't the sort who gave her body—or her heart—freely. Deep inside, he was forced to admit a truth that was easier to deny. He wanted much more from Jael than mere physical intimacy. He wanted to be her friend as well as her lover. He wanted to hold her all night long. To talk and laugh, to share secrets and confide dreams. Added to his amazement was the fact that he not been repelled by the notion of her carrying his child. Instead, the prospect touched a chord that had stood silent for years.

Expelling a sigh, he shook his head, disgusted at his wayward thoughts. What was he thinking indeed?

Jael's quick, agitated steps echoed softly in the night. She raised her face to the wind and allowed the tangy sea breeze to cool her flushed cheeks and sift through her hair. The memory of Nathan's proposition still heated her blood to the boiling point. His suggestion had been insulting. Degrading. What kind of woman did he take her for? Did he really believe that she would gladly tumble into his bed each night? Was she nothing more than a convenient receptacle for his male needs?

He seemed to labor under the mistaken notion that she would meekly agree with his outrageous suggestion. That he could use her, then once they reached their destination, just as casually discard her. Pay her off. Mark the account closed. And all because, as he described it, they had both found lovemaking agreeable.

She stopped walking and leaned against the rail. Forcing herself to breathe slowly, she willed the anger—and the hurt—to seep away. Gradually she became more attuned to her surroundings. It was a beautiful night, dark and serene. A full moon hovered above the horizon like a shiny silver medallion and played hide-and-seek with the clouds. Waves sloshed against the hull as the valiant little ship plowed through the water, the sound as soothing as a symphony to her jangled nerves.

She closed her eyes and saw Nathan's face behind closed lids. She had lashed out at him like a wounded animal. He had hurt her, and she had wanted to retaliate. Finally, now that she was calmer, she could acknowledge the truth. While finding his proposition abhorrent, part of her had been tempted to accept. He had been right on target when he'd said that both of them found making love agreeable. She loved loving Nathan—not just the act itself—but afterward. The cuddling, the closeness, the warmth. The contentment.

"Nice night, ain't it?"

Jael's eyes flew open. Simon Pulver's voice shattered the stillness, scattering her thoughts to the four winds.

"Yes, it is." From over her shoulder, she watched in dismay as he sauntered toward her.

"Ain't seen the cap'n much." He occupied the space next to her at the rail. "Whatsa matter? He too busy to walk with his pretty little bride?"

"My husband has work to do," she answered stiffly. She didn't want to be rude, but didn't want to encourage him either.

"Ah," he replied knowingly. "You two had a tiff?"

Jael could scarcely believe the audacity of the ship's officer. "What transpires between my husband and myself is none of your business, Mr. Pulver."

"Maybe, maybe not." He tore off a hunk of tobacco from a pouch he kept in a jacket pocket.

As upset as she still was with Nathan, his company was preferable to that of his third mate. "My husband will wonder what's keeping me," she said, her tone cool. "If you'll excuse me . . ."

She turned to leave, but Pulver shifted his stance so that his burly frame blocked her retreat.

Apprehension drifted over her like a chill wind. Reflexively Jael pulled the shawl tighter around her shoulders.

Pulver read her fear and chuckled in amusement. "What's the matter, little lady? Think you're too good to socialize with the hired help?"

Jael let her gaze roam with studied casualness. No help was in sight. Except for a crewman at the wheel some distance away, the deck was deserted. Besides, she'd feel rather foolish screaming for help when all Pulver had done was talk to her. She didn't want to create a scene and cause trouble. Nathan had implied that already her presence was the reason for dissension.

Pulver grinned at her from around the plug of tobacco. Juice dribbled out of the corner of his mouth and ran down his chin. He swiped at it with the back of his hand and rubbed it on his pants. "Not many folks around this time o' night," he observed blandly. "Jest you 'n me."

Simon Pulver made her distinctly uneasy. She didn't trust the man for a minute. But she wasn't about to be cowed. She had faced disagreeable, even dangerous, men before and survived. "If you're trying to frighten me, you're going to be disappointed," she said, doing her best to sound stern.

Pulver's swarthy face creased into a broad grin. "Now why would I want to scare you?"

Because you're a bully, Jael wanted to shout. *Because you enjoy picking on victims smaller or weaker than yourself.* Instead, she chose her words with care. "You've made no secret since the beginning of our voyage that you weren't pleased to find me aboard."

"Us seamen are a superstitious lot. Women bring bad luck." He caught a long strand of her windblown hair and rubbed it between his thick fingers. "'Specially them redheaded ones like you."

Jael tugged the lock free. She tried to move around him, but he stretched one arm so that it rested on the rail and obstructed her exit. "What's yer rush?"

"You're in my way," she said, hoping he didn't hear the slight tremor in her voice. "Please, step aside."

He ignored her request, chomping on the cud in his mouth. "Heard rumor you was one of them missionary folk. All prim and proper you was. Until," he chuckled, "the cap'n come along."

Jael felt color sting her face. "Need I remind you again, Mr. Pulver, my business is none of your affair."

"Ain't you grand?" Pulver aimed a stream of tobacco juice over the rail. "It caused quite a stir 'round here when you and the cap'n disappeared fer days on end. Folks did plenty of speculatin'."

"I was abducted," Jael defended hotly. "Since Captain Thorne was familiar with sailing vessels, a dear friend of my grandfather's, Reverend Hadley, requested that he search the perimeter of the island. By doing so, he saved my life."

Pulver smirked. "Heard, too, that preacher pal of your granddad's had to do a lotta coaxin' to persuade the cap'n to make a honest woman outta you."

Thomas Hadley, it appeared, had been right to be concerned about her reputation. Gossip of this sort had probably circulated throughout the islands. "Are you finished, Mr. Pulver?" Jael asked quietly. "Or do you still have more to say?"

Pulver inched closer and lowered his voice to a conspiratorial level. "Just wanted you to know that if the cap'n ain't willin' . . ." He gave her a lewd wink.

Jael balled both hands into fists. Never in her life had she struck another human being, but she was sorely tempted to do so now.

"Get out of my way," she said in a strained whisper.

"This man givin' you any trouble, ma'am?"

The leer dropped from Simon Pulver's face at the sound of John McFee's voice directly behind him.

Jael breathed a sigh of relief at John's timely appearance. She had been so engrossed in her conversation with Pulver, she had failed to hear John's catlike approach.

"Me and the cap'n's lady were just gettin' better acquainted." Pulver shrugged and backed off.

"Mr. Pulver was just taking his leave," Jael said quietly.

"Well, then, I'm the lucky man." With a roguish grin, John extended his arm to Jael. "Perhaps, ma'am, you'll accompany me for a final turn around deck before retiring."

"I'd be delighted, Mr. McFee." Jael stepped out from around Pulver and gratefully accepted John's arm. She looked pointedly at the third mate, then dismissed him with a curt nod. "Good evening, Mr. Pulver."

Pulver slunk off in the direction of the officers' quarters, muttering and shaking his head.

"He certainly is an odious man." Jael couldn't suppress a shudder of revulsion as she watched him depart.

"Cold?" John asked solicitously.

"No, I'm enjoying the fresh air—or at least I was," she said with a small laugh. "The cabin was getting a little too warm for comfort."

John nodded sagely but made no comment. They strolled for a while in companionable silence. Jael needed time to regain her equilibrium after arguments first with Nathan, then Pulver.

"Mind if I smoke?" John asked.

"Not at all. I rather like the smell of pipe tobacco," she confessed shyly.

They paused in the shadow of the windlass while John pulled a pipe from his pocket and went through the motions of lighting it. "Some say smokin' is the devil's habit," he said between puffs, "but I find it relaxing. Some men, like the cap'n, could use a vice or two to take their minds off what really ails them."

Jael caught a strand of hair as it blew across her cheek and tucked it behind her ear. "Are you implying Nathan has a problem?"

John grinned. "All men have problems, ma'am. All women, too, I'd wager."

Jael grinned back. "An artist and philosopher?"

"Don't spread it around," John warned. "I have my reputation as a fightin' man to protect."

Jael laughed. "I can keep a secret."

They resumed their stroll as John puffed thoughtfully on his pipe. "Nathan's a fine man, the best. I'm proud to call him my friend."

Jael looked at him curiously. "I haven't known you very long, John, but I know when you're leading up to something."

"Remind me never to play poker with you, darlin'. You'd call my bluff in a heartbeat." He gave her a rueful smile. "What I'm tryin' to say is that Nathan got a bit more than he bargained for the day he bumped into you. He's still got some figurin' out what to do. But if I know the cap'n, he'll make the right choice when all the cards are played."

"I hope you're right, John. With all my heart, I hope you're right." Jael fervently wanted to believe that when the game was finally over and the *Clotilde* docked in New Bedford, Nathan would be convinced that marriage to her would be the coveted prize and not an unwanted item in the discard pile.

"Keep the faith, darlin'." John patted her hand.

She placed her other hand lightly over his. "Regardless of how the game ends, I want you to know that I consider you a friend."

"I'm honored." John cleared his throat, genuinely touched by her declaration. "Now let me see you safely below decks before the cap'n comes charging up here lookin' for you."

They paused at the top of the companionway that led to the captain's quarters, and John's usually affable expression turned serious.

"If Simon Pulver dares step out of line one more time, you come to me. It'll be my pleasure to take care of the problem for you."

A lump rose in her throat. Jael realized she had found a champion—as well as a friend—in John McFee. She caught his hand and gave it a quick squeeze. "Thank you, John."

Her spirits lifted, her steps lighter, she descended the companionway. And she had John McFee to thank. John had given her more than his willingness to intercede on her behalf—he had given her new hope. New Bedford was still months away. Months.

Ample time for all the cards to be played.

Chapter 19

"**T**here she blows! She blo-o-ows!"

Jael felt anticipation run through her. She strained against the rail, scanning the waves for her first sight of the mighty creature that roamed the seas.

"Where away?" Nathan called as he raced from below decks.

"Two points off the lee beam."

"How far?"

"Mile and a half, sir."

"Call all hands! Stand by to lower."

At Nathan's command, the ship shuddered to life. Men scrambled down the rigging and burst from the forecastle. While the mates shouted orders, the remainder of the crew raced toward the whaleboats, kicking off their shoes as they ran. Their bare feet thudded on the wood deck.

"There she breaches," the lookout called again.

In the commotion, Jael doubted whether anyone else had heard the lookout. She craned her neck just in time to see a huge beast leap straight up out of the water. She sucked in her breath. The whale seemed to hang suspended for a prolonged period of time, its ponderous bulk black and glistening against a rich blue canvas of sea and sky. It was a sight to behold, one she wouldn't quickly forget. Then the whale crashed back into the ocean with a splash that sent water shooting in every direction.

"Lower away!"

Amidst a whir of tackle, the first of three whaleboats was lowered from the davits, a sort of crane used shipboard. In preparation for this event, wooden tubs filled with hundreds of feet of line were placed aboard. Harpoons, lances, cutting spades, oars, rudder, and a mast as well as a few emergency provisions were already stowed in readiness for this moment.

His face animated, Nathan came to stand beside her. Green and gold lights flashed in his eyes. "It's a sperm whale. Biggest I've seen in a god's age."

Jael's brows drew together. "How can you tell? We're so far away."

"From the spout." Nathan's gaze darted about the deck, mentally accounting for each man's swift performance of duties. "The spouts of all whales are vertical, except for the sperm's. His inclines forward."

John joined them to better view the proceedings from Nathan's vantage point. His wiry frame nearly vibrated with excitement and energy. "Looks like a lone bull."

"If so, we're in for a battle."

A grin spread ear to ear across the first mate's face. "Nothin' I relish more than a good fight, be it on land or sea."

"So I can attest by the number of broken bones I've had to set," Nathan commented dryly. "I've patched you more times than the sails."

Jael glanced anxiously from one man to the other, but could detect no animosity between them, only a rare camaraderie that she envied.

"Can't think of a better way for a man to go than with both fists flying." John swung his leg over the side of the ship before the first of the whaleboats touched water. His eyes held a devilish twinkle. "What about a contest? First man to land a harpoon wins a kiss from the pretty lady."

Nathan lifted a brow askance and looked at Jael. She moistened her lower lip with the tip of her tongue, unconsciously relishing the taste of Nathan's mouth on hers, and nodded her assent. Nathan's eyes smoldered with unspoken promise. "Bet's on."

Jael watched as Nathan, with a confident grin, slid down the davit tackle and dropped catlike into the whaleboat. The rest of the men followed suit until a crew of six manned each of the three boats. Nathan, along with John and Swede, acted as headsman. Simon Pulver remained aboard to pilot the *Clotilde* with a skeleton crew. The headsmen stood on small platforms in the stern, handling the steering oar and commanding the craft while the others rowed. Only the headsmen faced forward, Jael noticed. All others kept their backs to the quarry.

"Give way, lads! Give way. Pull, I say!" Nathan shouted.

John shook his fist for emphasis. "Don't let those other boats beat you. Pull like the devil's chasin'."

"Earn your salt, men," Swede exhorted. "Put your backs into it."

The headsmen entreated their crews to greater speed. Their shouts echoed across the expanding stretch of water between the whaleboats and ship.

Eyes riveted on the enfolding drama, Jael watched and waited. Only the hump of the whale was now visible. A geyser ten or twelve feet high spouted from the whale. The whaleboats looked minuscule in the roiling sea. The whale, on the other hand, even though mostly submerged, looked enormous. Overcome with wild excitement, the men treated this as a sport—a game of sorts. John's tales sprang to mind, and she realized anew the danger involved.

A crewman wearing a tarred, flat-crowned hat and smoking a pipe sidled up next to Jael. He folded his arms on the rail and leaned forward. The expression on his thin face was avid as he followed the progress of the whaleboats. "Men call me Cooper 'cause that's my trade. Been so long since I heard it, I forgit my God-given name." He pointed his pipe stem in the direction of the boats. "Soon as one of 'em gets close enough, they hurl a harpoon."

True to Cooper's prediction, the harpooner who rode in the bow of the lead whaleboat stood, his weapon poised and ready. Just as he hurled the harpoon, a wave caught the little boat broadside, tossing it about like a piece of driftwood. Instead of biting deeply, the weapon glanced off its target. The botched attempt enraged the whale.

"Uh-oh." Cooper wagged his head. Worry furrowed his brow. "Now they're in for it."

"I don't see the whale. Where did it disappear to?"

Even as she voiced the question, the whale reemerged. Its massive head protruded out of the water. Jael watched in a mixture of fascination and horror as the creature slowly milled about the whaleboats, bobbing up and down until he made a complete circle.

"He's pitch poling," Cooper offered as he puffed on his pipe. "That's not what we call a favorable attitude."

"What is he going to do next?"

"You'll see."

They didn't have long to wait. Rolling over on its back, its head out of the water, the whale took aim on the offending craft. Men dove over the side, barely escaping with their lives. Lashing out with his lower jaw, the whale attacked the hapless boat, snapping it in half, then chewing it to splinters.

"He stove the Swede's boat, that he did."

Jael let out a shaky breath. The nearest whaleboat, headed by John, rowed toward the men thrashing about in the water.

"The sperm is a born fighter. Somethin' like McFee." Cooper chuckled at his own humor. "In combat, a whale generally directs his efforts against the boat that attacked him. McFee, on the other hand, will knock the stuffin' out of anythin' his arm can reach."

Reassured that Swede and his men were about to be rescued, Jael swung her attention back to Nathan. He was approaching the flukes of the whale from the right side.

"Harpooner! Stand by your iron!" His voice rang loud and true.

Jael tensed as she saw one of the crewmen stand in the bow, balance carefully, and aim his long harpoon. When the boat was but a few feet from the whale, the harpooner flung the harpoon. This time it penetrated deep into the whale.

"Give him a taste of iron!" Cooper urged.

Panicked and furious, the gallied whale ran across the surface of the water, ruthlessly towing the small craft in its wake at a high rate of speed.

"The captain's in for a Nantucket sleigh ride," Jael's self-appointed guide crowed with delight.

Finally, as the whale tired, the crew hauled in line, drawing the boat nearer with each mighty pull. Nathan, who had been steering the boat, now changed places with the harpooner in the bow. Raising a long lance, he stabbed deep, trying to reach a vital organ.

Maddened by pain, the dying whale thrashed in circles.

"It's doin' what we call a 'flurry.' Pretty soon it'll get tuckered out."

The whale swam furiously, around and around, in smaller and smaller circles, spouting dark blood with every breath. Then it beat the water with its tail, gave a tremendous shudder, turned over on its back, fin out, and died.

After a hole was made in the whale's head with a cutting spade and a line attached, the men rowed toward the *Clotilde*. The men in small boats, straining against the oars while they towed a gigantic corpse, made a strange funeral procession under the evening sky.

Upon reaching the ship, they dragged the carcass alongside and passed up the tow rope. The fluke chain jangled as it was positioned around the tail. Simon Pulver directed a team of men at the windlass, and the whale was soon made fast to the side of the ship.

Hungry and tired, the crew was greeted with the aroma of coffee as they clambered aboard. With renewed energy, they secured the whaleboats in place.

Nathan planted hands on his hips and gazed back at the horizon. The sun had hidden behind the clouds, and the final light of day was quickly waning. "The day is too short for the task ahead. We'll begin cutting-in at first light."

"Dinner, all hands!" Cook called from the galley. "Double rations tonight!"

Amid a clatter of pots and pans, the ravenous crew stampeded aft until only Jael, Nathan, and John were left standing on the deck. Butterflies fluttered in the pit of Jael's stomach as she remembered John and Nathan's parting wager. Did Nathan remember it as well? She couldn't blame him if he didn't. After all, he had had more pressing matters on his mind in the convening hours. Still she dared hope.

Finally there were no further tasks left to oversee. The crew was already partaking of the evening meal. John swaggered up to her with a grin, put his hand at her waist, and pulled her close, then lowered his head.

Jael froze, eyes wide. Had she been mistaken? Had John and not Nathan won the wager?

"Not so fast, you scoundrel." Nathan placed his hand on John's shoulder and turned him about. "The prize is mine."

"Can't blame a tar for tryin' to steal a kiss from a pretty gal, can you, Captain?" John gave Jael a rueful smile. "If I hadn't stopped to fish the Swede and his men out of the drink, I'd have won the prize hands down."

But Nathan wasn't listening. Wasn't waiting.

And neither was Jael.

Nathan's kiss was long and hard. Hungry. Equally ravenous, Jael melted against him. Her ardor matched his. When his mouth attempted to plunder hers, she willingly surrendered its honeyed bounty. She welcomed the invasion of his tongue, challenging it to a lover's duel.

"Guess I'll go below and get me some grub," John grumbled, then sauntered off.

At last, Nathan drew away with great reluctance. Drawing in a ragged breath, he sought to temper the wild craving that devastated resolution with hurricane force. His willpower eroded by the subtle fragrance of jasmine, he yielded to temptation for another sweet taste with a series of nibbling, teasing, playful kisses.

At last, he set her from him with a heavy sigh and rested his forehead against hers. "John will never know what he missed." He tried to keep his tone light, but there was nothing casual in the look he gave her.

"That greeting was reserved strictly for you."

He caught her chin between thumb and forefinger. "Your kisses are far more potent than Jamaican rum. One touch goes right to my head. Annihilates my judgment."

There was a trace of sadness in her smile. She was willing to give him much more than mere kisses. More than just her body. He could have her heart—her soul. It pained her to know that while she loved him without reservation, he didn't return her affection. *Never call it love,* he had told her. She would be wise to heed his warning.

"Come on, woman. Let's eat." Nathan draped an arm over her shoulder, and together they strolled toward the main cabin. Neither paid any attention to Simon Pulver, who stood at the wheel.

The third mate watched them walk away with ill-concealed interest. "Women on board bring nothin' but ill winds," he muttered. He already had some of the men convinced of this truth—and the voyage had just begun.

Later that evening, Nathan made entries in his journal while Jael prepared for bed. She waited until he replaced the pen in the inkwell, then scooted to the far side of the bed and patted the mattress. "Sleep here tonight, Nathan. You said yourself tomorrow will be a full day. You'll need more rest than the sofa can afford."

"The sofa suits me just fine."

Stung by his refusal, Jael battled a sudden rush of tears. Then resolutely she cleared her throat. "At least let me exchange places with you for the night."

"I'm accustomed to the constant roll of the ship. You're not." He blew out the lamp, and she heard him undress in the dark. "I don't want you suffering from mal de mer."

"Oh." So far she hadn't demonstrated any sign of seasickness, but neither had they encountered rough seas. His consideration helped defrost his cold refusal to share her bed. She placed her hands behind her head and stared up at the beams. "Nathan," she queried softly.

"Mm-hmm."

"Do you enjoy what you do for a living?"

"Whaling is the only way of life I've known since I hired on as cabin boy at the age of twelve."

"But do you enjoy it?" she persisted.

There was a long pause before he finally answered. "I used to."

"But not any more?"

"Occasionally I consider trying my hand at something else. Whaling no longer brings the satisfaction it once did. I've been at sea nearly twenty years. In that time, I've seen whales become increasingly scarce as whaling grounds are depleted. Now there's talk of a bomb–lance gun being developed. Who knows what will happen then. It could expedite killing off all the ones that are left."

In the course of that afternoon, she had been by turns fascinated, fearful, and finally repulsed by the process. By the end of the long day, she had even felt a strange sympathy for the whale. She had admired the valiant struggle it had waged before its capture. "They are certainly magnificent creatures."

"That they are, pagan flower. One can't help but respect their tenacity. Now," he said as he turned on his side, "enough chatter. You said yourself that there's a full day ahead."

It came as no surprise to Jael the next morning when she woke to discover Nathan already gone. He worked as hard or harder than the lowliest of his crew. Conversation with a variety of crewmen confirmed that this dedication had won him the respect of every man aboard. She ate a biscuit, washed it down with a cup of tea, then hurriedly dressed.

With the whale's huge carcass lashed alongside, the ship bumped and tossed awkwardly. The wind had picked up. Waves rolled and tossed beneath the ship, making the spars and beams creak in protest. The cutting-in, as it was called, was already in progress when she came up on deck.

Nathan, as well as John McFee and Swede Iverson, stood on a cutting stage, a long platform made of planks suspended over the carcass by means of ropes and tackle. The rough seas made it necessary to send a man overboard. Jael observed with interest as a harpooner, secured by a lifeline, descended onto the whale and began the slippery job of securing an immense iron hook into a hole cut between the eye and the flipper.

Scores of seabirds circled overhead. Rough seas continually broke over the carcass, often obscuring it. Sharks glided through the water as silent as shadows. Then they'd rush the dead whale, tear off a hunk of flesh, and glide away. She shivered, chilled in spite of the bright sunshine.

The harpooner groped for the hole made near the flipper as waves surged and broke. Twice the man was washed from his task. Only the rope around his waist saved him from being crushed between the side of the ship and the dead whale. Meanwhile, Nathan, John, and Swede, their backs braced against

Inside Paradise

the handrail, fended off sharks with cutting spades. Jael gripped the ship's rail so tightly her knuckles bleached white. Her mouth went dry.

Everyone seemed to be shouting at once and calling out advice.

The harpooner signaled that he was ready for a third try. Once again he started to ease the blubber hook into the hole. Suddenly the ship yawed; the tackle jerked and tightened. A hollow rending sound could be heard above the screeching of the seabirds. A blood-dripping semicircle of blubber lifted from the carcass and landed with a plop on the cutting stage. Caught by a violent swell, the ship heaved to the opposite side, lifting a third of the bulky carcass from the water as it did so.

Nathan grabbed wildly for the handrail on the staging. Borrowing tricks he had learned from Hawaiians who rode surfboards, he flexed his knees and struggled to maintain his balance.

John, too, lunged for the handrail. But before he could wrap his fingers around it, his bare foot encountered the greasy chunk of blubber on the staging. The blubber shot across the narrow planking, leaving behind a slippery track of oil and blood and water. He was unable to right himself. With a strangled cry, his arms pinwheeling in a frantic attempt to regain a foothold, he slid into the shark-infested waters.

Just as suddenly as it had yawed, the ship rolled back. The movement sent Jael sprawling on the deck. Her first thought—her only thought—was for Nathan's safety. Had he managed to stay on the narrow scaffolding?

She was afraid to look.

And afraid not to.

She clawed her way upright in time to see Nathan, his arm outstretched, grasping air. A stricken expression contorted his face, making him almost unrecognizable. Swede, his usually ruddy complexion a sickly green, clung to the handrail and stared downward. Fins knifed through the waters. An empty space gaped between the two men.

The space John had occupied only minutes ago.

John bobbed to the surface, arms flailing. Terror distorted his features into a gruesome mask. A red stain spread across the water like spilled wine as sleek, silvery sharks churned the water into froth. John screamed again as he was dragged beneath the surface.

"Jo-o-ohn!" Nathan's anguished cry echoed above the wind singing through the rigging and the slosh of waves against the hull.

A frenzy of flashing silver. A gnashing of teeth.

Then a deathly stillness.

Jael pressed her hand against her mouth. Bile burned her throat. An ever-widening stain spread outward like ripples in a pool. Gulls wheeled overhead, their hoarse cries adding to the stark sense of unreality.

Still no one uttered a sound. Shock and horror registered in varying degrees on the weathered faces of the crew. The blubber hook jerked high in the air, then fell against the deck with a loud clank.

The clatter roused Nathan out of his stupor. His expression dazed, he glanced about. With tremendous effort, he rallied every ounce of self-discipline. His jaw set with determination; his mouth hardened into a grim line. "All right, men," he barked. "We have a job to do. Look alive!"

Jael couldn't believe her ears. Nathan acted as though nothing out of the ordinary had transpired. As though he hadn't just witnessed the brutal death of his best friend. How could he be so callous? So uncaring?

She felt nauseated, light-headed, and gulped in air. She was afraid she was going to faint. On legs that felt rubbery, she made her way across the deck and down the companionway. She barely reached the cabin before she ran for the basin and lost the contents of her stomach.

Chapter 20

Jael felt as though she had stepped straight into the bowels of hell. Not even Grandfather's most vivid sermon about hell's horrors had prepared her for the scene that confronted her. Night had fallen since she had last appeared on deck. The ship now resembled some seagoing devil's floating kitchen. Sparks flew from the brick tryworks where fires burned beneath bubbling cauldrons. Long tongues of flame greedily licked the air above the funnels, the lurid glow reflected by the sails.

Black smoke rose taller than the masts. A dark cloud hovered above the entire ship, carrying with it the miasma of burning and boiling. Of blubber and oil and grease. Jael pressed her handkerchief against her nose and mouth to block out the ghastly stench.

"Bible leaves! Bible leaves!" shouted a man at the try-pots.

In the reddish glow, she recognized Cooper. His narrow face gleamed with sweat from the intense heat of the fire. She watched others lug blocks of blubber that had been cut so that only thin slices remained attached to a rind, the configuration resembling a book with pages spread. These so-called books were then speared into the try-pots. Several crewmen skimmed off hot oil, then dumped it into barrels.

Her eyes roamed the deck, trying to pick Nathan out from among the toiling figures that teemed about like a colony of ants. She gasped in shock when she spotted the whale's head lying on the deck. One whaleman, sunk to his shoulders in the tanklike cavity, bailed a pulpy, dripping substance from the case.

"Damnation, woman! What are you doing up here?"

Jael turned in the direction of Nathan's angry voice and watched him carefully wade across the slimy deck. She noted his feet were bare and his pant legs rolled to the knees to keep them from dragging in the ankle-deep slush that had formed from the combination of blood, raw blubber, and oil.

"What are you doing up here?"

"I . . . ah . . . needed to see you," she blurted. She desperately needed to see him, to be reassured of his safety. John's horrifying accident had left her deeply shaken. It had brought home the fact that life is fragile and must be carefully guarded. But most of all, it had made her realize how deeply she loved Nathan. The man glowering at her, however, was a far cry from the smiling rogue who had captured her heart.

"Can't you see I have work to do?"

"I realize you're busy." Her eyes smarted, but she didn't stop to question whether it was from the suffocating black smoke or from Nathan's harsh welcome.

Nathan impatiently shoved a lock of hair from his brow and in the process added another smudge of dirt to his face. "Make it quick."

Jael thirstily drank in the sight of him. His shirt, damp with perspiration, clung to him like a second skin. He was filthy dirty and smelled like oil, but to her he was infinitely precious. "Cook said you haven't stopped once since morning. Not even long enough for a bite to eat."

"In case you don't remember, we're a man short."

Jael winced at the cruel reminder. "How could I forget?" she asked in a choked voice.

Nathan knew she wanted to soothe his hurt, but he wasn't able to accept her sympathy. Not when guilt rode him hard. Instead he lashed out. "Take a good look around." He made a broad, sweeping gesture with his arm. "This is a scene straight from the pages of Dante's *Inferno*. You'll have quite a story to tell all the new friends you'll make once we dock. Is this what you came on deck to see?"

"I brought you some supper." She held out a sack of biscuits and salt beef.

She made him feel small. He snatched the sack from her hand. "All right, you've accomplished what you set out to do. Now go below."

She started to turn away, then hesitated. "Nathan..."

"Yes," he said tersely. "What now?"

"About John..." Her voice was tentative, but her eyes remained steadfast even though Nathan's expression grew formidable at the mention of his friend's name. "Don't blame yourself for what happened." Then, she turned and walked away.

Nathan watched her go. Foolish woman. Didn't she know John's death *was* his fault? He had stood by helplessly while his best friend was torn apart. He didn't want her sympathy. Didn't deserve it. His emotions were riotous; his body weighted with fatigue. He clamped his jaw to contain the raw hurt that threatened to overwhelm him.

Swede materialized out of the satanic night to stand beside him. "You all right, Captain?"

"Here, take this." He thrust the bag of food at him. "From now on you'll assume the duties of first mate."

Swede bobbed his head in acknowledgment. "I'll try not to disappoint you, sir."

Nathan rested his hand briefly on the man's shoulder. "You won't."

They worked all through the night and far into the morning. One watch replaced another. Twenty hours of backbreaking, spirit-bending toil. Nathan cut himself no slack. He worked harder and longer than any crewman. He was everywhere at once. He carried the larger horse pieces from the blubber room to the block to be minced into Bible leaves. At the tryworks, he pitched Bible leaves into the boiling pots. He fed the fires with cracklings, scraps of blubber that already had the oil boiled out, and hauled full barrels to the hold. No task was too demeaning. He was a man chased by his own personal demon.

At long last there was nothing more to do. Every last bit of blubber had been tried out, the oil cooled, poured into barrels, and stowed in the hold. The crew swarmed over the ship with buckets and brushes in a massive cleanup operation. They scrubbed, scraped, and polished until the *Clotilde* shone from their efforts. When the ship gleamed, they washed themselves and donned clean clothes. Once again a lookout was posted in the masthead. The entire process was ready to be repeated.

Nathan made a final tour around the deserted deck. Except for the lookout and Simon Pulver, half awake at the wheel, the crew was sound asleep in the forecastle. Assured every detail had been attended to, he retired to his cabin.

In the tiny washroom adjoining the stateroom, he stripped off his grimy shirt and stepped out of pants stiff with whale oil. He sudsed his hair, then washed every inch of his body until his skin tingled. Too tired to dress, he wrapped a strip of linen around his waist and knotted it. He nodded brusquely at Jael, who sat on the sofa mending one of his shirts.

Having driven himself to the point of exhaustion, he swayed on his feet as he crossed the cabin. His eyes burned like twin coals, and his head felt airy as a balloon. He had a vague memory of swallowing a mug of scalding coffee, but couldn't recall when he had last eaten. Or if he had eaten.

Concern mirrored in her blue-violet eyes, Jael put down her sewing and rose from the sofa. She steered him toward the large captain's bed, and he lacked the energy to protest. The sheets had already been turned down. The bed looked fresh, inviting.

"Get some rest." Jael urged him down on the mattress.

Nathan dropped down on the bed. He was fast asleep before she pulled the covers over his shoulders.

She stood for a long time gazing down at him. Her heart welling with such tenderness she feared it would burst with emotion. She brushed the damp hair from his brow, a luxury she couldn't afford earlier when he spurned her help. Dark circles of fatigue ringed his eyes. Bearded stubble covered his cheeks, in her mind making him look even more vulnerable. Even in repose, his face looked strained, burdened.

"Sleep well, my love," she whispered.

She kept vigil in the cabin. She didn't want him to face the day with no one to share the heavy load when he finally woke. Each time he stirred in his sleep, she hurried to his side. Once or twice he called out and she soothed him as a mother would a child suffering with a nightmare. Then, each time, he lapsed back into an uneasy slumber.

She picked up his shirt and resumed mending, but her mind wasn't on the torn seam. She desperately wanted to help Nathan, but didn't know how. Didn't even know if he would accept her offer or push it aside. What could she possibly say that would ease the pain of John's loss? The thread became as twisted as her thoughts until it was hopelessly tangled in knots.

"Hold on, John! Don't..."

Jael tossed her sewing aside and rushed to the bed where Nathan thrashed restlessly.

"Oh, God, please..." he whimpered in his sleep and flung his arm over his eyes. Hoarse, racking sobs broke from his lips while salty tears trickled from the corners of his eyes.

It was sheer torture watching him suffer. Jael felt as though she, too, were being ripped apart. She realized that only in sleep could Nathan release the grief he tried to deny in his waking hours. A sorrow so great it dogged his dreams and robbed his rest. Responding to instinct, knowing only she wanted to console, to make him forget, she removed the pins that held her hair in a neat coil. A shake of her head sent her hair tumbling to her waist. Undressing quickly so as not to lose her resolve, she slipped into bed next to him and took him in her arms.

"It's all right, love." She brushed a kiss across his brow.

"Why John? Why?" he asked, his voice raspy, tormented.

"Hush, my darling." She cradled his head against her breast as he wept. "Shh," she crooned. "I'll help you forget."

A spasm rippled through his lean frame. Then he wrapped his arms around her and held fast. She held him tenderly, whispering endearments and soothing words of consolation until the storm spent itself and he grew still. When she thought he was asleep, she started to ease from the bed, but his hold tightened. She sighed. A feeling of profound contentment settled over her. There was no place on earth she'd rather be than in the enchanted circle of his embrace. Being close to him was a precious gift. Heaven couldn't hold greater happiness.

Emboldened, she spread kisses, delicate as dewdrops, across his brow. Unable to resist, she brushed her mouth across his ever so lightly. A spark to tinder. Desire ignited at the mere touch. Jael found herself staring into hazel eyes. Fascinated, she watched green and gold lights kindle and flame. She smiled then, a smile as ancient as Eve. With feline grace, she teasingly rubbed her body against his. Soft, ivory curves challenged taut, bronzed flesh and hard muscle.

"Let me love you," she whispered. She took his head between her hands and kissed him. Lingeringly. Lovingly. Her cheek grazed his once, then again. The contrast between bristled and smooth further excited her. Her lips made a playful foray down his neck, caressing, nuzzling. She traced the rim of his ear with the tip of her tongue, then lightly nipped the base with her teeth, then soothed the hurt with her tongue.

"Ah, pagan flower," he rasped in a voice thickened by emotion, "you weave a powerful spell."

Jael's smile grew triumphant. She could feel his lean, muscular body thrum with awareness. And passion. The knowledge brought with it a primal surge of power. Dipping her head, she renewed her sensual assault. She combed her fingers through the thick mat of auburn curls covering his chest and stroked the flat buds of his nipples. Gratified when they hardened into tight pebbles, she tasted him as he had once tasted her, delicately at first, then greedily.

He jerked spasmodically in response and grabbed a fistful of her hair. "Work your magic," he entreated. "Make me forget."

Joyfully she accepted the challenge. She glanced upward and found his eyes closed. The lines of fatigue and despair that had etched his face earlier had been replaced with expectancy. Desire. The opportunity was golden. She didn't want to waste a moment of it. It was time to discover and explore, to learn the intimate secrets of his body.

Without further hesitation, she allowed her hand to stray lower, pausing when she encountered the knotted strip of linen slung around his narrow hips. Her fingers nimbly unfastened the knot at his waist and freed the ends. "You can't hide your treasure, love. I want all of you."

Nathan's manhood sprang free. She stroked him from tip to base then back again. His shaft was tempered steel sheathed in fine silk. His breathing quickened and he moaned with pleasure at her tentative touch. Jael summoned a boldness she hadn't known she possessed. With a touch as light as a butterfly's, she retraced its length with her fingertips, then with her tongue.

His body arched like a bowstring. "You set me on fire."

"Let's burn together."

Nathan rolled onto his back, taking her with him. Startled, Jael stared into smoldering hazel eyes. Before she could utter a sound, his mouth covered hers.

Flames of passion raged out of control, incinerating fear and pain, guilt and regret. At each touch, each kiss, they burned hotter, brighter. Nathan's hands traversed the curve of her hips and molded her buttocks. Her pelvis cradled his. She moved subtly and felt the hard bulge of his manhood clamor at the portal of her femininity.

She clutched at him. Her nails dug into his back and made slight crescents in his flesh. Then she shifted slightly, wrapping her legs around his waist and wordlessly inviting him to claim the prize.

To unite and become one.

To attain the ultimate solace. The ultimate bliss.

Nathan plunged into her, then retreated. She cried out, her nails digging deeper, her legs twined tighter. Locked together, she tilted her hips, begging him to take her with him on a soul-shattering excursion. He levered above her, a fierce, primitive smile curving his mouth, then with slow deliberation thrust into her again and again. Stretching. Filling. With erotic thoroughness, he stroked her hot, slick vault, driving her wild with wanting. She writhed, consumed by mindless need.

Spasms of exquisite pleasure racked her. He let her hover on the very brink of ecstasy, and then with a final thrust, sent her spiraling beyond. With a shudder of surrender, he plunged after her into an abyss of sublime rapture.

Jael floated back to earth on a cloud of contentment. "I love you, Nathan Thorne, and I always will."

But he didn't hear her declaration of devotion.

Spent, Nathan slept soundly. This time without reliving terror. Without dreaming.

The crew assembled at sunset to pay their final respects to John McFee. Few scars remained of the hellish scene of the previous night. If not for the greasy, sooty stains on the mast and sail, it would be easy to pretend it had never occurred. That and the fact that

John's easy grin and friendly manner were conspicuously absent.

Nathan, his face drawn and somber, stepped in front of the group and opened a worn Bible. He opened it to a passage in the New Testament and in a subdued tone quoted from Mark:

> *"No one knows, however, when the day or hour will come—neither the angels in heaven, nor the Son, only the Father knows."*

He closed the Bible and looked at each of his men in turn. "John McFee was snatched from us suddenly, without warning, and will be dearly missed. John lived life to its fullest without malice toward any. Though not a churchgoing man, he was a God-fearing man. A good man. And that's how he would want to be remembered. Now," he said, bowing his head, "if you'll join with me in the Lord's Prayer."

Jael repeated the childhood prayer along with the crew. She wondered if anyone else had seen how the muscles in Nathan's throat had worked as he fought for control. Or if anyone had heard the catch in his voice when he said John would be dearly missed. No one would mourn John's passing more than he. She ached for him.

"Cook will pour a hearty serving of grog with each man's supper. Raise your glasses in a toast to John's memory. Few enjoyed a good drink or a good fight more than he."

The men quickly disbanded.

Jael wasn't ready to join Nathan in the main cabin. Instead she took a turn around the deck, stopping at the rail to gaze out over the water. The sun painted the sky and water in shades of scarlet and vermilion. The wind had died off, and the sails rippled in the evening breeze. Peaceful. But the day before yesterday had been peaceful too—until a whale had been sighted.

A lump lodged in her throat. Nathan's assessment of his friend had been accurate. John was a good man. She only wished she could have gotten to know him better. Somehow she sensed they would have become friends. If only there had been more time....

First man to land a harpoon wins a kiss from the pretty lady.

Jael's eyes brimmed with tears as she recalled his cheeky wager. She pressed a kiss to her fingertips, then blew it out to sea. "This one's for you, John McFee."

"John would have liked that."

Startled, Jael swung around, blinking back tears.

"Here," Nathan said, handing her an object. "John had just finished it. Since he didn't give you a proper wedding gift, he wanted to give you this."

Through a sheen of tears, she could barely make out the whale's tooth that bore an intricate carving of the *Clotilde*. Her hand shook as she took it from him.

"He was keeping it for a surprise." Emotion

thickened Nathan's voice. "I found it when I went through his things."

She couldn't squeeze words past the constriction in her throat. She didn't know who made the first move, only that somehow she was in Nathan's arms. She wanted to be brave for his sake, yet now she was the one in need of comforting. Her tears dampened the front of his shirt, but he didn't seem to mind. Their hearts ached in unison for a fallen friend.

As the sun bled into the horizon, they drew comfort from each other.

Chapter 21

"Red sky at night, sailors' delight. Red sky at mornin', sailors take warnin'," Simon Pulver recited in sepulchral tones as he stirred another spoonful of sugar into his coffee. "Sky this mornin' was as red as John McFee's blood when the sharks ate 'im."

Jael set down her fork. Her stomach revolted at the graphic reminder.

Nathan slammed his cup on the table. "Enough, Pulver! I'll listen to no more talk of that sort. You're forgetting there's a lady present."

"Don't pay him no mind." Swede tried to ease the tension.

"True ever' time," Simon insisted, wolfing down the last of his breakfast. "Last time no one believed me either. Before the day ended, a storm blew up the likes of which I never hope to see again. Hurricane, the captain called it. Lucky we weren't all killed."

Jael sipped her tea, but left the rest of her meal untouched. The men finished eating in silence, then adjourned to their duties on deck.

The feeling of unease that started at breakfast followed Jael throughout the day. She was restless, edgy, ready to jump at shadows. She tried to read, but when that failed to distract her, she put the book aside and picked up her sewing. After she pricked her finger for the third time, she gave up on that, too. Trouble was brewing. She briskly rubbed her arms to erase the sudden chill.

Hoping fresh air might cure her doldrums, she donned her new straw bonnet and, after a final peek in the mirror, went off in search of Nathan. She instantly spotted his tall figure at the wheel. Not wanting to appear desperate for his company, she leisurely strolled around the deck. Cooper returned her greeting, but rebuffed her attempts to engage him in conversation, which she found a bit odd. Usually he loved to chat. The rest of the crew pointedly ignored her. This added to her feeling of isolation.

"Have I done something to offend the crew?" she asked as she came to stand at Nathan's elbow.

He kept his gaze trained on the horizon. "What do you mean?"

Jael shrugged, feeling a trifle foolish. "They suddenly seem..."—she groped for the correct term—"...unfriendly."

"Don't worry about it."

His brusque tone immediately put her on alert. "I wasn't worried. I merely sensed a difference in their attitude."

Nathan wasn't proving much more amiable than his crew. Ever since the brief memorial service for John two nights ago, he seemed to have constructed some invisible barrier between them. He was polite to a fault, but distant. She had hoped their mutual sorrow would narrow the breach between them, but it seemed wider than ever. He spent as little time as possible in the cabin and when he did, he was always bent over his journal.

Gamely she tried again to enlist his attention. "Pulver must have been wrong about the weather. There's hardly a cloud in the sky."

"Seamen are a superstitious lot." He consulted the compass, then corrected his course. "A calm sea and gentle wind can be deceptive."

Finally Jael gave up on her quest for companionship. Disheartened, she returned to the cabin, where she spent the remainder of the afternoon rearranging the contents of her sea chest. Her lower lip jutted in vexation. She had gone to extra trouble with her appearance, and Nathan hadn't even noticed she was wearing the saucy straw bonnet he had purchased for her.

The atmosphere hadn't improved by dinnertime. Nathan seemed tense, irritable, answering Swede's questions in monosyllables. Pulver's gaze kept shifting back and forth between the two of them, a gloating expression on his swarthy, pockmarked face. Jael maintained a watchful silence. The ship pitched suddenly, sending **everyone** reaching to steady their mugs of coffee.

"What'd I tell you," Pulver smirked.

Swede watched the oil lamp sway. "She's going to air up, all right."

Nathan shot his mates a black look, and they subsided.

As soon as Nathan signaled the meal was over, the mates took their leave. "I'll check the hatches, sir," Swede volunteered as he left.

Nathan turned to Jael, who was still seated. "If you'll excuse me, I have duties to oversee."

"Of course," Jael returned, equally as formal.

Confused and saddened by his aloofness, she stayed at the table for a long time after they had left. Was Nathan grieving for John? Or was there another reason for his behavior? Considering how much he hated marriage, was he angry that they had made love? That idea was particularly painful.

The solitude of the cabin loomed before her. She found the prospect daunting. Deciding to postpone the inevitable, she ventured on deck. She paused at the top of the companionway and looked up at the sky. The darkness was absolute. Not a single star was visible. Boiling black clouds filtered out even the faintest glimmer of moonlight. Slowly she made her way toward the bow, where Nathan and Swede conferred by lantern light.

A gust of wind caught a sail and snapped it loudly. The ship heeled, and the deck slanted beneath her feet. Nathan barked orders and men scaled the rigging and began to trim the sails. Jael concluded she had seen enough and beat a hasty retreat to the relative calm of the cabin.

The full fury of the storm struck at midnight. In one practiced motion, Nathan tossed his blanket aside and shoved into his boots. Jael, awakened by the heaving ship, braced herself on one elbow. "Is this a hurricane?"

"Probably just a gale, but these things can take a day or two to blow themselves out." He reached for his jacket. "Stay in the cabin. Whatever you do, don't go up on deck. I'll have the steward bring your meals."

Then he was gone.

The *Clotilde* bucked and tossed. Wind whistled through the rigging; timbers creaked and groaned. The valiant little bark seemed to climb heavenward, its bow pointed at an impossible angle, then plunge into a steep trough with gleeful vengeance. Jael huddled under the quilts against the dampness that stole around the caulking, grateful for the captain's bed, which minimized the movement.

Day and night became one and the same. Nathan returned to the cabin only long enough to change his sodden clothing and to snatch an hour or two of rest. Jael worried ceaselessly. He looked gaunt, haggard.

Just when she thought it impossible, the wind grew even more demonic until it sounded like a hundred witches howling. She listened fearfully and wondered if the noise would ever abate. She dozed fitfully, but woke with a start when Nathan returned. He fell fully dressed on the sofa and was immediately asleep. Jael carefully made her way across the cabin and spread a quilt over him, then returned to her own bed. She was almost asleep again when a mighty crash vibrated through every beam of the ship.

The *Clotilde* trembled from the brutal blow.

Jael bolted upright and clutched the bedclothes. "Are we going to sink?" Wide-eyed, she watched and waited, expecting to find water seeping through the floorboards.

Before Nathan could answer, a crewman banged on the cabin door. "Sir, wake up. A mast split and a greenhand fell from the rigging. He's hurt bad—real bad."

Nathan snatched the surgeon's kit from its storage place beneath the sofa.

"Let me help . . ." Jael was already on her feet.

"No!" Nathan said curtly. "Stay here. This is my job."

Dejected by his refusal of her assistance, Jael bundled a quilt around her shoulders and waited in the dark for his return. At first she failed to notice that the howling wind had diminished to a persistent whine. The ship no longer bucked and rolled in the rough sea. Pearly gray light was visible through the porthole. The storm had subsided.

Two hours later, Nathan eased open the cabin door, but he needn't have bothered to be quiet. He found Jael wide awake, waiting and full of questions. Knowing his wife, this didn't come as a surprise. She had proven herself a full partner above and beyond his expectations.

"The greenhand. Is he . . . ?"

"He's alive." He shrugged out of his jacket and slipped off his boots. "Whether or not Martin Kellogg ever walks again without a crutch is another matter. Only his Maker knows the answer."

She digested this information for a long moment before asking, "What about the mast? How serious is the damage?"

Nathan sank down on the sofa and with a heavy sigh ran his fingers through his already disheveled hair. "Serious enough that we have to return to Lahaina for repairs. If that isn't bad enough, most of the deck gear was washed away and has to be replaced."

"I'm sorry, Nathan. I truly am."

He managed a rueful smile. "Maybe Pulver was right all along. Perhaps this voyage was doomed from the beginning."

She looked at him, aghast. "Surely you don't believe that nonsense."

"Think about it." Nathan lay on his back and stared balefully at the beams above his head. "We lost a whaleboat at our very first sighting. Next came John's . . . accident. Now the storm. Not only is the ship damaged, but a crewman is seriously injured."

He didn't reveal to her the rumblings he'd overheard from the crew. Many of the men, it seemed, put a great deal of credence into Pulver's dire predictions. Pulver was fast convincing them that a woman on board was bad luck. Nathan knew he'd have to keep a tight rein on his men in the long days ahead. With the *Clotilde* crippled, progress would be slow.

Wearily he scrubbed a hand over his jaw. He still didn't understand how the equipment could have been lost. He had personally checked to see that it was properly secured. And why had a greenhand been sent into the rigging during a raging storm?

The *Clotilde* hobbled toward Lahaina under shortened sail.

Jael sensed the hostility the instant she stepped foot on deck. Instead of friendly smiles—or polite nods—crew members quickly averted their gazes. Whenever she passed a small group, they whispered among themselves. Nathan, too, she observed, received different treatment than previously. Their expressions sullen, men reacted sluggishly to his commands. A few pretended they hadn't heard his orders until he was forced to repeat them.

Nathan joined Jael at the rail after she had completed her stroll. She noticed with alarm that he wore a pistol strapped to his waist. Swede sauntered up to them, his usual smile absent. "I don't like the feel of things."

"Neither do I," Nathan replied with a frown. "Keep your ears open. Let me know what you find out."

"Sure thing, Captain."

Nathan and Jael watched Swede cross the

deck to where two crewmen were greasing the spars and heard him offer the pair a bit of advice. The men looked to Pulver first for direction. At the mate's nod, they reluctantly did as Swede suggested.

Nathan lowered his voice so it wouldn't carry. "I don't want you up on deck unless I'm with you."

"But why, Nathan? What's going on?" She looked pointedly at the gun in his belt. "And why have you started carrying a weapon?"

His hand lightly rested on the butt of the Colt revolver. "It's just a precaution."

"A precaution against what?"

Nathan leaned against the rail and, feigning an interest in a dolphin diving in the ship's wake, didn't answer her question. Simon Pulver swaggered up to them, wearing an insolent smirk. Nathan turned his head and regarded him coldly. "What's on your mind, Pulver?"

He hitched up his pants and aimed a stream of tobacco juice over the rail. "Well, Captain, me and the crew's been talkin' things over."

"Out with it, man! Don't beat around the bush."

A wily smile curled Pulver's thin mouth. "Me and the men don't think it's necessary to return to Lahaina. We can manage fine just the way we are."

"Is that right?" Nathan's tone was as chill as Arctic ice.

Tense, Jael wrapped her hands around the rail. Animosity arced like lightning between the captain and his mate. Pulver obviously enjoyed provoking Nathan's temper. She cast a swift glance around. The crew had ceased their tasks and avidly watched the confrontation between captain and mate.

Pulver rocked back on his heels. "Can't fill barrels with oil if we're sitting at anchor."

"Listen up and listen good." Nathan ignored Pulver and addressed the crew.

As the men gathered around them in a loose semicircle, Jael didn't read any encouragement in the weather-beaten faces. Their expressions were guarded, wary.

"I sympathize with your concern. The *Clotilde*'s been out for two and a half years. It's understandable that you're anxious to return to your families." Nathan looked at each man in turn. His voice hardened with authority. "But that's the way it is with whaling. You knew that when you hired aboard."

The whalemen shuffled their feet; many refused to meet his look.

"We can't fill the hold with oil if we can't maneuver," Nathan continued. "Unless the mast is repaired and the gear replaced, our efforts will be severely hampered and will take twice the time."

"And what then, Captain?" Pulver snarled. "When we sail again will this still be a hen frigate? Ain't we had enough bad luck?"

Nathan's jaw worked as he struggled to control his anger. "You're stepping beyond your bounds, Pulver. You're forgetting *I'm* captain of this ship."

"I'd make a better one."

A collective gasp went up at his bold statement.

Nathan kept his voice level. "What you're suggesting sounds very much like mutiny."

Mutiny? Nerves tied Jael's stomach in a knot at the mere mention of the word. It was a serious charge with dire consequences. Governments and shipowners saw to it that mutineers were hunted down and prosecuted. The penalty was usually death. If the crew did revolt, Nathan and Swede were only two against many. She slid a glance in their direction. But if Nathan shared her fears, he kept it well hidden.

"You'd like to be captain, wouldn't you, Pulver?"

"Damn right I would. I'm sick and tired of bein' passed over by pretty boys like you. Heard the only reason you got this ship was because you banged the shipowner's daughter. I served my time. I deserve my own command."

"You deserve nothing."

"You shoulda made me first mate, not that dumb Swede."

A murmur passed through the onlookers. Men grew increasingly uneasy. It was one thing to complain about a woman on board—another to talk mutiny.

"There's something else we need to settle." Nathan stepped closer so that he stood toe-to-toe with Pulver. "I was going to conduct this conversation in private, but you seem to enjoy being the center of attention."

"I ain't afraid of nothin' you have to say." Pulver assumed a belligerent stance.

"Just before the storm struck, I personally checked to see that everything was tied down. Not long afterward, it was washed overboard."

"What are you implyin'?"

Nathan shrugged, the gesture casual, his eyes hard, speculative. "I find that a bit strange, don't you?"

"Lotsa things are strange," Pulver fired back.

"I can't help but wonder if *someone* deliberately sabotaged the gear for the sole purpose of creating trouble."

"You accusin' me?"

"Simply making an observation, Pulver. Why are you getting so hot under the collar?"

"Don't like you pointin' a finger at me when losing the gear was yer own doin'. If you weren't so busy sniffin' after your wife's skirts, you'd be takin' care of business like you oughta."

The assembled crew nodded and mumbled their agreement.

Encouraged, Pulver stabbed Nathan's breastbone with a grubby finger. "This ship deserves a real captain. Not one who's gotten lazy and careless. You coulda gotten us all killed."

Jael swallowed nervously as the crew drew around them in a tight knot.

Nathan's hand rested lightly on the butt of his gun. "I wanted to find out why the gear came loose so I did some investigating. Want to know what I found out?"

"Don't know about Pulver," Swede spoke out before the third mate could reply, "but I sure as hell would like to know."

"I found the lines slashed clean through just as though someone had taken a sharp blade to them."

"You can't prove nothin'," Pulver sneered.

"There was a witness."

The terse statement dropped like a stone into a still pond. Surprise and disbelief rippled through the spectators as one and all turned to discover the owner of the bold proclamation.

A slender young man, his expression resolute, stood supported by makeshift crutches at the top of a companionway leading from sick bay.

"Liar!" Pulver yelled, his face purple with rage. "The night was dark as pitch."

Martin Kellogg hobbled across the deck. "Not so dark I couldn't recognize you by the plaid jacket you always wear. I didn't realize what you were up to at first. Wasn't until this morning after Cooper happened to mention half the gear had been washed overboard by the storm that I pieced it all together."

"Tell me what you saw," Nathan ordered, his voice terse.

"While I was on watch, I saw you come by to make sure everything was tied down. Soon as you went below deck, Pulver came along. At the time I thought he was just double-checking the lines. When he saw me watching, he shoved something into his jacket." He adjusted the crutches to a more comfortable position. "Looked like a pocketknife."

"Who do you believe? Him or me?" Pulver looked around frantically, seeking support from his shipmates. But the crew seemed unable to meet his direct gaze.

Nathan gazed at his third mate with loathing. "You've been trouble on every ship you signed on, Pulver. You begged me to give you another chance, but I'm sorry I listened."

"Why, you bastard!" Pulver lunged forward and plowed his fist into Nathan's jaw.

Caught unaware, Nathan reeled from the blow, then recovered. Jael couldn't believe her eyes when, instead of drawing his pistol, he calmly unbuckled his holster and handed the gun to Swede, who had edged closer.

"There," he said. "Now no one can say this wasn't a fair fight."

Pulver outweighed Nathan by a good thirty pounds, yet no one appeared inclined to intervene. *John McFee wouldn't have let Nathan face the brute alone.* The thought flitted through Jael's mind. *He would have stood by with fists ready.* Pulver came at Nathan again, but this time he was prepared. He feinted to one side and the blow glanced off his shoulder. Pulver cursed soundly.

The two men circled each other. Pulver lashed out, but Nathan, as agile as a cat, danced out of range. Before Pulver could counter the attack, Nathan landed a powerful jab with his left fist. While Pulver was momentarily dazed from the blow, Nathan nailed him on the chin with a right hook. Pulver went down like a felled oak.

Nathan stood over him, fury emanating in hot waves. Blood trickled from the corner of his mouth. "Seize him and haul him to the rigging."

Swede stepped forward and grabbed Pulver's right arm. Cooper latched onto the left. As Nathan rolled up his shirtsleeves, an ominous pall fell over the men.

Someone handed Nathan a length of tarred rope knotted at one end.

With dawning horror, Jael realized what was about to happen. "No, Nathan. You mustn't," she pleaded, tugging on his arm. "Such treatment is inhumane."

Nathan's mouth firmed into a hard line. "Ned," he said, addressing one of the crewmen. "Please escort Mrs. Thorne below deck. See to it that she stays there."

"Yes, sir!" The young man caught Jael's arm and hustled her toward the companionway. She tried to pull free, but to no avail. She cast one final look over her shoulder before she disappeared down the stairs. And instantly regretted doing so.

Nathan leaned his weight behind the cat-o'-nine-tails and landed the first blow across Pulver's bare shoulders. She heard Pulver's hiss of pain through clenched teeth.

She didn't wait for more.

Chapter 22

Nathan checked the compass and made a correction in their course, then pulled up the collar of his jacket against the chill. The night was cool, but not as cool as the atmosphere in the cabin was sure to be. He dreaded facing Jael. Dreaded seeing the censure in her eyes. All her illusions about him had been shattered. How could he make her understand that he was only performing his job? And protecting her safety?

If he hadn't dealt with Pulver harshly, he would have lost the respect of his crew—and control of his ship. He had intercepted the looks a few of the more unsavory crew members cast in Jael's direction. It made his skin crawl to imagine what might have happened if they had overrun the ship. In all likelihood, he would have been killed and Jael left to their mercy. Once a mutiny occurred, the perpetrators were doomed outcasts. Criminals. They had absolutely nothing to lose. A woman's honor would hold little value. He had been forced to quell the uprising before it became full-blown.

His thoughts turned to Pulver. The use of the cat sickened him. Nathan tightened his grip on the wheel reflexively. The mere idea of flaying a man's back raw and bloody was barbaric. Repugnant. Only on rare occasions had he had to resort to a whip. While the thought of wielding it didn't please him, the thought of what might have resulted if he didn't pleased him even less.

"I'll take over the watch, Captain," Swede offered, tugging on a thick pair of gloves.

Nathan reluctantly relinquished the wheel to his first mate. "See that we don't veer off course. I'm anxious to return to Lahaina as quickly as possible."

"You can count on me, sir."

Before turning in for the night, Nathan went below decks to check to see how well Martin Kellogg was faring. He found the young man resting comfortably in his bunk, his injured leg propped on pillows.

"No sign of infection," Nathan announced after inspecting the young man's limb.

"That sure is good news." The youth's smile quickly faded. "Sure glad that business with Pulver is settled. He's a mean one. He's been tryin' to rile the crew ever since we pulled anchor."

"Well, you can rest easy. Simon Pulver won't be causing any more trouble for the remainder of the voyage. Now get some rest so you can try out those crutches again tomorrow."

Nathan's next stop was to look in on Pulver. His former third mate lay stretched on a cot in a locked storage room, snoring softly. Nathan nodded approval at the half-filled cup of rum sitting on a crate next to him. He had instructed Cook to see that Pulver got a heavy draught to ease the pain. He grimly stared at the fretwork of welts. As the ship's doctor, the task of applying a medicinal balm to the bloody welts had fallen to him. Already some of the redness was beginning to fade. He closed the door and relocked it, sincerely hoping he'd never again have to lay his weight behind a whip. Once they reached port, he planned to release the recalcitrant mate rather than turn him over to the authorities. The man had already been severely punished. Hopefully he had learned his lesson.

Wearily Nathan trudged up the steps and across the stern. He dug his hands deep into his pockets, his shoulders hunched against the wind. God, but he was tired of seafaring life. It no longer held the magic. No longer exerted its power over him. Somewhere along the way, the excitement and exhilaration had vanished. For years he had enjoyed pitting his wit and brawn against the huge beasts that roamed the seas. But no longer. He didn't want his life to end the way John's had. With no family and few friends. He was greedy. He wanted more.

Mentally girding himself for the battle he

faced, Nathan took a deep breath, then entered his quarters. He found Jael sitting stiffly on the edge of the bed, her expression stony. "You must think me an animal."

"How could you?" she choked.

"I had no choice," he replied, his tone neutral.

"No choice?" Her voice rose shrilly. "No choice but to strip the flesh from a man's back?"

"I don't expect you to understand."

"You're right." She shuddered. "I'll never understand how one human being can inflict so much pain and cruelty on another. *Never!*"

Nathan took in her ghostly pallor, her clammy skin, then crossed the cabin and dampened a cloth with cool water. Kneeling in front of her, he gently bathed her brow. "There," he said. "Are you feeling better now?"

She hugged her arms around her midriff for warmth. "No."

Nathan sighed inwardly. Her feelings for him had altered drastically. The trust that had slowly flourished between them had been destroyed. Nathan felt the fragile hope that he had nourished wither and die. Hope that her feelings for him would be resilient enough to withstand even this obstacle.

"I never suspected you capable of such brutality." Jael rose from the bed, and walking as far from him as the cabin permitted, presented her back to him.

He went to her and gently placed his hands on her shoulders. "Jael . . ."

She shook off his touch. "Please, don't."

"At least hear me out." He let his hands drop to his sides. There was too much at stake not to try again to make her understand. "The crew was on the verge of mutiny. I did what I had to in order to protect my ship, my command. Pulver left me no choice."

"I realized this afternoon that I don't know you at all. You're not the man I thought you were."

Her words bounced hollowly off the cabin walls. Nathan's heart felt equally as hollow. Until this very moment, he hadn't realized just how important it was that she understand. Understand and accept. But he couldn't fault her reaction. What gentle, sheltered woman could witness such an abomination and remain unmoved? Even seasoned sailors cringed when the cat whistled through the air.

He shoved both hands through his hair and, charged with a restless energy, paced back and forth like a caged animal before coming to an abrupt stop in front of her. "Dammit, Jael!" He grasped her shoulders and forced her to look at him. "I'm a ship's captain. I was only performing the duties expected of someone in my position. Not because I derived any pleasure from whipping a defenseless man, but because I had to. I have an obligation to the ship's owner, to the rest of my crew, to assure them a safe passage. Mutinies are violent, bloody revolts against authority. Men—even rational men—tend to commit savage acts. I had to protect you." He gave her a small shake. "Protect us."

His passionate appeal to logic slowly penetrated the thick barrier of resistance she had erected against him. She blinked up at him. He hadn't flogged Pulver out of malice. Hadn't raised the cat-o'-nine-tails in anger. Duty, not rage, had prompted the whipping. She moistened dry lips and tried to explain. "The whole time all I could think of was Grandfather hitting me with his cane—over and over again."

"Oh, my sweet little Jasmine," he groaned and pulled her against his chest.

She slipped her arms around his waist and leaned against him. "I always felt so . . . helpless. There was nothing I could say, nothing I could do, to make him stop."

He smoothed her tangled hair, then pressed a kiss into the bright tresses. "You have me now. I swear, as long as I'm alive, I'll never let anyone hurt you ever again."

Jael listened to the steady thud of his heart. She realized that in spite of his tender declaration, he didn't want to be wed and would soon leave her. Losing him, she knew, would be far more painful than any beating she had ever endured.

There was a subtle difference in Lahaina. Jael sensed it immediately upon stepping foot on solid ground. A certain tension. A strained look on usually happy faces. Thomas Hadley ended the mystery when they stopped at his home to inform him of their return to the island. The kindly minister seemed to have aged in the short time they had been away. His face appeared more deeply lined, the twinkle in his eyes had dulled.

"Smallpox," Thomas replied in answer to Jael's question.

"When?" Nathan asked.

"How did this happen?" Jael voiced her question simultaneously.

"A passenger arrived on the *Charles Mallory* in February who was riddled with the disease. While the doctors bickered among themselves about vaccination versus inoculation, the disease spread."

"It's feared the disease will ravage the islands." Alice Hadley poured tea into china cups.

Nathan added a spoonful of sugar to his tea. "How bad is it?"

"Very bad and getting worse with each passing day."

Alice nodded sagely. "Doctors predict the worst is yet to come."

"Weren't precautions taken?" Jael looked to Thomas for an answer.

"Of course, my dear." Thomas removed his glasses and pinched the bridge of his nose. "Three commissioners of health were appointed to effect measures designed to prevent the spread of the pestilence, but, unfortunately, they weren't successful. Now, months later, the disease is reaching epidemic proportions. The brunt of the scourge is striking Oahu even as we speak."

"So far only a handful of cases have been reported on Maui." Alice helped herself to a small iced cake. "My heart goes out to the Hawaiian people. They appear the most vulnerable."

"Corinne sailed on a packet bound for Boston last week. Alice is understandably relieved that our daughter is out of danger." Thomas gave his wife an indulgent smile. "Corinne never had the disease, but I insisted that she be vaccinated. Speaking of which, Jael, do you need to be vaccinated?"

"It won't be necessary." Jael sipped her tea, which had grown cold. "I had a mild case of smallpox when I was a small child before I came to live with my grandparents. Fortunately I wasn't scarred."

"Really!" Thomas replaced his spectacles and looked at her with renewed interest. "I don't suppose you'd consider joining a group we've been recruiting to send to Honolulu to nurse the sick."

"No!" Nathan's reply came swift and emphatic. He surged to his feet and paced the length of the parlor. "How can you even suggest such a thing, Thomas?"

"Help is desperately needed, Nathan," Thomas remonstrated. "This is a crisis. We all need to do what we can to be of assistance."

"I refuse to allow my wife to put her life in jeopardy." The notion of Jael in the midst of a raging smallpox epidemic was untenable.

INSIDE PARADISE

If anything should happen...

If he should lose her...

He couldn't bear to consider the possibility. Gradually he became aware that the others were watching him curiously. Well, let them. He didn't give a tinker's damn. "I can't imagine why you would even mention this preposterous idea, Thomas," he said, still incensed by the clergyman's suggestion.

Thomas raised an eyebrow, mildly amused by Nathan's vehemence. "If Jael had smallpox as a child as she claims, then she's immune to the disease."

Jael set her cup down and pushed it aside. "Nathan, I'd like to be of help...."

"Absolutely not!" Nathan wheeled on her. "I will not permit my wife to subject herself to pestilence. I expressly forbid it!"

Jael lapsed into silence.

Alice tactfully changed the subject. "The cottage is still yours to use for as long as you like. I'm sure Mahie and Inaika will be happy to perform any services you require. They seem quite fond of you."

A short time later, Jael and Nathan took their leave. Thomas helped load their belongings into the back of a borrowed wagon and waved them off.

Jael cast a sidelong glance at Nathan, who sat tight-lipped on the seat next to her. She waited until they were nearly home before broaching the subject again. "Nathan, I'm sure I'd be in no danger in Honolulu. Besides, it would make me feel useful while you're seeing to repairs on the *Clotilde*."

"Don't even think about it." He speared her a look that made her lapse into silence. "I don't want to hear another word on the subject."

Afraid she had already pushed too hard, Jael pretended an interest in the passing scenery.

They spoke little the remainder of the afternoon. After dinner, Nathan made entries in his journal while Jael hemmed a dress. Finally it was time to retire for the night.

Nathan replaced the pen in the inkwell and closed the journal. He cleared his throat to gain Jael's attention. "As soon the mast is repaired and the gear replaced, we'll set off again."

Jael neatly folded the garment she had been working on and replaced it in the basket. "How long do you think that will take?"

"A few weeks perhaps. A month at the most."

"Well, ah, good night then." Feeling awkward and at a loss for words, she rose from the settee and started toward her bedroom.

"Jael." Nathan's voice stopped her. "This doesn't change anything. It's only a temporary delay. You'll get your divorce—and your freedom—as quickly as I can arrange it."

She couldn't push a reply past the knot in her throat. After a quick nod of agreement, she forced herself to walk at a sedate pace to the bedroom. Once inside, she leaned against the door and closed her eyes. Tears squeezed from beneath their lids to trickle down her cheeks. Nathan apparently was as determined as ever to regain his independence. To legally sever their relationship. Why didn't she feel the same single-minded determination? The same urgency?

Instead the thought of divorce filled her with a sadness bordering on despair. She didn't want to be free of Nathan. She wanted to be a part of his life, and he a part of hers.

Chapter 23

"**M**issus, Captain said you stay home," Mahie scolded. "He said you not go away. He not want you get sick."

Jael folded one of her dark, serviceable dresses and stuffed it into a valise. She was glad she had saved them. They would serve her in good stead in Honolulu. "I have to do what I can to help those stricken with the disease."

"Captain be plenty mad." Mahie wrung her hands in distress.

"The captain is spending the week aboard his ship supervising the repairs. He won't even realize that I've gone."

"But, missus, what you want I tell him?"

Jael looked up from her packing and frowned. The young woman was clearly distraught at the prospect of having to inform Nathan of her departure. "Just tell him the truth, Mahie," she sighed. "Tell him the epidemic has worsened, and I wanted to help."

"He be plenty mad," Mahie repeated, then

her expression brightened. "I ask Inaika to tell Captain."

"You're a coward, Mahie." Jael laughed at the girl's ploy.

Mahie nodded her head vigorously. "Yes, missus, Mahie big coward."

"Be sure the captain knows that I'll be back long before he's ready to set sail." Jael snapped the valise shut with finality.

Mahie followed her out of the cottage, clucking after her like a mother hen. "You be very careful, missus, you not get sick. Reverend Hadley say smallpox very bad. Many die."

Jael gave her friend a quick hug. "Don't worry, Mahie. Smallpox won't hurt me. I'll be safe."

Inaika was waiting for them outside. He tossed her valise into the wagon that Thomas had provided and helped her climb into the seat. He climbed in after her and, with a snap of the reins, the conveyance rolled down the sandy lane. Jael settled back and stared ahead without seeing.

Nathan would be livid when he learned she had disobeyed him. In the past she had tested his temper in small ways, and he had passed with high marks each time. But the tests were never of this magnitude. He had expressly forbidden her to go to Honolulu, yet she was openly defying his order. Would she regret her decision? Somehow she didn't think so.

Not even Reverend Hadley's dire predictions had prepared Jael for the chaos that greeted her in Honolulu. Cases mounted into the thousands and the death rate was high. Yellow covered wagons creaked through the city's streets, gathering their dreadful burden of bodies. Gray smoke constantly hovered over the city as infected houses were burned by the order of the health commissioners. She had been assigned to one of the crude hospitals that had been established in an attempt to isolate and care for the unfortunates. Rows of cots filled with people in various stages of the disease lined the makeshift hospital.

The sun beat down mercilessly, the heat adding to the patients' misery. A peculiar, sickening odor specific to smallpox victims pervaded the air. Jael's shoulders slumped wearily as she dipped a cloth into a basin and sponged the feverish brow of a boy she guessed to be about nine or ten. He tossed restlessly in the throes of delirium. She inspected his body for the first telltale sign of a rash that would herald the next phase of the illness, but so far his skin was unblemished. She moved on to tend the young woman in the next cot. Her body was hideously swollen and covered with purulent blisters. Jael raised the woman's head and pressed a cup to her lips. Unable to swallow because of the sores in her throat, the water dribbled down her chin. Experience told Jael that this woman would be dead before morning.

She sighed. How long could this horrible plague continue? How many more lives would it claim?

Mary Cummings, eldest daughter of Elijah Cummings, a friend of Thomas Hadley's who had a small mission near Twin Falls, came over and laid a sympathetic hand on Jael's shoulder. "You look as though you're ready to collapse. Why not go and have a bite to eat or a drink of juice?"

Jael summoned a wan smile. She admired Mary's even-tempered, no-nonsense attitude. It was a pity the disease that she had contracted when only a toddler had left her blind in one eye. "No thanks, I'm fine."

"Go now," Mary insisted. "If there's any change in your patients' condition, I'll call you."

Jael straightened her sagging shoulders and tiredly left the crude building. She walked a short distance and sank down on a bench under a spreading banyan tree. Eyes closed, she leaned against the trunk. Since she and the small band of missionaries landed in Oahu last week, she had gotten little rest. Her thoughts drifted to Nathan as they always did when she had a free moment. She wondered what he was doing at that very moment. Had he discovered yet that she was gone? If so, was he angry? She fervently hoped that he hadn't taken his anger out on Mahie.

"Mrs. Thorne! So it is you!" Jael's eyes flew open at the familiar voice. She found herself staring into the face of none other than Simon Pulver.

"Didn't think there could be too many women with your hair color."

"Mr. Pulver," she gasped. "What brings you here?"

"Government's gone and recruited me."

Jael saw the yellow wagon behind him and began to understand. She had heard rumors that prisoners had been enlisted to transport the stricken to hospitals and to bury the dead.

Pulver's next words confirmed her assumption. "They came into the jail askin' if any of the prisoners had had the pox. Ain't much," he shrugged, "but it beats goin' stir crazy starin' at the walls."

"Then my husband did turn you over to the authorities?"

"Naw, Captain set me loose the minute we landed. Got a soft streak, I guess." He took off his cap and wiped his brow with his shirtsleeve. "Thought I'd try my luck in Honolulu, thought maybe a change of scenery would do me good. Got in a brawl my first night here and got tossed in the brig."

"It's time I get back to my patients." Jael rose to her feet. "Good luck, Mr. Pulver."

"Good luck to you, too, Mrs. Thorne." He jammed his hat on and shuffled off.

As she went about her duties, her mind kept returning to the chance meeting with Simon Pulver. The man seemed to bear Nathan no ill will; he seemed respectful even. Undoubtedly he understood and accepted the code espoused by seafaring men. She felt deeply ashamed for ever believing Nathan could inflict such cruel punishment unless absolutely warranted.

The young woman died before sundown, and her body was taken away. An old man, his skin sloughing off, took her place, and then he, too, died. Disheartened, Jael turned her attention to the boy. A rash had appeared and spread from his face to his arms, chest, and back.

"Be strong," she pleaded as she spooned water down his throat. "I survived and so can you."

"Jael?" Mary Cummings tapped her shoulder. "There's someone here to see you. He's waiting outside."

Jael left the boy in Mary's capable hands and hurried out of the hospital. Expecting to see Simon Pulver, she was stunned to find Nathan instead. "Nathan..."

He turned at the sound of her voice. She took an eager step forward, then froze. Fury emanated from him like heat waves. "How dare you come here when I specifically forbade you to?"

"Nathan, I'm not in any danger." She spread her hands in placation. "I told you before, I've already had the disease. I'm immune—safe."

"Do you have any idea of the hell you've put me through?" He advanced on her and grabbed her shoulders as though he wanted to shake some sense into her. "All this time I thought you were at the cottage out of harm's way. Then I learned the minute my back was turned, you disregarded my orders."

Jael had never seen him so angry. His fingers bit into her flesh, and his voice shook with barely controlled rage. But strangely enough, in spite of the anger, she didn't fear him. She knew beyond a doubt that he'd never physically harm her, and from that knowledge came strength.

"I'm sorry you're upset, but I refuse to let you bully me." Nathan seemed taken aback by her strong words, but she didn't take time to savor her victory. "I did what I felt I had to do, just as you did aboard the *Clotilde*." She waited for the full import of her words to register.

Nathan grew very still. A jungle of emotions darkened the hue of his eyes, making green and gold lights flash. "I've been out of my mind with worry."

Jael placed her hands lightly on his chest and pressed her advantage. "Just as you had a responsibility to protect your ship, I felt a similar responsibility to do what I could to help these poor people. Please try to understand."

"If anything had happened to you..." His voice was raw with emotion.

"But nothing did." She smiled up at him, touched that he cared so deeply. Her eyes hungrily roamed his features. She reached up and lightly traced the lines of strain bracketing his mouth.

He studied her in return, his expression equally intent. A puzzled frown pulled at his brow. Then a realization slammed into him with the force of an anvil. He marveled at the change he detected in her. This timid, untried girl had become a woman brimming with quiet confidence. A woman in every sense of the word. Caring. Generous. Passionate. The metamorphosis was complete. A lovely butterfly ready to spread her wings...

... and fly away?

Butterflies need freedom. The thought of losing her started a debilitating ache in the region of his heart, then spread throughout his body. Pain as real as a broken bone. He wrapped his arms around her and held her as though he would never let her go.

After a long moment, he cleared his throat and purposely set her from him. Keeping his hands on her shoulders, he gazed into her upturned face. There was still one final piece of unpleasant business left to conduct. "I came to take you home with me."

"No." Incensed, she jerked away from him. "How can you even ask such a thing when you see so much suffering all around you?"

"Jael, listen to me...."

"I can't leave now." She gestured wildly toward the hospital. "Not when there's still much work to be done."

"Jael," he pleaded, catching her shoulders before she could turn away. "It's your grandfather...."

Eyes wide, Jael searched his face. "What about Grandfather?"

"He contracted the disease and is very ill. Thomas thought you should know."

Silas Kincaid, her indomitable grandfather, near death? After all the suffering—all the misery—he had subjected her to, she should rejoice. But she felt neither sadness nor joy. Only a deeply ingrained loyalty, a pervading sense of obligation. "How soon can we leave?"

Upon their return to Lahaina, they went directly to Silas Kincaid's home. Smoldering rubble was all that remained of the cottage Jael had once shared with her grandparents. Thomas and Alice Hadley waited nearby.

Alice greeted Jael with an affectionate hug. "I'm very sorry, dear, but your grandfather died this morning."

"The Lord released him from his misery. It's a blessing." Thomas wagged his head sorrowfully. "You wouldn't have wanted to see him in that condition."

"He hemorrhaged," Alice confided. "Black smallpox is always fatal."

Thomas patted Jael on the back. "If there's anything Alice or I can do, please don't hesitate to ask."

"That's very kind of you," Jael murmured as her mind struggled to cope with a myriad of emotions.

Thomas rested his hand on Nathan's shoulder and spoke in a voice low enough for only him to hear. "I'm glad she's not alone, that she has you to look after her."

Nathan's thoughts mirrored those of the clergyman. Jael hadn't spoken more than a dozen sentences since he had told her that her grandfather had contracted smallpox. She appeared wan and frail, thinner after her week in Honolulu. He watched her anxiously. He wished she would cry, or at least voice what she was feeling, but instead she seemed to have retreated inside herself.

"It was thoughtful of the both of you to be here," Jael told the minister and his wife in a soft, emotionless voice.

"I wish we could have greeted you with good tidings." Thomas took Jael's cold hand in his and squeezed it sympathetically. "Unfortunately..."

Nathan put his arm around Jael's shoulders as they watched Alice and Thomas Hadley depart, then turned his attention to his wife. "Are you all right? You've been quiet ever since we left Oahu."

She tried to smile, but failed miserably. "Just give me a few minutes alone."

"I'll wait down by the water."

Jael slowly wandered around the perimeter of what had once been a cottage. It had been a house, but never a home. A place of lectures and harsh discipline. Never a haven of affection and laughter. She expected to feel... something. If anything at all, she felt... pity. Pity for a miserable old man who had never learned simple kindness. A man who preached eternal damnation, but never love and forgiveness. Who existed but never lived. A man who, though living in a paradise, was blind to its beauty. A wasted life.

She didn't want to share the same fate. She

was determined to have more—with or without Nathan. Squaring her shoulders, she turned her back on the past.

Nathan turned when he heard her approach and anxiously scanned her face.

She smiled, a fleeting smile that reflected sadness and pain, and reached for his hand. Her slender fingers meshed with his hard, callused ones. "Let's go home."

Together they slowly made their way along the beach. The setting sun, the bright yellow gold of a ripe pineapple, was sandwiched between a band of mauve clouds and the deeper violet of the Pacific. A stand of palm trees was silhouetted against the colorful sky, their fringed fronds outlined in stark relief. Jael absorbed the beauty, knowing she would always remember this moment in time. Always remember the feel of Nathan's hand in hers.

When they reached the cottage, they went inside. Though night had fallen, Jael didn't bother to light a lamp. The shutters stood open, and moonlight slanted through, filling the room with a pale, silvery glow. She stood in the center of the room, untied her bonnet, and took it off. "There's something we need to discuss."

Nathan's gaze was glued to hers, his stance tense, expectant. "All right, I'm listening."

She drew in a deep breath and let it out slowly. "Now that Grandfather has died, it's no longer necessary for you to take me away from the islands. I've decided to remain on Maui."

"When did you decide all this?"

"It's all I thought about on the return from Oahu, and I believe it's best for both of us this way." Nervously she fiddled with the trim on her bonnet, twisting the ribbon round and round her finger. "Have your attorney draw up the divorce papers when you reach New Bedford and send them for my signature. You'll have your freedom, and I'll have mine."

"If that's what will make you happy." His voice sounded stiff, foreign, the voice of a stranger.

Happy? Jael nearly choked. She had never been so miserable in her life. But she wouldn't bind him to her out of pity. Wouldn't shackle him out of a sense of duty. He had made it perfectly clear on numerous occasions that he prized his freedom. Spending time together during a long sea voyage would only make the final parting all the more difficult. She had offered her heart, but he hadn't wanted it. She didn't think it could withstand another rejection.

Bereft of words, Nathan turned and left the cottage.

There seemed to be nothing more to say.

Chapter 24

Nathan leaned against the rail of the *Clotilde* and stared across the expanse of water with his gaze locked on the dark stretch of beach where Jael's cottage stood. It had been a week since she had informed him of her decision to remain on Maui. A week since she had declared her willingness to proceed with a divorce. A week of pure hell. The longest—and most miserable—of his life.

Be careful what you wish for, John McFee had once warned. Nathan's mouth twisted into a bitter grimace. Once again, John's advice proved sage. He had all the blasted freedom in the world, yet now the world seemed a cold, desolate place.

He felt in the pocket of his jacket and drew out the scrimshaw brooch he had bought the afternoon he had watched Jael mesmerize a group of island children with a fairy tale. Curious about her business transaction with the wily Mrs. Ka'ano, he had returned to the marketplace and impulsively purchased the brooch. Later he planned to surprise Jael with it, but had hesitated, waiting for just the right opportunity. The opportunity had never materialized. Now it never would.

Dear God! What had he done?

His fist tightened convulsively around the brooch, the edges biting into his palm. His chest pounded heavily, though he didn't understand how it could when surely it must be an empty cavity, hollow as a drum. Jael had effortlessly captured that vital organ that used to be his heart and held it hostage.

He slowly opened his fist and gazed at the bit of jewelry. His vision blurred. Instead of seeing a flower delicately carved, he saw her face. Incredibly lovely. Poignantly sweet. He shook his head in wonder as a simple truth staggered him. Knocked him senseless. Almost knocked him to his knees. *He loved her.* It was as indisputable—and as natural—as breathing. She was his world. His present, his future, his immortality. Why had it taken him so long to realize it? What a fool he had been.

Jael, he knew, had loved him once. He desperately hoped she still did. But first he needed to prove that he was worthy of her affection. She deserved a home, children—and her newfound freedom. Not for all the riches money could buy would he clip her glorious sense of independence. He needed to convince her that their greatest freedom and power would come from their combined—not individual—strength.

For Jael he'd even give up whaling. After

nearly twenty years at sea, he was ready for a change, a challenging new adventure. Only days ago, an acquaintance had approached him with a proposition to form a partnership for a sugar plantation. The plan certainly had merit.

With a shock, Nathan acknowledged relinquishing life at sea wouldn't require a great deal of sacrifice. The past voyage had affirmed his growing disenchantment. John's death had made him realize that he wanted something more for himself. A dream he allowed himself in rare moments of soul-searching began to crystallize. Dreams of a family and home. Dreams of a loving companion, someone to share life's triumphs and disappointments. With Jael all things seemed possible. Beautiful, loving, passionate Jael.

He smiled for the first time in days as his mind began to plot an extravagant plan to woo and win her favor.

Jael lifted the lid of the polished teak box and removed the exquisitely carved brooch from its velvet bed. It had arrived that very afternoon. No card had been attached; none had been necessary. Lovingly she traced the tiny jasmine carved in whalebone with the tip of her finger. Only one person would have been so thoughtful. It had been more than a week since she had seen Nathan. During that period, he hadn't made any effort to contact her. Repairs on the *Clotilde* had probably been completed and he was ready—and eager—to set sail. Tears suddenly clogged her throat, and she swallowed them back. This must surely be Nathan's way of bidding her goodbye. His farewell gift.

With trembling hands, she fastened the brooch to her nightdress, directly over her heart. She wanted it close even while she slept. After blowing out the lamp at her bedside, she drew the mosquito netting around her bed, then lay back and closed her eyes. She should be exhausted from a day spent cleaning and scrubbing a classroom in preparation for her first students in the new mission school. She was grateful for the position. The income from teaching along with extra money she made from her sewing would allow her to live comfortably though not luxuriously. But independence was bittersweet.

Rather than lesson plans, Jael's thoughts strayed to Nathan. He was seldom out of mind for long, never out of her heart. She missed him dreadfully. If she believed for a second that she could change his mind about marriage, she would have journeyed with him to the ends of the earth. But never had he given her any reason to think otherwise. Reluctantly she had released him from wedding vows he had been loath to make in the first place. Tears squeezed from beneath her lids, and she dashed them away. More continued to fall. At long last she fell asleep, their wetness still on her cheeks.

* * *

She awoke feeling disoriented. She lay unmoving and tried to recall what had disturbed her sleep. Certain impressions shifted through her mind like bits of colored glass in a kaleidoscope. A night as dark as velvet in a jeweler's case. Mosquito netting swaying in a ghostly waltz. And the heady fragrance of flowers.

Jael smiled drowsily. The room smelled like a garden.

She smoothed the sheet and her fingers encountered a silky-smooth object. With a slight frown, she picked it up, surprised and delighted to discover a flower. Wide awake now, she sat bolt upright. Flowers—armfuls of jasmine—blanketed the bed. Enchanted, she scooped them up, buried her face in the soft petals, and inhaled their sweet essence. She felt like a princess in a magical bower. All that was lacking was a storybook prince. And perhaps for this one night, their last night together, her prince had come to love her.

Cautiously she pushed aside the bedclothes and climbed out of bed. To her amazement, a trail of petals led from the room. She followed their path through the parlor and out the front door. Oddly enough, she experienced no fear, only a burgeoning sense of anticipation. She sensed Nathan was behind all this. Just as she stepped onto the porch, a figure emerged from the shadows behind her and placed his hands over her eyes.

Jael sucked in her breath in alarm.

"Don't be frightened," a male voice whispered. "I'm not going to harm you." Quickly, before she could see his face, Nathan whipped out a silk scarf and used it as a blindfold, then swung her into his arms.

Jael's arms automatically wound around his neck as he bounded down the steps. She would play his game. "Who are you? Where are you taking me?" she demanded in an oddly breathless voice.

"Be patient," came the amused response.

Rather than outraged, she was intrigued. She had been kidnapped once before—and had feared for her life. But this time was entirely different. Instead of trepidation, an inexplicable excitement began to build, tickling nerve pathways until her entire being thrummed in response.

As a result of being blindfolded, all other senses seemed heightened. Jael became acutely aware of the crunch of footsteps on sand, the chatter of night birds, the cool kiss of trade winds on fevered flesh. Her cheek rested against the starched smoothness of a man's shirt. Beneath it, she felt a solidly muscled shoulder. Her midnight phantom had a delicious, purely masculine scent of musk combined with the salty tang of the sea and a hint of sandalwood.

Jael kept one arm looped around his neck while she commenced a leisurely exploration down the strong column of her abductor's throat. She thrilled at the strong pulse beating there. Her fingers slipped into the opened shirtfront and encountered crisp curls.

"Later, love," her abductor chastised with a low chuckle. "You're distracting me."

Jael stifled a giggle as she suppressed the urge to tweak the chest hair to test his reaction.

When they had gone a short distance farther, Jael felt herself lowered to the ground and placed on a bed of leaves of some sort. Once again the scent of jasmine filled the air. The blindfold was removed and Nathan filled her vision.

"Nathan," she murmured dreamily.

"I've missed you so. I thought I'd go crazy without you." He kissed her with all the pent-up longing and yearning in his heart.

The instant his lips touched hers, Jael was lost, hopelessly, mindlessly lost in a haze of sensation. She plummeted headlong into a bottomless chasm of taste, texture, and emotion. As his mouth played over hers, she absorbed his essence until she felt a part of him, and he a part of her.

"You make me come alive," she sighed against his lips.

"And you make me burn." His gaze never leaving hers, he swept the nightdress from her slender body, then hastily discarded his own clothing.

She reached out, welcoming him into her embrace. "You're a beautiful man, Nathan Thorne. Both inside and out."

Nathan caught her wrist and pressed a kiss into the cupped palm of her hand. "It's you who are truly beautiful."

Jael smiled up at him, her love shining in her eyes.

His lips claimed hers in a kiss that left them both breathless and wanting.

Perfectly attuned to every nuance of her expression, every incoherent sigh, every delicate shiver, he stroked each curve and hollow with languid ease until she purred like a kitten.

Slow, tantalizing caresses.

Soft, lingering kisses.

Jael succumbed to the magical spell he wove. Under his tutelage, she became equally creative and playful. Her hands roamed over his hard muscled form to lightly tease, then stroke. Her tongue darted out to playfully torment and taste.

The fire burned hotter, brighter, its heat more intense. He entered her with a powerful thrust. A paroxysm of intense pleasure exploded inside her as she cried out his name. A powerful shudder ripped through Nathan seconds later as he, too, gained the ultimate satisfaction.

Gradually their pulses ceased to race and returned to normal rhythm. Nathan held her snugly against him, her head resting against his heart. Content to just hold her, he smoothed her tangled mane with gentle fingers, then watched the fiery strands sift through his fingers. "Do you think, perhaps, you could love a sugar baron as well as a ship's captain?"

Jael propped herself on one elbow and stared down at him. "What do you mean?"

"I've decided to make some changes in my life—a life I want you to be part of." He smiled that lazy rogue's smile that had always charmed her, then turned solemn. "This is the place we first made love. I thought it only fitting that I bring you here tonight and beg, if need be, for a second chance. I love you, Jael."

Jael closed her eyes as pure bliss flooded through her, washing away doubts and fears. Every fiber of her being sang with joy. "Oh, Nathan, I nearly despaired of ever hearing you say that. I love you, too. I have almost since the beginning and always will."

"Can you ever forgive me for being too stubborn—and too stupid—to admit the truth until it was almost too late?"

"Just as long as you never stop loving me."

"Always, pagan flower." He eased his fingers through her hair, and cradling her head, urged her mouth down to meet his. As their lips met, a commitment was sealed. A destiny welcomed.

Epilogue

Nathan stood on the edge of the veranda and stared out across the blue waters toward the fleet of whaling vessels. Just that morning, the *Clotilde* had sailed through the channel between Maui and Molokai to anchor off Lahaina. Seeing her from a distance, knowing she was under the command of a new captain, brought back a flood of memories. Most of the memories were good ones. Others tinged with sadness.

He still sorely missed John McFee. He could never think of his friend without regret, without sadness. Thomas had told him that time would heal all wounds. Nathan would have to put his trust in the clergyman's wisdom and hope that someday the pain would ease.

If anyone had told him three years ago that he would give up the sea to become a farmer, he would have told them that they were crazy. But that's exactly what had happened. And he had never been happier. He was firmly convinced that Hawaii's future revolved around a plant that grew wild—sugarcane. Besides sugarcane, the island's rich soil produced a bounty of fruits and vegetables that were in high demand in places as far away as San Francisco. His venture into farming was proving highly successful. The plantation house had just been completed, and he was about to purchase additional land to plant sugarcane.

Strange, he mused, the unexpected twists life could take. He always thought he'd spend his entire life on the seas. Carefree and unencumbered. Master of his own fate. Jael told him once that her mother had called life a grand adventure. With Jael at his side, that was exactly what his life was turning out to be. An adventure more grand than any he could have imagined.

As though sensing she was the object of his thoughts, Jael joined him on the veranda. She came to stand next to him, her eyes anxiously following the path of his.

"Do you regret your choice?" she asked quietly.

He smiled at her over the head of their two-year-old son, who was asleep in her arms. His son, he thought with a burst of pride. John Thomas had golden brown hair like his own, but he had his mother's eyes. Soon there would be another child. Nathan secretly hoped for a red-haired daughter.

"Regrets?" He pretended to ponder the matter, but sobered when he realized the depths of her concern. He looked toward the *Clotilde* bobbing at anchor, then back at his wife as she stood cradling his son. "Nary a one, my love. It scares me senseless to think how empty my life would be without you. You're my world."

If Jael had any lingering doubts, they were instantly dispelled as his lips moved over hers, demonstrating without words the depth of his passion.

If you enjoyed this book, take advantage of this special offer. Subscribe now and get a

FREE
Historical Romance

No Obligation (a $4.50 value)

Each month the editors of True Value select the four *very best* novels from America's leading publishers of romantic fiction. Preview them in your home *Free* for 10 days. With the first four books you receive, we'll send you a FREE book as our introductory gift. No Obligation!

If for any reason you decide not to keep them, just return them and owe nothing. If you like them as much as we think you will, you'll pay just $4.00 each and save at *least* $.50 each off the cover price. (Your savings are *guaranteed* to be at least $2.00 each month.) There is NO postage and handling – or other hidden charges. There are no minimum number of books to buy and you may cancel at any time.

Send in the Coupon Below

To get your FREE historical romance fill out the coupon below and mail it today. As soon as we receive it we'll send you your FREE Book along with your first month's selections.

Mail To: **True Value Home Subscription Services, Inc.**, P.O. Box 5235
120 Brighton Road, Clifton, New Jersey 07015-5235

YES! I want to start previewing the very best historical romances being published today. Send me my FREE book along with the first month's selections. I understand that I may look them over FREE for 10 days. If I'm not absolutely delighted I may return them and owe nothing. Otherwise I will pay the low price of just $4.00 each: a total $16.00 (at least an $18.00 value) and save at least $2.00. Then each month I will receive four brand new novels to preview as soon as they are published for the same low price. I can always return a shipment and I may cancel this subscription at any time with no obligation to buy even a single book. In any event the FREE book is mine to keep regardless.

Name		
Street Address		Apt. No.
City	State	Zip
Telephone		
Signature		
(if under 18 parent or guardian must sign)		

Terms and prices subject to change. Orders subject to acceptance by True Value Home Subscription Services, Inc.

0-380-77372-4